Holly Jackson was born in January 1971 in a small country town in South Australia.

Married at 22 years of age, she had four children from the marriage before their separation in 2007. As a single mother of four children, Holly completed her education at the age of 36 and obtained a degree in business management and administration. Holly then proceeded to design and develop her own fashion design business which flourished for three years before she closed the business and put pen to paper.

Over the next six years, Holly concentrated her efforts on her new direction of writing. In 2017, Holly relocated to her hometown in South Australia and rebuilt her life after a long struggle; financially, physically, and mentally. Determined, self-taught Holly then went on to complete her first book *Reality* over a period of six years and obtained a publishing contract with Austin Macauley Publishers, London. Holly's vision was to encourage and inspire other people to reach past their present situation and follow their dreams, inspirations and goals and never be discouraged by others.

"You are your own success."

To all who have known the hardships, heartbreaks, and the struggles of life.

To the strength within us all.

Keep the Faith.

Holly Jackson

REALITY

AUSTIN MACAULEY PUBLISHERS™

LONDON • CAMBRIDGE • NEW YORK • SHARJAH

A CIP catalogue record for this title is available from the British Library.

ISBN 9781528931212 (Paperback)
ISBN 9781528966580 (ePub e-book)

www.austinmacauley.com

First Published (2020)
Austin Macauley Publishers Ltd
25 Canada Square
Canary Wharf
London
E14 5LQ

To the wonderful person whom I met during my journey of writing this book, whose encouragement and support made this dream come true.

From the bottom of my heart, I truly thank you.

To my beautiful children whose unconditional love was a source of inspiration.

May your lives be blessed with joy and happiness.

I love you always.

To Austin Macauley Publishers and their dedicated staff for giving me the opportunity and support to fulfil this dream.

Inspired by True Events

Loss of Innocence

Three twenty five am: Jade awoke to a familiar presence in her room. She felt the movement near her bed, smelt the familiar smell of alcohol on his breath, the familiar movement of the bedcovers lift from off her body as his hand slid under the sheets. She felt her breath tighten within her throat as she pulled at the bed covers, wrapping them around her tightly. "Peter, no, get out of my room," she whimpered quietly, fearfully in the quiet morning hour.

Her eyes opened wide in fear as she moved away from the hand that crept beneath her sheets, and crunched herself into the corner of the wall next to her bed. "No Peter, please leave me alone, she whispered in a ten-year-old whisper of her innocence.

She saw his face through the darkened shadows of her room. A creepy smile, his eyes burning into her innocence, a look she had come to know so well. Jade held the covers up to her neck, her feet pressed tightly together, blocking his path, a touch of his wild abandonment of decency and trust. She could smell the intoxicating smell of his alcohol stained breath, breathing closer and closer against her skin.

"Please, please leave me alone Peter," Jade whimpered again, only louder this time.

"Let me see your titties, Jade," Peter said quietly in a vulgarity of his indecent intent that terrified her and crept in prickles up her spine. "I will show you my dick. Boys have a dick, want me to show you, it's fun. I will take you for walks and rides in the car. I will give you twenty dollars if you let me touch you," Peter continuously said bribing her in his unadulterated onslaught of indecency.

"No Peter, No," Jade replied fearfully as the tears fell down the terrified look upon her face.

Jade just wanted this to stop, the night terrors of her brother's hand that crept into her bed without warning and terrorised her in bad dreams and in reality.

She would not allow her brother to steal her innocence, she fought against the fear, she fought with her tormented thoughts of the assault. How would she escape this nightmare?

"If you don't leave my room I'm going to tell dad," Jade warned in a timid voice. Finally Peter turned and walked from the room in silence as Jade breathed a sigh of relief and the tears that had pooled in her eyes began to fall down her soft young cheeks.

That night Jade lay restless in her bed her mind constantly planning her escape, she wished her brother would leave her alone and that she could live somewhere else safe, happy and away from the assaultive abuse of her brother's incestuous intentions and the suffering of his debasement would end.

Jade awoke the next morning early and sat at the kitchen table across from her brother. She shuttered under the stares and glares of her brother's threatening eyes and felt helpless, alone in the onslaught of his abuse within the darkened hours of the night.

"Mum won't believe me anyway," Jade muttered under her breath to herself. "Why can't they understand who I am?" "Why don't they love me?" Jade had always felt different like she didn't belong she loved to sing, dance and perform as she had numerous times, with the neighbourhood as her audience. Jade dreamt of her escape and start a career in acting, she waited to be noticed and waited and longed for her big break to begin but it never came.

That day Jade sat up in the big, old almond tree in the middle of her back yard and looked down upon the world. "Why me?" Jade asked, looking above herself to the heavens. "Please save me from this," she prayed incessantly.

Four am: Jade awoke to a familiar presence in her room again. A tear rolled down her soft cheeks as her eyes opened and she crouched into the corner, pulling the blankets up around her neck. "Please go away Peter," Jade pleaded again and again. The words slurred from his mouth as his breath breathed the smell of his intoxication.

Jade listened fearfully to the abusive words of her attacker as he refused to leave her room, "Come on Jade, I'll give you twenty dollars if you let me touch you," Peter slurred. Peter slid his hands under the sheets reaching for a forbidden touch of her young flesh. Jade looked at Peter, her eyes wide and fearful as he raised to his feet and stood over her, slowly sliding the zip down upon his pants and revealing his naked flesh, and started to touch himself in front of her.

"No Peter. No, get out of my room," Jade pleaded again and again. "I'll tell Dad if you don't leave me alone."

"You tell Dad and I'll tell him that you're making it up and being weird," Peter replied, pulling forcefully at the bed sheets. Terrified, the tears rolled down her young cheeks.

"Peter he will believe me, now get out," Jade pleaded again only louder this time.

"Okay Jade. I'll leave you alone," Peter replied, turning his back and walking out of her bedroom and back to his own room.

Jade laid in her bed terrified, crying and confused, not knowing what to do or how to stop it from happening. She placed her face into her hands and wiped at the continual tears that kept falling from her eyes until she finally fell back asleep exhausted.

The next day her neighbourhood friend, Katherine, came over. Jade loved Katherine and her willingness to join in the numerous adventures, plays, and dances that Jade constructed for her neighbourhood production, although had not been of Katherine's interests had encouraged Jade and excited her and made her love her even more.

Katherine watched Jade shine as she performed her plays, wrote her songs, dance moves and made the invitations for all the neighbours and set up the stage on her mother's unfinished porch.

She knew this made Jade happy and it's what she wanted to do with her life one day.

They had been friends for many years ever since they were very young having lived within the same neighbourhood and knew each other inside and out and although Jade was the more ambitious of the two making all the plans, Katherine was happy to stand in her lime light and follow in her footsteps. Jade was always fashionable and creative and led the way within her circle of friends within the small township of Copper Cove, her presence a shining beckon to many of her friends who loved and admired her dearly.

"Let's build a cubby house," Jade announced, smiling as she greeted Katherine by the back gate of her back yard.

"Where are we going to build that?" Katherine asked.

"Over there," Jade replied, pointing to the abandoned chicken pen situated on a large block across the narrow dirt road. Jade had found an abandoned old shed across the road from her home, part of the tin was missing from the front of the run down establishment, but the door was still intact and swung freely upon the abandoned large tin shed. Jade stood back looking at the establishment, a picture forming within her mind of the finished project.

"Okay," Jade thought. "I could get the timber and tin from over there. Dad has nails and a hammer I could use. I'm going to fix it up and make it mine. My special place. " She showed Katherine the shed she had found and told her what she planned on doing.

Katherine thought it was a great idea and quickly joined in the renovations and rebuilding of the property, helping her carry the tin and hold it in place as Jade nailed it to the bare timber railings. While rebuilding the property Jade called out orders like a boss and requested the things she needed as Katherine ran around gathering the equipment for her dutifully.

Finally, at the end of the day they stood back and looked at all their hard work. Jade and Katherine looked at each other with a big smile and threw their hands in the air playfully and giggled before letting themselves in through the big wooden door of the establishment. "Ours," Jade announced, opening her arms and spinning around on her heels smiling.

The next day Jade took some old blankets and sheets, that her mother had given her, over to her special place. She started to hang the sheets up like walls to make rooms in the cubby house and gathered old furniture, pictures, old kitchen appliances, plates and cups and coordinated the kitchen and loungeroom of the cubby house. She took her books, pencils, paints and paper and all of her craft gear out to the cubby house and placed them into the small green-painted cupboard. Jade felt like the cubby had become her home away from home, a place where she felt she could relax and be alone in her creativity without any disturbance.

Jade heard the jingle of the little bell tied to the front door of the cubby house and walked over to the door and opened it.

"Hi," came the voice standing at the door.

"Hi Katherine," Jade replied, smiling. "Come in. How do you like our house?"

"It's awesome," Katherine replied giggling looking around at what Jade had done. "I like it."

The girls both sat down on the old lounge and Jade got out her books. "Which one would you like me to read to you today," Jade asked. Jade loved to read and often read books to Katherine and her little brother, Mason, who thoroughly enjoyed it and quite often requested it.

Katherine picked the book and they both sat back down and she started to read the magical adventures out loud. Katherine sat silently on the lounge settee next to her as Jade began to read. A broad smile lit up upon her face as the book took her into a world of magical imagination and the words seeped into the depths of her mind forming wonderful pictures.

Suddenly Jade heard the bell ring on the front door again. She placed the book on the lounge and got up and opened the door.

"Peter." Jade's heart sank into her stomach at the sight of her brother standing in the doorway.

"What are you two up to?" Peter asked, walking into the cubby house.

"Nothing. Just reading and hanging out," the two girls replied in unison.

"Well," Peter replied, pulling a small box out of the pocket of his jeans. "Look what I have." Peter flashed the box around in front of them as if he had found a prize.

"What are they?" Jade questioned a curious furrow forming across her eyes.

"Cigarettes," Peter answered. "I'll give you one and show you how to smoke like a grownup." Although they were only eleven and knew that they shouldn't touch the cigarettes, fascinated and curious Jade and Katherine agreed and took one each.

Peter lit the cigarettes as the girls sat down upon the old lounge settee and puffed at the lit stick of tobacco.

"I don't feel well," Jade announced, holding her head and stomach.

"Neither do I," Katherine announced also, holding her stomach, and turning slightly pale.

"Why do grownups do this?" Jade asked, throwing the cigarette to the floor and stomping on it.

"Cause it makes them look cool," Peter replied. Jade's faced frowned into an inquisitive confusion as she reached for another one and lit it.

"Cough, cough," Jade coughed choking, her throat irritated by the smoke. Peter laughed as he sat on the lounge puffing at his own cigarette.

"Jade. Peter. It's time to come home," came their mother's voice calling across the road from the backyard of their house.

Jade turned to Katherine with a smile, "Did you like the cigarettes?"

"No," Katherine replied, stomping on the butt and throwing it into the bin. Jade started to giggle as she rose from off the lounge settee and placed a cigarette into her mouth, prancing around the room pretending to smoke it like an adult.

"Come on crazy girl. We've got to go," Peter said, walking through the cubby house and out of the front door with Jade following not far behind.

The next day after school Jade and Katherine met in the cubby house again. As Jade reached for her books she noticed a book that had not been there before. "The Trucker's Wife," Jade said, reading the title and flicking through the pages of the book. Jade stopped on a page and began to read. Her mouth dropped open as the promiscuous words ran through her mind and forced her hands to close the book.

"Oh Katherine, it's full of naughty words. Whose is this? I'm not reading it," Jade said, placing the book on top of the little green cupboard. "I'm taking it home to Mum."

Jade heard the bell ring on the front door and walked to the door and opened it.

"Peter. Go away," Jade demanded. "This is our place not yours."

"Don't you want a cigarette?" Peter asked enticing his way into the cubby house. Jade and Katherine looked at each other, a cheeky smile forming across their young faces.

"Okay," they said. "Come in." Peter sat down between them on the lounge settee and passed them both a cigarette and lit it for them. Peter giggled at them as they both began to prance around puffing at the cigarettes showing off.

"Do you like them now?" Peter asked a cunning grin forming across his face.

"Yes," Jade replied glancing at Peter with a cheeky smile.

"Okay, I've got to go," Peter replied walking towards the front door before coming to a sudden stop his eyes glancing at the book sitting on top of the little green cupboard.

"What's this?" Peter asked picking up the book from off the cupboard and began to read the first couple of pages.

"Oh no," Peter said. "Have you read this?"

A red hue formed across Jade's cheeks as her mouth searched for the right words to say. "We had a quick look but I couldn't understand what they were doing. I put it there so I can take it home to Mum. Is it hers?" she said quickly, turning her head back and forth between Katherine and Peter.

Peter flicked through the pages quickly. "Would you like me to read it to you?"

"No thank you," Jade replied sternly, placing her hands over the red hue upon her cheeks. Peter looked at Katherine devilishly before walking over to the lounge and sitting down next to her with the book in his hand. "Would you like me to read it to you Katherine?"

"Yes okay," Katherine replied, the naivety spreading across her young face. Peter started to read the book. Within moments of Peter starting to read the book Katherine started to ask questions about the references within the book. Unabashedly Peter started to explain.

"Well this is your pussy," pointing towards Katherine's vagina. "And this is my…"

"That's enough," Jade piped up angrily, quickly interrupting. "You have to leave now Peter."

Peter didn't argue and raised to his feet quickly and walked out with the book in his tight grip. Although Jade had stipulated to Peter to give the book to their mother she knew deep within her that he would not, as he walked out of the cubby house and back home.

Jade loved the weekends and waited patiently for Saturday to arrive when she could do her plays for the neighbourhood. She had worked on it all week and had written all the invitations and had sent them out two days before the big day of the production.

She walked around the neighbourhood putting them in all the letterboxes a big smile on her face in anticipation and excitement.

On the Saturday morning, Jade set up the makeshift stage on her mother's unfinished back porch. She hung the old curtains up as stage curtains, placed all the props into position, placed the stereo system on the floor near the make shift stage and waited for Katherine and her younger brother, Leon, to arrive.

Over the previous week Jade spoke to Leon and Mason about joining the show and after explaining what they would have to do, they both agreed to play the characters written in the script but both refused adamantly to be a part of the dance scene. Jade accepted their refusal gracefully and rewrote the play, removing the dance scene so the two boys could be in the whole play. Within moments of setting up the stage Katherine and Leon arrived and changed into their costumes. "Okay, showtime," Jade announced, smiling at Katherine, Leon and Mason.

Jade opened the back gate and waited for the audience to arrive. One by one the people from the neighbourhood started to come through the back gates. Masan stood confidently at the back gates collecting the tickets and greeting the audience as they arrived and ushered them towards their seats. Jade felt the excitement tickle her stomach as she stood behind the make shift stage curtains, standing in position ready to perform. The audience clapped as the curtains opened and giggled as the children performed the show and raised off their chairs and clapped joyously through the last performance as the children took their bows and closed the stage curtains.

Jade wrapped her arms around Mason and her friends and thanked them for their performance. "Well done guys. Here are the lollies I promised you," Jade announced, handing the bags filled with mixed lollies to all of their outstretched hands before sitting on the back step next to Katherine, smiling and giggling at their performance.

"Mum, can Katherine stay over tonight?" Jade called out from off the back step through the open kitchen door.

"Yes love," Sienna replied.

That night Jade and Katherine played joyfully in her bedroom, pulling out all the board games while they listened to their favourite music on the stereo. Although Jade did not have a sister, Katherine had felt to her the closest thing to having a sister in her life and spent most of their spare time in each other's company.

"Two peas in a pod," Jade's mother had commented, poking her head through the bedroom door as the girls played continuously together.

Jade and Katherine woke the next morning, words leaping instantly from their mouths as their eyes began to open. Katherine loved Jade's spontaneous nature and the many stories that she would tell her. Katherine had always been the quieter of the two and often found herself sitting quietly and listening as Jade told of her numerous stories of her own imagination that formed magical creative pictures within their young minds. Dominant and confident Jade always led the way as they travelled many exciting adventures together and performed their artistic talents for their neighbourhood audience.

"What are we going to do today?" Jade asked, laying in the top bunk of her bed.

"I don't know," replied Katherine.

"Maybe we should finish that board game," Jade suggested.

The two girls climbed out from under the soft, warm bed covers and walked to the kitchen and sat at the kitchen table. Jade reached for the cereal as Peter entered the room and sat at the kitchen table with them.

"Would you like to play boardgames with me after breakfast?" Peter asked, looking at Jade and Katherine through cunning eyes.

"Yes," the two girls answered with anticipation in quick succession.

"And cards."

"Could you show us how to play?"

"Yeah sure," Peter agreed, nodding his head.

After breakfast Jade went to her bedroom and fetched the boardgames from out of her large bedroom cupboard that spread the width of the bedroom wall and took them into the loungeroom.

"Let's play snakes and ladders first," she suggested, entering the loungeroom.

"No let's play cards," Peter suggested, placing the pack of cards down upon the lounge room floor and sitting down in front of them.

With enthusiasm, Jade quickly placed the boardgames away onto the coffee table and sat on the floor with Peter and Katherine. Just then Peter and Jade's parents entered the room. "We're leaving now," they announced, picking up their sports bags and walking out of the front door. "Bye, "the children all called out in unison. Jade and Peters parents had always attended sports on the weekends and quite often left the children at home by themselves of which the children had grown accustomed to but had remained within walking distance from their home, their sports club located only metres down the road.

"Okay," Peter said, glancing a devilish grin at the two girls. "I'm going to teach you to play what we play at our cousin's place."

"What are we playing Peter?" the girls asked, looking at each other curiously.

"Poker. We are going to play strip poker," Peter announced, a cunning grin spreading across his face. The girls didn't really understand but naively agreed to play anyway.

Peter dealt the cards out one by one and explained to them how the game was played. At first the girls thought it was funny, beating someone so they had to take pieces of their clothes off. Over the course of the game Katherine had been reduced to only wearing her underwear and lost the next hand. Katherine raised to her feet and slowly went to pull down her underwear as her cheeks started to turn red.

"No," Jade piped up, quickly raising to her feet from off the loungeroom floor. "We're not playing anymore." Peter laid his cards on the loungeroom floor and shrugged his shoulders. "Okay, how about we play something different then.

I know. Let's play hide and seek," Peter suggested, raising his head as a devilish smile formed across his face. "You girls hide, and I'll find you," and started to count, "one, two, three…"

The two girls quickly ran off through the house giggling innocently as they hid in the many hiding spots of Jade's bedroom. "You hide under the bed," Jade said, giggling. "I'm going to hide in the cupboard." The girls climbed into their hiding spots giggling uncontrollably and waited to hear Peter coming. "Shhh," Jade whispered. "He's coming." The two girls fell into deafening silence as their faces remained in a broad smile within their hiding spots.

Jade heard her brother's footsteps creep into the bedroom and walk pass the cupboard. Slowly and quietly Jade slid the cupboard door open slightly so she could peak

16

through a tiny gap. She watched silently as Peter approached the bed and lifted up the covers. "Oh no, he's found her," Jade whispered to herself, holding her breath and the playful giggle that threatened to escape from her lips. Jade peaked through the tiny gap as Peter climbed on top of the bed and reached his hand down into the gap between the wall and the side of the bed. Jade heard a loud giggle come from under the bed then the room fell into an unsettling silence. Peter's arm stayed firmly down the side of the bed for what seemed like hours but were only minutes as Jade kept watching inquisitively within the cupboard. Peter climbed from off the bed and reached under the quilt that swang over the edge of the bed and pulled Katherine out from under the bed and placed her on top of the covers as his hands slipped under the rim of her skirt and under the soft lining of her underwear.

Jade swallowed hard, terrified and unable to move, as tears welled within her eyes. "I'm sorry Katherine," Jade sobbed in a whisper, placing her hands to her gasping mouth, her words frozen within her throat and unable to move. Jade watched horrified as Peter removed Katherine's underwear, opened her legs and slid up in between them. Horrified and unable to move gripped in her fear Jade froze, her breath held tightly within her young throat as she placed her hand over her opened mouth once again.

Within minutes Peter stood up, pulled his pants back on and walked from the bedroom. Jade quietly but quickly slid the cupboard door open and stepped out of the cupboard, rushing to the side of the bed and placed her hand on Katherine's shoulder who lay motionless upon the bed.

"Are you alright? Did he hurt you?" Jade asked, a concerning tone quivering within her young voice as her tear filled eyes looked into her friends flushed face.

Katherine raised from off the bed and slipped back into her clothes in silence. "I'm so sorry Katherine, I didn't know what to do," Jade sobbed, wrapping her arms around her in concern and guilt.

"It's okay," Katherine answered looking down at the ground. "My stepfather does that too."

Jade's mouth dropped open, before tears welled up in her eyes and fell down her young cheeks. Silently Jade walked Katherine out of the house and to the back gate and she left.

Jade sat up in the large tree in the backyard of her parents' home as her mind remembered in horror over the events of the day. "What if that is what her stepfather was trying to do to me that night," Jade whispered to herself, placing her hand over the gasp that leapt from her mouth. Jade did not like Katherine's stepfather and remembered the night that she was going to sleep over. Jade complained of the ache within the muscle in the top of her thigh. Katherine's stepfather had got a cream for her and had offered to rub it in, stretching his hand out to touch the top of her thigh. "No, no thank you," Jade said, pushing away his hand and quickly walking from the room and telling Katherine that she had to go home as she wasn't feeling well. Jade could not fathom what was happening around her and sat in the tree gasping fearfully as she remembered.

She tried to put the image out of her head but little pieces of it kept creeping in, she closed her eyes for five seconds counting then opened them again.

Within moments of opening her eyes Jade heard the familiar sound of her parents car pull up in the driveway. "Yes," Jade said climbing down the big branches of the tree and landing on her feet on the ground and walking into the house. Jade looked at Peter who sat silent on the lounge as she walked past him and out into the driveway. She ran to her parents' side, a big smile spread across her face. "I'm so glad you're home," Jade said, wrapping her arms around her mother's waist. Jade never said a word to her parents about what had happened that afternoon to Katherine and remained silent in the secrecy.

The following week seemed to past so fast as the next weekend arrived so quickly.

Jade's parents had decided to go dancing for the weekend and left the children in the care of their nanna. Jade watched as her mother carefully applied her makeup and got dressed into a beautiful flowing blue dress. Jade's fascination had grown for creams and makeup and watched with eager anticipation as her mother prepared for her big night out.

"You look beautiful," Jade said, sitting on the end of her parent's queen size bed, smiling up at her mother.

"Thank you love," her mother replied, returning the smile and walking out of the bedroom joining Jade's father in the kitchen. "We'll be back soon okay kids," their parents called out through the house. Jade followed her parents to the front door and watched as they got into the car and drove down the narrow dirt road towards her nanna's house. Moments later Jade's parents returned with their nanna and two of her cousins who were also staying the night. Jade ran out to the front porch to greet them and wave goodbye to her parents before returning back to the confines of the house. "We won't be home until late," her parents called out of the wound down car window before driving off down the narrow dirt road and headed towards the outskirts of the township.

"Let's play Cowboys and Indians," Peter yelled out playfully. Jade giggled as the boys tied her to the clothes line and rushed around her in a mad flurry of laughter and giggles. Peter suddenly ran into the house and within minutes returned with Jade's favourite doll and proceeded to tie it to the clothes line and spun it around, hitting the doll with a cricket bat. "Nooo!" Jade yelled out. "Stop it, Peter!" Just then the children's nanna walked out from the house. "Time for bed kids. It's time to come inside."

Peter and her cousins were sleeping in the bedroom on the other side of the narrow hallway across from Jade's bedroom. The house was only small, a miners cottage that had been renovated and now consisted of only two bedrooms that were located on either side of the narrow hallway that ran through the middle of the home. At night, Jade would quite often hear her brothers playing games whilst they were supposed to be going to sleep. The boys made Jade giggle with their crazy antics as she listened with curiosity as she laid in bed at night while her brothers talked to each other until the late hours of the evening.

The children all got ready for bed and said goodnight to their nanna who then settled herself upon the lounge within the loungeroom. The loungeroom was situated at the end of the small hallway divided by the heavy wooden door that was always kept closed and shut off from the hallway and the children's bedrooms.

Jade climbed into her bed and started to sing herself to sleep in the quietness of the still evening.

One hour later as Jade lay in her bed still awake she heard the turning of her bedroom door and a crack of light start to appear as the door slowly started to open. She quickly sat up as her throat tightened and she swallowed hard and watched as the door slowly creaked wider. "Oh no," Jade whimpered fearfully to herself, holding her palm to her opened mouth. Jade watched as her two cousins peeked around the corner of the door and snuck to the side of her bed.

A smile formed across Jade's face as her chest began to rise and fall in relief as her throat unclenched and her breathing returned to normal. "What are you guys doing?" she asked, giggling as she watched them crawl around on their hands and knees. "Shhh. Be quiet. We don't want nanna to hear us."

"We've got some lollies for you. Do you want some?"

"Yes please," Jade replied, reaching out her opened palm as they placed the lollies into her hand. "Thank you."

Jade opened up the lolly wrappers and started to eat them while her cousins sat on the bedroom floor sharing their lollies with her before quietly sneaking back out the door and returning to their bedroom. She tucked the rest of the lollies into the draw of her bedside cupboard and laid back down in her bed and slowly drifted off to sleep.

Twelve thirty five: Jade awoke as the tucked-in bedcovers began to pull away from off her and a hand slid beneath the bedcovers and came to rest on the soft inner flesh of her thigh and slowly crept up to touch the bare crevice of her exposed vagina. Jade's voice froze in her throat as she tried to scream out for help but only allowed for a whisper to be muttered from her young lips. "Peter no," Jade whimpered, trying to console herself as the tears fell heavily from her terrified eyes. "Stop, please stop," Jade pleaded, as her cousins stood around the bed giggling and watching before they started to slide their hands under the bedcovers as well. Jade heard the loungeroom door open. "What are you doing?" their nanna called out from within the door way. "Get out of there and back into your beds."

"We're just giving her lollies," the three boys explained, holding out a palm full of lollies and running back to their bedrooms quickly.

Afraid to close her eyes, Jade walked over to the light switch and turned it on and grabbed a book from off her cupboard and returned to her bed and begun to read. The stories filled her with hope and inspiration as she read the wonders of the words as her mind drifted into a realm of magic and fantasia and eventually closed her eyes and fell to sleep.

The next morning Jade awoke early, full of energy. Although Jade had not got much sleep the night before disturbed by her brother and cousins her body and mind had grown accustomed to the numerous disturbances that plagued her through the night within the family home and her senses remained on full alert.

She tiptoed through the house trying not to waken anybody as her hand held its tight grip around the top of the bag of lollies, giggling, as she started to place them into her mouth one by one and savour the sweet nectar of the sugar against her tongue. "Mum won't know," she giggled walking through the back door of the house to the back yard and climbed the big old almond tree until she reached the top branches.

She sat in the branches looking at the morning sky; the birds flying, the cool morning breeze blowing through her hair; it was her favourite place and spent many hours sitting lost in thought within the tree as she pondered life and her dreams.

She let out a loud sigh as she sat still eating the lollies one by one. "I wish…"

Suddenly Jade heard the click of the backdoor handle and the door creak as it started to open.

Jade looked down above the backdoor. "Dad," ran through her mind as her eyes sighted the tall, willowy figure that stepped through the back door and out into the unfinished laundry.

"Jade, Jade, are you out here?"

"I'm up here dad," Jade said smiling and climbing down the big branches of the tree until her feet hit the ground. "I'm here dad," Jade announced, walking over to her father and wrapping her arms around his waist. "I love you," looking up at him, a smile forming across her young face.

The family sat around the kitchen table talking as her parents and nanna drank their morning cups of coffee and delighted in the conversation of the children as they ate their breakfast. As her parents and nanna were talking to one another Jade drew in an anxious breath and held it tight within her throat as she awaited for her nanna's denouement of the truth about her brother and cousins sneaking into her bedroom the night before, while her parents were away. But her nanna said nothing and remained silent in her knowledge.

19

Jade's face dropped with disappointment as her eyes fell to the floor dismayed.

"Well I think it's time that I went home," her nanna announced, raising to her feet from off the kitchen chair and gathering her belongings. Jade's father raised up from off the kitchen chair and reached for his car keys from out of his jeans pocket and headed towards the front door. "Well then, if you're ready to go Shirley, I'll take you home." Jade's eyes quickly darted towards her nanna in silent anxiousness before dropping her glare onto the floor in saddened disappointment. Jade had hoped that day her nanna would speak up and save her from the cruel, vile violation of her brother's hands and betrayal. But she never did.

That weekend Mason moved back into Jade's bedroom, unable to share a room with Peter anymore, the age gap, causing continuous conflict to arise between them.

"I'm having the top bunk," Mason argued as he scrambled to the top bunk to claim his position.

"Fine," Jade replied not really minding which bed she took. Jade felt a shift in oppression as her spirits lifted and she felt a sense of safety settle under her skin as she watched her younger brother start to move his belongings into her room. Within an hour Mason had positioned his furniture and belongings into the bedroom and had started to settle in. "Now, you can't touch this. And you can't go there," Jade explained, mapping out the rules of the bedroom like a commander.

Mason nodded in compliance without putting up a fuss.

He knew she was bossy, and would tell their father if he didn't follow her rules having made herself clear on several occasions. But the two got on perfectly anyway, they had always been best of friends, he to her a sister substitute, dressing him up in makeup and dragging him into her plays and girly games whenever she could. Mason just went along with it and never seemed to mind his sister's playful antics.

That night as they got ready for bed, Jade and Mason started to playfully swing the pillows at each other between the top and lower beds, laughing and squealing as they played until they heard their mother call out to them to go to bed. Jade quickly climbed out of her bed and switched off the light before climbing back into her bed and pulling the covers up around her.

"Goodnight Mason."

"Goodnight Jade," he answered before snuggling down underneath their bed covers and falling into a deep sleep.

Midnight: Jade woke startled, awoken by the click of the bedroom door latch. She opened her eyes and rolled over as she watched the bedroom door slowly open and feet appear coming through the doorway. She looked at the pair of feet and followed them up the legs, the body to the face. It was her brother, Peter. "Nooo," she whimpered in a terrified, soft whisper pulling her blankets tightly around her neck. Fear, dread filled the young girl; she froze with terror not knowing what to do, or unable to call out as the words stifled within her throat by fear and would not leave her mouth. Peter walked towards her each step, terrified her until he was at the side of her bed. He crouched down, he stayed so silent, his movements quiet but fast, he didn't speak, not one word; he slid his hand under the blankets of her bed; her hands trying to stop his, fighting against the invasion, but was not able to against his strength; her brother was too strong.

Then he whispered quietly, "This is what boys will want you to do," as he slid his hand inside her panties and forced his finger deep inside of her, breaking his younger sister's untouched hymen. Her eyes filled with tears as her stomach clenched tightly and she winced in pain, her soul filled with fear, disgust then shame. Then he left, walking from the room silently and clicked the bedroom door shut again. Jade held her stomach as it ached and pulled her knees into a tight ball around her chest.

"Why Peter, why," Jade sobbed with shame, a young innocent girl no more; her body, her innocence, her choice, now stolen by her older brother and the incestuous indecency of his hands.

It was the last time Peter came to her room, Jade remained silent and had never said a word to anyone, not her friends, Mason or her parents. She felt ashamed, scared and disgusted in herself that she could not stop him that it was her own brother that had stolen her innocence. She wanted no one to know of the indecency she had suffered and felt her parents would blame her, hate her and she would be abandoned for bringing such shame to the family.

Jade didn't want to disappoint her parents, she didn't want them to look at her in that way to think she was a bad girl. As time passed, Jade allowed the indecency and insult of that night to fade into the background of her mind and grew into a strong, independent young lady and had remained silent in the admission until she was fourteen years of age.

Jade stood stern, her hands on her hips in her flaired confrontation with Peter, the courage rising up her spine as the truthful words finally spilt from her mouth in anger. "You're just a disgusting pig," she yelled at him. "I hate you, you had no right to…"

Just at that moment, their mother walked in on the children's yelling and arguing. Jade's eyes narrowed into an angry slant as the two of them glared at each other and then her mother before returning the animosity back towards her brother.

"To sneak in my room and hurt me. You touched me down there," she yelled, pointing between her legs. Her mother's face dropped as it turned a pale shade of white shocked by the impact of what she had just heard and looked momentarily silenced at her children.

"What," their mother finally said loudly.

"He's been sneaking into my room for years, touching me and forcing me to do horrible things to him Mum," Jade sobbed, breaking down and placing her head into her hands.

Her mother's eyes darted towards Peter, glaring at him in disbelief as her mouth opened with shock but remained silent in her words. Peter stood motionless as he stared back at his mother and remained silent in the accusation. Jade shook her head and ran to her bedroom and closed the door, crying in relief of the secret that had just spilled from her mouth and freed from her soul.

Jade never knew what was said to her brother; her parents never asked her anything about it or even asked her if she was okay. It just stopped, and her brother never entered her bedroom again and the threatening stares that had intimidated her constantly throughout the home just stopped. It was never spoken about or mentioned again but the family was never the same and Jade, was never the same, the sweet creative naïve young girl; replaced by a trail of self-destruction that followed her like a black shadow, as she suffered a trail of bad choices and a cycle of continued abuse, a shadow of her brother's incestuous hands.

For the First Time

"Jade. This is Kevin," Peter introduced, stepping towards his girlfriend's brother in a gesture of introduction as they stood on the footpath in front of their parents' home.

"Hi," Jade answered, her naive sixteen-year-old voice falling into a state of shyness.

Jade blushed as she stood staring at Kevin's dark, handsome, good looks and searched for the words within her mind to speak within her shyness Kevin eventually spoke first within the awkwardness and shyness, bridging the silence between them. "Would you like to go out for dinner tomorrow night?" he asked courageously. A smile formed across Jade's face. "Yes, that would be nice," she replied. Kevin smiled sweetly as he continued to look into her eyes. "I'll pick you up at five o'clock then." "That would be great," Jade answered looking back at him coyly. "Okay, I'll see you then," Kevin replied before kissing her gently upon the cheek and leaving with her brother.

The next evening Jade fussed tendentiously over her outfit as she flung clothes this way and that way from her bedroom cupboard in preparation for her date with Kevin. Finally, she settled on a pair of blue jeans and a silky blouse that buttoned up down the front and hung softly over her shoulders and the slender curves of her waist. After touching up her makeup, she settled herself on the lounge and awaited Kevin's arrival.

"Five o'clock. Right on time," Jade said, looking through the loungeroom window at the car that parked on the dirt footpath at the front of the house. "He's here mum, I'm going now," Jade called out through the house. "Okay love, have a good time," Sienna replied calling out from the kitchen.

Jade beamed with excitement as she walked towards the front door, straightening her clothing before opening it. "Hi Kevin," she greeted with a smile, as she walked out of the front door and followed Kevin to his car and got in. "Where are we going?"

"We're going to Montana Bay," Kevin replied.

"Nice," Jade replied, reaching her hand over to place hers into his that lay empty against the middle console of the car as they continued to talk until they arrived at the restaurant in Montana Bay.

"So what do you do?" Jade asked, nibbling at the fresh bread rolls seated at the dining table within the restaurant.

"I'm a truck driver. I drive semi-trailers. Anything actually but I transfer goods between Alterro and Copper Cove."

"Oh," Jade replied. "Are you allowed to have passengers?" she asked curiously.

"Yes. My Mum goes with my dad sometimes when he does the interstate runs," Kevin explained.

"I would like to go with you sometime," Jade replied smiling. "It sounds interesting."

"What do you do Jade?" Kevin asked, reaching for one of the bread rolls and placing it into his mouth.

"I have two part time jobs. I'm a supervisor for the checkout area of the local supermarket and I work part time at the local take away store," Jade replied.

"Ahh and which one do you prefer?" Kevin continued to ask.

Jade giggled. "Well they are much the same and pay the bills," she replied giving him a wink. Jade could feel the attraction growing within her as they sat together enjoying their meals, locked in conversation and continual flirtation. She tilted her head slightly and smiled as she listened to his many adventures and his enthusiasm for motorbike racing, of which he regularly travelled to many locations within the countryside and metropolitan areas to compete.

"Oh, I'd like to come watch you sometime," Jade said enthusiastically.

"Sure. I'm going to a race meeting in two weeks' time, you could come to that," Kevin explained.

"I'd love to," Jade replied, her smile beaming in enthusiasm, jumping excitedly in her seat.

Two weeks later Kevin pushed the motorbikes into the enclosed steel trailer and strapped them down tightly before walking out of the trailer and back out onto the ground. "You ready to go," he called out from behind the trailer as he closed the trailer doors. "Yes, ready," Jade called out in here reply, rising from off the seat placed near the back door of his house, walking to the car and placing her handbag into the front passenger side seat and climbing in.

Kevin and Jade chatted continuously as they made their way along the highway until they reached the outskirts of Alterro and parked the car in the motor cross circuit carpark.

"I'm looking forward to this," Jade said smiling as she helped to unpack the helmets and protective gear from the back of the trailer, as Kevin pushed the motorbikes out of the trailer and onto the grassy plains of the pits and continued to prepare them for the race.

Jade roared with the crowd as the motorbikes jumped over the man made hills as they raced along the winding track of the extensive dirt circuit. As soon as the race had finished, Jade walked the perimeter of the dirt circuit track to the finishing line where she met Kevin who was rewarded with a third place ribbon. "Congratulations," Jade applauded, throwing her arms around Kevin in a tight embrace.

Over the next six months Kevin and Jade became frequent visitors to the dirt circuit tracks as Kevin indulged in his hobby of motorbike racing and Jade worked the flags on the track and acquainted herself with the other people who also enjoyed the sport. As Jade's popularity at the dirt circuit track grew steadily it had caused a constant irritation and frustration to develop within Kevin as the couple fought continuously over the attention she received from the other males who frequented the circuit.

"That's it, I'm not going anymore, I've had it with your false accusations," Jade yelled, slamming her foot down onto the ground and marching off. Kevin followed her as they continued to quarrel. That night Jade did not budge from her decision and held steadfast to her stance of annoyance as Kevin tried to convince her that he was wrong and that he would not accuse her anymore.

That summer Kevin pulled out of motorbike racing as Jade stood fast to her decision and refused to accompany him anymore.

One month later: Jade lifted her foot up to the first step and slowly climbed the ladder leading to the passenger seat of the semi-trailer. "I'm in," she giggled, climbing into the seat and doing up the seat belt, before turning up the music on the stereo that sat in the dashboard of the rig. "Yes, let's cruise," Jade giggled again as she looked forward to her first ride in the semi-trailer. Kevin climbed into the driver's seat smiling and started the engine. "Here we go," he smiled, pulling the truck out of the large shed and steering it towards the highway. Kevin and Jade chatted incessantly and sang to the music as they travelled the two hour drive to the outskirts of Alterro, where they pulled into an open yard that contained numerous large warehouses full of goods wrapped in plastic and loaded onto wooden pallets. As Kevin steered the truck into one bay of the warehouse a crew of four men gathered around each side of the truck and started to undo the tie down strapping that was holding the load firmly in place.

Jade and Kevin climbed down out of the cab of the semi-trailer that they had arrived in and walked over to the prepared tray top truck that sat idle and loaded with goods within the bay of the warehouse in preparation for deliveries and climbed into the front seats and started the engine.

Deliveries within the metropolitan areas of Alterro took hours as they drove from one location to another unloading the wrapped goods that sat on the back of the truck. Jade looked down at the watch on her arm as an inconspicuous glaze covered her eyes in an impatient slant.

"OH NO," Kevin yelled out suddenly, as they started to weave in and out of the lines of traffic.

"What is it?" Jade asked, alarmed at the tone of Kevin's voice.

"Jade, the brakes. We've lost the brakes." Kevin pulled at the gear stick urgently, quickly gearing the truck down, as he pumped hard at the brakes continuously. "Oh god hang on," Kevin yelled, as the truck kept rolling towards the back of another tray top truck that had stopped at the red traffic lights ahead of them. BANG went the metal to metal as the truck rammed into the back of the tray truck and shunted it forward. Jade quickly held onto the sides of her seat tightly as the trucks collided and she was flung forward in her seat towards the large front window. "Are you alright?" Kevin asked concerned, reaching his hand over to touch her arm.

"I'm not hurt. I'm not hurt," Jade answered quickly, slightly stunned as she looked over at the truck in front of them. Kevin climbed out of the truck and walked towards the other driver who stood waiting at the back of his truck. Slightly shaken, Jade sat in the front passenger seat of the truck watching in silence as the two men conversed in conversation. Within moments Kevin returned to the truck and climbed into the driver's seat.

"He's not hurt and there's no damage done to either truck so he's not too concerned. He's more concerned at how we're going to drive this thing back."

"How are we going to drive it back?" Jade asked, her hands trembling slightly.

"Slowly," Kevin laughed. "It's alright Jade, there's air in the brakes, I just have to use the gears and go slow. We'll be alright."

"Okay," Jade replied, tightening her seatbelt and facing forwards in her seat.

Although it was a slow trip weaving in and out of the lines of traffic, Kevin slowly navigated the truck back to the warehouse where they parked the truck and waited another three hours for their semi-trailer to be reloaded, ready for its return to Copper Cove.

That evening Jade made the decision that she would not accompany Kevin on his truck runs again as she now had a different perspective and now worried continuously about Kevin's safety also.

Six Months Later

Jade sat alone waiting as the long fruitless minutes passed into hours and she tried to reach Kevin on the telephone. "Where are you Kevin?" Jade complained, checking the time on her watch once more. Hours later Kevin finally arrived at her parents' house and knocked on the front door.

"Where were you? I was waiting for you," Jade asked, opening the front door.

"I was having dinner with my parents," Kevin explained, dropping his head slightly to the left side.

"Well, didn't you think to invite me," Jade answered abruptly, her words poisoned with agitation.

"I'm here now aren't I," Kevin answered quickly, his words a display of his disrespect.

Although Jade held onto the animosity that surged through her, she gathered her handbag disgruntled and headed out the front door and got into Kevin's car and they headed for the nightclub situated within the next town.

"I'm moving to Alterro," Kevin blurted out, leaning close to Jade, raising his voice against the loud mellifluence of the music.

"Alterro? What about us?" Jade answered, her voice filled with concern.

"You can come see me on the weekends and vice versa," Kevin answered, his voice loud against the music.

"Or I could move with you," Jade said speaking loudly over the music, smiling.

"Well, I suppose that you could," Kevin replied, dropping his head slightly.

"Then its settled, I'll talk to my Mum about it and start to make the arrangements," Jade replied, frowning as her smile held the firm slant of bewilderment, as she studied Kevin's reaction.

Two weeks later after leaving from their lunch date earlier than expected while arguing about the move to Alterro Jade drove towards Kevin's house along the back streets of the dirt road that wound up through the narrow streets of Montana Bay to take him home when all of a sudden Kevin yelled out, "Stop."
Jade quickly stomped on the brakes of her car and felt her heart leap into her throat as suddenly the car drifted into a sidewards slide before turning completely into a half circle and coming to rest onto two wheels against the embankment in front of his house before falling back down onto the four wheels of the vehicle. "Whoa. That was lucky," Jade said, gripping her hands tightly around the steering wheel and catching her breath. Jade drove steadily into Kevin's driveway, shaken by the incident as Kevin sat silently in the front seat next to her. "Take it easy on your way home Jade," Kevin said exiting slowly from the vehicle and standing by the open front passenger side door. "Yes, I will," Jade replied shakily. "I'll talk to you tomorrow okay. Bye," she continued as he closed the door and she reversed back out of the driveway and headed towards the highway to Copper Cove.

The next day Jade sat down with her mother and explained that Kevin was moving to Alterro and that she wished to move with him.

"But you're too young," her mother argued.

"I am not. I'm old enough," Jade snapped back. "Besides I don't want to live here anymore, not with him," Jade growled gesturing towards her brother Peter, who stood in the kitchen doorway listening. Jade felt the animosity rise within her as she stood looking at her brother as the memories of that horrendous violation came flooding back. "I fucken hate you," Jade mumbled under her breath. Jade growled as her eyes formed into tight narrow slits and focused their intent at Peter. "Get out of here Peter," Jade growled again, pointing him towards the narrow doorway. "I want to move out of home," Jade yelled, her stance stern and strong, as she stood facing her mother with her hands on her hips.

"You can't move out legally until you are seventeen years of age Jade," her mother replied in a calm voice, taking charge of the situation.

"Then I'm moving out then," Jade replied calmly and walked away.

Over the next two weeks while Kevin was away and settling into his new premise in Alterro Jade scoured the newspapers looking for employment within the metropolitan area of Alterro and applied for numerous positions until finally she got accepted for an interview.

"It's car detailing," Jade explained to her mother, as her mother questioned the description of the job. Peter agreed to drive Jade to the job interview in Alterro in the coming week and invited his friend to come along as well for the day.

Two weeks later: Although nervous, Jade entered the building and saw a man with blondish brown hair sitting in the office and approached the man looking for where she had to go for her interview.

"So you're Jade. Come on in, I've been expecting you," the man greeted, rising from off the chair and shaking her hand.

"Hi," Jade greeted back, shaking the man's hand before sitting on the seat in front of the desk opposite him.

Thirty minutes later, Jade left the office smiling and elated as she felt that the interview had gone well and that she had a good chance at acquiring the position.

Two weeks later; Jade received a phone call.

"I've got the job," Jade replied, the telephone held tightly to her ear. "Thank you very much. I'll be moving in two weeks' time, is that okay?" Jade asked. Jades new employer accepted her terms of when she could start the position and finalised all of the details with her before ending the phone call. Excited with the great news she had just received Jade quickly rang Kevin as soon as she hung up the phone. "Kevin, guess what," she said excitedly down the phone as he answered. "I've got the job," Jade announced quickly before Kevin could even answer.

"Great," Kevin replied, his voice a cause for concern as it quivered and hesitated in his reply. "Where have you got a job too?"

"In Alterro baby. I've got a job as a car detailer. I'll be coming down in two weeks' time." Kevin grimaced on the other end of the phone as Jade's smile spread across her face in enthusiasm. Two weeks later on her seventeenth birthday, Jade packed her belongings into her small two-door vehicle and headed towards the highway in her drive to Alterro. Independence beamed through her eyes as the image of Copper Cove fell slowly into the background in the rear-view mirror, as she drove away.

"I can do this," Jade told herself, touching the boxes that sat in the passenger seat next to her.

On arrival Jade was greeted by Kevin and Tony, Kevin's best friend and flat mate, who proceeded to carry the heavy boxes from out of her car and place them into the loungeroom of the two bedroom unit.

Although the two bedroom unit was small it sufficed its intention of housing Kevin, Jade and Tony and they formed a comfortable union within the unit. The unit consisted of a loungeroom, kitchen and an open plan living area having two bedrooms and a bathroom leading from off the loungeroom and although small, housed the trio perfectly.

That night as Jade slipped under the covers of the couples queen size bed for the first time Jade felt the nervousness that crept through her overwhelm her all of a sudden as Kevin rolled over towards her and began to caress her lips with his sensually.

"I... I... I haven't done this before baby," Jade whispered into the dark.

"I love you," Kevin whispered back, his hands sliding up the soft fabric of her negligee to caress the soft firm flesh of her young breasts.

"Mmm," Jade moaned nervously, her lips pressed against his. Jade felt his hand slide down her stomach and his fingers reach under the smooth fabric of her panties. "I'm a virgin baby. I mean I haven't done this before, you are my first boyfriend I've ever had." Kevin stopped suddenly and slid his hand out from under the soft, warm fabric.

"I love you baby, I won't hurt you," he replied, kissing her gently on the lips, as his fingers trailed back down her stomach and under the soft fabric of her panties once more. Jade felt the sudden mixed rush of excitement, nervousness and fear as Kevin slowly slid her panties down off her hips, down her legs and off her ankles leaving them in the bottom of the bed.

He slowly, gently opened her legs with his hands and lifted himself on top of her to nestle between her parted legs and began to caress her breasts as he slowly kissed her neck and shoulders.

"Mmm," Jade moaned, the excitement within her, building. "I love you," Jade whispered as Kevin pushed slowly inside of her.

"Ohhh," Jade moaned, feeling the sudden thrust as he entered her deeply for the first time.

That night Kevin kissed Jade differently as he made love to her for the first time and held her in his arms afterwards as they slowly drifted off to sleep.

The next day Jade started her first day in her new employment position as a car detailer. Although the work was long and arduous Jade loved the freedom the employment position gave her as she travelled all over the city delivering cars or running errands for the office. Within two weeks of her employment position Jade had received a promotion and was asked to do promotions for a famous car, which the owner of the car yard owned. Jade was delighted and humbly accepted the position without delay. That night Jade went home excited and told Kevin of her big promotion and informed him that she was starting on Monday and that she would be travelling around the local supermarkets of Alterro to do promotions for the famous car. Kevin was delighted for her and congratulated her on her new promotion which they celebrated that evening. Jade awoke on Monday morning full of enthusiasm and excitement as she got ready for work that morning and arrived at the car yard ten minutes early as planned.

Crowds of people within the shopping malls gathered and buzzed excitedly around the famous car asking questions about the cars origins and having their photos taken sitting in the famous car. Jade loved her new position and eagerly participated in the promotions of the famous car and looked forward to working the set every day.

One evening when Jade arrived home, she was greeted by an angry look written upon Kevin's face, who sat in the loungeroom waiting for her to return to the house after work.

"So who is he? The bloke you're working with," Kevin questioned angrily.

"Who, Alex," Jade replied with a giggle, not realising the seriousness of his questioning.

"I don't want you working there anymore," Kevin growled, his voice, a gruff damnation of authority.

"Kevin, he's forty four years of age. You can't possibly think that he would be interested in a girl like me, god I'm a teenager." Kevin suddenly flew into a jealous rage and forcibly pushed Jade into the bedroom where he pushed her down and pinned her to the bed by her hands and the weight of his body.

"You're my girl," he roared, staring down above her, spitting in her face in a gesture of disrespect. "You're not doing this work anymore, do you understand."

Tears welled up in Jade's eyes as she tussled to get her arms free from the tight grip of his hands and remove the weight of his body that pinned her to the bed.

"Yes Kevin, I understand," finally spilt from Jade's lips as the tears rolled down her flushed cheeks and onto the bed spread cover. That night Jade rolled into a ball into the corner of the bed as the tears fell down her cheeks until she eventually fell asleep exhausted.

Over the next six months Jade noticed a considerable change in Kevin's attentions towards her and his sudden interest in Dana, Tony's girlfriend. His once usual smile faded into a tight gritted grin each night as he walked through the door when he arrived home from work and their once active sex life started to dwindle to a mere kiss at the end of the night and backs turned towards each other.

Jade's suspicions started to gather as Kevin's work hours began to stretch past his usual working times and often returned to the unit exhausted and silent.

"Where's Kevin?" Jade asked, her mind questioning his whereabouts one particular day, as she walked through the length of the small flat looking for him.

"I don't know where he is," Tony replied, sitting on the lounge settee in the small loungeroom.

"Where's Dana?" she continued, shrugging her shoulders in her questions and lifting her arms bent into the air at the lack of his usual appearance within the unit.

"She won't be coming over until later," Tony replied, the concern non-existent in his voice.

Jade had taken notice of the considerable change in Kevin's attitude towards her and the way he would portray himself in Dana's presence which had struck her as unusual and odd and made Jade watch their interaction carefully. Tony and Dana had not been dating for very long and were still in the thresholds of a new relationship and getting to know one another. Dana was a constant presence at the small flat but had not been visiting quite so often within the previous months, which was starting to cause a concern of suspicion in the pit of Jade's stomach. That evening in Kevin's long unexplained absence from the unit Jade paced the bedroom floor for hours deep within her own thoughts until finally she heard the familiar sound of the front doors latch open and she quickly walked out into the loungeroom.

"Where were you?" Jade questioned sternly as Kevin finally walked through the front door.

"I had to work late Jade," Kevin replied, plonking himself down on the lounge settee and placing his feet up in a folded motion upon the coffee tables surface. "What's for tea?" Jade's face dropped into a tight scour of anger and disbelief as she stomped out of the loungeroom and entered the kitchen.

"I'll give you what's for tea," Jade grumbled to herself as she rushed around the kitchen preparing the evenings meal.

The next evening at five o'clock Jade went to the location of Kevin's employment in search of his whereabouts. "No he's not here Jade," his supervisor answered. "He knocks off at four o'clock normally." Jade nibbled upon her lips nervously as the information settled under her skin in a tight web of suspicion and deceit.

"He's been lying to me, he's cheating on me," Jade whispered to herself, the thoughts of her suspicion rushing into her mind as she hurried towards her parked car.

Jade's intuition sounded loudly in the pit of her stomach and the nervous tension within her body rose to a tight ball that sat in the depth of her throat as she travelled the streets towards Dana's house.

Jade felt the angry nervousness tighten her grip around the steering wheel as she rounded the corner and parked her car behind Dana's in the narrow driveway of Dana's home. "There's his car," Jade whispered to herself angrily, peeking out from her car window at Kevin's car parked out on the street in front of Dana's house.

Jade exited the vehicle and marched up to the front door pounding her fists against the modern wooden panelling of the front door in an agitated state. "I know you're in there," Jade yelled. "Kevin, Dana, I know you're in there." Suddenly the front door opened just a crack and a set of eyes peaked through the small crack of the door. "Jade. What are you doing here?" Dana asked nervously.

"Where is he Dana?" Jade growled back, her voice angry and stern.

"Where's who?" Dana replied, faking a bewildered look that spread across her face.

Jade reached her hand out and pushed the door open and marched her way past Dana and into her bedroom. "You bastard. You fucken bastard," Jade roared, the vision of Kevin sitting in the bed naked a bitter slap in the face.

"Jade, Oh fuck. Jade," Kevin called out, the trembling in his voice hard to disguise startled by her sudden appearance and having been caught in the act of his deceit and betrayal.

"I'm going to kill you," Jade roared, rushing towards Kevin sitting on the bed.

Kevin leapt from off the bed dodging her attack and rushed down the narrow hallway naked and locked himself in the small storage cupboard situated in the wall space of the narrow hallway.

"You fucken coward. Come out of there," Jade roared, angrily pulling on the small handle of the cupboard. Jade looked to her right as a shadow caught the side glance of her eyes as Dana ran for the safety of her bedroom and locked herself in. "Dana. You fucken bitch. How could you. I trusted you in my home, what about Tony, you fucken bitch."

Jade stomped out of the house angrily and stood in the front yard yelling profanity in their direction before walking over to the hose sitting on the front garden bed and picked it up and pulled it over to Dana's car winding down the window sticking the hose through the gap before winding the window back up to enclose it in the gap tightly. "I'll fucken teach you," Jade roared turning on the tap unleashing the water into the vehicle and walking away to her own parked car, reversing fast out of the driveway and speeding down the streets until she reached her home.

Two hours later Kevin came home, sulking in through the front door and approached Jade nervously. All that night he incessantly swore that it was his only mistake and that he wholeheartedly loved Jade and promised that it would never happen again. Jade finally dropped her eyes to the floor and stood down from her stern stubborn refusal to relent and forgave Kevin and promised Kevin that she would never tell Tony of his illicit affair with Dana that could end their friendship. Jade never said a word and remained steadfast in her promise.

Six months later Tony and Dana's relationship ended and Tony remained oblivious to Dana's deceit and betrayal and remained living within the dwellings of the small two bedroom unit as Kevin and Jade moved out of the two bedroom unit and into a unit of their own.

Kevin and Jade moved into their new unit situated only ten minutes from their previous residence but within another suburb of Alterro and closer to Jade's employment.

The unit, a one bedroom unit with open plan living spaces served its purpose well and was situated within walking distance of Jade's employment positions at the car yard and at the local suburbs supermarket where Jade had now found another employment position. Although Jade had enjoyed doing promotions for the famous car it was fraught with arguments and jealousy from Kevin and she had to decline the invitation to travel overseas to further her career in promotional work. Although she fought tenaciously against Kevin's jealousy she could not overturn his decision and missed out on the opportunity that had presented itself to further her career.

Over the next six months, Kevin and Jade's relationship was fraught with continuous arguments and disagreements and his lashings of abusive words and jealousy tore strips away at her confidence and escalated into a torrid affair of animosity and bitterness. Jade could not stand it anymore and had lost all hope of salvaging the relationship and came to a decision. One afternoon after another bitter argument, Jade growled angrily and precisely as the words left her lips.

"I'm leaving you Kevin," Jade growled, placing her hands on her hips in a stance of sternness. Kevin stood momentarily stunned at her outburst but remained silent in his defence.

Two days later Jade placed her belongings into her car and returned to the small township of Copper Cove and moved back in with her parents. Kevin did not stop her.

Six months later Jade met Christian.

Entrapment

It was a hot summer's day and the sun shone down in glorious rays upon the group that congregated upon the shore line of the bay. Jade had always gone to the bay, her group of friends calling to her as they grouped together in pools of laughter and excitement. But this night was different, a party had erupted in the crowd as Jade made her way towards the small town of Montana Bay.

"Come with us Jade," Jamie said, enticing Jade towards the party of people she had not met before. "I'll introduce you." Jade procrastinated over the invitation before finally agreeing to participate in the party of revellers that were congregating at a house within driving distance of the bay. "Yes," Jamie said gleefully, climbing into the front passenger seat of her vehicle as the crowd started to disperse from the bay and head towards the home of where the party was being held and Jade and Jamie followed them in their pursuit of joining them.

Although Jade had always been the life of the party and enjoyed her time with her friends, this night felt different, something sat nervously within the pit of her stomach, something did not feel right. Jade had always portrayed tomboy traits choosing to play with the boys in a sense of excitement as she rode the motorbikes, kicked the football and leapt from the tallest of the sand dunes and playing Eightball with her brothers but tonight she did not feel like letting herself go and joining in the usual antics of fun, something that she could not place her finger on and held her back from wanting to indulge in the usual excessive consumption of alcohol and fun that she had always indulged in with her friends.

Jamie and Jade arrived at the two story house and walked up to the front door and knocked loudly announcing their arrival.

"I hear footsteps," Jade said, smiling in Jamie's direction listening intently to the sounds of the house.

"Hey Tim," Jamie greeted as the door opened. "This is Jade."

"Hey mate, Hi Jade," Tim replied flashing a smile in her direction.

"Hi," Jade answered, stepping through the front doors of the house and following Tim and Jamie up the stairs to the games room where their friends and the other people who they did not know had congregated into a scene of excitement.

Jade looked around the room, noticing the Eightball table positioned in the middle of the large games room, before focusing her gaze back around the room at her friends and the strangers that stood in circles within different areas of the room.

"Who's that?" Jade asked, touching Jamie on the shoulder in curiosity as she noticed the tall, dark-haired girl standing next to the bar at the back of the room.

"That's Christian's sister, Vicky. That's who's holding the party tonight," Jamie answered, subtly pointing towards Christian. Jade confidently approached the dark-haired girl standing at the back of the room next to the bar.

"Hello Vicky, I'm Jade," she said, introducing herself.

"Hi," Vicky replied, pouring herself another drink from the arrangement of chilled liquors stored behind the bar. "Would you like a drink Jade?"

"Yes please," Jade answered, leaning her body against the wooden bar as her eyes scanned the crowd of gatherers. Although Jade was now nineteen she had tasted her first drink at the tender age of fourteen, to which she had taken a liking to the intoxicating sweetness of alcohol and had favoured the scene of the many parties, of which she had been invited to and had not known any different as she watched her brothers and relatives indulge in alcohol and parties over her youthful years.

As Jade stood talking to Vicky next to the bar Jamie re-entered the room shortly followed by Christian, a younger man of whom Jade had guessed was close to eighteen who Jade had not seen before or recognised as one of the people who had been known amongst her group of friends. "Jade," Jamie called to her, inciting her attention. Jade walked in the direction of which they stood and held out her hand as an introduction to the younger man.

"Hi, I'm Jade," she said smiling confidently.

"Hi Jade, I'm Christian," the younger man replied, holding out his hand to place into hers as a broad smile spread across his face. Within moments of being introduced Christian and Jade struck a chord with one another and started chatting incessantly in a mellifluous flow of conversation and comfortability. Jade felt the flutter of attraction within her as the two stood close to one another engrossed in their own conversation and intrigue as the night escalated itself into a loud roar of chatter, music and laughter around them. "How old are you Jade?" Christian asked.

"I'm nineteen," Jade replied, smiling. "How old are you?"

"I'm eighteen," Christian replied, returning the smile.

"Excuse me a moment," Jade said placing her drink down upon the table next to them and turning her attentions towards Jamie.

Jade walked towards Jamie, who was standing at the bar, smiling to herself as she walked away from Christian.

"Hey Jamie, are we going to be staying at your place tonight?" she asked curiously.

"I don't know Jade, just give me a minute and I'll find out." Jamie walked over to Christian for a brief moment before quickly returning to Jade's side. "We're all going to stay here for the night Jade."

"Brilliant," she replied giggling as she walked over to the bar and grabbed another drink and placed her car keys on the hook that sat behind the small wooden bar. "I'll just ring my parents and let them know I won't be home tonight. Can I please use your phone?" Jade asked, walking back over to Christian.

"Yes of course, I'll show you where it is," Christian replied, leading her down the small stairwell and into the kitchen.

After calling her parents Jade returned to the games room and joined the many revellers who had turned up the music as the party started to become more boisterous and loud.

"Do you smoke?" Christian asked, leaning towards Jade as he passed her the bong filled with pot.

"Yes," she replied with a coy smile, reaching her hand up to grip the smoking apparatus and place it to her lips.

Jade could feel the invigorous intoxication of the alcohol and pot swirling through her senses instantaneously spreading a smile across her face and form giggles within her mouth that spontaneously flowed from her lips. She walked over to Vicky and pulled her gently to her feet from off the seat she was sitting on the other side of the room. "Dance with me," Jade said giggling as the loud music swam through her soul in garrulousness and moved her feet in rhythmic motions to the thumping music.

"No Jade, I don't dance," Vicky replied giggling, wrestling with her to get back to her seat.

"Oh come on," Jade continued, pulling her towards the middle of the room.

"You crazy girl, okay," Vicky replied, allowing the music to move her in time with the tunes.

"Watch out," Jade called out suddenly as Vicky took a step backwards. But Jade was not quick enough and in her intoxicated state Vicky lost her balance and tripped on the table leg, crashing to the floor. The room burst into ebullient laughter as Vicky lay on the floor slightly embarrassed holding her stomach wracked in laughter. "Oh my," Jade said laughing, rushing to help her up from off the floor. "Are you alright?"

"Yes," Vicky replied, her giggles still escaping from her lips as Jade helped her to her feet.

"Who wants to play Eightball?" Jade called out to the crowded room, quickly leading Vicky over towards the Eightball table. Numerous hands reached into the air as a crowd gathered around the Eightball table and organised their turns for a game. They all wrote their names on a little piece of paper and placed it into the wide brimmed hat before Jamie placed his hand into the hat and pulled out the names. As Jade stood by the pool table she glanced over at the bar where the other younger men were standing in a congregated group. One of the men pulled a small plastic bag filled with a white powder out of his jacket pocket and began to pour the white substance out onto the bar and formed it into lines across the bench top of the small wooden bar. The man looked up and noticed Jade's eyes staring at them in curiosity. One of the younger men walked over to Jade smiling friendly. "Would you like some?" he asked a questioning smile forming across his face.

"Umm, No. Not tonight, thank you anyway," she answered coyly. "I don't even know what that is," ran through her mind in her naivety as the man turned and walked away back to the bar. He pulled a fifty dollar note out of his wallet and began to inhale the lines of fine white powder into his nostrils one by one, changing sides of his nostrils as Jade looked on inquisitively. Jade giggled then turned her attentions back towards the pool table and had her shot smiling as the ball ran its direction of her placement and settled next to the pocket.

As the darkened evening turned into the light of day, the party had begun to wind down and sleepy eyes filled the room. Vicky walked over to the stereo and turned down the music before walking to the narrow staircase and descending to the bottom floor. "I'm going to bed," she called out on her descent down the staircase.

"Me too," echoed through the room from the other people standing within all corners and areas of the room. Jade followed Christian down the staircase and into the large carport situated underneath the house. "Here Jade, grab these," Christian said, holding out an armful of blankets and pillows which he placed into her arms. Jade followed Christian into the loungeroom and placed the blankets and pillows onto the lounge settee. Within moments the other people from the party had congregated in the loungeroom and began to pull together their make shift beds upon the floor and loungeroom chairs. "Goodnight," echoed through the room one after another as they all settled into their make shift beds and began to drift off into a solemn slumber. Jade crawled into the large makeshift bed next to Christian as he embraced her into his arms comfortably and fell asleep.

Jade awoke early the next morning to a throbbing headache. "Ohhh," she moaned holding her head. "I need water." Jade crawled out from under the blanket quietly as to not to disturb Christian or the other people sleeping within the room and tiptoed around all the people still asleep as she made her way to the kitchen. "Water," she muttered to herself, searching for the glasses in the kitchen cupboards. Jade filled the glass with water and sat at the kitchen table sipping the water slowly.

"Oh my, I feel terrible," she moaned holding her head in the palm of her hand as her elbow sat neatly on the table top. "Never again. Who's that?" she said suddenly to herself, listening to the footsteps approaching the kitchen from the loungeroom. Jade raised her head from off the table top as her eyes scanned the direction of the footsteps. "Oh it's you Christian," she said smiling, greeting him for the morning.

"Hey," Christian said, walking in holding his head in his hands.

"Water," Jade replied giggling but sympathising.

"Yes please, "Christian replied sitting at the table next to her in a silent stupor.

"When are you going back?" Christian asked, sipping slowly at the glass of water that she had gotten for him.

"Soon," Jade replied. "I have to get going soon."

"Could I see you again, soon?" he asked. A sweet smile formed across Jade's lips as her eyes met his.

"Okay," she blushed, looking slightly down at the table coyly. "That would be nice."

Christian reached for the note pad sitting on the cupboard bench top placed near the table and began to write his phone number on it and handed it to Jade.

"I'll give you a call sometime tomorrow okay," she said smiling placing a kiss upon his cheek.

Jade raised to her feet and walked to the loungeroom to gather her belongings and returned to the table. "I've got to go now okay. Thank you for a good night."

Christian stood from the table and walked her to the front door. "I'll see you soon," Christian said, leaning forward and placing a kiss upon her cheek.

"See you soon," Jade replied, smiling, as a little coy giggle slipped from her lips and she spun on her heels and walked towards her parked car and left.

Over the next two days Jade continuously pondered in her thoughts of the young man of whom she met at the party and the attraction of which she had felt towards him.

She pulled out the piece of paper from her purse and unfolded it, revealing the phone number that he had given to her before she had left that morning and held it within her fingers.

"He's charming," Jade whispered to herself, biting nervously upon her bottom lip and fiddling the piece of paper indecisively between her fingertips. "I'm going to call him," she said suddenly making a snap decision and walked nervously to the phone.

Jade rang the number and waited nervously. "Hello," answered the phone.

"Hey Christian. It's me," Jade replied shyly.

"Oh Jade, It's nice to hear from you," Christian replied, a pleased tone held within his voice.

"Would you like to come to my place? I haven't got my licence or a car," he confessed giggling slightly embarrassed.

"Yes," Jade replied. "I'll be there soon."

Jade hung up the phone and walked to the bathroom, retouched her makeup and picked up her handbag sitting on her bedroom cupboard and drove to Montana Bay.

Over the next three months Jade spent every spare moment of her time with Christian as their interaction with each other began to deepen and grow. Although Jade had been very attracted to Christian sexually and she knew that the attraction was reciprocated Jade had decided to wait and had continuously pushed his hands from between her legs as their kisses deepened into a sensual embrace of seduction. Jade had wanted to wait until she really knew Christian until they approached their first sexual experience and continuously told him no upon his feverish touch. She felt embarrassed to confess to her innocence of having had only one lover before him and held the secret deep within her with each kiss that tantalised her senses.

"Would you like to stay?" Christian asked one evening while sitting within the privacy of his bedroom, the palm of his hand gently caressing the side of her face.

"But I'm not in love," ran through Jade's mind before she finally answered. "Yes," unable to resist the temptation of their sexual attraction anymore.

Their eyes stared into one another's as their lips touched and his embrace swept her into a world of abandonment. Jade nervously unbuttoned her shirt slowly as Christian slowly removed his T-shirt and unbuttoned his jeans, sliding them to the floor. "Ohhh," Jade moaned as he lent forward and kissed her deeply as his hands unbuttoned her jeans. Jade laid down upon the bed as Christian slid between her legs and pushed his hardened length into her. "Ohhh," she moaned as his body began to move in rhythmic unison with hers. "Mmm, ohhh," moaned from the bedroom in sexual ecstasy until their final movements came to an end and he wrapped her into the warmth of his arms, and they fell asleep.

Jade awoke early the next morning to an unperceived indifference as she lay next to Christian in his bed. As they lay together talking softly, Jade noticed a shift in Christians disposition towards her. No longer was he the charming polite young man that she had come to know and grown to care deeply about and now held an air of uncertainty about him.

"I have to go," Jade said nervously feeling uncomfortable by the sudden change in Christian, raising herself from off the bed and slipping back into her clothes and reaching for her car keys from out of her handbag.

"I'll see you tonight," Christian replied arrogantly, pulling the blankets around his neck and rolling over to his side away from her. Jade felt the bitter disappointment of her sexual abandonment wash over her and settle under her skin, as her eyes glanced over at Christian in a formidableness of disappointment.

Jade walked from out of the bedroom and got into her parked car and drove home, her mind searching for the answers of which he portrayed that morning after their night of intimate sexual pleasure. Jade parked her car in the driveway at her parents' home and sat silent momentarily, bewildered by the sudden change in Christian's demeanour. "Did I disappoint him last night?" she questioned herself within her mind. "Why was he not so reciprocating this morning? Maybe he doesn't like me now." That evening Jade decided to stay home and give herself some time to think things through and tossed and turned continuously under the covers of her bed sheets that night, as her mind meticulously searched for the denouncement of Christian's shift in attitude towards her.

Jade awoke the next morning feeling slightly better about the circumstances although still confused but decided to put it behind her and go and see Christian.

On her arrival Jade knocked on the front door of Christian's house but there was no answer. She walked through the open carport to the back gate and called out. "Christian, are you home? "

"I'm in the pool room," came his voice from out of the large brick building situated in the back yard of the house. Jade walked through the back gate and over to the pool room and opened the door.

"Where's your mum and dad?" she questioned, entering the pool room. "No one answered the door when I knocked on it" "They are at Rivergum Plains on their houseboat for the weekend," Christian replied, flashing a wicked smile in her direction.

Jade knew of Christian's parents' activities and that they had regularly left the children home alone while tending to their houseboat at Rivergum Plains which had been revealed to her in their continuous conversations of getting to know one another. Although there were four children in the family the parents were rarely home and gallivanted all over Rivergum Plains in their family business of running a chartered houseboat and also their roof tiling business which meant the children were quite often left home alone to take care of themselves. Christian had complained about it on numerous occasions and disliked the responsibility he was left to face as the carer of his younger sibling Scott.

Jade sat quietly in the chair next to Christian, the birds chirping in the background in the aviaries that covered the long back wall of the pool room as they began to talk.

"What's wrong with you today?" Christian asked, his eyes staring into hers in an inquisitive glance.

"What do you mean?" Jade replied, tilting her head slightly to the side covering the truth of her thoughts that still plagued her mind.

"You're not your usual chatty self today."

"I'm okay, just feel quiet today that's all," Jade replied, keeping her thoughts to herself as she forced a smile to spread across her lips.

Christian rose to his feet then bent down on one knee in front of her and wrapped his hands tightly around the tops of her arms squeezing down upon her soft flesh. "Don't fucken start with me," he growled looking viciously into her eyes. Jade froze as a foreboding sensation swept up her spine and rose her to her feet quickly. Christian raised off his knee to stand over her facing her in a confrontational stance and glared intimidating daggers into her eyes before walking out of the pool room. "Coming inside," he yelled out from the back yard as Jade stood fearfully frozen on the spot where he left her.

Jade hesitated, her feet stood still, bewildered by his sudden change in attitude towards her before finally taking that first step and followed him through the back yard to the confinement of his bedroom.

Jade walked through the bedroom door and into the room where Christian had started to undress. "Take your clothes off and get in my bed," he demanded angrily, stepping towards her in a slow moving stance. Christian reached his hands out and grabbed her around the tops of her arms and pushed her down hard upon the single bed and kissed her roughly, forcibly. Jade laid there motionless, fearful, nervous and stunned by his actions and behaviour and closed her eyes blocking out the truth of his assault as he took her roughly until he had finished with her.

After he was finished he looked viciously into her eyes as he lay hard down upon her, his body pinning her to the bed and wrapped his fists around her throat. "You try and leave me and I'll kill you. Do you hear me. You're mine girl. You are not going anywhere. You're mine."

Christian got up from off the bed and stood glaring down upon her in an aggressive stance before turning and walking from the room. Jade laid upon the bed motionless stunned by what had just taken place as the terrified emotions that rushed throughout her welled tears within her eyes that slowly began to trickle down her soft, pale cheeks and onto the pillow case.

"Oh my god," Jade whispered. "What am I going to do? What should I do?"

Jade felt an overwhelming foreboding sweep down upon her in a confusion of fear as she raised from the bed, reaching for her clothes and began to dress. Her mind could not fathom the sudden change in his demeanour and darted fearfully over the repugnant attack which had just occurred.

Jade left the house that day terrified, unable to believe what had just happened but feared not returning as he had stipulated and had threatened in his assault upon her life that if she didn't return he would hunt her down and hurt her; he had made that very clear to her that day.

That night under Christian's strict instructions Jade returned. She was greeted at the door by his mother which gave Jade a sense of relief as she thought Christian could not harm her in their presence within the family home. Jade did not speak of the incident which had taken place that day, out of fear and repercussions of Christian's viciousness and assault.

That night while Christian was away at his friend's house, upon his orders Jade waited patiently for his return, sitting in his bedroom. Without warning she heard a knock on the bedroom door. "Come in," she called out, curious to who was at the door.

"It's just me," Christian's older brother, Matt announced. "How are you?"

"I'm fine," Jade answered biting nervously on her bottom lip.

Matt walked through the door and into the bedroom placing himself down upon the end of the bed and looked at Jade through admiring eyes. "You know I've liked you ever since I met you that night at the party," Matt continued. "You're too good for my brother," reaching his hand out to stroke her hand.

"Matt. I don't know what to say. I am with your brother. We can't do this," Jade replied hurriedly, pushing away his hand. Jade let out a nervous uncomfortable giggle as her eyes darted to avoid his contact. "You know, I could set you up with one of my girlfriends," she announced. "And don't worry, I will never tell Christian about what just happened here, it will be our little secret."

Matt nodded his head and dropped his gaze from her eyes. "I'm sorry Jade, I should have not come on to you like that." Jade smiled and reached out her hand to stroke his arm.

"It's okay, I understand Matt," Jade muttered cautiously as his brothers hand laid deeply entrenched upon the soft vulnerability of her flesh.

"I appreciate you keeping this to yourself," Matt replied, rising from off the bed and walking from the room.

"Oh god," Jade whispered to herself, holding the palm of her hand to her forehead. "That was so weird."

Over the next couple of days Jade's mind tangled constantly with the fearful agitation that overwhelmed her in confusion and held her to Christian in a fearful state. She feared being alone with Christian but feared more not to abide by his orders and did not know how to escape as his vicious temper tormented her mind and held her in a state of fear for her life and an overwhelming sense of damnation.

"What do I do?" Jade whispered to herself, laying under the covers of her bed at her parents' home placing her trembling hand to her forehead. "How do I get myself out of this? I will have to be brave and tell him I don't want to be with him anymore but what if he." Jade stopped suddenly, the words ceasing to fall from her mouth as she drew in her breath and felt the courage of her decision raise up her back bone.

The next day Jade went to Montana Bay and met Christian. They drove down to a hollow in the sand dunes and sat in the car talking to one another as they had within the first six months of knowing one another. Christian exhumed his natural charm and looked at Jade with a sweet smile that spread across his face.

Jade paused momentarily and went silent as her intuition dictated the right words and time to announce her departure from the relationship. She looked at Christian as she drew in a deep breath and allowed the words to spill from her mouth in an act of courage and self-preservation. "I know we've had some really good times together and I really like you but I really don't think we are going to work out. We are too different. I don't want to be with you anymore Christian." Jade's heart beat nervously at a fast pace within her chest as Christian paused silently and stared at her. Christian sat motionless in silence that had seemed like hours but were only minutes as Jade held her breath and his eyes fixated upon her before his face took a sudden change.

"Oh no," ran through Jade's mind as she braced herself for the onslaught of his terrible rage. Christian remained silent as his eyes unexpectedly welled with tears that began to fall down upon his cheeks.

"Oh my god," Jade whispered to herself, the strength of her courage draining and falling to the floor in a state of compunction and compassion. "Please don't cry. I'm sorry. But. "

Christian quickly interrupted before she could say another word. "Please don't leave me, please. I love you very much. I'm so sorry I have been a little mean. Things have been going on and I was wrong to take it out on you. I'm very sorry," he pleaded sobbing as he reached out to stroke the top of her hand tentatively.

Jade sat there motionless and speechless, stunned by his unexpected reaction and was once again confused as her mind darted back and forth engulfed by her heart that implored sympathy. "Okay," she said finally shaking her head in disbelief, her eyes softening in line with her sympathetic heart. "I won't leave you. We'll just take it slow and see how it goes okay. But please, you cannot treat me that way Christian. I don't like it."

Christian took her hand into his gently and lovingly and slowly lent forward and kissed her softly on the lips. "I won't, I promise. I won't ever do that again," he whispered, trailing his kisses down the softness of her neck.

Jade remained silent not knowing what to say next as her mind wondered what was going through his head. "Does he want me to say I love you too? But I don't," ran through her mind in silent admission.

Finally Jade spoke. "I like you a lot too." She had hoped that that was enough, she couldn't lie to him and say that she was in love with him when she wasn't; the truth was she feared him and could not fall for such a monster but now felt sympathy for him which had remained her secret.

Jade started the car and drove back to Christian's house and they spent the afternoon swimming and frolicking in the pool and sitting together talking in the backyard under the warmth of the summer sun that shone down upon them. That day Jade left Christian's house with a content smile that showed upon her face.

Over the next couple of days Jade and Christian spent time apart busied within their employment positions. Jade held two part-time positions in the small town of Copper Cove, stacking shelves in a busy supermarket at night and a cleaning position during the day hours that were arduous and tiresome. Christian worked for his father's roofing business in Montana Bay but had mentioned that he was looking for another employment position as he found it hard to work with his family and the days would quite often end in bitter arguments and quarrelling .

Although they had spent two days apart Jade did not feel the pull of her emotions at all and had not missed Christian in their absence from each other's company as she felt that she should have and spent the time away from him to forgive his wrong doings and move herself forward from the aggressiveness of his behaviour that had plagued them in the beginning of their relationship. Jade had hoped that his words were true and that she would not suffer another blow from his viciousness and aggression and that he truly meant it when he said that he was sorry.

On the Friday night Jade busied herself in her bedroom trying on many different outfits in her quest to look beautiful and wanting to look special and attractive for Christian. Jade drove to Christian's house confident and excited and smiled broadly as she walked towards the front of the house and knocked on the large wooden front door of the family home. She heard footsteps coming quickly to the door; the door opened.

"Oh hi Matt," Jade greeted Christian's brother who stood within the open door smiling. "Is Christian home?"

"Come in Jade. He's in his bedroom." Jade walked up the long, narrow corridor to Christian's bedroom and knocked on the door.

As she entered the bedroom Christian did not get up to greet her but lay sullenly on top of his bed covers, devoid of his usual charms that she had come to admire. His eyes glared at her without a welcoming smile as he lay silent upon his bed. Jade felt her heart beat quicken in her chest, her breath tighten within her throat as her mind was suddenly bewildered by the sudden change that represented itself again. "Oh no," ran through her mind in a sudden rush of panic and fear wanting to make her run from the room.

"Why are you wearing those?" Christian finally said his words spiked with aversion and agitation, looking at her new tight jeans. "You look terrible. You have a big fat arse. You shouldn't wear them and your hair is horrible. Blonde doesn't even suit you, you know. You should have been born with dark hair not blonde. You are so ugly," he repeated incessantly ramming the words into her psyche. "I don't know why I even bother with an ugly girl like you. You're not even worth it," he continued suddenly rising to his feet from off the bed and rushing towards her pushing her hard up against the solid brick wall, her cheek hitting the wall so hard Jade could feel the heat of the bruise already starting to form across her cheek bone. Christian grabbed her arm in a tight grip of his hand and twisted it up behind her back as his gritted teeth gnawed at her ear. "Now you listen to me. You are my girl and you'll listen to me from now on. I want you to move in here with me. I have already asked my parents and they have agreed. You'll be staying here tonight and tomorrow we will go and get your things from your parents' house. Do you understand?" Jade nodded her head in silence his furiousness terrifying her into a silent scamper that welled in tears within her eyes and trickled down her face as she trembled against his powerful strength and viciousness. Christian slowly loosened his grip upon her twisted arm and released her from the entrapment against the wall and sat on the end of the bed glaring at her.

That night Jade spent hours in fear for her life as Christian's brutal assault was executed through his violent aggressiveness and scornful hateful words and an incessant abuse of physicality. His violence was shocking as he wrapped his fingers tightly around her throat taking her breath away from her and swore to kill her as he looked deep into her eyes with his scornful black eyes that pierced deep into her mind, her soul before throwing her down upon the bed and repeatedly raping her.

She knew that he meant every word he had said and that night he had shown it too.

The next morning after Christian's insistence, they got into Jade's car and drove back to her parents' home and gathered her possessions and loaded them into the car. Jade's parents had not been home at the time to which Jade was grateful as she did not know how to explain the numerous inflictions of bruising and grazes that covered her face and parts of her body. Jade picked up a pen and paper and began to write them a note:

Mum and Dad
I have moved out of home and have gone to Montana Bay with Christian.
I am Okay so please don't worry about me. I will give you a call on the weekend
Okay. Love Jade

And left it on the kitchen table.

Over the course of the next month as Jade remained trapped within the terrifying grips of Christian's relentless abuse, removed from her parent's watchful eye, the violence escalated and grew more horrendous.

"Wake up Jade," Christian said leaning above her, the large diver's knife gripped in his hand and held viciously to her throat.

Jade awoke abruptly as if awakening from a nightmare as she felt the knife come down against the soft skin of her throat, nicking her slightly like a paper cut. "Please let me go," Jade pleaded terrified, streams of tears falling down her cheeks. "Christian, god, let me go."

"You're my girl, do you hear me? If I can't have you then no one can," Christian growled through gritted teeth, his face only millimetres away from hers." You won't go anywhere will you. Cause if you do, I'll kill your family. And then I'll kill you." Jade trembled under the power of his viciousness and threats and nodded her head as her widened terrified eyes slowly closed hoping she could disappear from where she was entrapped.

Jade bore the marks of his viciousness with each newly formed bruise that lay upon her face, arms and body as he executed his power over her every day. Although Jade was terrified and her mind shattered into a submissive state of abatement she remained aware and conceptual and started to notice a pattern in Christian's behaviour as his violence escalated on the days before he would leave her alone in the house to go diving. Jade's mind escaped deep into thought as she planned numerous outcomes and scenarios if she was to make her escape, each time that she withstood his attack and viciousness. Jade did not know what to do but she was not going to allow him to destroy her and her thoughts of escape grew with each passing moment that she lay gripped within his abuse. Jade waited for the day when she could run.

"I'm going diving," Christian yelled from the front door.

Jade sat up off the double bed and walked down the narrow hallway to the front door and stood in front of him.

"Okay," she replied meekly, her mouth arched downwards removed from the once happy smiles that once graced her face. Flashes of the tempestuous abuse of which she had been suffering gripped in his hands incessantly repeated themselves within the dark corners of her mind and her eyes dropped towards the floor. Jade stood motionless and submissive within a trance like state as her mind replayed each moment when suddenly she felt Christian rush towards her.

"No Christian, let me go," Jade pleaded sobbing as she felt the hands of her lover wrap around her throat tightly and push her hard up against the wall. "Please Christian, I can't breathe." Jade's eyes darted in desperation as the world around her took on a pale shade of black and the air she tried so desperately to breath became thin. Life began to flash past her in memories as her mind told her that she was going to die. Just as Jade desperately took one last gulp of air she suddenly felt the tight grip around her throat loosen. She fell to the floor onto her knees as Christian loosened his grip completely and removed his hands from off her throat.

"Come here," Christian growled, pulling at the front of her shirt and lifting her to her feet. "You ugly little slut. You're worthless. I'm going to kill you bitch."

"Oh my god, you nearly killed me," ran through Jade's mind in a terrified realisation of his threats as she turned her cheek to the side and broke all eye contact. Jade felt helpless to escape, alone and entrapped, isolated within her terror that remained unnoticed by the world or the other people within the house. Every day she felt the longing, the endless waiting for the moment when she could break free and leave and save herself from the vicious onslaught of the abuse.

Terrified, Jade gulped at the air within her throat that was now sore and constricted by fear and held her hands submissively behind her back as Christian growled his orders at her. "I'll be home at four pm. I expect you to be here."

"I'll be here. I promise," Jade whimpered complacently. She kissed Christian on the cheek and turned away towards the hallway and walked towards the bedroom, her prison of which he held her captive day after endless day within his abuse and sat on the end of the double bed, placing her head into her hands. "I can't do this anymore. Please someone help me," Jade sobbed again and again, the tears falling heavily from her eyes and rolling down her pale cheeks. The tears stopped falling as if they had dried up as Jade's broken submissive mind suddenly retorted from the oppression and formed a strategical plan within her mind.

Day after day Jade grew stronger from each lashing of abuse as she spent her time devising the moves of her plan to escape from the hell that her life had become. With each horrendous chokehold around her throat, suffocation of the pillows placed upon her face while she slept or violent punches that bruised her soft flesh, Jade grew more and more distant from Christian, as her mind disconnected into its own world where her fear did not overpower her and she planned her escape from the fearful hold which he had over her.

Three months later Christian and Jade moved out of his parents' house and relocated to Copper Cove into an older style house with three large bedrooms and a quarter of an acre block located on the back of the property.

One evening Christian received a phone call from his friends in Alterro.

"We're coming up for a visit," the voice said down the phone excitedly.

"Excellent," Christian replied. "When are you coming?"

"Tonight mate," he informed him.

Jade took a deep breath and relaxed, she knew Christian well enough to know that she was safe from his hands tonight and tonight in his friends presence safe from the fear and worry of his onslaught, tonight would be her freedom even if for just a short moment.

She walked from the hallway and sat on the end of the bed, placing her head into the palms of her hands. "Maybe tonight," Jade whispered to herself. "Tonight I will escape while he's busy with his friends." Jade would not give up, her life so precious to her, her dreams too important, she had to escape.

That night Jade heard a car pull up in the backyard. She had not met Christian's friends before but hoped that they were not like him, vicious and cruel and heavy-handed with their girlfriends. Jade waited for Christian's instructions as she stood at the backdoor watching his friends exit the vehicle. "Yes," Jade whispered to herself looking to the ceiling in relief as she watched a girl exit from the back seat of the vehicle.

"Hey mate," Christian greeted his friends. "This is Jade."

"Hi," Jade answered tentatively, as they offered her a drink that they had brought with them in an esky. Jade knew that she wasn't meant to drink as she had been on medication for six months as a result of the terrible debilitating anxious condition that she now suffered as a result of Christian's constant abuse but took the drink anyway and joined in the celebration.

"Let's start a bonfire," Christian suggested as his friends followed him into the backyard and began to gather wood and kindling and throwing it into a pile within a clearing and setting it alight. "I'll get the guitar mate," Christian called out walking back into the house.

Within minutes Christian returned to the site of the bonfire and started to play the guitar as his friends sat around the fire listening to him play and talking and drinking. Jade sat down on the big log next to the other girl and started to talk. She felt a sense of calmness with the other people around. She knew Christian would keep his hands off her tonight which had served to be a god send and enabled her to regroup and recover momentarily from the strain. "Coward, gutless coward," ran through Jade's mind as she sat and watched each stroke of his fingers upon the guitar strings.

Late into the evening that had slowly turned to darkness, heavily intoxicated Jade went in search of Christian and the girl who had disappeared from the crowd.

"Where's Christian?" Jade said, standing off the log and not receiving an answer from his friends before she walked off towards the house and entered through the back door.

"What's that?" Jade whispered to herself as she stood listening to the strange noise coming from the end of the house. Jade walked along the wide long hallway that ran through the middle of the large house towards the noises which led her to the main bedroom.

"Christian are you in here?" she called out, poking her head around the doorway of the bedroom door.

Jade's jaw dropped open as her eyes focused on the two people in her bed. "Christian, what are you doing?" Jade said, standing at the foot of the bed startled. Christian slipped his hands from out of the girl's pants and sat up right on the bed. Jade turned on her heels quickly and rushed from the bedroom. "Come here," Christian yelled from the bedroom ordering her to come back.

Jade walked back into the bedroom, her head held low before raising her head once more to look at the girl who lay on the bed half naked.

"What Christian?" Jade said standing at the end of the bed.

"I want to see you two girls together. Take your clothes off and come here." Without question Jade did as she was told and started to take her clothes off dropping them to the floor before crawling onto the end of the bed and joining the girl on top of the bed in a sexual embrace. "Lay on top of her," Christian demanded smiling devilishly.

Jade complied submissively, laying down upon the naked girl and started to kiss her as Christian joined them on the bed as he pushed Jade aside and opened the legs of the girl and entered her aggressively. "Ohhh, stop," the girl moaned intoxicated and semi unconscious. "I'm out of here," Jade said, slipping back into her clothes and rushing from the bedroom.

"Come here, you little slut," Christian yelled, running from the bedroom and punching her in the arm. "You fucked all this up." Christian led Jade back into the bedroom pulling her by her arms and to the side of the bed, picking up the intoxicated girl from off the bed and giving her to Jade who led her stumbling and leaning upon her out of the bedroom and towards the bathroom.

"Did you know that I use to date him?" the girl slurred, taking off her clothes and stumbling into the shower. Jade drew in a deep breath. "Would you like to date him again?" she questioned, secretly hoping the answer would be yes.

"No," answered the girl. "Aren't you two an item?"

"No," Jade replied quickly. "We have split up, he's all yours if you want him."

"No. I don't want him, it was just sex Jade," the girl answered giggling incoherently, grabbing the towel off the towel rack and drying herself.

Jade walked out of the bathroom and re-joined the group in the loungeroom.

"Want a drink Jade?" Christian asked. "And one of these," grabbing the packed bong off the coffee table and handing it to her.

"Thanks," Jade answered, her scowl hidden behind the fake smile on her face.

As the party continued and the intoxication of the alcohol started to escalate, tempers started to flair and arguments between the friends and Christian started to erupt. As their backs were turned Jade quickly stood up off the lounge settee and rushed out of the house and towards the road. "I'm out of here," Jade yelled out as Christian came rushing out of the house.

"Get back here," he demanded yelling down the street.

"No," Jade yelled back and kept on walking, stumbling along the road in the dark.

Jade kept on walking until she finally came to her parents' house and let herself in through the front door.

"What are you doing here?" her mum asked surprised by her appearance.

"I've had enough, Mum," Jade answered angrily. "I'm so angry, you should have seen what he was doing tonight."

Within moments of her arriving they heard a loud knock on the front door.

Sienna rose to her feet and opened the front door.

"Christian. What are you doing here?"

"Is she here?" he asked angrily.

"Yes, she's in the kitchen," Sienna answered allowing him entry into the home.

Christian walked through the narrow hallway that led to the kitchen. Jade's eyes opened wide to meet his angry glare before narrowing to a tight angry slit. "What are you doing here?" she growled. "Get out of my parents' house, you're not welcome here." Jade raised from off the kitchen chair and rushed at him pouncing on him and knocking him to the ground in a scuffle.

"You motherfucker," Jade yelled, swinging her fists that landed down upon Christian in short succession. "I'm going to kill you," sitting down upon him and wrestling him to the floor as her fists kept pounding at him hard.

"Jade, No," her father yelled out, running to pull her off Christian. But Jade was too angry, the strength of her anger holding her in place against her father's hands and kept swinging her fists until finally her father and her brother, Peter who came running from his bedroom pulled her off him.

"You crazy bitch," Christian yelled. "Get her off of me."

"You have to leave Christian," her father demanded, pointing him towards the front door. "Now"

"Don't worry, I'm leaving," Christian said, straightening himself and walked out of the front door of the house.

"Can I stay the night please Mum?" Jade pleaded, her face flushed with her frustrations and anger.

"Of course you can love," Sienna answered, walking to the laundry cupboard and gathering blankets and handing them to her.

Jade felt the rage swirl around her as her mind fumed with hatred and animosity as she climbed into the make shift bed upon the loungeroom floor. She laid motionless silent trying to calm the overwhelming rage she felt inside of herself. "I've got to go to the bathroom," Jade whispered to herself, her face still flushed with anger and frustration.

As Jade snuck back quietly through the house and re-entered the loungeroom she could not let go of the rage that had consumed her and snapped out of control. "Fuck him. I'm going to kill you," Jade roared inside of herself as she paced the length of the loungeroom back and forth. "Fuck him," Jade growled quietly in her intoxicated state. "I'm going to get him."

Jade looked at the front door biting her lip nervously as a flash of her parents stopped her in a moment of hesitation. Jade looked back towards her parents' bedroom at the other end of the house before refocusing her anger upon the exit of the front door. "Fuck it," Jade growled one last time and rushed out of the front door.

Her feet walking at a fast pace out into the nights darkness as she stumbled through the bushes, over the rocks in the paddocks and hid within the confines of people's front yards as she made her way back to the house where Christian was in a commando style trance.

Finally, she made it back to the house and quietly crept into the back yard along the outside of the fence line and poked her head just above the fence and saw Christian standing on the back porch having a cigarette. Jade lowered her head quickly and peaked through the nail holes of the fence watching him as she crept the length of the fence to the entrance of the back yard, thinking about her next move. Jade picked up a log that lay on the ground next to her and hid it behind her back and crept out of the darkness and started to approach Christian standing on the back porch.

As she took that first step out of her hiding place a sense of logic suddenly overtook her. "What are you doing?" she thought to herself. "No girl, this is not the way," and dropped the large wooden log to the ground next to the fence.

Jade stood up straight and walked towards him, starling him in her appearance. "What the fuck are you doing here?" Christian yelled. Words trembled in Jade's throat that constricted her of any sound as she tried to speak suddenly gripped back into her fear and came to a stop, standing motionless within the moment. Christian stood silent momentarily glaring at her before rushing in her direction, raising his fist and swung it down hard, landing his fist upon the soft tissue of her eye socket, knocking her off her feet and to the ground, splitting the soft skin on her brow. The blood gushed down her face and into her hair as she sat on the ground shaking her head slightly dazed and stunned, before jumping back onto her feet in one swift movement.

"How dare you," she growled, yelling the words through gritted teeth as her feet quickly marched her forward towards him. "I hate you." Christians face dropped to a pale shade of white as his arms spread open and entrapped her in a tight bear hug, holding her arms down by her side as she continued to struggle and fight his grip.

"Stop it Jade," he yelled, carrying her towards the front of the house. The profanity poured out of Jade's mouth as she was carried to the front of the house, when all of a sudden she stopped as the sight of her parents came into her view. "Your parents and the police are here," Christian said quietly, releasing his grip instantly from around her arms, dropping her to the ground. Jade's father exited the car quickly and walked towards the police car that was parked behind them, his face a pale shade of white as he sighted Jade's eye bleeding profusely down her cheek and into her blonde hair turning it red. Jade quickly walked over to her father standing near the police car before being led back to her parents' car by her father and placed into the back seat.

"Oh Jade," her mother cried, viewing the state of her daughter covered in blood and her eye swelling and changing colour. "I was so worried Jade."

"I'm sorry Mum. I'm so sorry," Jade cried in the backseat, placing her head into her hands. After talking to the police officer briefly Jades father returned to the car leaving the police officers there and drove them home.

That night Jade arranged to move back into her parents' house.

The next morning Jade awoke to the mumbling of voices coming from the front yard of her parents' house. She stretched her arms up in her sleepy state and stumbled to her knees upon the bed and pulled back the curtain of her bedroom window.

"Oh it's my brothers," Jade said, quickly jumping to her feet and slipping into her clothes.

"Hey Steve," Jade said, stepping out of the front door of the house, her damaged bruised swollen eye weeping blood down the side of her face as she dabbed at it, trying to stop the blood from trickling down her face.

"What happen to you?" Steve questioned rushing to her side looking at her eye intensively, worried and concerned.

"Christian king hit me. Last night," Jade said. "He knocked me to the ground, one punch"

"The fucken little prick. I'll break his fucken fingers," Steve roared pacing up and down the footpath.

"No, you won't," Sienna said standing straight up to her son and looking him in the eyes.

"No, I just need you to help me move my stuff out of the house," Jade interrupted quelling the tension between her mother and brother.

"Okay, okay," Steve replied turning away from their mother and facing towards Jade, calming his voice. "When?"

"Now, today," Jade replied, a worrisome look covering her face. "I don't know if he's still there but I know he won't dare do anything while your there."

"Okay, let's do it," Steve replied, gesturing towards their other brothers and the friend that he had brought there with him.

Jade entered the house cautiously with her brothers walking close behind her. She walked into the loungeroom where she quickly viewed Christian sitting on the lounge settee. "Christian I've come to get my things. I'm moving out," Jade said confidently within her brother's presence, her backbone straightening and looking directly at him. A slight smugness spread across Christian's face and curled his lips as he looked at her face and the damage that he had inflicted the night before. "Okay," he replied and his words fell silent.

Jade walked out of the house and grabbed the big cardboard boxes from the back of the car seat and took them into the house and started to pack up her belongings. One by one her brothers carried the numerous packed boxes out of the house and placed them into the car and trailer.

"Is Christian here?" Jade asked, calling across from the other side of the garden.

"No, he left," Steve called out replying. Jade walked over to the packed car and trailer to where Steve and her brothers stood waiting for the last of the boxes to be loaded into the trailer by Steve's friend.

"Okay, we're done here," Steve said. "We'll take this home for you now."

"Thanks Steve." Jade replied, "I'll see you at home."

Jade walked up to the back of the house; it was quiet; no one was there; she couldn't see anyone, hear anything as she entered the house to check to see if she had forgotten any of her belongings and walked into the loungeroom. Suddenly she heard a noise coming from the bedroom that was located directly off the loungeroom. The door suddenly rushed opened.

"Oh hi," Jade said, startled by the sudden appearance of Christian's friend who stood in the doorway.

Christian's friend smiled broadly, smugly, "No he isn't. He said that he would be back later."

Suddenly Christian rushed from out behind him and walked straight up to her. "You fucking little cunt you got me in trouble with the police," Christian growled through gritted teeth, pushing her aggressively to the floor, scrambling with her pants.

"No Christian. Please god no," Jade cried out, tears of fear rushing down her cheeks. "Please Christian, No," she cried, pleading with him. Christian ripped her pants down to her ankles and pressed himself down on top of her and pushed his hardened length in, in one swift movement. Jade let out a cry as she lay pinned to the loungeroom floor. "Please god no. Christian please stop. Oh god, stop," Jade cried out as she heard the cheers and clapping in the back ground coming from his friends who watched the abuse taking place. Jade's eyes looked over at the fish tank as the bubbles rose to the surface slowly as it etched into her mind and her eyes rolled shut until he had finished his violent abuse.

"You little slut," Christian yelled, rising to his feet, spitting at the ground next to her. Jade laid on the floor motionless shocked before curling into a tight ball crying.

"That didn't just happen. My god no," Jade sobbed, holding her knees to her chest.

Jade never told anyone what had happened on that fateful day on the loungeroom floor alone in that house and had held the secret within her tightly ashamed and humiliated by the actions of Christian and his friends.

Jade had been at her parents' home for a week.

While sitting peacefully in the loungeroom she heard a knock at the front door. Jade rose to her feet in joyful anticipation waiting to greet the person on the other side as she opened the door. "Oh hi," Jade greeted as her eyes widened nervously and her face dropped in appearance.

"Hi Jade," greeted Vicky, Christians sister.

"What are you doing here?" Jade questioned, her mind suddenly rushed into a state of trepidation.

"I just came to see you," Vicky answered. "Can I please come in?" Jade paused momentarily in deep thought before finally answering hesitantly.

"Yes, okay, come in," Jade said opening the door. Jade sat nervously, quietly in the lounge chair as she listened to Vicky talk.

"He misses you, you know. He's very upset about what happened."

Jade dropped her eyes to the floor and raised her fingers to her mouth, chewing on her fingertips before raising her eyes back up to meet hers that had remained looking at her. "What can I say," Jade finally answered. "I can't go back Vicky, you don't understand." Vicky's eyes dropped their stare to the floor from out of Jade's view.

"Okay, I understand Jade, I do," Vicky finally replied.

Jade rose from off the loungeroom chair and walked over to Vicky with her arms spread and wrapped her arms around her before gesturing towards the front door.

"I'm always here if you need someone to speak to okay," Vicky said upon stepping from the front door and walking the narrow cement path to her car as Jade followed her.

"Thank you," Jade replied, leaning against the car's open window as Vicky climbed into the driver's seat and placed the keys into the ignition.

Jade raised her eyes above the roof of the car to look towards the next door neighbour's house as something moving caught her eye. "Who's that?" she questioned puzzled. Suddenly Christian ran from the neighbour's yard and rushed towards her. "No, No, it's Christian." Jade cried out, stepping back away from the car as she felt the tightening of her throat, her words froze within her voice as she held her breath in her gasp. "Please, no," she said. "I'm not going back to you. It's over Christian," Jade said, raising her hands up to shield her face in a defensive pose.

"You are my girl," Christian growled. "Get in the fucken car." Christian reached out and grabbed her arm and opened the back door shoving her into the entrapment of the back seat of the car before climbing in himself. "Go Vicky, go now," he yelled frantically. Vicky started the engine of the car and sped down the dirt road and out onto the highway that led back to Montana Bay.

That night Christian violated her violently and showed her what would happen if she tried to escape from his captivity again.

That night trembling and terrified, battered and bruised and ordered by Christian Jade rang her parents and was answered by her father. "If you stay there Jade don't ever come back home. I'll disown you." Jade was devastated and dropped her head into her hands. "He doesn't know, he doesn't understand," Jade whimpered. "He said that he would kill you if I left again."

Three Months Later

Christian and Jade were swimming in the pool room when Tim, Christians friend unexpectedly entered the room. "Would you like to come with us diving mate?" Tim asked. Christian stopped momentarily and glanced his eyes over at Jade, furiousness blazing in his eyes, before directing his view back to Tim.

"Yeah mate. Love to," he answered cheerfully, pulling himself out of the pool and reaching for a towel.

Jade followed Christian into the house and into the bedroom.

"You know the rules Jade," Christian growled. "You know what will happen."

"Yes Christian, I know," Jade answered complacently.

Christian left with Tim, walking to the beachfront leaving Jade alone at his parents' house for the first time since he had kidnapped her and returned her back into his tight grip of abuse. Jade watched out of the bedroom window as the two men walked the narrow dirt track down to the beachfront and slowly disappeared. Jade's heart began to pound fast and loud within her chest as she quickly walked away from the window and reached for her handbag, swinging it over her shoulder and running for the front door of the house. She rushed into the driver's seat of her car, her trembling fingers frantically scrambling to place the keys into the ignition and started the engine, reversing the car back quickly and sped down the back streets of Montana Bay until she came to the highway that led to Copper Cove and continued to speed down the highway until she reached her brother's house. Jade pulled her car to a stop, her tyres slightly skidding along the road in front of the house and frantically scrambled out of the car and ran to the back door of the house.

"Steve. Steve are you there," Jade cried out desperately, frantic to hear his voice.

"Jade what is wrong?" Steve called out rushing to the back door and opening it to let her inside.

"Oh my god Steve. It's been terrible. Oh Steve, I'm so scared, I've just escaped from Christians house," Jade cried the tears rushing from her eyes and streaming down her cheeks. Steve looked at his sister, he had never seen her in that state before and walked up to her wrapping his arms around her and held onto her tightly until the tears started to stop. That evening Jade revealed the truth of the abusive violent threatening behaviour of which she had suffered within the tight grips of Christians abuse and entrapment. That night Steve agreed to Jade staying at his place for a while until the dust settled and she felt safe to return to her parents' house.

The next day Steve left for work and left Jade home alone. Each day, terrified she would be found by Christian, Jade crawled behind the large brown lounge that sat up against the loungeroom wall and tucked her legs into a curl as she listened intensively to the silence of the house until her brother returned at the end of the day. After three days there was a knock at the door.

"I'll get it," Steve said, standing from the kitchen table and walking to the back door.

"Mum, come on in," he greeted Sienna, opening the door.

"Is Jade here?" their mother asked concerned.

"Yes, in there. She's been here for three days. Have you known what has been going on?" Steve asked looking questionable at his mother. "Not really love," Sienna replied walking into the house.

Jade's mother walked into the kitchen and saw Jade sitting at the kitchen table sullen, trembling, her head in her hands.

"Sweetheart are you alright. I got a call from Christian. He understands that it's all over. He said that you can go and get your things," stepping towards her and placing her hand upon her shoulder trying to comfort her.

"I don't want my things," Jade replied. "I'd rather stay here." Jade felt the trepidation creep up her spine and fill her eyes as she looked at her mother trembling.

"We'll go with you Jade," her mother replied, her eyes a frown of her concern.

"Okay, I'll go," Jade finally agreed dropping her head to the floor in a behaviour of defeatism lacking the strength to argue with her mother.

Jades parents drove her back to Christian's house in Montana Bay and they all walked up to the front door together and knocked on it. Christian answered the door. "You're here," he said, standing with his hands behind his back in a military pose.

Suddenly and unexpectedly Christian reached his hand out and grabbed Jade by the scruff of her neck and pulled her inside the house in one quick movement and put the knife to her throat, before slamming the door shut as her parents stood there helpless and shocked.

"You fucking little cunt. I told you. I told you if I can't have you then no one can. Today you die bitch," he growled in her ear, holding the knife hard up against the tender flesh of her throat. Terrified and frantic Jade struggled and broke free of his grip and crouched near the kitchen table. "Come here bitch," Christian growled through gritted teeth like a demon possessed, grabbing her by the shirt and placing the large blade up against her throat once more.

"No Christian please, you don't have to do this," Jade pleaded, her tears streaming down her whitened cheeks as her body trembled uncontrollably within his grasp.

"Please let me go, please," Jade pleaded desperately. Christian started to lead Jade towards the back of the house when suddenly they heard a knock at the front door of the house.

"Open up. It's the police," a voice yelled into the house from the locked front door.

"Get fucked. Get the fuck out of here," Christian roared profusely.

"Sir, come to the front window where we can talk," the officer replied calmly.

Christian turned Jade around and walked her through the kitchen and into the dining room and approached the window with the knife held directly into her back. He slowly approached the window closer and closer as he pushed Jade out in front of him with the knife jabbing into the skin of her back through her clothes. Jade stared at the police officer through the closed window as her lips sounded the words, "Help me please."

Christian reached around her and slide the window open slightly.

The police officer saw his chance and rushed at the window with his hands and slid the window open quickly and grabbed Jade by the shirt, pulling her out through the window in one swift movement. The officer wrapped his arm around Jades shoulders and walked her to her parents who wrapped her up in their arms and began to cry in relief. Jade lay in her parents' arms in shock, she was not crying and stared off into space in a trance as if the air around her could swallow her whole and her very existence had been erased. Within moments, another police car arrived, two police officers quickly exited the vehicle and rushed to the house and apprehended Christian who was then removed from the home and taken to the local police station. That day Jade sat in front of her parents within the police station and told the horrendous story of the abuse of which she had suffered over the last twelve months within the entrapment of Christian. Jade's parents turned a shade of white as they listened and cried when they heard the horrendous truths spill from their daughter's lips. The police officer who had rescued her from out of the window advised Jades parents to get her counselling. But they never did.

The next morning, organised by the police officer who pulled her from the window Jade went to the court house and got a restraining order against Christian.

Jade was also informed that Christian was not eighteen but was seventeen years of age, he had lied to her. Christian was never prosecuted and walked away without any charges being laid against him.

Christian left the small town of Montana Bay two weeks later.

Jade had been told that he had relocated to a major city but he had been involved in a nasty accident that involved being hit by a tram and had both of his legs broken from the hips down. Jade did not know what to think or whether to believe the rumour. Two weeks later Jade saw Christian in the small township of Copper Cove as she sat with her parents in the safety of their car limping on crutches and covered in plaster from the hips down. The rumour was true.

For six months Jade did not leave her parents' home and suffered from the debilitating effects of Agoraphobia, until finally the day came when she decided she was going to leave the house and get on with her life.

The Marriage

As the house began to stir and fill with the sounds of her family rushing to and fro in their bustle of preparing for their day, Jade was awoken from her peaceful slumber, stretching her arms upwards towards the ceiling as she swung her feet from under the warmth of her blankets, placing them firmly on the carpeted floor of her bedroom.

"Mmm. What a beautiful morning," Jade said quietly as she pulled back the curtains of her small bedroom window and was greeted by the kiss of the morning's sunrise shining down on her through the pane of the window.

Jade had awoken early that morning, a strange notion swimming through her thoughts, as she greeted her mother in the warm summer's breeze that came through the kitchen window and settled upon their skin like a soft welcoming to the day.

She slowly sipped at the coffee as she sat at the kitchen table contemplating the thought that played and roamed within her mind.

"I'm going to meet my husband-to-be today," unexpectedly spilled from her lips.

Jade's mother looked at her, a puzzling giggle written all over her face and spilling from her lips.

"What love?" she finally asked questioning the disparate of Jades comment.

"Today I will meet my husband," Jade answered, raising her eyes to look at the puzzled expression that had formed upon her mother's face.

"Okay," her mother answered, a slight disbelief giggling within her voice as she placed her coffee mug down onto the kitchen table and sat down in the chair, sipping slowly at the warm brew.

Jade giggled too, puzzled at her own strange notion that had wedged itself into a corner of her mind and played with her thoughts as she continued to sip at the warm coffee in front of her at the kitchen table.

Jade rose from off her chair, placing the empty coffee cup upon the sink, inconspicuous in her thoughts as she walked away from her mother and entered the bathroom and proceeded to dress into a picture of attractiveness before leaving the house in her pursuit of the vision that had entered her mind that morning.

Jade entered the local hotel and walked up to the bar and sat down upon a stool, ordered herself a drink and waited patiently in anticipation, intuition beating in an unrelenting conformation within the pit of her stomach and surging through her thoughts.

"I know he'll come," Jade whispered to herself, trying to pass the time by busying herself around the eight ball table joyfully playing with the numerous patrons of the hotel that came and went.

Jade looked at the clock that hung above the long straight bar of the hotel. "Mmm 6.30 pm," she said to herself, her hopes starting to dash in a subsequence sense of her own reflectiveness.

Jade lowered her eyes to the hotel floor feeling slightly embarrassed by her own illogical notion that had remained within her mind like a stubborn propensity.

"Maybe just a little longer," ran through Jades mind, smiling down at the ground hiding the illogical secret, transfixed in her own reasoning of staying. Jade sat on a stool at the long bar staring into the hotels facilities of the adjoining room that contained numerous gamblers that came and went in a joyous commotion of smiles or a dispelled disappointment of frowns, as the winning numbers were displayed across the face of the television that was fixed to the wall.

As Jades eyes precariously glanced over the numerous people that came into her view as they lined the perimeters of the next room Jade was suddenly struck by the vision of three strangers that entered through the heavy set doors of the gamblers facilities and approached the television screen that hung on the wall.

A gasp rose into Jade's throat as her heart began to quicken in tempo within her chest and she felt a sudden rush of unexplainable excitement swirl within her stomach as she intensively continued to watch the three strangers walk to the board fixed to one of the walls displaying the winning numbers.

"It's him," raced through Jade's mind in an intuitive acknowledgement of enlightenment. "This is strange, how did I know that he would be here," Jade whispered to herself, placing her fingertips to her mouth. "This is like déjà vu." Her eyes continued to carefully study each movement of one of the strangers who had caught her eye and of who she was drawn to as he moved around the room and approached the gamblers desk at the back of the room. "It's really him," Jade whispered, the unexplainable attraction beckoning her to approach him.

Jade tentatively rose to her feet from off the stool and walked through the open doorway that separated the two rooms of the hotel and strategically sat down at the round table placed within the middle of the gambling room in anticipation of being noticed by the man that had instinctively caught her eye.

"Hi," Jade said confidently exerting a joyous smile, her eyes fixated upon him as the unknown man flashed a shy glance at her sitting at the table.

"Hello," the tall dark haired man answered shyly re-directing his glance back towards his friends who had momentarily paused near them in their intrigue of the interaction. "Would you like to sit down with me?" Jade asked, her smile an inviting fascination of attraction.

"Yes, thank you," the tall dark haired man said, smiling shyly at the ground as his eyes led his hands towards the stool that he pulled out from around the table and reservedly sat down.

The friends that had accompanied the man looked on with astonishment at the unexpected view of their mates interaction with the unknown woman who had approached their friend so confidently and of who had invited him to sit with her. "Would your friends like to join us?" Jade asked, looking at the man's friends and gesturing towards the table in an invitation to join them. The two other men looked at each other and smiled peculiarly before walking the few steps towards the table and pulling out a stool each and sat down. "I'm Jade by the way," Jade introduced herself giggling, feeling a little foolish for not introducing herself straight away.

"I'm Derek and this is Brett and Rick," the dark haired man replied, introducing himself and his two friends who joined them at the table.

"Do you live here in Copper Cove, I haven't seen you before?" Jade asked, suddenly feeling a touch shy and less confident within the attraction that had started to arose her senses while eyeing Derek as she sat with him and his friends.

"No, we come from Werrington, we're just passing through the town on our way to go camping and thought that we would stop for a drink and check our bets in our travels," Brett answered smiling. "Oh, you like camping, I've never actually been camping before so I wouldn't know what it is like," Jade replied, sipping at her drink that was placed on the table in front of her and smiled in Derek's direction.

Jade's attention faulted on the other two men as her attentions swung reflectively towards the attraction she was feeling towards Derek who had remained shy and reserved in her presence as his eyes continued to lower and raise from the table as he looked at her.

"We've been planning this trip for quite some time now and finally we're here," Derek added smiling cautiously at Jade.

"So you've never been camping before?" Derek continued curiously. "No, never," Jade replied smiling. "Then maybe," Derek said hesitating as his eyes darted towards his friends in a questioning glance before dropping his eyes back to the table and then raising them again.

"Would you like another drink Jade?" Derek asked, raising to his feet from off the stool.

"Um, yes, that would be nice," she answered, clasping tentatively at the empty glass before her aware of the amount of alcohol that she had consumed over the course of the afternoon and the effects that she had started to feel. Derek returned a short time later carrying two drinks that he placed down on the table as he sat down on the stool before sliding one of the drinks over to Jade and re-joined the conversation that had now become comfortable and flowing. Derek's reservation and hesitance within Jades presence slowly began to fade as his eyes constantly focused on her in a look of appeal and his attraction towards her. Jade smiled back flirting with his attraction and drawing him into her attention as each moment ticked over into hours and ignited their enthusiasm of getting to know one another.

"Would you like to come with us?" Derek asked unexpectedly, smiling confidently at Jade, looking as if he was holding his breath for her reply.

"Umm," Jade replied hesitating in her answer as her mind accessed the situation and considered the offer to go with the men that she had only just met.

"Okay, yes that would be fun," Jade finally replied a mellifluent smile forming across her face.

Derek's face lit up in an exuberant smile as his face unclenched and he looked as if he had heard the words of which he had wanted to hear. Brett and Rick looked at each other astonished before allowing a muffled laugh to escape from their mouths.

"Oh, I hope that's alright with you guys," Derek said looking at his two friends, fidgeting slightly.

"Yeah, that's okay, mate. More the merrier," Brett replied flashing an omniscient smile in Derek's direction.

That weekend Jade followed the footsteps of her newly found friends and her attraction towards Derek, who treated her with respect and kindness throughout the weekend of camping and endless fun.

After a two hour-drive along the highway that led to a dusty back road travelling east from Copper Cove the car finally came to a stop at the camping ground. A clearing of brilliant white beach sand dazzled under the bright sun and was surrounded by wild bushlands that numerous species of wildlife inhabited.

"Where are we?" Jade asked, looking around at the unfamiliar surroundings.

"Cape Lyzza," Derek replied, smiling. "Haven't you ever been here before?"

"No," Jade answered. "It's got a beach and everything. Would you be able to please show me around, I'd love to see?"

"Sure. Straight after we set up the tents if you'd like," Derek replied, stepping out from the back seat of the vehicle onto the clearing of the camp grounds.

Jade exited the vehicle and stretched her legs and arms after the long drive and waited patiently as the three men pitched the tents in preparation for the evening hours.

"All done," Derek said approaching Jade placing his arm around her waist and leading her towards the beaches and surrounding areas of the campgrounds.

"It's beautiful here," Jade said looking out over the spectacular views of the beaches water fronts, cliff faces and wild terrain of the bushland as she followed Derek from one sight to the next. "I didn't even know this place existed," Jade continued smiling up at Derek before pointing to another location that came into her view. "What's over there?" Jade pointed to a rocky area within close proximity to where they were standing, a cliff face that in her eyes resembled a place she had visited while on holidays with her parents as a young girl.

"Wait for me you guys," came Brett's voice that echoed within the not-too-distant space between them.

Jade and Derek smiled at each other as they stood waiting for Brett to catch up and join them in their exploration of the area.

The cliffs edge of the cliff face below displayed no safety barrier to the crashing waves below allowing sightseers access to stand on the edge of the cliff which although Jade had thought dangerous, it intrigued her curiosity to look at what it held below.

Jade felt the rush of the wind push against her body and swirling around her feet as she leant forward over the cliffs edge to view the crashing waves slapping and crashing against the rocky cliff face and the sea bottom below.

Suddenly Jade felt the urgent rush of arms wrap around her waist pulling her back away from the dangerous edge of the rocky cliff face, that plunged to a depth of a watery rocky bottom.

"Be careful. You could have fallen," Brett said, shaking his head in disbelief, the concerned look that had formed upon his face turning into a worried frown.

"I'm sorry I scared you, I just wanted to see the bottom," Jade answered, a slight hint of embarrassment blushing upon her cheeks. "But thank you, my hero," she continued, an awkward giggle escaping from her mouth, trying to erase what she had done and change the sombre mood of the moment. Brett shrugged his shoulders glancing a wary grin in her direction before stepping away from the area and walking towards the direction of the pitched tents in the clearing of the camping grounds.

As the day passed and settled into the night, the groups stamina started to waiver as they began to wind down from the long day of travelling and exploring the vast area of the beaches and surroundings and built a camp fire that flickered and illuminated in red and yellow splendour under the setting sun.

The bright full moon shone down upon the beach sand around them and cast shadows upon the land as the flicker of the fires shadows reciprocated each movement of the people that sat around the fire to keep warm. Jade loved the idea of camping, the freedom and fresh air of the outdoors and wilderness had inspired her mood into a mellifluent exuberance of her senses that were also induced by the intoxication of the alcohol that she had consumed over the course of the day but now sat idle and resting by the camp fire next to Derek.

Tired and weary, she laid her head upon the blanket that she had formed into a pile against her and relaxed into the quietness and tranquillity of the night that eventually fluttered her eyes until they closed and soothed her to sleep while listening to Derek and Brett continue in their quiet conversations of reciprocated stories.

Hours later Jade awoke unexpectedly to the soft sounds of the crackling firewood slowly burning in the early hours of the mornings mist and the eerie black eyes that stood above her and stared down upon her.

"Oh my god," Jade whispered placing her hand to her open mouth startled by the dark image of the large wild emu that stood hovering above her, precariously perched on its large feet that sank into the soft beach sand.

Startled and frightened, Jade quickly looked around the abandoned area of the camp in a moment of silent panic.

Jade leapt to her feet and ran to the unlocked car parked metres away in the darkened distance and rushed into the back seat, locking all the doors in her terror of the large, wild bird and hid behind the front seats.

"Where are you Derek, where have you gone?" Jade whispered , trying not to draw the attention of the emu towards the car as she poked her head up to look around the camp grounds and watched the animal as it walked around the clearing in the soft beach sand.

She glanced her eyes momentarily over at the tents on the other side of the clearing, her mind quickly analysing the location of where Derek may be and which tent he was located in as she intensively watched the emu's movements that silently, slowly moved in the direction of the bushland that surrounded the clearance.

Finally the large, wild bird slipped into the covering of the bushlands and disappeared out of Jades view.

"Oh, thank god," Jade whispered taking a deep breath upon the breath that had been stifled and held tight within her throat before slowly opening the car's door and tip toeing over to the pitched tents, opening one of the door flaps to peak inside and crawling into the cuddle of Derek's arm that felt her movements appear next to him.

The next morning the group awoke early and crawled out of the tents into the bright morning's sunshine. "You'll never guess what happen to me early this morning," Jade said, covering her mouth as the embarrassed giggle escaped from her lips.

"What?" the men all said in unison, their eyes forming a curious glance at her.

"I awoke by the campfire to an emu standing over the top of me, I was petrified and ran to the car and locked myself in." The men looked at each other then let out a burst of laughter. "Did you think that it was going to open the door," Brett teased laughing. Jade dropped her head slightly, embarrassed by her story and her irrational actions but joined in the laughter before they set their sights on packing up the camp grounds and loading the tents and equipment into the boot of the car.

"Where are we going now?" Jade said inquisitively to Derek as they sat in the back seat of the car together.

"First we are going to find another camping ground on the way, one with showers so we can get cleaned up before we go to the footy," Derek answered, looking over at Brett as if he was going to ask him a question.

"Football," Jade answered with a giggle. "This really was a boy's weekend hey."

"I did warn you," Derek replied, casting a little smile in her direction.

"That's alright, it will be my first time," Jade answered, returning a cheeky smile.

The group left the camp grounds and continued in their journey back along the highway until they found a caravan park stopped to shower before continuing in their journey to the football stadium in Alterro. Over the course of the weekend Jade and Derek's attraction to each other blossomed as they lavished each other's attention upon one another and became comfortable within each other's presence.

That summer, only two weeks later after they had first met Jade moved to Werrington to be with Derek. Although Derek was in the midst of a divorce from his first wife of nine years, and was responsible for three little girls from that marriage, it had not fazed Jade as she stepped into the role of being a step parent with the greatest of ease and grace, and enjoyed the weekends playing step mother with his three little children as Derek and Jade started to build a life and future together.

Two years later

"I'm pregnant," Jade announced unexpectedly, her eyes wide and anxious within the situation as she looked at Derek.

"What? But you were infertile. What happened?" Derek questioned, a look of bewilderment forming across his face.

"I don't know," Jade replied, shaking her head and rubbing her hand gently across the fabric of her stomach. "I never thought that I could get pregnant," Jade continued. "This wasn't meant to happen, I'm freaking out Derek, I'm only 21 years old, I wasn't expecting to be a mum, I had all these other plans for my life." Derek flashed a smile in her direction before walking over to her and placing his arms tightly around her, comforting her as the stark realisation of the moment sunk into their reality's.

"I guess we're going to have a baby," Derek said kissing Jade upon the head and rocking her slightly back and forth within his arms. That summer Derek and Jade moved to a secluded farmhouse in Botana Way to be closer to Jade's family for the birth of their first child. Four months into the pregnancy, upon an appointment to her local doctor in Copper Cove Jade came home, an anxious bewildered look formed across her face.

"What is it?" Derek asked, rushing to her side concerned by the look upon her face.

"Ohhh. Umm," Jade hesitated. "Everything's alright, there's nothing wrong with the baby. But Derek, we're having twins," Jade announced, rubbing her larger than expected extended stomach.

"Oh my god, twins," Derek replied, his face a glow with the possibilities. "One might be a boy. Or they both might be," he said gleefully placing a hand gently against her stomach. Derek's mood exuberated into a state of ecstatic joy upon hearing the news of the unexpected pregnancy of twins and quickly rushed to the telephone to call his family in Meltona.

Two months later: Derek had started to display unusual moody behaviour and had become over bearing in his jealousy of Jade and any attention that she would show her family or friends which had started to cause Jade to distance herself from the people close to her to ease the situation. Although Jade was aware that his attitude towards her had taken an unusual turn from the man that she had come to know before the pregnancy she found herself making excuses for his behaviour within her nativity and felt committed to the relationship due to her pregnancy and took a step down from her own assertiveness to stay by his side.

Derek and Jade sat arguing in the front seat of the car as they returned from the small township of Botana Way with their purchases. "Don't speak to me that way Derek," Jade replied angrily as Derek growled accusations and insulted her with profanity.

"Get out of the car," Derek growled, reaching across her lap and opening the front door of the car. "Walk home."

Jade looked at Derek astonished and upset before climbing out of the front seat of the car and placed her feet down onto the heavily gravelled dirt road and stood up. "You're a terrible person Derek, I'm pregnant and with twins." Derek pulled the front door of the car shut tempestuously and placed his foot down onto the accelerator and sped off down the road leaving Jade standing there alone in her state of pregnancy.

Jade started to walk along the long gravel road towards home but within minutes Derek returned and circled the car around to come to a stop at her side.

"Get in," Derek demanded angrily, opening the door and gesturing to her to get into the vehicle.

"Don't you ever do that again Derek," Jade said angrily, animosity filling her voice as she placed herself into the front seat of the car and buckled up the seatbelt. The drive home was silent, not a word was spoken between them until they finally reached the front gate of their property.

"I'm sorry," Derek finally muttered looking over at Jade and reaching for her hand, stroking it softly.

"I'm sorry too," Jade replied, touching his hand gently before leaning over to place a kiss upon his cheek.

One month later: "I think that we should go to Meltona to buy the furniture and things we need for the babies," Derek suggested unexpectedly sitting in the loungeroom chair as they watched TV together.

"But I'm seven months pregnant and getting very uncomfortable," Jade replied looking back at Derek, a concerned frown forming across her face.

"No, I think it would be cheaper to buy the things we need there, besides when are we going to get another chance to go without the children," Derek replied convincingly, almost demanding.

"But. I guess," Jade finally agreed submissively, not wanting to start an argument.

The twelve-hour trip was fraught with numerous stops as Jade tried desperately to stay comfortable in the front seat of the car as her stomach pressed down hard with all the weight of the two babies travelling inside of her. Not wanting to upset Derek, she hung on desperately and bit her tongue to stop the words leaving her mouth when she felt the need to stop and uncomfortably travelled to the next township despite having to shift the weight of her pregnancy upon the small frame of her body, stretch her legs or to use the bathroom. Finally they arrived at Meltona and drove to Derek's parents' house and was happily greeted by the family upon their arrival.

"Oh my god, look at you," Derek's mother cooed, placing a hand onto Jade's extended stomach as Jade smiled in return at her joy. Derek's mother guided Jade through the house to the bedroom of which she and Derek would be staying as Derek unloaded the car and placed their luggage into the bedroom.

"Oh no, I forgot my creams," Jade said looking around at Derek as she unzipped her suitcase and began to unpack.

"You'll be right," Derek answered showing no concern, looking over his shoulder at her as he sat on the end of the bed. That week Jade felt the agonizing pain of each tear as it tore across the delicate stretched flesh of her stomach amongst the extended breach of her capacity as the mass of the babies growing inside of her over stretched her skin and tore at the inner walls of her muscles.

"Please Derek, I need my creams," Jade pleaded rubbing at the skin on her stomach in pain.

"I'm not going and getting them, you'll be fine," Derek answered, refusing to help her to purchase the much needed personal items to stop her skin from tearing and ripping at the seams which caused her so much pain and discomfort.

" Besides I'll only know those marks are there, you'll never be with anyone but me now anyway." Jade sat down on the bed exasperated and gobsmacked as she rubbed gently at the skin on her stomach trying to fathom the extent of Derek's thinking and refusal to help ease the discomfort, she was in. "Is this the way it is going to be," Jade asked herself, her mind trying to depict the future, a life with Derek.

Two weeks later: Over the next three weeks of the pregnancy, Derek and Jade occupied a caravan in Alterro in a caravan park as they awaited the birth of their twins, the doctors having insisted on them being close to the city hospital in preparation of the birth. Although the pregnancy had been relatively carefree the twins had started to absorb the nutrients from each other which was robbing one of the babies of all sustenance and placing it into danger and they had to be induced three weeks early.

"You're going to have your babies tomorrow Jade," the doctor announced. "We can't wait any longer."

Jade felt the nervousness of the reality that was about to come as the doctors words settled under her skin but was quickly replaced by joy.

"Tomorrow. I'm going to be a mum tomorrow," Jade finally muttered, a big smile spreading across her face. That night after ringing Jades parents and informing them of the expected induced birth of their babies scheduled for the next day Derek and Jade nervously packed up the caravan and took photographs of themselves to memorialise the moment before they became parents and snuggled up in bed early in preparation for the big day ahead.

They arrived at the hospital at 8.15 am as arranged with their doctor and took the lift to the birthing ward.

"Today's the big day Jade," the nurse greeted them smiling, seating Jade on the hospital bed within the birthing ward and handing her a hospital gown to get changed into. "Okay, let's get you started," the nurse said as Jade finished changing into the gown and laid down upon the hospital bed, Derek placing himself in the chair next to the bed.

"Oh my," Jade moaned as the first contractions squeezed down upon her stomach and then continued to come in short succession. As the labour continued the doctors advised Jade that it was time to insert the epidural into her spine releasing the pain medication that would numb her from the waist down, administered for the safety of her babies' birth. Within moments of the epidural being put in place Jade felt no pain with each contraction and quickly fell asleep for the next twelve hours.

"Jade, wake up. It's time," the doctor announced, after one last examination. "Hold on Jade, We've got a slight complication here. Jade I have to use forceps on the first baby and the second baby is breech. I need you to push when I say."

Jade followed the doctor's instructions and pushed down hard as the doctor maneuvered the forceps onto the first baby and gently helped the baby out of the birthing canal. The first baby James bellowed out a cry as he entered into the world. "Okay Jade, we've still got some work to do here. Now stop pushing Jade, I'm going to have to reach for this little one and pull him out." Jade felt the pressure of the doctor's hand as he reached for the feet of the breeched second baby, Nick, and gently pulled him through the birthing canal and out into the world. Within seven minutes of each other's births the twins were born. But Nick did not cry as he entered the world as James had and lay limp, lifeless and blue within the doctor's arms. Jade felt the tears well up into her eyes instantly in her panic and fear as Derek stood over her holding James in his arms.

"What's wrong with my baby?" Jade cried out, her voice fraught with panic and anxiousness. "Derek, what's wrong with him?"

"He's not breathing Jade," Derek said. "He's not breathing."

"Oh god, please be alright. Please be alright," Jade prayed holding her breath tightly within her throat as the doctors and nurses worked frantically over the baby inserting tubes into his mouth and patting him on the back gently.

"Waaa," came the cry they had all been waiting so anxiously to hear as Nick finally took his first breath and announced his arrival in the world.

"Oh thank god," cried Jade, placing her hands to her mouth, the tears of relief rushing in streams down her face as she smiled up at Derek whose panic had started to subside as he stood next to her holding James tightly in his arms.

"Here's your little man," the doctor said, placing Nick into his mother's arms.

"Hello there little one," Jade said, looking into his soft, tiny face and holding his tiny hand. "You gave us quite a scare." Jade was allowed to hold Nick for a brief moment before he was taken from her by the nurses and taken to another ward within the hospital for observation.

"Oh they're so beautiful Derek. They're so beautiful," Jade said smiling broadly exhausted but elated emotionally at the birth of her two little boys.

Eighteen months later: Derek, Jade and the twins moved from the small township of Botana Way to Meltona to be close to Derek's family and within two years Jade announced her second pregnancy.

"I'm not having another baby out of wedlock," Jade stated, the traditional upbringing of her own parents now causing an impact upon her decisions.

"Then let's get married," Derek suggested. "Well, we are engaged, we should get married before this little one's born," Jade agreed smiling and rubbing at her stomach.

Over the next six months Derek and Jade rushed to make the arrangements for their wedding and sent out the invitations.

Jade's parents had informed her that they would make the journey to Meltona from Copper Cove to attend their wedding but did not inform her that her brother Peter would also be attending and had been an unexpected uncomfortable surprise to Jade upon their arrival.

On the day of the wedding while waiting to drive to the registry office to get married Derek and Jade began to argue incessantly over unimportant issues of Derek's concern.

"But I'm not going to get to watch the football if we don't get back by that time," Derek argued.

"But it's our big day, it's our wedding, can't you put it off for one day," Jade argued back dismayed and disappointed at Derek's lack of importance for the proceedings of the day.

After two hours of arguing and bickering Derek and Jade placed James and Nick into the car and drove out onto the highway that directed them towards the registry office.

"Oh no," Derek said as the car began to suddenly splut and shudder down the highway before coming to a stop. Derek pulled the car over to the curb and got out of the car. "I don't know what's wrong with it," Derek said frantically, fiddling with the plugs and battery of the car. Suddenly the car's engine fired up again. "Yes," Derek called out, slamming down the bonnet and getting back into the car. "It's fine. We're going to be late though," he continued agitated, a scowl covering his face in a bleak mask of irritation.

Derek and Jade arrived at the registry office and hurried towards the building and into the altar in their tardiness of lateness, quickly followed by a small number of family members and friends who had gathered outside the building waiting for them and rushed inside with them in their attendance and the wedding began without any further delay.

"Do you take this woman to be your lawful wedded wife?"

"Yes."

"Do you take this man to be your lawful wedded husband?"

"Yes."

Within moments of arriving Derek and Jade walked from the entrance of the registry office as husband and wife and after their family took numerous photographs of them and standing with family members they got back into their car and returned home. Within minutes of arriving back at home while waiting for the celebrations to begin, Derek and Jade began to argue once more. The bickering continued over the next hour until it was time to proceed to Derek's mother's home for their wedding reception.

Although the wedding reception was beautifully adorned with decorations, food and their wedding cake it also held an air of uncomfortability as the numerous guests that had been invited were unknown to Jade and Derek and mainly consisted of Derek's families friends and neighbours organised by his mother and sisters. Near the end of the reception Jades mother approached her and asked Jade if Peter could reside at her place for the evening instead of having to stay in a hotel. Jades face dropped in a stance of refute at the inconsiderate question that had been forced upon her.

"No mum," Jade answered standing her ground. "This is my wedding day and I don't want him around my children or me." Sienna stood back a little astonished by the answer then dropped her stance and just nodded her head. "Alright love, we'll work something out."

Although at times awkward and uncomfortable the celebrations lasted into the early hours of the morning when everybody finally retired for the night and Derek and Jade returned home husband and wife.

Jades pregnancy was uncomplicated and she glowed in the face of motherhood once more and rejoiced in the knowledge that she was carrying a daughter to join her family of boys. Jade gave birth to a beautiful little girl, Monique, who enriched her life with the joy of having a daughter to love as well as her beautiful boys. Although Jade loved her children and was joyous in her role of motherhood she could not settle into the business and lifestyle of the city which was often fraught with danger of which she faced upon her husband's absence from the family home while he was at work and longed to be returned back into her humble, safe country surroundings of Copper Cove.

"I'm not raising the children here," Jade yelled, as the two of them fought continuously and tenaciously standing their grounds.

"Then where are we going to go?" yelled Derek, fighting back in his defence, throwing his arms up into the air.

"I want to go back to Copper Cove," Jade yelled. "I want to be near my family." Finally after months of numerous arguments and frustrating moments Derek relented and gave in.

Six months later; Derek and Jade moved back to a small township located near Copper Cove and one year later during the Christmas period Jade announced her third pregnancy. Nine months later, their fourth child was born, a beautiful baby boy Cody, who was to be their last child.

Two years later

Derek and Jades relationship remained a tumultuous battle of arguments and tenacious grips of power as Derek fought to take control of Jade and treat her as if she was his possession and kept her from the graces of her family and friends by causing arguments each time she wanted to visit them, which drove her into a distance from the people she was close to and entrapped her within his control and eventually Jades confidence began to waiver and she became submissive to his demands. Unexpectedly and without consulting Jade or taking her feelings and opinions into consideration Derek made a decision. "I've got a job in Meltona," Derek announced, telling Jade what they would be doing. "But we're going to have to stay with my parents to begin with." Although Jade did not agree with moving her family back to Meltona she no longer had the courage or strength to disagree with Derek overwhelmed by his constant empowerment over her and the exhaustion of raising four children to which she received no help from Derek and submissively agreed anyway. One week later the family moved back to Meltona and into Derek's parents' home. The housing arrangements although at first had run smoothly had diminished over the duration of time and turned to arrogant glances and irritation directed at the children and at Derek and Jade continuously from Derek's mother and stepfather. Although Jade did all she could to keep the children quiet and out from under their feet tensions grew daily within the household which had started to feel very uncomfortable. Jade constantly searched for their own accommodation while Derek was at work but could not find anything within the same district as his family that was affordable and within their budget and Derek refused to move elsewhere outside of the district, to which the couple argued constantly about in the privacy and confinements of their bedroom.

Six weeks later

In the early hours of the evening Jade was bathing Cody when she heard a noisy shuffle within the confines of the kitchen and quickly lifted Cody out of the bath to investigate the noise.

"Get out," Derek's mother yelled at Derek as their children stood around dumbfounded and anxious at the argument that was erupting.

"What's going on?" Jade said, stepping into the kitchen followed by Cody who was holding his mother's hand.

"I want you all out of here tonight. I've had enough," Derek's mother continued to yell. "If you don't leave tonight, I will call the police."

Derek and Jade walked over to his mother and tried to console her. As Jade reached her arms out to comfort her Derek's mother swung out and landed her fist down upon Jade's cheek, hard.

"Now get out," she yelled.

"How dare you," Derek roared, gathering the children and walking out of the front door, placing the children into the back seat of the car before rushing to the front of the car and climbing into the driver's seat as Jade rushed into the front seat and they drove off down the road towards his sister's home.

As the couple arrived at Derek's sister's house and pulled up into the driveway, the front lights of the house suddenly were turned off and the curtains of the house were pulled shut.

"What now," Derek roared. Derek knocked on the door but quickly returned to the car as his knocks went unanswered. "We can get our stuff out of the shed tomorrow," Derek said, returning to the car. Derek and Jade went to his brother's house who welcomed them into their home and where they stayed for the night.

The next evening Derek and Jade arrived at his sister's house and started to empty his sisters shed of their belongings and load them into the trailer. "Get her out of here," came a voice from within the house. "Get her out of here or we'll call the boys on her," pointing at Jade through the window of the home.

Derek stuck his finger up at his sister in a stance of profanity and angrily ignored her plea and continued to pack their belongings into the trailer until the shed was empty and they left, returning to Derek's brothers house. "What are we going to do Derek?" Jade cried that night once alone in their bedroom. "We can always go back to Copper Cove," Jade suggested lifting her head up to look into Derek's eyes as her eyes flowed with tears. Without question or argument Derek agreed.

That week Derek and Jade made the twelve-hour trip back to Copper Cove and moved in with Jade's parents. That weekend Jade's parents moved into the caravan at the side of the house and allowed the family to live in their home. Nine months later

Derek and Jade bought a house in the small township of Suisania Bay and began a new life.

Although the family had settled into Suisania Bay well and the children had made friends within their schools and the township and were thriving in their new surroundings Derek and Jades marriage remained fraught with tension and constant arguments which escalated to Derek's abuse of control through harsh, cruel words and physical abuse of which was hidden from the children within the confines and secrecy of the bedroom.

Two years later Jade met Sherri.

It was seven thirty pm; time to wind the house down, bath the children and start getting them ready for bed. It had been a long day but enjoyable as the family attended their usual activities of recreational sports on the weekends. James and Nick who had joined the local football team attended their football matches of the Saturday mornings as Monique who had joined the local netball team for her school played netball. Although Jade tried to spend equal time with all of her children in support of their chosen sports she found it hard to spread herself between all of their activities and had encouraged Derek to show support as well and attend their games when she was not able to.

To Jades surprise Derek wholeheartedly agreed and quite often attended the football matches of their sons while Jade attended the netball games of their daughter.

"Good luck boys," Jade said, stepping from the car and gathering her things as they parked at the netball grounds to drop off Jade and Monique. "See you soon," smiling at Derek. Things had grown steadily worse between them and the marriage was fraught with bitter arguments and violent behaviour by Derek who constantly demanded control of Jade and the family, although they had been married for fourteen years, Jade had already made the decision to remain a dedicated mother and refused to leave although she did not love Derek anymore and had spent numerous hours dreaming of a life without him as she went about her household chores or spent time out in her garden alone. Everyday Jade placed on her mask of perfunctory and smiled her way through the day a smile that was impregnable to the animosity that it hid. Derek remained oblivious to the resentment and loathing she felt within his presence and remained none the wiser as Jade continued to fake her way through each moment of their life together for the sake of her children.

Jade took Monique to her sports that day enjoying the freedom of her unwatched interactions with the other parents and people around her in Derek's absence.

Jade was asked often to score for the game and accepted wholeheartedly in her support of Monique's interest and her team. She enjoyed helping whenever she was needed and was made to feel like a valued supporter and often volunteered to work in the canteen as well when she was able. Near the end of the season the coach of her daughter's netball team had pulled Jade aside and had indicated that her daughter was being moved up to the next grade the following year and that she had hoped that Jade would be interested in the coaching position. Jade was elated that she had been asked and agreed to take the position wholeheartedly and was encouraged by her daughters approval and excitement of having her mother coach the team. Jade had played netball for seven years as a child and had participated in the sport as an adult and felt that she could handle the position although she had never put her hand to coaching before but looked forward to taking on the challenge.

That morning while sitting on the sidelines scoring for the game, Jade joyfully chatted endlessly to the numerous parents that sat along the sidelines with her watching their daughters play and felt an air of freedom within the space of not being within the constant control of Derek's eye and demands.

"Yes. They won," one of the parents called out elated at the end of the game, clapping their hands, as the team shook the hands of their competitors and walked from the court joining their parents. "Well done sweetheart. Congratulations," Jade said, leaning down to kiss her daughter on the top of the head. "Let's go get an ice-cream."

Jade and Monique walked towards the canteen and purchased an ice cream before leaving for their walk home. Monique spoke incessantly about her friends and their joyful antics as she walked alongside her mother in their walk home.

Jade smiled and giggled as she listened to her daughter telling all the tales of her friends playfulness and their times together and loved to hear all about it as they strode along the footpaths of Suisania Bay. Although Jade shared a close bond with her daughter her thoughts had started to wonder just how long it would last as Monique was starting to reach that level of maturity of becoming a teenager. Jade knew that she would have to lavish her childish attention and closeness over the next couple of years until that time would arrive. She had learned from the experience of raising James and Nick who had now reached their teenage years and started to move into the difficulty of becoming a teenager and creating the gap as they started to drift and form their own level of independence. After a long walk along the streets of Suisania Bay Jade and Monique finally made it home and let themselves in through the front door.

They had been home about ten minutes when they heard the familiar sound of the families car pull up in the long gravel driveway at the side of the house.

"Mum. Mum," James and Nick called out excitedly, rushing through the front door and running down the long, wide hallway that led towards the kitchen followed closely by their younger brother Cody. "Mum, we won."

"Well done boys, congratulations," Jade cheered, rubbing them on the shoulders and taking in the view of their excitement. Although Cody did not play football or held any interest towards any sports, he loved to go to the boys games as Sherri was there with her children and Cody enjoyed running the grounds of the football oval and playing with them until his brothers football match had finished. Derek quite often sat with Sherri at the football which gave Jade a sense of relief as she did not have to chaperone her husband who was quite reluctant to attend social gatherings by himself and demanded that Jade attend any function with him including going to the shops. Jade trusted Sherri with Derek, their close friendship having had stood the test of time without any cause for alarm or mistrust and Derek had always been an honest, faithful man who had always shown respect for their relationship by not attracting the attentions of other women.

Sherri was Jades second cousin by marriage although Jade had no relationship with the family member that she had married and only knew of his name but did not know the man well she still regarded Sherri as family, although they had not met before they had moved to Suisania Bay. Sherri now separated from her husband, the marriage ending six months earlier had become a welcomed frequent visitor of her home along with her four children who stayed with Jade playing with her children on a regular basis, often staying for days at a time while Sherri tended her employment position or was having a hard day because of her ex-husband.

After enjoying the evening meal and cleaning up the kitchen Jade suggested that she would like to invite Sherri and the children over for the night and asked permission from Derek and if he was up to it. Although Derek liked Sherri and her children he still liked to regain a certain amount of control over Jades friendship and interactions with her and would impress that upon them with his constant interruptions of phone messages or calls while they were out at a café having a coffee together or at Sherri's house causing Jade

71

to often flee the scene under his constant harassment and comply to his demands. Jade felt she had no choice but to always ask for Derek's approval before making any plans of her own.

Tonight Derek agreed to Sherri and the children coming over and Jade rushed to her phone excited to send an invitation to her friend and sent Sherri a message.

"Hey Sherri. Would you like to come over and spend the evening with us?"

Within minutes of sending the message Jade received a reply and picked up her phone and began to read.

"Hey Chicky. Yes we'd love to. We're on our way. Be there soon."

"She's coming," Jade announced to the family smiling. "Okay, I'm just going to go to the shops to get the lollies, chips and drinks and I'll be back soon," Jade said walking quickly out of the kitchen to gather her handbag from out of the bedroom and left the house through the front door. Jade rushed through the shop and gathered the things she needed for the night of entertainment and returned home placing the supplies upon the kitchen bench and told her children to prepare for the evening. The family enjoyed there weekend get-togethers with Sherri and the children which were always spent in laughter and spontaneous fun. Derek and Jade had bought a large house on a quarter of an acre block of land which served perfectly for the children's electric go-karts, scooters, bikes and gave them plenty of space to run around in and enjoy playing together. The large shed on the other side of the block located away from the house had been renovated into a sound proof workshop to accommodate the woodcraft business of which they had started together, but also served as an entertainment area where the stereo could be turned up loud and the adults could unwind peacefully.

"Can we light the bon fire tonight, please dad?" James asked, pointing at the large pile of branches and garden matter that sat in a pile in the middle of the acreage.

"We'll see mate, "Derek replied smiling and patting James on the shoulder.

Thirty minutes later Sherri arrived with her four children and the household became a flurry of noise and boisterous activity. Although Jade was a relaxed person and didn't mind the children running around having fun, she made them adhere to the rules of the house which was a well-known fact amongst all of the children.

Jade and Sherri tended to the children filling up the bowls with chips and lollies and filled up a glass with soft drink for each of them before sending them on their way. " Okay you older boys we're going outside now so please keep an eye on the younger kids okay, we'll be out in the shed," Jade told James, Nick and Sherri's son as they collected their bowls of goodies from the kitchen. As they always had the children divided into their groups and went and played within the bedrooms of the house or the loungeroom while Derek, Jade and Sherri, vacated the house and ventured towards the large renovated shed located in the back corner of the quarter acre block.

Jade turned on the stereo, selected a CD and placed it into the compact disc player and increased the volume. "Let' party," she said, spinning on her heels excitedly to face Derek and Sherri, an unfettered smile spreading across her face. Derek unlocked the shed cupboard and reached for the bong, placing it down onto the shed bench and packed the cone piece with the marijuana he pulled from his jacket pocket and handed it to Jade. "Thanks," Jade said, smiling, placing the bong to her lips, igniting the drug and inhaling it deep into her lung before handing the bong back to Derek. Although Sherri did not partake in smoking marijuana and preferred to drink alcohol as her choice of habit of relaxation she did not bat an eye lid at their recreational habit and held no judgement towards them as they sat together laughing and talking.

As the loudness of the music played its rhythmic tunes that transpired their minds and souls into a mellifluous sound of melodies Jade and Sherri rose to their feet from off the chairs and started to sway their hips in rhythm to the music in the middle of the shed floor smiling and giggling in joyful playfulness. Their nights together were always filled with spontaneous fun and playfulness as the intoxication of alcohol rose through their systems and sent them into a state of uninhibited grandiose.

"Do you remember that night we played on the go-karts and got dressed up in the kids dress ups and put those wigs on and raced around the paddock?" Jade asked laughing as the memories filled her mind. "That was so funny and so much fun, do you still have the movie we made?" Sherri replied laughing with her. "Yes, we do I think, don't we Derek," Jade said her eyes diverting into Derek's direction as he sat close to them on one of the chairs laughing with them. "Yes," he replied. We should watch it again one day." Jade let out a loud laugh as they continued to talk and she remembered another incident of that evening. "Do you remember when I fell off the scooter and scun up my knees and elbows? Oh my god that was so funny but I was so embarrassed as well," Jade continued laughing at herself. The laughter continued and grew into a tessellation of memories and laughter within their conversation.

The hot summers sun that had shone down upon the hot tin roof of the large shed that day had left a warmth of humidity within the inner walls that now hung in the air all around them and was making them feel uncomfortable with the rise of the alcohol also warming their senses. "Let's go into the next room and put the fans on," Jade suggested raising off the chair and leading the group into the next room and placed the fans into a position on the shed floor to blow the cool air upon them.

"I'll be back in a minute," Jade said giggling flashing them a cheeky smile as she left the room and walked towards the house.

Within minutes, Jade returned and entered the shed armed with an armful of water pistols. "Let's play," she giggled handing Sherri and Derek a water pistol each. Derek and Sherri leapt to their feet spontaneously laughing as they reached for a water pistol and ran out of the shed and into the yard squirting each other and laughing uncontrollably. One by one the children alerted and curious by the sound of the loud laughter that echoed across the paddock and in through the windows of the home walked out of the back door and over into the paddock to where the adults were enthralled in their playfulness. "Oh we want to play," the children yelled out in unison their faces lighting up into exuberant smiles as they started to run towards the fun.

Derek, Jade and Sherri drenched in water and laughing continuously handed the water pistols to the children and watched them run around the back yard chasing each other as the adults had, squirting each other as they laughed and squealed.

"Want to play darts?" Jade suggested, gesturing back towards the entrance of the large shed.

"Yes, let's," Sherri answered, her mouth still full of laughter as they turned and walked back through the shed doors and came to a standstill in the next room in front of the dart board that hung on the wall. "Let's add a twist," Jade suggested, a cheeky giggle escaping from her lips. Jade walked over to the shed cupboard and collected a note pad and a bunch of pens and handed a piece of paper and a pen to Derek and Sherri.

"Okay, let's play truth or dare dart-style," Jade suggested laughing.

"Ha-ha," Derek laughed. "Okay, why not."

The three of them secretly wrote down their questions and suggestions onto their own separate piece of paper and placed them into a container.

"Okay. Who goes first?" Jade asked, picking up the container and waving it high into the air announcing the game was ready to be played.

Derek and Sherri sat paused, motionless continuously looking back and forth at each other giggling waiting for the other one to make the first move.

"Oh you chickens. Okay, I'll go first," Jade piped up, walking towards the dart board with the darts in her hand. Jade steadied herself in front of the dart board and threw the first dart. "Bullseye," she yelled clapping her hands in excitement. "Next."

Sherri rose to her feet from off the stool as Jade walked towards her enthusiastically and placed the darts into her hands and sat down on a stool to watch.

"Oh no," Sherri laughed spinning around to look at Derek and Jade, the dart missing the board altogether and puncturing the shed wall.

"Ah ha, you must pick a note out of the container," Jade said, holding out the container shaking it in front of her giggling. Sherri placed her hand into the container and picked out one of the notes and unfolded the piece of paper, her eyes widening as she started to read the written inscription.

"Oh no. no, no, no," Sherri shrieked laughing her cheeks starting to turn a slight red hue. "I'm not doing that."

"What is it?" Jade asked jumping to her feet from off the stool giggling, a curious smile forming within her eyes and across her face as she walked towards Sherri to read the piece of paper.

Sherri giggled slightly embarrassed as Jade approached closer and closer until she stood before her. Sherri closed her eyes in disbelief, a strange little sigh leaving her lips before dropping her head down and unexpectedly placing a kiss upon Jade's soft lips.

"Oh my," Jade said jumping back within the unexpected approach as a blush quickly formed across the top of her cheeks and a loud laugh burst out of her mouth, her eyes quickly diverging towards Derek. "I wonder who wrote that," Jade said cheekily winking her eye at Derek and handing him the darts.

Jade knew that Derek had written that suggestion upon the piece of paper that night which had intrigued and alerted her mind and made her look at Derek differently. What was Derek hiding within the depths of his thoughts? What were his true intentions?

That night Jade's intrigue within her mind grew in momentum as she uncovered each one of Derek's suggestions written upon the small paper notes folded up and concealed within the container behind the walls of the large shed located on the quarter acre block.

The Forbidden Secret

Jade had noticed things different in her husband lately, his oddesy, a cause of concern to dwell within her as his constant interest in the computer as the children were placed in bed for the night had alerted her mind to something, although the reason had remained unknown.

Jade remained silent, watching, listening to his movements, a suspicious intrigue developing within her curiosity. The large loungeroom within the family home was designed with a separate room attached that housed their office and computer and although separated by the thick stone walls the doorway remained open devoid of a door and visible from the point of which she sat on the lounge chair in front of the television as she rested from the long hard days of raising her family.

One evening as Jade sat upon the chair within the loungeroom and Derek sat quietly within the confines of the office suddenly the precariousness of her perception rose her to her feet and stepped her into the office doorway and glanced her eyes towards the images upon the computer screen.

"Oh my god," flashed into her mind as her eyes widened and viewed the vivid images flashing across the computer screen. "You're kidding." Jade's mouth dropped open in astonishment as the raw truth of her husband's interest in the computer sent her into a state of disbelief.

As Jade's feet grazed the thick carpet in a hesitant silent footstep the thought of confrontation flashed through her mind, but diverted in a divergence of her own interest of collecting the movies off the shelving hidden behind the corner of the office wall.

Derek had not noticed her interest in the computer screen as he obliviously typed away at the computer key board, his eyes locked to the screen as Jade collected the movies and returned to the loungeroom and sat back down on the chair.

"So this is what he's been doing for the last three months?" Jade whispered to herself touching at the frown that formed and burrowed into her forehead. "Naked women and explicit sexual images." Jade did not know how she felt, her image of her husband was distant from the actions she had now viewed.

Jade and Derek's sixteen-year marriage had held her in an innocence and inexperienced state of affection and sexual intimacy, a flat line of the passionate woman that lay within and hid within the moral upbringing of which she was raised and had lived. The exploitation of the naked brazen women shocked Jade but the explicit words of their sexual advances towards her husband did not ignite an emotion to erupt as her reaction remained dormant in the act of her husband's betrayal.

"I thought he had been playing computer games," ran through Jades mind, paused and entrenched in deep thought that distracted her attentions towards her usual enjoyments of relaxing at the end of the day. "So this is what he's been doing, wow," she whispered a grin that almost represented a giggle forming across her mouth.

Although Jade had felt the disdained shock of Derek's consumed interest in the explicit material, she had not wanted him to stop and felt the unusual encouragement towards his act of betrayal. She had hoped he would continue and that his world of fantasy would detach him from her and entice him into a pursuit of another woman. Although Jade loved her family with her whole heart her children had remained her focus and world of love and within the last five years of their marriage Jade had spent it in a world of planning her escape from the excessive controlling abusiveness of her husband's behaviour.

Jade no longer expressed affections or sexual advances towards her husband and remained distant from his presence within the family home over the period of the last eighteen months and now portrayed an image of a dutiful wife, a smile that was hidden behind a mask of animosity and perfunction.

Jade quietly rose to her feet sneaking to the office door, her eyes fixated on the computer screen as the images of the explicit naked profanity flashed in changing screens before her.

"Would you like a coffee?" Jade asked unexpectedly, a surreptitious grin hidden within her words.

"Ohhh, Umm, yes," Derek replied stuttering, his fingers quickly stretching towards the keys of the computer keyboard, flicking the screen to a computer game that sat hiding in the background.

"So what's her name Derek?" Jade asked profoundly. "What are you doing?"

"I…uh…um… I was just having a look," Derek replied lost for words and red-faced in the confrontation as his mind searched for the words to conceal the truth.

"Relax Derek," Jade giggled smugly. "Truthfully, I really don't care."

"I'm so sorry Jade. I was just curious and I… I…" Derek answered, wriggling in the perception of the moment of being caught in the act. "I should not have done this, we are married and."

Jade interrupted the embarrassed admission of his betrayal as he sat squirming in his chair. "Please, god. Truthfully, Derek, I don't mind. Can I see though, I am intrigued, curious."

"Umm, yes, I suppose, if you want to," Derek answered, covering the embarrassment of his flushing cheeks with the palm of his hand, still squirming in the uncertainty of her reaction.

"I'll go make a coffee Derek, so don't switch the screen," Jade said giggling as she left the confines of the office and walked down the long hallway and into the kitchen before returning with two cups of coffee in her hands.

Jade sat in the empty chair next to Derek at the office desk and sipped at the hot coffee held within her hand as her eyes stayed focused on the computer screen.

"Hmm. Show me," Jade said softly, looking into the uncertainty of Derek's face.

Derek changed the screen back to the explicit sexual site on the computer, displaying the naked images and poses of the site's participants brazen sexuality.

"Oh my god. I can't believe people are so brazen. I've never seen anything like this," Jade gasped blushing in her innocence, her eyes opening wide at the nakedness of the explicit pictures, shocking her mind. Although Jade felt shocked by what she was seeing the graphic view of the sexual poses ignited curiosity and intrigue within the depths of her mind, her cheeks flushing continuously in an innocent blush of nativity.

"How long have you been doing this Derek?" Jade asked curiously.

"People really do this, oh my god. I've never seen anything like this before, ever. Do you really like this Derek, these explicit pictures? They show everything, even close ups of peoples intimacy and men's orgasms spread all over the women's body parts."

"Umm, yes I do Jade. I'm sorry," Derek replied hesitantly.

"Ohhh, don't be sorry, if that's your thing, well, that's your thing Derek."

"Oh my though, it's really rude," Jade continued giggling and blushing. "I've seen enough, I'll leave you to it okay."

Jade rose to her feet picking up the coffee cup off the computer desk and returned to the loungeroom , placing her coffee cup down upon the coffee table slightly shaking her head in disbelief within a grin that had spread across her face.

"I'm going to watch a movie now okay." Derek turned around to watch the slow movements of his wife's blushing introduction to the loss of her naivety as she moved around the loungeroom calming her mind and placing a DVD into the player. "Are you sure Jade. You don't mind?"

"No, not at all, knock yourself out. If that's what you like Derek then go for it," Jade replied flashing a cheeky smile in his direction.

As Jade sat down upon the loungeroom chair her properness of decency suddenly flashed into a precarious curiosity of the naked pictures within her mind, the profound words of which she had been exposed to by Derek's wandering mind and brazenness intriguing her further. Jade had not known of this kind of existence of brazen sexual gestural indiscreetness and sat shocked in the exposure for a moment before returning to the empty seat next to Derek giggling.

"Can I see some more?" Jade smiled coyly, biting at her bottom lip and dropping her head slightly. Derek smiled as his hand reached for the keyboard.

Over the continuing weeks, Derek had frequented his contention of discrepancy upon the explicit sexual site without the motions of covering his actions and focus with Jade's approval.

Jade giggled at the naughty conversations, intrigued by the other peoples brazenness of nakedness and brash words of naughty enticement. Derek poured over the many numerous profiles of rude photographs and brazen fantasies nightly, intrigued and enticed into an unadulterated curiosity.

Although Derek had not revealed himself or shown the nakedness of flesh choosing to abstain from the enticement to reveal himself, a question flashed into her mind as Jade sat next to him sharing in the images and sexuality.

"Aren't you worried that they'll find you a little creepy, just a sightseer," Jade finally commented, pouring over the nakedness of the men's graphical images. "Oh my, this is rude," she giggled.

Derek paused in his thoughts before directing a glance over in her direction. "Do you think I should?" he asked, a bright red hue quickly flushing through his cheeks.

"Well," Jade answered, a cheekiness in her voice. "I think it's only fair to reveal who you are." Derek looked at her strangely before finally answering, "Well, I wanted to but I... I..."

"You didn't want me to catch you did you?" Jade replied giggling, placing her hand to her mouth girlishly.

"No Jade I did not, I didn't want to disrespect our marriage either," Derek replied, a concerned smile spreading over his lips.

"Well, since you have my approval, I don't see the harm in it, it's just pictures like everyone else. It's not like you're going to ever meet these people," Jade smiled curiously but impressed by his answer.

Jade smiled sweetly, encouragement within the smile that flashed within a cheeky grin that then formed upon her face, the secret of her own intentions well-hidden.

That evening Jade took Derek into the bedroom and pleased him sexually before leading him to the reprobation of his nakedness, snapped in photographic imagery.

Derek uploaded the image of his nakedness to his profile exposing himself to the viewing pleasure of the other participants of the site who showed great interest and left numerous comments for all to read.

Derek had not known the intentions of Jade's encouragement, the secret locked within her silent thoughts and dutiful actions and remained oblivious in his brazenness to go further into his devilishness upon the site.

Jade blushed and giggled like a little girl as she viewed the rudeness of his brazen photograph sighted by the rest of the world. She could not believe that what they were doing was legal at first, the naughty site once shocking had now become a novelty, a sense of intrigue and indulgence to her senses that kept drawing her to it.

"Well, what can I say. That's a nice picture of your…umm…bits," Jade continued, giggling at her cheekiness.

Jade kept her next intention well-hidden, a secret buried deeply within her strategical, planned motions. She had hoped Derek's new-found interest would attract a woman to entice him out of the marriage and into the arms of a sorted affair but she knew Derek, his loyalty a saintly quality that had attracted her from the first time they had met and would not be so easily led.

Every night Jade snuck into the computer room to sneak a peek at the computer screen, an intrigue that had grown in proportion. The naughty pictures pulling her into a motion of unabashed reprobation.

She giggled at the naughtiness, intrigued by the brazen nakedness flashing in pictures upon the computer screen. Tempted by the sweet seduction of the brazen women's advances towards her husband, the thought passed through her mind of answering the delectable messages of sexual advances.

Jade knew within her that the marriage was over, the integrand behaviour of her thoughts now spreading much further into her actions. "This was her way out," she thought. "If only I can entice him into a lucid affair of words with the other women." Jade did not love him anymore, she knew this to be true, although her devotion had remained to her children, her marriage had turned into a sacrifice of her own sanity and emotions, a truth she had kept well-hidden deep within her.

Jade's executed plan of attempting to place her husband's affections into the arms of another woman ran into a mission of fanatical temptation of the words of suggestion and encouragement each night as she sat next to Derek's fantasies upon the computer screen. She wanted him to be happy, she had not lost the respect for him, that always played in the background of her thoughts. She knew it would be hard to leave the controlling hands of her husband, she knew that it would be a war of bitterness once she did, but still she could not stay anymore and dreamt continuously of the day she would leave.

Every night Derek and Jade visited the explicit site of naughtiness in their curious state of sexual temptation and adultery. It had not ignited their sexuality towards each other but rather a sordid, lucid affair of fantasy and fascination towards the profiles of the other people. The explicit photographs excited Derek. Jade knew this and watched with anticipation of her own interests, her strategical, planned, escape into her own directions.

Then the night came when something in Derek changed.

"Would you like to start a profile Jade?" Derek asked smiling devilishly.

Jade's eyes opened wide in astonishment at the proposition, Derek's encouragement of naughtiness.

Derek had always been very protective and jealous of Jade, a possessiveness that had built a wedge between them, his possessiveness of her attention had drove her into a state of loneliness and frustration over their sixteen-year marriage, a contribution towards her reason of planning her escape.

"Absolutely not," Jade answered, gasping and trying to soften the embarrassment with a little giggle. Jade rose to her feet off the chair shaking her head, giggling before stepping away from Derek's side and directing herself away down the hallway and into the kitchen.

"I can't believe he asked me to do that," Jade whispered to herself, turning the kettle on and placing two coffee cups upon the kitchen bench. Jade's cheeks blushed as the fascinating thought rolled within her mind. "No, No, I just couldn't do that," she whispered again holding her palm to the side of her blushing cheeks.

As Jade sat motionless in the loungeroom chair for many hours within the enticing thoughts of Derek's suggestion she suddenly raised to her feet and approached Derek, who was still sitting at the computer desk engrossed in the naughty site of erotica. "Okay, let's do it," Jade said her cheeks a slight red hue of shyness and embarrassment. "Really," Derek replied. "Yes," Jade answered and walked out of the room and into their bedroom and fossicked through her wardrobe for the right outfit to wear. That evening Jade risked the exposure and allowed the curvature of her back that slimmed to her waist and curved around the soft curves of her slim hips to be viewed by all, and unzipped her dress for the first time and allowed Derek to take a photograph for the site.

Jade poured over the profile, although her profile was an innocent view of her womanhood, the sexy image impressed provocativeness and tantalization in the tastefulness of the temptation, as she uploaded the image to the computer screen.

Jade sat silently, patiently watching for any words to highlight upon the computer screen within the profile. Within moments of uploading the photograph a complimentary man introduced himself, *"Hi sexy lady, I'm Max."*

Jade felt the rush of excitement swirl through her mind and body as she read the words from the unknown man and quickly placed her fingers to the keyboard and replied in her a nervousness of playful wit and humour.

Within moments the stranger replied and directed her to his personal message box upon the naughty site.

That evening Jade spent hours glued to the computer screen, enticed and enthralled by the letters that bounced back and forth between herself and Max in playful humour and appreciation, while Derek played numerous computer games in silence upon the big screen television situated within the loungeroom only metres away. No longer did Derek rush to the computer screen at the end of every day but was delegated to the loungeroom by Jade who rushed to beat him to the computer after placing the children in their beds and had become increasingly fascinated by the intrigue of the site and the stranger who had contacted her on that first evening.

Each night the infatuation grew in intensity with each word that bounced between the email services upon the naughty site, as Jade and Max ignited each other's senses of intrigue and fascination.

One by one Jade replied to each word written upon the computer screen which had developed into a nightly ritual of infatuation and admiration for Max. For the first time Jade felt her heart crush upon the stranger who had become her steady companion each night after she had tucked her children into bed. Jade felt the lingering tingles that sat beneath her skin, and the words of the letters swirling in her mind, her fascination with Max pulled at her every night and within two months, Jade and Max had left the site and had started an online affair of personal stories that ignited into passionate love stories of an erotic nature through their own personal email addresses.

As her fantasies with Max intensified and deepened, Jade fell into a distant enchantment of a delusional imagination, which had carved a form of her own reflection of passion and wickedness within the image within the mirror that stood before her.

Max was a breath of fresh air from the staleness of her relationship with Derek, a marriage that had served its purpose and had now felt the ever-growing pressure of the oddness and bitterness towards each other.

She had never told Max of the deep dark secret that dwelled within her, of her planned strategical moves leading to the end of her marriage, a marriage that had become her prison of isolation, emotional despair and desperation to leave.

One evening Jade sat down with Derek at the computer, who fumbled nervously at the computer's keyboard as he logged into the erotic site. Jade looked at Derek as the pictures on his profile site emerged upon the computer screen.

"Oh my god," Jade gasped, her opened mouth telling a dozen stories of astonishment and disbelief. "I can't believe they do that for all to see."

Jade sat motionlessly stunned as the numerous array of photographs revealed the intimate sexual pleasures of other's relationships, one night stands or voyeurism.

Jade could not believe what she was seeing and sat silently blushing at the numerous erotic photographs that flashed before her eyes having never been exposed to such explicitly before.

Derek giggled to himself as he looked at Jade, cheekiness and unabashed erotica burning within the depths of his eyes, as he stared back at her fumbling for the words to hide the truth of his extent of enticement and pleasure.

"Yes. I do," he finally confessed. "But." Jade quickly interrupted and cut his words of one by one as he stumbled within his sentence of excuses.

"But, oh my god Derek. They don't leave anything to your imagination do they."

Jade sat back and watched as the uploaded video of a woman masturbating with a vibrator taking it from her intimate parts to her mouth and back again played vividly in front her and her husband.

"It's X-rated porn, live for all to see," Jade continued, chewing at her bottom lip. "I don't know if I can watch this Derek. I had no idea that they went that far."

"It's soft porn Jade," Derek smiled, feverishly punching away at the keyboard in his response.

It had made Jade feel uncomfortable, although she had not felt betrayed or irked by Derek's fascination, she had not wanted hers to go that far, and held on tightly to her moral innocence, that she felt had slipped into a secret passion with Max of her own intrigue and betrayal.

"How about we do that?" Derek suggested, pointing to the numerous erotic images flashing across the computer screen.

Jade's eyes opened wide in her response before the words tumbled from her lips, "We haven't even had sex for eighteen months Derek. Absolutely not. I could not do that like those people. Absolutely not."

Derek hindered in his response as the bright hue of his blush covered the cheek bones upon his face and slanted his head down in an embarrassment of his own repugnance.

"It's okay Derek truly, if you like that stuff, you continue, but I've seen enough," Jade commented, rising off the seat and taking herself to the loungeroom.

Derek had not moved from the light hue of embarrassment that lingered under his skin, although he portrayed disappointment from his eagerness of erotica he had kept his respectable dissipation and slightly giggled as Jade left the room.

That evening Jade's moral disposition was shocked at the visual display of what was in her mind, a virtual filthiness of the site goer's immoral behaviour, and asked Derek to remove her profile from the site.

Derek did not hesitate at Jade's request and went to instantly delete her profile from the site without question as Jade returned to the office and stood over him watching.

"Wait a minute," Jade said as her eyes began to wander over the many comments that came in layers upon her profile page.

"Oh my," Jade whispered, a blushing hue covering her cheeks, as she started to read the sexy comments written by the site seers participants. Jade bit at her bottom lip and held her palm to her open mouth as the comments ignited the innocent passion hidden deep within her.

"Oh my," Jade repeated, her words leaving her mouth before she could withhold them. "Is that really what they think of me," ran through her mind as she continued to read the numerous comments, a coy smile spreading across her mouth. Jade had never known such admiration of her body before, marrying her third lover, Derek who had kept her in an innocent degradation of his own control and had not lavished her with such adoration or complimentary behaviour.

The admiration of the erotic site goers' comments fascinated Jade and pulled her into a night of intrigue and mellifluent fantasia as her mind ignited into a passionate abandonment of her usual benevolence.

"Can I play on the site too?" finally spilt from Jade's lips with an innocent smile covering her spark of intrigue and interest.

"Yes Jade, that's fine with me," Derek replied shifting from off his chair where he sat in front of the computer screen and allowing Jade to take his place.

Jade kept reading the comments, blushing and smiling coyly as the comments sparked a deep hidden smile within her.

"Hey Blondie, You have the sexiest little back I would love to unzip that dress a little further. Could we chat? :-) Kiss, kiss, kiss."

That night Jade spent the evening viewing the virtual naughtiness of the site's visual pleasures in an erubescent glow of her secret admirers. That night Jade did not speak to Max. The fascination that had become her erotic worldly passion of secret exotic stories hidden deep from the knowledge of her husband.

Jade left the site that night in a natural glow of intrigue and the admiration of the numerous comments of which she had read over and over even from the other women who were asking for more photographs of what they had commented, of her beautiful body. Jade had not known such admiration trapped within her loveless marriage of convenience and necessity.

Each night giggles and laughter escaped from out of the office walls as Jade visited the erotic site nightly pulled by the incredible admiration of the sites visitors.

"Oh my," a giggle slipped quietly from Jade's lips as her online affair with the exotic deepened in fascination and infatuation, as Derek played his computer games in the loungeroom oblivious to the addiction of which was forming.

Jade rose off the office chair and walked slowly towards the loungeroom and joined Derek at the side of the loungeroom chair, situated in front of the large screen television.

"Derek. Do you think it would be okay to take another photograph for my profile," Jade asked, smiling confidently broad, waiting in baited breath for his reply.

Derek pressed the pause button on the computer game controller and slowly turned his head towards Jade. "Of course, Jade,", he replied smiling.

Jade smiled broader in return, her cheeks flushing just a little,

"I was thinking that maybe you could take them for me? Please."

"Yes, of course, I would love to."

Jade smiled once more as Derek rose from the loungeroom chair and was led away into the confines and privacy of the bedroom walls, as he followed Jade to her daring role of provocative exposed voyeurism.

"I think I'll get the office chair," Jade said flippantly, waltzing out of the bedroom door.

"Okay, do you want to go out while I get ready and I'll call you," returning from out of the loungeroom with the office chair, positioning it within the middle of the open space in front of the cupboard mirror.

Within minutes Jade started her heavy search for just the right outfit. "I know," Jade said to herself, raising her head from out of the confines of the bedroom closet. "This one. My legs, a photo of my legs," Jade giggled, emerging with her favourite dress.

Jade quickly, nervously got into the dress and covered her legs in a soft covering of body lotion.

"I'm ready Derek. You can come in, I'm ready now," she called from the bedroom, placing herself upon the office chair, crossing her legs and sliding the hem of the dress up high upon her thighs revelling her soft, silky crossed legs.

"Weit wil, nice," Derek whistled softly as to not wake the sleeping children within their bedrooms situated along the long hallway that ran through the middle of the home. Jade's smile lit up across her face, it had been a long time since Derek had showed a provocative interest in her or complimented the sexiness that had sat hidden within her, and ignited at the introduction to the erotic site. But in Jade's thoughts lay not the interest of her husband but the sweet provocative comments that lay hidden within her profile upon the site, locked up in secrecy by a secret password.

Emerging nervously from the confines and privacy of the bedroom, Jade entered the office clutching at the photographs contained upon her mobile phone.

"Oh my, I don't know about this now Derek," Jade admitted, scratching at the back of her hair, as they pushed the cord into the slot of the computer to upload the photographs.

"Have you seen what they put on here Jade?" Derek grinned.

"Hmm, yes," Jade giggled, giggling away the integrity of the innocent woman holding back at the curiosity that had sat hidden within her coyness. "Okay do it, just do it Derek," finally spilled from her mouth courageously.

The next day as Jade busied herself in the large vegetable plots that she had built behind the shedding of the painting shed, the erotic site and her online lover, Max, swirled in excitement throughout her mind, the comments repeating in a tessellation of admiration and appreciation igniting her curiosity to monumental heights.

Jade giggled to herself her mind ablaze in erotic photographs and comments of the sites participants as she continued to lavish in her love of gardening.

Jade loved to garden, she had built the four plots of raised beds herself using the resources that lay abandoned waiting to be used at the newly bought property three years earlier and was proud of her accomplishment.

She loved the feel of the earth between her fingers, sitting and watching as each plant grew in the sunshine, and blossomed into the fruits of the loving labour. Jade remained isolated and separated from Derek's reach throughout the day engrossed in her own thoughts and the love of her garden until the children had returned home from school that afternoon and it was time to make the evening meal.

"Did you have a good day at school kids?" Jade asked her children who sat at the kitchen table as she served up the evening meal, her mind still engrossed and reminiscing over the erotic site upon the computer.

That evening after placing the children to bed, Jade snuck away to the private confines of the office, her heart beating nervously harder within her chest as she turned on the computer.

"Weit Wil. Sexy Girl. Nice legs," read the numerous messages.

Jade blushed and giggled like a schoolgirl as her eyes poured over the many complimentary messages left in her inbox upon the erotic naughty site.

The site had touched and awoken the hidden woman that had sat suppressed within the control of her mentally and emotionally abusive marriage of sixteen years and ignited into an exuberant exploration of the sexual provocativeness that had laid hidden and unprovoked within her.

One comment upon the site in particular had caught Jade's eye in a familiar sense of deliberation and precise eloquence. "Max," Jade giggled and smiled, navigating her response to his personal message box.

"Hello Max," Jade wrote back in reply, giggling joyfully as they continued to correspond throughout the entire evening.

The next evening Jade sat down at the computer screen and wrote a letter to Max.

"Hello sexy man." Jade's fingers began to type. "I would love to have a spa with you."

Within moments a reply rushed back into her inbox. Jade quickly opened the message and began to read as she playfully bit at her bottom lip in excitement at his enticing words of erotic playfulness and intrigue, before typing a message in her response that evoked a continuous reply of words. Their interaction that evening continued into an eruption of an erotic match of words and escalated into Max and Jades incessant infatuation with each other that spilled into a nightly ritual of intrigue and naughtiness.

With each day that passed in the avoidance of the tessellation of her husband's incessant oppugnancy, Jade's animosity grew stronger and stronger, as the sweet mellifluence of Max's words beat louder and louder in her heart and mind, pulling her into a world of passion and fantasy.

Jade's concentration beat loudly with the site's fascination, the comments a repeated tessellation within her mind daily, the ignition of her passions with Max precipitating into an uncontrollable passion.

His every word hanging delicately from the tip of her tongue, sounding in a silent celebration of life and lust. "Oh my," Jade giggled to herself as she went about her daily duties caring for her family and the family home within her avoidance of Derek. "I can't believe I'm so caught up with all of this it's just a person on a computer."

But Jade was caught up in all of it as her mind raced over the numerous comments and the letters from Max as her heart beat fast in excitement, at the anticipation of her nightly ritual.

That evening Jade put the children to bed and rushed towards the office and switched on the computer , no longer did she hesitate or withstand the waiting of her turn to use the computer or wait for Derek's approval and proceeded to fulfil her own whims of fascination.

"Oh, you're keen tonight," Derek commented, smiling in Jade's direction as he stood within the doorway of the loungeroom.

"I, um, I'm just curious as to what they thought of my new photo," Jade replied, biting nervously at her bottom lip, hiding the truth from her husband.

"You don't mind do you?"

"No, of course not Jade, you go first tonight if you want. I just felt like playing games tonight anyway. Have fun."

Jade smiled and turned directing herself towards the kitchen where she made two coffees and quickly returned to the office. Within moments of her return to the office Derek returned from the confines of the bedroom producing a bag of pot and a pipe which had become their nightly ritual of relaxing while the children slept peacefully in their bedrooms.

"Do you want a smoke Jade?" Derek asked, packing the marijuana into the stained pipe.

"Yes please," Jade answered, smiling gratefully as he handed her the pipe and she proceeded to smoke the sweet intoxication of the marijuana before handing the pipe back to her husband and turning her attentions to the computer. That night Jade remained on the computer until the early hours of the morning until her eyes drooped in a sleepy succession of fluttering eyelids, engrossed in her affair of intrigue and fascination as she opened the emails and comments one by one reading them eagerly.

That night Jade's curiosity pulled her into the other areas of the sites functions of interacting with the other participants as she explored the other options available to her.

"Oh my," Jade whispered. "I didn't know that you could chat instantly to people. There's a chat room." Jade felt the nervousness of her apprehension and hesitance as she ventured further into the functions with the numerous sites participants whom requested to speak to her.

Jade hesitated within her nervousness as her fingers hit the keyboards buttons. "I should not be doing this," ran through her mind as her fingers ignored the incessant nervousness within her mind. "I'm a married woman." But Jade longed for the stimulation of the outside world, her naivety craving to be set free, her growing curiosity pulling her into the unknown of the exotic sites responses.

Jade fumbled with the keys of the computer, her unfamiliar, inexperienced fingers finding a common interest with the words that lit up upon the computer screen. Jade felt so inexperienced compared to the experienced voyeurs that expressed their uninhibited ventures of exotica upon the site. Encouraged and provoked by her own curiosity Jade took a deep breath then entered the chat room.

A broad smile spread across her face as a familiar greeting caught her interest and attention. "Hi there, Blondie." "Max," Jade whispered with an air of excitement as she giggled.

A slight panic of the unknown came over her suddenly, a feeling of nativity hesitated within her fingertips as she reached for the keys. "Okay, what do I do now," Jade thought to herself, not wanting to ask the question to her husband who sat oblivious in the next room.

Jade pressed down upon the keys one by one as an exuberant smile spread across her face and she proceeded to type the words in her response that set the scene of an ignited instant attraction to the one who sat waiting in his anticipation: Max. The quick-witted humour of Jades response ignited the pair into a quantitative of humorous attentiveness that bounced excessively and naturally, as the pairs adventurism ventured beyond the boundaries of private messaging and escaped into the world of instant chat messaging, that sounded in a tessellation of laughter from Jade bouncing within the walls of the open plan office space.

Jade turned her head to the view of her husband's eyes glazing down upon her. "You sound like you're having fun."

"Hmm," Jade answered in a hesitant hum, hiding the gleam that lay hidden deep within her eyes. "Would you like to use it now Derek?" she meekly asked.

"No, I'm just about to make a coffee, would you like one?"

"Yes Please, thanks," Jade replied, containing the ecstatic excitement that lay hidden under her smile of appreciation.

Jade knew that Derek sat oblivious to her well-hidden secret, she knew the infatuation could lose her rights to using the computer on the site again. She knew it was wrong and although she had caught her husband on the site, he had not developed an obsession with the site or a close infatuation with another woman as she had hoped, although he had a select download of naughtiness and provocativeness of photographs. That night Jade fell in love with the man hidden behind the computer screen, Max.

Jade sat in the driveway that Friday afternoon, a silent long pause, a heave in her chest of hesitation and dread as she thought about entering the house with the shopping and having to be within the presence and company of Derek once more. Her marriage, an infliction of which she longed to be set free and to be able to rebuild a life of which she dreamed of and craved to experience. Jade had grown tired of hiding the truth, of smiling in silence from within inside of herself, a smile that had grown in perfunctory when formed upon her face, a love that no longer existed , the marriage had come to an end.

Jade had had a hard week, the kids a constant source of pleasure and exhaustion but always her first priority. While taking care of the numerous chores within the household and for her family Jade often found her mind exploring different options out in the world, and within, escaping into her own imagination and desires.

That weekend Jade invited Sherri over for some drinks to indulge in, their usual evening of kicking back and relaxing while the children played together. Even though Jade had known Sherri over a long period of time and their bond had deepened during the traumatic time of Sherri's divorce and they had formed a high level of trust between them, Jade held onto the deep-seated secret of her interaction and participation upon the erotic site and her infatuation and feelings she felt for Max and had held the secret close to her chest although the thought had entered her mind at times.

"Do I tell her?" Jade whispered to herself in her perfunctory form of preparing the families' dinner as the children ran around in the yard and she stood watching and looking outside of the kitchen window. Jade wanted to share the secret that she hid deep within her, to share the excitement but held back through the judgemental aspects of her own moral denouement. She knew it was wrong.

Sherri had decided to stay the night instead of running the risk of driving home while under the influence of alcohol and brought in the children's bedding from her car as Jade busied herself in the kitchen.

Within moments, Jade had whizzed up the children's meals and had settled them into their usual routine of movies while they sat and ate their tea, while the adults vacated the house and walked down into the direction of the large shedding situated on the quarter acre of land at the side of the house.

"Brrr, it's a little cold," Jade said on entry to the shed. "Should we go back inside? We can play music in the loungeroom instead."

"I agree Jade," Sherri answered, rubbing her cold arms with the palm of her hands. "We just have to go outside to smoke that's all," Jade answered, gathering their things and walking back towards the house and setting up for the evening in the loungeroom.

Jade sat patiently in the cold stillness of the night air as Sherri enjoyed her cigarette. Jade had quit smoking when she was pregnant with the twins and had not picked up another during her sixteen year marriage and felt proud of her accomplishment of resisting the temptation of the addictive nicotine although surrounded in it on a regular basis as Sherri lit one up in her presence regularly.

Jade's mind wandered into a realm of fantasy as it drifted into the depths of her secrecy as she stood waiting for Sherri to finish her cigarette. "Where is your mind tonight Jade?" Sherri asked.

Jade giggled as she was snapped from her deep thoughts. "Well, oh I was just thinking to myself. Thinking about the kids," Jade lied, hiding the truth from her friend's knowledge in a fastidious necessity of her own preservation.

Jade did not know Max properly yet and had the feeling she had not wanted to share her secret of her online affair with anyone. She wanted it. She needed it. She wanted it all for herself. For Max and their fantasies to be exclusively hers.

As the night drifted into a full swing of intoxicated excitement and laughter bellowing from out of the loungeroom walls as Jade, Derek and Sherri shared stories while they poured the cold liquor into the tall glasses placed onto the loungeroom table, Derek suddenly went quiet and turned his head towards the office.

Derek rose from the loungeroom chair and walked towards the office turning on the computer. "What are you doing Derek?" Jade asked instantly, walking over to stand by Derek's side.

"Do you think we should show Sherri the site?" Derek asked, a devious smile forming upon his face.

"I don't know what she would think," Jade replied, placing her fingertips to her bottom lip.

"Don't know about what?" Sherri asked, pushing her head into the space between Derek and Jade, looking at the computer screen.

Jade giggled loudly, "Oh my Sherri I don't know if you're into this or not."

Derek unabashedly loaded up the page of the naughty exotic site and revealed its contents for all to see. Although she giggled loudly and blushed slightly, Jade had the notion Sherri was no stranger to such erotica and had been exposed and involved in such sexual advances before.

"Have you seen this site before Sherri?" Jade asked, a slight hue covering her cheeks in the presence of her friend.

"No," Sherri replied. "But my ex-husband was into porn so I've seen this kind of material before. I find it quite funny actually. All these naughty people."

"Derek," Jade squealed. "Oh my." Derek loaded up his profile, his photographs staring in the face of her friend, exposed in all of their intimacy. Sherri giggled incessantly in her intoxicated state of surprise.

Jade stood silently, her eyes a nervous gaze of sideway glances toward her friend as each exposed photograph revealed more and more of Derek's nakedness. Jade did not know what to say and was silent in her gestured response towards the photographs as her palm reached for the openness of her mouth in front of her friend. The encouragement came in a point of the finger as Jade dispelled all emotions from her marriage as her fingertips reached for the blind truth of her husband's discretion.

"Ohhh," Sherri gasped as Derek's nakedness rose into her view while Jade stood and giggled.

Derek pointed at the nakedness of one of the site's visitor's photographs, exposed in a full erotic rapture of an unadulterated pose of voyeurism.

"Are you on her Jade, do you have a profile?" Sherri asked, curiosity spreading across her face and into her cheeks.

"Oh my," Jade whispered to herself. "Yes, but not full view like Derek or the other people on here. I'm just not that game," Jade replied, a blush covering her cheeks. "He told me to do it," she giggled nervously held within her embarrassment. "I was just experimenting Sherri, honestly." Sherri looked at her sideways, a devilish smile forming upon her lips.

Derek entered Jade's profile and entered the password which they had constructed together. But the password continuously refused entry to the profile.

"Wrong password," Derek remarked.

"What's going on. It won't load Jade?" Derek queried, turning to face her.

"I'm not sure," Jade lied, looking at Sherri. "Go to the chatrooms Derek," Jade insisted, quickly steering him away from her profile, hiding the naughty secret that sat deep within her, her own secrecy of the changed password.

"Okay," Derek answered laughing in his intoxicated state. "Can I take some photographs of you to together? Just pretend." Sherri and Jade looked at each other before bursting out laughing as the intoxication of the alcohol uninhibited their rational minds.

"Yes, okay. Let's do it," Jade finally answered, lifting the bottle of liquor to her lips. "How do you want us?"

Derek strategically set an office chair up in the middle of the room, placing the two women into a provocative pose. "Yes, just like that," Derek commented, snapping at the photo shoot of his mobile phone. Suddenly Jade fell heavily to the floor laughing, slipping from the safe support of the office chair and into an intoxicated state on the office floor. Sherri's face flew into a rapture of laughter as she held her hand out to pick Jade up from off the floor and back into the seat of the office chair.

"Kiss her," Derek said, a devious devilish smile spreading across his cheeks.

"Touch her breasts. "

"No," Jade squealed giggling.

"Okay," replied Sherri, a devilish intoxicated grin covering her face.

Without any more persuasion, Jade reached for Sherri, her hand cupping the fullness of her breast as she stood and placed her soft warm lips against that of her friends, as Derek snapped the camera and captured the moment in photographic images. Derek hummed to himself as he greedily snapped at the forbidden photographs capturing the women in all of their prowess with each other. Within that moment Jade asked Sherri to stand against her pressing their naked flesh together and reached around palming her friend's slender waist and covering the nakedness of her breast with the cup of her palm, while Derek's eagerness captured the moment in all of its glory ready to upload to the erotic provocative site. The girls stood giggling in the intoxicated provocative moment.

"Oh my god. It looks like we're really doing that," Jade commented, covering her open mouth. "Oh my." Jade asked Sherri to go outside with her. "I need a joint," Jade commented, slipping the paper-filled joint into her fingers, directing her friend towards the outside of the house and to the back veranda, hiding the truth from the children who had remained within the confines of the bedrooms out of view.

"Jade, why wouldn't your profile load before?" Sherri asked curiously.

"Umm. I changed the password so Derek wouldn't know," Jade confessed. "Please don't tell him," Jade pleaded. "I haven't told Derek Sherri, but I have a little secret," Jade confessed further unable to no longer contain the secret she was hiding.
"But he's been talking to all the girls on the site."

"Umm," Sherri replied giggling. "I don't care Jade, I really don't, I understand."

"I just can't tell him Sherri, it would start a fight. Please don't tell anyone."

Sherri looked at her friend giggling. "God, no," Sherri replied. "Mums the word."

That night Jade awoke to an unusual sound of unexpected giggling coming from the location of the office and approached the noise with an open mind, as she viewed the empty sheets of her bed next to her.

"What are you doing?" Jade asked, as her friend sitting with her husband in front of the computer screen came into her view.

"Nothing Jade," Derek answered quickly. Jade stood smiling omnisciently at her husband's reply before turning to leave from the room and climbing back into her bed alone.

Jade awoke the next morning, a hangover sitting heavily over the frown that formed upon her forehead. "Ohhh," Jade grumbled, filling up the kettle and turning it on.

Jade walked down the hallway and into the office to check on Sherri. Sherri's eyes opened as Jade entered the room and greeted her good morning.

"Would you like a coffee?" Jade asked.

"Yeah, sure," Sherri replied, climbing out from under the covers of her bed.

It was a nice sunny morning, the sun rising in the sky to form a beautiful, warm glow over the earth's surface which illuminated in the eyes of the two women as they entered the back veranda.

Sherri and Jade sat down at the table that was located under the back veranda, their coffee cups warming their hands as their minds began to stir and awaken from their sleep.

A strange smile formed on the bridge of Sherri's lips as she sipped at the hot coffee in the comfort of the country's warm morning air.

"Well, what can I say," Jade finally said, giggling at the night's antics.

"How long have you been on that naughty site?" Sherri finally asked. "What is it exactly?"

"Oh god," Jade uttered under her breath as she started to blush. "Ohhh, it's," stumbling over her words. "Please, please don't say anything, do not tell a soul please," she begged. "The truth is I caught my husband on it; he was uploading pictures and looking at pictures and talking to other women who were sending him naked pictures of themselves upon his request so I thought I'd take a look. I was curious, shocked at first but very curious, so I asked if I could have a look, he didn't seem to mind. So then I asked if I could have a profile of my own," Jade blushed as she continued to explain.

"Ohhh. But why wouldn't your profile open Jade?" Sherri asked, curiosity streaming through her voice. Jade felt a sudden centrifugal as her mind searched for the right lie to tell. "She's forgotten," flashed through Jades mind in comfort.

"Didn't you like it?" Jade finally said, sipping deeply into her hot coffee. Jade bit at her lips as her mind reminisced over her secret interaction with Max.

"Don't you care Jade, about what your husband is doing?"

"Nah, no, I don't; whatever makes him happy, Sherri. It's his choice. Anyway," Jade replied, changing the subject. "Would you like some breakfast? The kids will be awake soon."

Jade rose from the seat and walked towards the entrance of the back door. "Please don't say anything about it," Jade pleaded.

"Don't worry Jade, I won't say a word," Sherri assured her.

Suddenly the back door slid open revealing the first signs of the awakening of the children.

"Hey Cody. Do you want some breakfast?" Jade asked, holding Cody's head against her side, running her hands through the thickness of his hair. "Here we go," Jade muttered, looking at Sherri placing a kiss at the top of Cody's head. "Time for breakfast." Jade rose from the chair and entered the kitchen and proceeded to make breakfast for the children as they awoke one by one and entered the kitchen and sat at the kitchen table to eat. Jade and Sherri stood by the kitchen bench as the children finished their breakfast enjoying another coffee and engaging in small talk that was filtered enough to be acceptable within the presence of children until the children had all finished their meal.

"Okay, time to clean up," Jade said, packing up the breakfast dishes and ushering the children towards their bedrooms. Sherri had become a regular visitor to the family home as her divorce unfolded in a torrent of dishevelling of the family and the family home and had become very comfortable within Jades family home. Jade had been a comfort to Sherri, a support, offering her help beyond her own capacity, although Sherri did not know that her own marriage was dissolving into an abandonment of commitment and Jade secretly longed to end her marriage also.

"Okay kids, time to go," Sherri called through the house. Jade walked Sherri and the children out to the front veranda and waited for them to be seated in their vehicle.

"Bye," Jade said. "I'll see you tomorrow night," waving to Sherri and the children as she reversed her car out of the driveway and drove down the road and disappeared around the corner of the street. "I'm going back to bed," Jade said to herself laughing as she walked back towards the front door of the house.

Over the next six months, Jade focused her efforts on her plans to depart from her marriage and constantly found ways to evade Derek's company as her mind intertwined with the letters of the exotic enticement of her infatuation with Max. She waited every night for the words of Max to entice her into a world of fantasy and eroticism. She longed to read his letters, his words, falling deeper and deeper into the excitement of their passionate erotic affair of words and his forbidden love that had reached her heart, a love that would never in person touch the depth or warmth of her aching heart or the depth of her passion, her flesh.

Her heart pounded at each word as he consumed her mind and of which she no longer had the strength or will to fight, she seeked his attention which evoked a natural force within her to erupt and crave him explicitly.

It had brought her back to life from a marriage that had run its course and had developed into a relationship of animosity and hardship and had sent her mind into a slumber of boredom and fastidiousness.

It wasn't something she had planned or expected to ever cross her path, she had lived the life of an obedient wife, a devoted mother, never tempting nor tempted, but here it was something she could not deny or deny herself of a temptation so sweet so erotic, it swept her away into a land of forbidden love, lust and words that sounded like sweet poetry to her mind and heart.

Jade hid the truth well, shielding her eyes, the dancing light that hid beneath the colours in her eyes denying the involvement, the emotional connection, hiding the truth she protected so fiercely even from herself, but she knew, she knew what she was doing was wrong but knew not how to walk away; the pull, the temptation, the connection was too strong for her to control as she reached for Max at the end of every day.

He had reached the core of her running his fingers through her soul stroking the very essence of her being, her womanhood, the woman who was locked away, the essence she did not know, her passion, her lust, her expression, bursting, bubbling within her, her desire to unleash her existence to feel alive.

She spent her days locked in anger, control, fear of the unpredictable behaviour of her husband, her nights engrossed in laughter, joy, excitement, lust and love; her nights with him: her Max.

Jade's life had become a double standard of pleasures and pain, not knowing which one was going to win, take her over and tilt her towards the path on which she would choose to walk. Max tempted her with his words, tantalising her with his pictures, she had not known a man like him before, she had not known these feelings he had evoked, teasing her soul, unable to leave, unable to say no, unable to stop.

She knew she was lost in him, his letters, his words, him.

Although they knew not what each other looked like, their identity hidden well from the world, from each other, it did not matter to them. With each stroke of the keyboard, they grew closer and closer every night until the night the question came, "Can I see your face?"

91

Jade held her breath, she had not expected that question to arise so soon and felt the nervousness and apprehension rise up her spine and fall into the pit of her stomach. "Oh, I don't know," Jade whispered to herself. She bit at her lip, wrapped in the nervous tension of his question, to show her true form, the face she had hidden behind the screen of the computer. Max's words flowed eloquently, each word written into a precise formation of defined paragraphs that exuded meaning and definition of the expression of which he wished to provoke. Jade knew that he was an educated man and felt pale in comparison. Although she held a business degree she felt his expectations of her were of a high standard and felt the falter within her own confidence of which had been wilted down over time through the abusive controlling words of her husband and felt she would not measure up to Max's expectations. Jade did not see herself as beautiful or alluring and shied at revealing her face, her true form.

"Oh Max, I don't know," Jade whispered to herself, nibbling at her finger nails.

She wanted to show Max the woman she was, who she was, but feared his reaction, she did not want to disappoint him. Would she still be the beautiful, sexy woman he had told her she was? The apprehension wrapping around her in a hold of tenaciousness. Jade so badly, desperately needed to see the man who she could not resist, who had her wrapped around his fingers, dangling, lusting him, loving him. She could not resist, she could not say no. "Okay," Jade replied. "But I hope you're not disappointed."

Jade's fingers fumbled nervously over the keyboard as she loaded the photograph of her face into the computer. Jade held her breath as she looked over her shoulder at Derek who sat oblivious in the next room. She turned her attentions back to the computer nervously nibbling on her bottom lip before finally pressing the key, send. Jade could not deny Max's request anymore and fell into the depths of her guilty pleasure of their secrecy. Within moments of sending the photograph Max replied, "Oh my god Jade, you are beautiful. A stunning woman."

Jade blushed coyly in the office chair, reading the words over and over as the blush spread across her cheeks and turned her nervousness into a broad exuberant smile that spread across her face.

"Thank you, Max. Now it's your turn," Jade replied, typing the words and sending the message through to his personal email box. Within minutes Max wrote back and sent his photograph through to Jade with a message attached. "I hope you're not disappointed."

Jade looked at the photograph with jubilation, *"Oh my Max, you are so handsome."* Jade looked at the photograph over and over before finally replying.

That night their infatuation deepened into an attraction beyond mischievousness enticement and entered into a world of adoration and affection.

As each night passed, Jade fell deeper and deeper into Max's love and admiration, the strong desire to touch him pulsated throughout her and grew stronger and stronger, she could no longer deny the truth of their connection.

His words a captivating cascade of beauty and sweetness that repeated themselves incessantly through her mind. The fantasy of his love stoking its fingers through her soul and sweeping deep into her heart.

"Ohhh, Max, I wish I could see you in person," Jade wrote at the bottom of her letter. That night Max's words roamed through her mind continuously as she lay awake next to her husband in their bed. Jade desired better, unable to fake her way through her marriage anymore. That night Jade made a decision.

Derek and Jade strolled the circuit the next day, watching their children as they attended the school gathering, evading the truth of the failing marriage. They did not hold hands, the distance between them a silent shudder of the inevitable. Derek had taken the time off work as it was their anniversary, a celebration spent in a silence of unspoken words or affection.

Jade strolled with Derek looking at the ground, thoughts rolling through her mind incessantly. She did not want to be there, not with him; her mind tangled in her online lover's words, her body longed for his touch and only his touch. Jade knew that day what she must do.

Derek and Jade returned home that day, sitting out in the big shed on the quarter acre block of which they had come to know so well as their own private space away from the children. That day Jade did not fumble or hesitate with her words as they freely and decisively spilled from her mouth.

"Derek. I want a divorce, I don't love you anymore, I can't do this anymore," Jade announced in a determined, confident but careful manner. "It's over Derek."

It's not something she had planned to do on this day, their marriage anniversary, the spontaneous words spilling from her mouth as she looked Derek in the eyes. It was not planned for that day in particular, as the courage straightened Jade's backbone and the words fell from her lips.

Liberation

That evening Derek and Jade sat the children down on the couch in the family loungeroom of their home and prepared to tell them the unsettling news of the unperceived circumstances that Jade knew would turn her children's lives upside down into a spiral of devastating consequences.

Jade sat silent in the large armchair of the loungeroom watching as her children's smiling faces fell from the innocence of happiness to the devastating effects of an unperceived dissolution as the words left Derek's mouth in an indignation of damnation towards Jade.

"Your mother doesn't want to be with me anymore. She's kicking me out. She wants a divorce," Derek scowled as he looked at the children staring back at him.

Jade could not believe her ears and instantly looked at Derek in disgust as the repertoire of contemptuous words left his mouth and without haste interrupted before Derek could say another damaging word of unconscionable recognition of his own children's emotional welfare.

Jade looked over at her children's sullen bewilderment as her face filled with the sorriness of her concerns for what her children had just heard and the devastating predicament she had just inflicted upon their lives.

"Kids I'm so sorry," Jade said in a quiet remorseful tone. "I know this is hard to hear but sometimes two people just can't be together anymore. No matter how hard they try, they just can't get it right."

Jade raised to her feet from the lounge chair and slowly stepped towards her children to kneel in front of them. "It doesn't mean that your father and I don't love you and you know that we are always going to be there for you. You'll always have Mum and Dad. That won't change okay."

Jade felt her heart sink into her stomach as she watched her children's eyes begin to fill with the tears of the devastating truth of the dissolution of their oblivious happiness and what they had believed was their world of family togetherness and joy.

Jade's eyes filled with tears as she watched Nick drop his head into his hands and break down into awash of inconsolable devastated sobbing and quickly raised to her feet to sit beside him and embrace him in her arms of comfort.

"It's going to be okay," Jade whispered softly as she held Nick tightly in her arms. "Oh sweetheart it's going to be okay." But Jade could not stop the flow of sorrow that flooded her son's cheeks and felt helpless within his grief and pain. "Oh god, what have I done," Jade whispered silently to herself as Nick leapt to his feet and marched out of the loungeroom and down the long hallway to hide within the confinement of his bedroom. Jade looked over at Derek who sat in motionless silence in the large lounge chair scouring a look of contemptuous impugnation at her before turning his face away in a stance of targeted tribulation. Jade looked around into the large, silent loungeroom as her children sat staring at her with tear-soaked eyes before finally raising to her feet and rushing to their sides to gather them into her arms of consolable concern.

"I love you. You know that don't you? I will always love you," Jade sobbed as the tears began to fall from her own eyes and roll down her cheeks.

"I know mum," Cody said in his young, innocent voice as he stroked his fingers through his mother's hair and kissed her on the cheek. Jade lifted her eyes off the direction of the loungeroom floor to look into her son's comforting stare as she absorbed the warmth of his unconditional love before kissing him on the cheek and pulling him closer into her embrace.

"I have to go and check on your brother to see if he's okay," Jade said quietly as she kissed her children one by one and released her arms from the tight embrace of her motherly comfort. "I'll be back in a minute okay." James, Monique and Cody nodded their heads in a recognition of unity as they watched their mother walk from the loungeroom and down the long hallway into Nick's bedroom where he lay in a devastated trance of tears and sadness. "Oh my boy, come here," Jade said softly as she sat down on the bed next to him stretching her open arms out to wrap around him. Nick lifted his face off his tear-soaked pillow and crawled into a ball inside of his mother's arms. "I'm so sorry sweetheart. I'm so sorry," Jade whispered as her throat tightened and struggled to choke back the tears of her son's grief.

"I love you sweetheart," Jade whispered as she held Nick in her arms and rocked him. "It's going to be okay I promise you. Don't cry sweetie. It's going to be okay."

That night after Jade tucked her children into their beds and said goodnight, she climbed into what was once the matrimonial bed of her marriage alone and cried for her children into the early hours of the morning until finally she fell asleep into a deep slumber of tear-soaked sadness for her children.

Over the next three weeks Jade and Derek walked the house in silence as they passed each other during their movements throughout the family home. Derek no longer slept alongside Jade in what was once the bed they had shared and had relocated himself and that of his personal belongings into the confinement of the office that was adjoined to the family home's loungeroom.

Although their silent avoidance of one another had developed into a state of separate living whilst under the confinement of the same roof, Jade continued to offer her assistance to Derek in his search for a new residence which he could now call his own in a desperate bid to hold onto a sense of civilizable perfunctory while in the children's presence. Within the three weeks of passing, Derek finally found a rental property on the outskirts of the Suisania Bay township and had made all of the necessary arrangements for his relocation from the familiarity of the matrimonial family home.

On the week leading up to Derek's vacating of the family home, Jade helped to prepare Derek's new rental property in a meticulous detailing of cleaning and purchasing of new furniture and household necessities in order for Derek to be independently adequate. As the precarious situation of their parting had fallen into a period of monitory depletion within their funds, Jade had agreed to allow the purchase of the household goods of which had been a necessity to Derek's standard of living to be debited to the credit cards of which had been applied for and placed in her name in the duration of their marriage with the promise of Derek's contribution to the repayments of the debts.

On the day of Derek's departure from the family home, Jade watched in shame and dismay as Derek chaotically bullied his way through their household and personal belongings in a tempestuous display of laying claim to all except the refrigerator, washing machine, Monique and Cody's belongings, one of the mattress's from the matrimonial bed, the computer and a few crockery items.

By nightfall Derek loaded up his car for the last time that day and ordered the children into the car before slamming the door of the house shut and disappearing around the bend of the road that ran adjacent to the house of which they had called home for three years.

As Jade walked around the empty rooms of what was once the family home she dropped her face in desolation towards the direction of the empty floors as she eyed the many broken items of furniture and her personal belongings of which Derek had discarded and scattered across each room of the family home in a contemptuous display of desecration. Jade stood in the silence of the long hallway as she stared into the nothingness that surrounded her and dropped to her knees in a flood of tears in a confliction of extreme grief and jubilation of her liberation as she stepped out from under the dark shadows of which Derek had held her within his control for sixteen years.

As Jade held her tear-soaked face within the palm of her hands and listened to the silence that surrounded her in the house that was once filled with children's laughter and chatter, a calmness began to swirl within her and fill her senses in a breath of her own freedom. Jade drew in a deep breath as she raised her head from out of her hands and eyed the emptiness of the dishevelled rooms of the house.

"It's done," Jade whispered to herself as she began to slowly raise to her feet from out of the curled position of her embattled disposition. "I'm free. I'm finally free."

She stood motionless in the empty long hallway staring at the slammed front door before finally drawing in a deep breath and stepping forward to take the first step towards her own sense of unfettered optimism. "Okay. Time to clean this all up," Jade said to herself as she stood in the doorway of the loungeroom that held the scatterings of Derek's unashamed display of impudent desecration.

As Jade walked from one side to the other of the loungeroom picking up the broken remnants of the thrown and scattered picture frames, household ornaments and re-standing the strewn remnants of the furniture that had been discarded as worthless in Derek's eyes her mind wandered into the realms of her unlimited imagination of her own aspirations for a future without restriction or derision of her soul.

After many hours of removing the shattered remnants of the household goods and broken glass of the strewn picture frames that lay around on the floors of each room that evening Jade finally sat down in the office chair that stood before the office desk and sighed her first breath of relief as she sipped at the chilled glass of wine that sat within the relaxed grip of her hand. "Okay," Jade said to herself as a small smile began to form on her lips. "Now it's my turn to do what I set out to do."

That evening Jade turned on her computer and wrote a long letter to Max explaining the outcome of her new liberated stance as a single woman and mother and the escape from her deliberation of manipulation and control of which she had suffered for the last sixteen years in the hands of her tempestuous marriage.

As Jade wrote the last sentence of her long letter to Max and pushed the send button a mellifluous smile of joy filled her face and spread throughout the exuberance of the endless possibilities that surrounded her future.

Over the next month Jade worked continuously embarking on her endeavour of meticulous research and study within the business plan of the services that occupied the small town of Suisania Bay and the surrounding areas while still maintaining a loyalty of endless selfless accommodation to Derek's needs as he stepped into the world of single parenthood.

With each passing day, Jade's strength grew, and her vibrant personality of optimism and confidence began to flourish within the confines of her own choices and ambitious passion to develop her own business.

Although Derek had remained on a vigilant path of keeping Jade close and within his reach at a moment's notice by embarking on an endless spree of text messages and phone calls, the dissolution of their marriage had not served as a battleground as Jade had feared in the five years of the apprehensive trepidation she had endured whilst in the midst of her irrevocable decision of separating from the marriage. Jade had remained a constant source of civilised assistance to Derek as she agreed to continue to do his household chores, laundry requirements and provide her meal preparation and cooking knowledge on a daily basis.

As Jade began to mass the daily hours of continuous research and meticulous study of the complexity of business and computer training while adhering to her virtue of her responsibilities of raising four children as a single mother, her attention to Derek's continuous demands of helplessness and acquirements of assistance began to waiver as she pulled herself away from Derek's hold and onto her own path of separation and independence from the structure of a matrimonial union.

As Jade's attention and assistance waivered from Derek's attention and drove her into a world of business clarification and associations with people of unfamiliar difference to the world she had previously known within her marriage, the civilised acquiescent she had once held within the perspectives of maintaining a stance of a peaceful camaraderie with Derek slowly descended into an acrimonious perplexity of contemptuous text messages and abusive phone calls.

With each refusal of Jade's willingness to assist Derek's whims of need the tension grew between their every correspondence with each other and started to weave a confliction of loyalties within the faces of their children.

Over the next few months, Jade drastically changed her diet and exercise routine to one which was that of an organic foundation and spent her days painstakingly and endlessly revising and analysing the information she had gathered while conducting the market and community surveys that were required to construct and develop the business that had become a passion within her soul.

Jade joined many charity-based programs that had been formed throughout the small community of Suisania Bay and had formed many new friendships outside of her usual circle of acquaintances and had found that her friendship with Sherri had blossomed into a tight bond of support and related issues as the ongoing chaos with Derek that had wound so tightly around her began to unravel into a complexity of unforeseen tribulation of Derek's vengeance of his broken heart and loss of control.

By day Jade worked endlessly into the night training herself into a world of a dedicated, ambitious drive within the business industry as she acquired the necessary knowledge and skills that were required in order to develop her own business. But as each evening fell into the dark depths of the moonlit night sky, Jade unveiled the image of her business style of perfection and slipped into the realms of her harlequin of infatuation with the man that had swept her into a world of exotic desire and erotic lust behind the secrecy of the walls that surrounded her office confines. No longer restricted by the bonds of her marriage vow to Derek, Jade and Max's infatuation and connection grew into a fantasy of their own reality for which neither had the strength or desire to say no to one another. Jade and Max's short letters of admiration erupted into a nightly ritual of endless emails of erotic pictures and exotic tales of fantasy as their connection and desire for each other stroked the essence of their souls and unleashed their unforbidden lust for one another.

Jade found herself lost in thoughts of Max as she went about her daily routines and wrote stories of passion and wild desire that she would send throughout the day, to send strokes of arousing tantalisation throughout his senses upon his return to his office the next morning. As each night passed Jade was drawn deeper and deeper into the magical moments of Max's every word that penetrated, intrigued and soothed her every desire and pulled at the heartstrings of her surrender of the truth, her heart.

That night as Jade wrote her last letter for the night to Max, she breathed a heavy sigh as she sat in the chair staring at the computer screen, wriggling her fingers across the letters of the keyboard.

As Jade sighed off on the bottom of the letter, her fingers spilt the confession that had laid hidden within her heart and whispered from her lips each night as their connection had grown but had remained frightful and cautious in her admittance until tonight.

To my amazing beautiful man.
"Max I love you."
Yours forever. Jade xx

Jade sat back deep into the back of the office chair as her nervous disposition at what she had just confessed sent her into a shutter of apprehension as she awaited the longed-for reply from her forbidden lover.

That night Max replied a letter of synchronised sincerity as he typed the words Jade had been needing to hear.

To my beautiful girl,
I have been waiting so long to hear you say those words to me. I have loved you from the first day we met. I love you too Jade.
Love always. Max xxx

Jade's eyes lit up as she read the loving words and felt the quick flutter of her pounding heart as she read the special words to herself over and over. "Ohhh, Max. I wish I could kiss you right now," Jade whispered to herself as she slightly tilted her head looking at the letter written on her computer screen. "I wish I could meet you." Although Jade knew that she would never meet her online lover in person she found herself dreaming about sweet moments of the day they would actually meet and got lost in her day dreams of his beautiful words. As the night fall slipped into the early hours of the morning, Jade said goodnight to Max and climbed into her bed and fell quickly into a peaceful slumber.

Over the next few months Jade's relationship with Derek declined and tangled itself into a web of Derek's jealous contempt as he struggled to let go of Jade and their marriage.

Day by day Derek's text messages and phone calls grew more and more vicious, insulting and frequent in nature and verged on the threatening persecution of Jade's safety as she slept alone in the empty house while her children were staying with their father. Jade found herself cringing with each flash of a message on her mobile phone as she feared the words that she would receive with each reading of Derek's attack of abusive crucifixion towards her.

Jade dropped her children off at Derek's house for their week-long stay with their father and returned to her daily routine of studying and research as she sat outside in the glorious rays of the summer sky. Within an hour Jade's phone began to flash and announce the arrival of text messages.

"Oh no," Jade said quietly as she picked up the phone in her clenched grip. "Please don't start Derek." Jade opened the message on her phone and began to read the vicious words that had been written to her from Derek. "I know you're not alone slut. I know you have a boyfriend and when I find out who, I'm going to kill both of you. You're nothing but a dirty little slut. You had no right to break up the family like you did. I will hate you forever." Jade dropped her head down from the sunshine that shone down upon her and warmed her skin. "Oh Derek. Why are you doing this?" Jade said quietly to herself as she placed the phone down on the outdoor settee refusing to be cohered into answering the abusive messages. Jade raised to her feet and walked back into the house through the large sliding doors that led to the kitchen's entrance and fetched the chilled bottle of wine from out of the refrigerator and poured herself a small glass of the chilled liquor before returning to sit on the settee under the sun's rays.

She looked down at the face of her mobile phone that had sat idle in her absence.

"How long are you going to do this Derek?" Jade said to herself as she looked out at the open space of the land that was situated in front of her. As Jade placed the chilled glass of wine to her lips and took the first sip a succession of flashes beamed across the screen of her phone as it sat on the outdoor bench.

"Oh god no," Jade sighed as she picked up the phone and opened the messages.

"You fucken little slut. I should come over there right now and kick your fucken heads in. You're an embarrassment to this family. I'm going to haunt you until the day I die you fucken worthless little bitch." Jade's eyes dropped into a deep furrow as she gulped at the vicious words that Derek had written over the four messages that she had received. "I'm not buying into this Derek. I'm not," Jade said sternly as she raised to her feet and began to pace the small patch of concrete path that separated the two patches of lawn situated outside of the shade of the back veranda. Over the next two hours Derek continued with his onslaught of threatening and abusive messages until finally Jade fled the house in a scurry of tremulous trepidation and headed for the safety of the confines of the sports tavern which she knew Sherri would be working the night shift. Jade hastily walked towards the front bar and sat on the tall stool waiting to sight Sherri as she sipped at a glass of wine that sat in her shaking hands. "Oh god Sherri. Where are you?" Jade whispered quietly to herself as her eyes glazed around the perimeters of the tavern.

As Jade was about to order another glass of wine, Sherri entered the bar from around the outside of the small hallway that led to the kitchen area of the tavern and sighted Jade who sat alone on the bar stool.

"Hey Jade, what are you doing in here? You never come in here," Sherri said with a greeting smile as she approached the end of the bar where Jade had placed herself. "Are you alright?" Sherri asked noticing the worrisome look that had spread itself and wedged into the furrows of Jade's frown.

"No, no I'm not," Jade replied trying not to let the emotions that had buried themselves tightly into her throat spill from her mouth while surrounded by people that lined the long bar of the tavern.

"What's wrong?" Sherri asked leaning forward in her concern. "I don't know what to do Sherri. Derek keeps sending me all these vicious text messages again and again," Jade began to explain in a quiet tone trying to keep the conversation between them. He threatened to come over to the house tonight and kill me," Jade continued as she placed her forehead into the palm of her hand.

"He's just angry. He'll get over it."

"No, No he won't Sherri," Jade quipped up as her worried eyes glazed directly into Sherri's, "He won't stop." Sherri stepped back as she viewed Jade's tremulous disposition and stood silently in the moment before stepping forward and lowering her head down to the level of Jade's once more.

"Do you really think he's capable of doing something?" Sherri asked quietly.

"Yes, yes he would," Jade spoke up raising her serious glare once again to meet Sherri's. "You don't know him like I know him Sherri. He would and I have no doubt that he will." Jade sat motionless in the stool staring at Sherri as her tears of anguish began to fill her eyes. "I don't know what to do, where to go," Jade began to sob as the tears began to fall down her pale cheeks. "Oh god," Jade said quietly as she secretly tried to shield her tears from the other patrons that surrounded her in the tavern.

"I'm going to go home okay," Jade said looking at Sherri. "I'm just going to go home."

"Okay," Sherri replied looking at Jade with deep concern. "Ring me if you need me alright."

"I will. Thanks Sherri," Jade replied before raising to her feet off the stool and heading out of the tavern's front doors and out into the car park. That night Jade lay awake alone tossing and turning on the queen size mattress situated on the floor of her bedroom as the constant tessellation of the flash of messages filled her phone sitting on the bedside cupboard and sent chills of trepidation throughout her senses and mind.

The following month after discussing her proposal with Derek, Jade contacted one of the local real estate agents of Suisania Bay and placed their large family home on the sales market. Jade had discussed with Derek the possibility of acquiring the home as her own through the delegation of selling the attached allotment of land for Derek's acquisition which would allow for the lowering of the price of the house and amount of the home loan of which Jade would have to apply for. But Derek refused to contemplate Jade's proposal of separating the two allotments of land titles and accused Jade of hatching a contingency plan to rid herself of his presence and possess the greater portion of the land ownership for herself.

Although Jade had felt the deep disappointment of Derek's refusal to allow her access to the proposal of acquiring the family home as her and the children's base, she proceeded with the renovations that were necessary to achieve the asking price of the home's sale and prepared herself for the change in location. Within a few weeks of the house being placed on the market, Jade received contact from the real estate agent informing her that an offer of $250,000 had been made and that the settlement could be met on the offer within the month. Ecstatic at the brilliant news she had received Jade instantly contacted Derek with the proposal of the two hundred and fifty, thousand dollars for his consideration. But Derek still refused to budge on any offerings of the house's sale price that had been placed at $280,000 and refuted the offer as an unsuitable amount.

Over the course of the next month Jade noticed an increasingly alarming difference in her children's demeanour when it was her turn for visitation with them. The smiles of adjustment that once adorned their soft cheeks no longer spread across their face and now held a contemptuous frown of disappointment and confusion. Jade held the ever increasing concern of her children's wellbeing as Derek embarked on a personal rampage of her dishonour and shame that in the vindictive confines of his mind she had brought upon him and the family. Jade stood by helpless as she watched the deterioration of Nick's inconsolable grief twist and turn into a fiery force of rage against her as his father pulled him further and further into the battle that stood between Jade and himself. Upon each visit of the children's return to Jade the week's quality of special moments spent together had descended into a tessellation of tempestuous bickering amongst the children which spilt out in a force of indignation towards Jade and her decision to leave their father. Jade struggled to keep her focus as the pull of her children's unbalancing tore her from her studies and research and into the depths of inconsolable anger and grief. She felt helpless as she tried constantly to console Nick who had embarked on a contemptuous rampage throughout the family home, lashing out at everyone who came close and twisted into a concernment of combative conflagration towards the household, smashing windows and belongings that stood within his path of destruction.

With each passing week Jade felt the extreme anguish of her concerns for her children and dealing with Derek's perpetualism of harassment which had sent her into a world of cautionary measures as she went about her daily routine. As Jade conducted her continual research and study programs throughout the business communities of Suisania Bay she had become aware that Derek had been following her and watching her and who she had within her circle of associations amongst the community.

As Jade stood in front of the local education centre speaking to one of the collegiate teachers, Don, after completing a day of studies she was astonished as she sighted Derek's car sitting in the large car park that ran parallel to the centre's building. "What is he doing?" Jade said quietly as she placed her hand to her mouth. "Excuse me," Don questioned as he stood next to Jade conversed in their discussion.

"Oh, Oh It's okay. I just saw someone I know, that's all. I'm sorry," Jade giggled in her nervous reply.

That night Jade noticed unusual sounds emitting from the back of the house towards the entrance to the laundry. As she crept along the long, dark, silent hallway towards the back of the house Jade was startled by the sudden loud sound of the door creaking against the force of someone trying to pry the door open. "Oh god," Jade whispered to herself as she jumped back against the wall of the kitchen entrance. "Oh god someone's trying to get in." Jade turned and ran back to the confines of her bedroom snatching up the large wooden beam that stood against her bedroom wall and slowly crept back down to listen at the kitchen's entrance. Jade stood motionless in silence as her heart pounded in tremulous palpitation and her ears strained against the silence of the dark night as she listened for the eerie sound of the unknown intruder at the back door's entrance. As the timber of the door shook and rattled under the weight of the strain being pushed from the other side echoing a loud thump through the silent walls of the house, Jade felt the tight swallow of her dry throat as she grasped for her composure from the terrifying vulnerability that sent chills through her senses of her unknown assailant.

With terrified courage Jade drew in a deep breath and walked swiftly to the laundry door of the emitting sound carrying the large wooden beam in the tight grip of her palm and fingers.

"Hey," Jade growled in a husky deep voice. "Get the fuck out of my yard now. I've got a gun in here pointing straight at you. Now fuck off."

Jade stood sternly against the wall of the laundry hallway as she listened to the sounds of the running footsteps that paved along the cement of the pathway that led out onto the gravel of the driveway at the side of the house. As the sound of the running steps rustled the gravel of the driveway and disappeared into the silence of the road Jade ran towards the front of the house and pulled back the long curtain that hung over the large glass window of the office and peered out into the darkness of the night that surrounded her home.

"Who was that?" Jade whispered as her eyes strained against the darkness. "What did you want?" As Jade let go of the curtain and lent back against the wall of the office, her mind raced in tremulous denouement as her heart pounded in perilous palpitations that sounded in her ears.

"Who would know that I'm here all by myself?" Jade questioned as her mind continued to race over all the possibilities of the unknown assailant.

Two weeks later as Jade was sitting in her office chair conversing in her erotic infatuation of her late night provocative fantasies with Max she heard an unusual sound coming from the direction of the back of the house. "What was that?" Jade said quietly to herself as her startled eyes swung around towards the direction of the strange sound. Jade quickly raised to her feet from out of the chair and hastily walked into her bedroom and grasped at the wooden beam that sat against the bedroom wall before slowly tiptoeing towards the back of the house and stopping at the entrance to the dining room area. "There it is again," Jade whispered as her heart began to pound in tremulous succession. Inch by inch Jade silently crept towards the laundry door as the strange creaking sound continued to emit waves of confused terror through her ears and senses. "Who's there?" Jade said in a loud stern voice before standing still once more in her silence. As the eerie sounds of the door standing firm against the force of the weight behind it escalated into a struggle of entry into the safe confines of the house where Jade stood alone in her own protection, she flew into a panic and ran to the phone that sat on the hallway stand and dialled the number of the local police. "Yes hello," Jade said softly as the police officer answered the phone. "I think someone is trying to break into my house. There's strange noises coming from the back door."

"Stay calm miss. We'll be there as soon as we can. There's an officer on the way okay," the police officer assured Jade.

Jade stood silenced in her fear against the hallway wall as she listened to the continuous cracks of the wooden door being forced upon from within the darkness of the outside perimeters.

"Oh god please hurry," Jade whispered to herself trembling as she tightly griped at the large wooden beam within her hands. As Jade started to take a step towards the laundry door, she heard a loud knock at the front door of the house which darted her eyes back towards the front of the house. "They're here. Thank god they're here," Jade said as she walked towards the front door and opened it to the police officers that stood calmly on the other side. "The noise is coming from the back door. Hurry," Jade announced to the officers as they entered the house through the front door and quickly walked down the long hallway to the laundry door. As the police officers paroled around the laundry door and the outside perimeters looking for signs of the unknown intrusion Jade stood assured and calm within their presence as she waited in the confines of the kitchen for the police to conduct their investigation.

"We can't see anyone miss," one of the police officers said as he walked back into the kitchen area towards Jade. "We can see marks on the door where it seems someone has been trying to jemmy it open. Were they there before?"

"No," Jade said as her eyes opened wide to the startling news. "No there weren't any marks on the door. It has only been freshly painted, ready for the sale of the house. My husband and I only separated a few months ago so I've been renovating the house so that it can be ready for the sale."

The two police officers looked at one another and then turned their questioning eyes back into the direction of Jade's waiting stance.

"Did you and your husband part on good terms?" one of the police officers asked carefully.

"Well, No," Jade answered, dropping her eyes to the kitchen floor. "No we didn't. It wasn't exactly a good marriage leading up to the separation and my ex-husband took it pretty hard. I left him," Jade explained, lifting her eyes back up into the worrying look of the police officer's glare.

"Do you think that maybe your ex-husband would do things to try and scare you?" the police officer asked once again. Jade held her lips in a tight slant of obscurity as her mind pondered the thoughts of the officer's direction of questioning.

"Yes, yes he would," Jade finally answered holding her hand to her forehead in dismayed disbelief.

"Okay. We are going to do a search of the neighbourhood and just keep an eye on things within this area for a few days just to make sure that everything is safe and secure okay," the officer reassured. "If we do find anything out of the ordinary we may contact you for some more information regarding tonight's call out to your home okay."

"Yes, that's fine," Jade answered placing the tip of her finger into her mouth as her mind continued to ponder the rationalization of the officer's comments.

Within the next hour, Jade heard a knock at the front door once again. As she raised to her feet Jade pulled back the curtain of the side window and sighted the two police officers standing on the front porch at the entrance to the front door. "Hmm," Jade hummed inquisitively as she walked towards the front door and opened it to the officers. "Yes," she answered as she opened the door.

"Hello again miss," the police officer answered. "We have just conducted a thorough search of the neighbourhood and sighted a blue Commodore parked on the opposite side of the road that leads to the direction of your house. Would you know who may be the owner of this car?" Jade stood for a moment in pondered thought as the realization of the officer's words washed over her in a retraction of her known truth. "No. No I don't," Jade answered shying away from the officer's questioning stare.

"So you have no idea who may own that vehicle?" the officer asked once again, looking at Jade's stance of desideratum.

"No," Jade answered once more holding her stare of intransigent acknowledgement. After speaking to the officers about her concerns that she held for her own safety while carefully concealing the truth that she feared in her own mind of Derek's involvement and infliction of his own controlling cruelty upon her, Jade returned to the confines of her office in a state of composed definition.

At the end of the week, Jade's moment of confrontational suasion of the subtle exchange of her awareness of Derek's actions drew near as she waited for the appointed time of the exchange of the children's visitation with their father. As Jade stood explaining to Derek of the events of the police officers call out to her home while in the absence of the children, that week she felt a satisfied glow rush through the depth of her impertinent disposition as she watched the acquiescent of conduciveness wash over Derek's face in a veil of tribulation and compunction.

Over the next month Jade laboured long, hard hours as she continued with her meticulous course of study and research into the development of her business plan whilst remaining under the pressurised grip of Derek's vengeful harassment and standover tactics.

On returning to the local education centre after the peaceful rest of the weekend Jade was confronted by the centre's manager and teaching collegiate with a concern of their safety and wellbeing after Don was confronted by Derek's jealousy of Jade's association with the members of the centre. Jade stood lost for words in her apology as she explained to the manager and Don of the perplexity of the situation that had been caused through her decision to separate from her husband. Although the manager and Don accepted Jade's apology and explanation as sincere they had advised Jade that in the case of their own protection and that of the other members of the class that accompanied her during the training course due to the nature of the threatening act of violence that Derek had expressed, Jade's presence within the learning centre would have to be expelled if Derek was to impend another threat towards any of the centre's members or staff.

That week as Jade exchanged the children's visitation with Derek she drew in a deep breath of courage as she stepped towards the confrontational capitulation of his continued aggressive behaviour that had now outstretched into the confines of her professional world. Although Derek had reacted negatively and had showed a high level of contempt towards Jade and the strict set of guidelines and the scolding of his behaviour towards the professional members of her associations he had surrendered to the rationalisation of the situation and had been in appliance to Jade's reformation of his behaviour towards the members of her business associations.

That weekend as Jade lay awake in her bed on the Saturday morning listening for the stirrings of the wakefulness of her children, she pondered over the many tribulations of the day's events that had to be shared in the foreboding presence of her ex-husband. Although she knew that the day held a special meaning of excitement for her children with the onset of the town's annual celebration of festivities and her daughter's inclusion of the festivals beauty pageant, Jade's enthusiasm in the stark face of Derek's presence wavered into a day of dread.

After moments of foreboding Jade finally pulled herself from under the protective covers of her blankets and walked over to her bedroom window and pulled back the curtains to stare out at the beautiful sunshine that had covered the land in its early morning glow.

Jade had made many preparations leading up to the day's events knowing how special it had been to her children and felt appreciative of Derek's agreeability to allow the children to spend the night with her and also the morning to prepare Monique for her special occasion before their visitation with their father that weekend. She had arranged with Derek for her and the children to meet him at the festivals beauty pageant staging area at twelve o'clock which had allowed for a thirty minute interval before the time that Monique was due for her appearance on the stage. Although Jade had felt the apprehension of being in Derek's acrimonious presence she had felt a reassurance of her safety amongst the gathering of the festivals attending crowds.

Jade walked into her youngest children's bedroom and softly touched her sleeping daughter on the shoulder stirring her from her peaceful slumber. "Sweetie," Jade said in a quiet voice smiling as she watched Monique open her big beautiful eyes and smile up at her. "Today's the day. It's time to get up baby girl." Monique stretched her arms out from under the covers of her blankets and wrapped them around Jade's shoulders in a loving embrace of excitement before letting a little giggle escape from between her smiling lips and climbed out of her warm bed.

"I'm really excited Mum," Monique said in her exuberance. Jade's face lit up into an omniscient smile of her daughter's delight and excitement as she walked over to her daughter's closet and pulled out the new dress that she had purchased for her special occasion.

"I know you are sweetheart," Jade replied flashing a smile in Monique's direction before walking back to her daughter's side and handing her the coat hung dress. "Time to get all dressed up in your new dress and have some fun at the festival, hey sweetheart."

"Yes," Monique smiled and giggled as she reached for her dress from Jade's hands and laid it down neatly on top of her bed covers.

Jade giggled at her daughter's excitement and softly kissed the top of her head before walking over to Cody's bedside softly touching him on the shoulder to stir him from his slumber.

"Time to wake up sweetie," Jade said softly watching Cody slowly wake and open his eyes to look and greet her with a smile. "Hey Mum," Cody replied in his young, soft voice sleepily sitting up in his bed.

"Good morning sweetheart," Jade replied flashing a proud smile straight back at him and kissing the top of his head before wrapping her arms around him in a loving, motherly hug. "Up you get," Jade said as she rose back up from the bent position of their embrace. "We're going to the festival today, remember? Then you're going to dad's for the weekend," Jade reminded her young son. Cody smiled a sleepy confused smile as he climbed out from under the warmth of his blankets and walked over to his closet to gather his attire for the day. Jade knew that at Cody's young age of eight, he had felt the confusion of the complexity of the situation the separation had brought upon the family's un-united disposition, but adored his willingness to overcome the obstacles of the obscurity and to just go with the flow of each day and moment that they shared together.

As Monique and Cody started to bustle around in their bedroom gathering their things and getting ready for their big day of fun, Jade walked from the room closing their bedroom door behind her and walked across the long hallway to her sleeping son's bedroom.

"James, Nick. It's time to wake up boys," Jade said in a soft voice gently touching each one on the shoulder stirring them from their deep sleeps of peacefulness.

"Wakey Wakey," Jade said once more smiling as James and Nick slowly opened their sleepy eyes and mumbled a groan of being disturbed from their slumber. "Good morning sweetheart," Jade greeted her teenage sons with a warm smile as their eyes focused on the morning. "Hey Mum," James and Nick both replied rubbing their sleepy eyes and stretching their arms up from under their warm blankets.

"What time are we going to the festival?" Nick asked sleepily as his mouth stretched into a wakeful yawn.

"As soon as we are all ready sweetheart," Jade answered. "But don't take too long hey. We want to get there early, okay." Jade smiled at the two boys who started to slowly, sleepily climb out from under the warm covers of their beds as she walked back out into the long hallway closing their bedroom door behind her and headed for the kitchen where Monique and Cody had situated themselves at the dining room table finishing the breakfast they had prepared for themselves.

As Monique left the confines of the bathroom after showering, Jade followed her back into her bedroom to help her prepare for her introduction into the stage world of beauty pageants.

"Let's do your hair and get you ready for your big day, hey sweetheart," Jade said with a smile of jubilation as she watched her daughter's joviality beam through her smiles and giggles of excitement.

Jade loved her daughter's young innocent energy of girlie mellifluence as she embraced the world in an oblivious journey of adventures and laughter which stirred and delighted the soul of Jade's inner child of wonderment and happiness.

As Monique completed the final touches of the outfit that she had chosen for the special occasion she walked over to the chair that Jade had placed in front of the large mirror of her dressing table that sat situated against the pink and purple painted walls near the back end of the bedroom and sat down ready for Jade to style her hair and apply the makeup to complete the image of grandiose.

As Jade reached for the makeup kit that she had fetched from her bedroom Monique spoke up in requested excitement of the colours that she wished for Jade to apply for the occasion. "Oh that one and that one," Monique giggled in her excited request as she pointed to the bright colours of the makeup palate.

Jade giggled as she watched her daughter choose the adult colours of a night out under the bright lights of the dancing scene and subtly persuaded her daughter to allow her to apply the softer colours of a young innocent girl. As Jade applied the last stroke of the soft makeup to Monique's face she took a step backwards to view the masterful creation of the young beauty within the image of the large mirror. "Beautiful sweetheart. You look beautiful," Jade said proudly as a large smile spread across her face and twinkled in her eyes. Monique's face lit up with the same large smile as she rose to her feet and admired her own reflection of innocent perfection twirling round and round, swirling her knee length skirt into a rhythmic dance of swaying twirls. Jade giggled and smiled as she watched her daughter glowing and swirling in her own young-girl amusement and excitement before walking from the bedroom and preparing herself in her own attire for the celebration of the day.

Within the hour Jade had finished her own routine of dressing and preparing herself for their day out amongst the local community of the festivities and announced to the children that it was now time to leave for the large showgrounds where the town's festivities were being held.

"It's time to go kids," Jade called out to her children from the front doorway of the long hallway that led out onto the front porch of the large family home. "Let's go have some fun."

Within minutes they had arrived at the car park that ran adjacent to the school that was situated a short walking distance from the large showgrounds of the festivities activities. As Jade parked the car and started to gather their hand held luggage of the day she turned towards the back of the car to where James and Nick had seated themselves. "So what rides do you want to go on?" Jade asked James and Nick inquisitively.

"Everything," the children all announced in giggling unison. Jade smiled and laughed at the children's enthusiasm as she reached for her purse that sat on the floor of the passenger side of the car.

"Okay," Jade replied as she handed the money to James and Nick who sat patiently excited. "Everything it is then." James and Nick held out their hands and grasped the money before placing it securely into the front pockets of their jeans.

"Thanks Mum," they both replied with a large smile before executing their departure from the car. As Jade and the children arrived at the front gates of the large showgrounds James and Nick sighted their large group of friends that had stood waiting for them to arrive at the foot of the sideshow ally and had quickly announced their presence and eagerness to join in the fun of the festivities.

"I want you to come and watch your sister's first pageant okay boys," Jade requested as Nick and James started for their departure into the large crowd of show attendances.

"Yes, okay Mum," the boys called out in reply. "We'll meet you at the stage, okay."

"Okay," Jade replied smiling at their compliance. "At twelve o'clock alright. Okay kids we have a little bit of time left before we have to head over to the stage to meet your father," Jade said as she turned back towards Monique and Cody standing behind her waiting for her to finish her organising with James and Nick. "What would you like to do?"

"We want to go on the rides," Monique and Cody squealed in excited delight looking over at the long ally of illuminated rides spinning around on their well-oiled axles.

"Okay," Jade giggled and smiled in her reply. "But sweetie you can't get dirty or messy yet as you have to go up on stage for the beauty pageant so maybe we should just enjoy the simple sideshows first hey." Although Monique and Cody felt a slight disappointment at not being able to enjoy the thrills of the spinning rides straight away they both understood their mother's point of view and humbly agreed to Jade's suggestion and followed her towards the direction of the sideshow ally of games and show bags.

After an hour of walking to and fro enjoying the variety of different games and sideshows, Jade announced to Monique and Cody that it was time to join their father on the other side of the large showgrounds at the designated spot of the stage setup, and led them towards the succession of people that stood waiting at the stage for the beauty pageant to begin.

As Jade and the children walked to the other side of the large showgrounds that accommodated the enclosures of animal stalls and a variety of different displays, Jade noticed a familiar face standing within the crowd of displayed sideshows and proceeded to approach the display to pronounce a polite greeting of recognition.

"Hi Don," Jade said with a smile as she approached the well-known collegiate from her training course of computer studies at the local education centre.

"Oh, hi Jade," Don replied with a surprised friendly smile. "How are you?"

"I'm really good thanks," Jade replied smiling politely. "Well don't you look quite spiffy in your fireman uniform," Jade teased giggling. "I didn't know that the fire brigade put on a display at the festival."

Don replied with a slightly flattered embarrassed laugh as Jade smiled and teased his adorn of uniform in front of the other uniformed members of his regiment but proceeded to inform her that the local fire brigade had been adorning a display of the workings of the fire brigade for a number of years to which he had been a member of for quite some time as well as working at the education centre.

As Jade and Don stood together conversing in their conversation of the festivities and various subjects Jade could hear the low hum of their assumed flirtation of Jade's arrival to speak with Don between the other members of the brigade who stood in close proximity to the polite conversation.

Jade giggled to herself at the men's notions of a startled eye interest in Don and found herself within an undeniable blush of embarrassed, mistaken intent of her actions.

Although Jade had thought highly of Don and the kindness and understanding that he had portrayed in his friendliness towards her their relationship had remained on a strictly professional level of educated collaboration within the confines of the education centre.

Derek's tessellation of unfettered impugnation towards her had made it impossible for her to willingly associate with anybody or feel the freedom of her newfound lifestyle whilst under the watchful threatening eye of his repugnant obsession with her.

Even though Don had shown a fearless disposition in her company and whilst in the comradeship of his fellow colleagues of the fire brigade Jade felt an uneasiness of Derek's close presence of contemptuous contingency as she stood within the conversation continuously looking over her shoulder.

"Oh no," Jade muttered as she gulped the tense tightening that wrapped itself around her throat as she sighted Derek's transfixed glare from across the crowded showgrounds. "What's wrong?" Don asked concerned.

"I'm so sorry Don. I have to go," Jade replied in a worrying voice looking down at the ground. "Derek's watching us."

Don smiled a comforting smile as he replied in a reassuring voice, "It's going to be okay. Don't you worry about me. You just try and have a nice day okay."

Jade lifted her head up as a comforted small smile formed in the corner of her lips, "Thanks Don. You too. I'll see you in class on Monday okay."

Jade took a deep breath of her suppressed apprehension as she coddled her composure into a stance of perfunctory courage and walked over in the direction of Derek's waiting glare within the crowd that stood in front of the stage of the beauty pageant parade.

Although Jade felt the dread of having to subside into the shadows of Derek's company of indignation, she had wanted this day to be special for her daughter and the joy of her children's excitement of attending the festivities and had formed a willingness of importance within herself to show a civil order of etiquette whilst in Derek's presence.

As Jade and the children approached closer and closer to Derek's position of waiting, Monique burst into a run of welcoming delight as she ran to the cuddle of her father's welcoming arms calling out his name. "Dad, Dad, You're here," Monique said excited as she threw her arms around her father's shoulders and hugged him tightly.

As Jade steps approached closer with Cody following close behind her, she sighted James and Nick's inclusion into the family gathering coming from within the opposite direction of the showgrounds and allowed a small smile of friendly submission to form along the lines of her lips and the tiresome endless beret of battlement to slide from within her mind of obscurity.

"Hello," Jade said calmly greeting Derek and standing in her position of perfunctory unity next to him. "Hi," Derek replied in a friendly submissive voice as his feet moved closer to her side in a gesture of allegorical togetherness whilst in the company of the town's fellow crowds that had attended the local festivities.

Jade rose to the tips of her toes watching above the heads of the crowd's mass as she sighted the other children of the beauty contestants being led around to the back of the stage in preparation for the parade.

"We have to go now sweetie," Jade said smiling down at Monique's eagerness of excitement. "It's time to go backstage and get ready." Jade reached out for Monique's hand and led her smiling daughter through the crowd's mass to the back of the stage and introduced her to the beauty pageant's organisers who were patiently placing the children into an orderly fashion of entrance towards the stage .

Jade kissed Monique on the top of her head and wished her luck before leaving to walk back out through the crowd to stand back in her position of the family's unity of her daughter's support.

As Jade weaved and dodged her way through the crowds of people waiting to watch the parade of beautiful children begin their stage entrance, she noticed Derek glaring a threatening glare of jealousy in Don's direction. "Oh god no," Jade whispered to herself as she looked over towards Don. "Not today Derek. Please not today."

On returning to her position within the realms of the family unit Jade stood a distance of apprehensive complacency between herself and that of Derek's side as she subtly moved Cody into the space of separation that would divide her susceptibility to the ability of Derek's jealous attack of speculation.

But the distance of Jade's position did not stop the beret of insulting accusations from leaving Derek's mouth as he lent over the top of Cody's small frame and started to growl the hush of words into Jade's ear.

"I saw you talking to the fucking pretty boy over there. You're an embarrassment to this family. You sicken me."

Jade felt her cheeks flush with a display of embarrassment as her copulated coupling within Derek's presence sank into her disposition of a perpetual persecution of his unashamed insults.

"I was just saying hello," Jade whispered calmly in her reply as she lowered her face towards the ground. "He is my teacher and I was being polite."

But Derek ignored the response as an excuse of Jade's desires and through the jealousy of his contemptuous eyes could not see the rationalisation of the truth as he moved closer and closer into the space that Jade had constructed between them.

Jade squirmed in Derek's demise of insults and accusations as she fought the sudden rush to escape back into the safety of the confines of her home away from the continuous onslaught of the impertinence of the situation of which their separation had become.

Jade lifted her eyes into a steadfast silent glare towards Derek as her mind established the matter of the importance of the days outing before turning her face to smile at her children and return her attentions back towards the direction of the stage front. As the stage illuminated into a colourful array of display Jade felt her heart warm her face into a proud smile as she watched her daughter enter the stage presence and perform her twirling attraction of joyous performance for the festival's crowd of onlookers. Derek and Jade clapped in a surreptitious display of harmony in front of the local crowd of attendance as Monique finished her performance with a smile and a curtsy before exiting the large open stage.

After the final performance had finished and the winners had been announced, Jade silently slipped away to weave her way back through the crowds of people to collect Monique from behind the stage entrance.

"Mum, Mum," Monique giggled and smiled in joviality as Jade arrived at the back of the stage. "I came fourth. Look at what they gave me," Monique continued in her happy enthusiasm.

"You looked so beautiful up there sweetheart," Jade replied beaming a smile of her daughter's happiness that spread across her face from ear to ear.

On returning with Monique to the position of where she had been standing with Derek and the children, the children began a campaign of their wish for Jade to stay and enjoy the grandeur of festivities a while longer before she returned back home to leave them with their time with their father.

Jade succumbed to the enticement of her children's wishes even though she had felt the need to escape Derek's sullen derision of antipathy towards her and continued in her children's delights of the joyous occasion of the festivities while in the presence of a family unit.

After spending another hour of striding up and down the long galleries of rides and sideshows smiling at her children's excited waves as they spun and rode the parade of rides, Derek had started his hateful jealous campaign of insult towards her once more.

"So are you fucking that fuck wit over there? You're nothing but a little slut," Derek said quietly as he stood glaring viciously at Jade.

"I've told you so many times Derek," Jade replied glaring back at Derek in an impertinent stance of her own innocence and defence. "No, he's my teacher. That's it, I've had enough."

Jade stood silent in the assault of insulting false accusations as she waited for her children to ascend from the confines of the strapped chairs of the spinning rides to join her on the sidelines with the other waiting parents.

"I'm sorry kids but it's time for me to go," Jade announced with a scrupulous smile. "You guys have fun with your dad okay. I'll see you after the festival when you come and pick up your things."

Jade bent over and kissed and hugged them all goodbye and began her trail back towards the car park of which she had parked her car. As she left the glare of her insulting ex-husband, Jade waved at a passer-by of which she had known the woman associate for many years but felt the inflictions of the cautious restrictions of Derek's jealous assault rise up within her warning her to conceal the friendly gesture from Derek's knowledge.

As Jade made her way down the short distance of the town's streets that led towards the confines of the peace and safety of her home she decided to pull into the local bottle drive through to purchase a six pack of bourbon to enjoy over her weekend of no responsibilities and relaxation.

"Ahhh," Jade sighed a heavy sigh as she pulled the car to a stop at the end of the long, gravel driveway at her home releasing all the tension she had felt whilst in the presence of Derek at the town's festivities.

Jade sat still in the front seat of her car for a moment in silent solitude absorbing the freshness of the peace that surrounded and enveloped her in a mellifluous blanket of inner peace.

"Okay time to relax," Jade said, smiling to herself as she reached for the six pack of bourbon on the passenger seat of her car before walking through the large side gates and entering through the back door of the house. Jade placed the bourbon into the refrigerator and fetched the small stereo system from within her bedroom and placed it on the kitchen counter facing the rhythmic sounds of the speakers towards the open back window. A large smile adorned across Jade's face as she reached for a can of bourbon from within the refrigerator and situated herself upon one of the outdoor bench chairs that she had placed in the illuminated warm glow of the summer's golden sun.

Within moments of Jade consuming the first sip of the chilled liquor she heard the familiar tone of the message alert ring of her mobile phone. Jade rolled her eyes in an omniscient foreboding gesture as she reached for the phone that sat next to her on the wooden bench chair. "Here we go," Jade muttered as she opened the text message and began to read.

"I'm just letting you know that I will be returning a little earlier than arranged with the kids to retrieve their things for the weekend. Derek."

Jade glanced her eyes back in the opposite direction of the phone in a surprised expression of the message's contents. "Okay," Jade said quietly to herself with a smile, "Well that was a nice message for a change." Jade answered the message quickly in agreeability and returned to her leisurely salute of enjoying the loud musical tunes of the stereo while sipping the chilled can of bourbon under the rays of the summer's sun.

As the day wore on into the late hours of the afternoon Jade had started to feel the effects of the chilled alcohol that she had consumed over the course of the relaxing hours she had spent sitting outside absorbing the warmth of the sun and decided to venture back indoors to prepare some light refreshments of an array of a deli platter of finger foods. While she busied herself in the kitchen slicing and arranging the platter of food she heard a strange noise coming from outside the kitchen window.

"What's that?" Jade said to herself as she raised her eyes to glance out of the open window to the back yard. Jade's eyes and mouth widened simultaneously into a startled expression of tremulous astonishment as she sighted the ring of her cats and dog that stood in a stance of intimidation around the tempestuous vulnerability of a large poisonous brown snake that was striking out this way and that as it followed the intrusion of its attackers.

"Oh my god," Jade said as she placed her hand to the opening of her startled expression before quickly rushing out through the back door of the house and over towards the circle of animals that surrounded the vicious agitated striking snake.

"No," Jade yelled frantically at the cats and dog trying to disperse the dangerous commotion. "Shoo! Leave it alone."

But the animals remained in their stance of a circled attack of the large brown snake which had now started to slither into the striking gap that it had formed between the circle of animals and had started to head towards the opened back door of the house.

"Oh god no. What do I do?" Jade said loudly as her frantic mind searched for the solution to stop the snake from entering into the back door of the house.

Jade hastily ran to the entrance of the shed door and grabbed the handle of the flat edged shovel that stood leaning against the iron of the shed walls and ran back towards the position of the slithering agitated snake that was still being pursued by the hunt of the circle of cats.

"Psss… Move. Get out of here," Jade yelled and hissed frantically at the cats as she positioned herself between the striking snake and that of the open back door.

As the cats took a slight scatter from the stance of Jade's oppugnation of dispersion, she felt the tight wrenching of the formidable omniscient within her stomach of what she must do.

"Oh god oh god oh god," Jade said loudly as she raised the shovel above her shoulder and slammed it down hard towards the direction of the snakes back. As the shovel landed upon the ground missing the snake it shook the handle from out of her tight grip and fell the shovel to the ground in a splayed out dishevelment next to the agitated large snake.

"Oh no," Jade cried out as she frantically bent over to retrieve the shovel from of the ground and raise it above her shoulder once more. "Oh please. I'm so sorry," Jade cried out as she slammed the shovel down hard once more striking the snake in the middle of its back and slicing half way through the long slithers of the wiggling agitated snake. The large vicious snake raised up onto its length striking out towards Jade in a vicious attack of its brutal assault as it began to slash around from side to side uncontrollably. Without haste Jade raised the shovel for the third time and slammed it down hard onto the large snakes head ending its life and pain of the assault in one swift blow.

"Ohhh, god," Jade said as she felt the rush of the unavoidable desecration wash over her in a torment of wrenching foreboding as she stood over the remains of the lifeless body of the large, venomous snake.

"I had no choice," Jade whispered softly to herself shaking her head from side to side in disbelief of the situation she had just been forced to face.

Jade placed the shovel against the wall of the back veranda and walked back over to the shed retrieving a plastic bucket before walking back to the position of the dead snake and placing its lifeless body into the coffin confines of the bucket.

As Jade sat back down on the wooden outdoor bench still wracked in the shock and still shaken from the terrible dangerous incident that had forced her to take the life of a living creature, within minutes she heard a beret of chatter and laughter echoing down the length of her driveway and enter through the gate of the backyard.

"Hey Mum," the children all called out in unison as they rushed towards her in their excited delight of having attended the local town festivities.

"Hey Jade," Derek greeted as he strolled in calmly behind the children.

"Hey Derek," Jade replied politely before returning her attentions back in the direction of her excited children.

As the children continued in their garrulousness of excitement and joviality of their delightful day that they had spent at the town's festivities, Jade's mind wandered back to the fearful situation of the dangerous plight she had been subjected to within minutes of their arrival back home.

"Oh wow," Jade whispered under her breath shaking her head. "That could have been so much worse."

"What's wrong Mum?" James asked with concern watching his mother's disposition change.

Jade raised her head from the direction of the ground and started to explain to Derek and the children of the unbelievable story of what she had just witnessed and the situation of having to be forced into a fearful foreboding decision of having to take the life of the large venomous snake as it slithered dangerously towards the confines of the household.

"No way," James and Nick both replied in disbelief as the children's faces dropped into an expression of astonishment.

Jade stood up from off her position of the wooden bench chair and led them over to the shed that held the bucket where she had laid the snakes lifeless carcass to rest.

"Whoa Mum," James and Nick both said as they stood viewing the lifeless remains of the large brown snake. "I can't believe you had to do that," James continued looking up at Jade with widened eyes.

"Yes I know. I can't believe it myself," Jade replied looking down at her children gathered around the contents of the bucket. "But I didn't like having to do that. Not at all," Jade continued to explain, "It still is a living creature but the animals were in danger and it was heading for the open door of the house and I knew that you guys would be home at any minute. It's a dangerous snake and if it had bitten one of us, we could have been in real danger."

James and Nick looked up at their mother in disbelieving awe of their mother's bravery as Monique and Cody screwed up their tiny noses in disgust of the bloody, lifeless carcass before running back into the confines of the family home.

Derek stood shocked at what he had just heard and the sighting of the lifeless snake laying within the bucket as his eyes glanced at Jade filled with a precarious submission of recognition of her courage and independent bravery.

Within moments of having arrived the children had packed their suitcases full of their belongings and had hugged and kissed Jade goodbye for the weekend before leaving to spend the weekend with their father.

"Bye kids," Jade called out waving as she stood on the footpath that ran parallel to the road out the front of the house before turning around and returning to the inside dwellings of the family home.

"What an afternoon," Jade said smiling, still locked in her disbelief of the events that had unfolded before her during the afternoon. "What a day."

That afternoon, after finally getting to finish eating the platter of food that she had begun to prepare for herself, Jade sat down on the stool at the kitchen bench in her own cogitative realm of thoughts.

"Hmm," Jade hummed as the thoughts of the festival ran this way and that way through her mind.

"Why not," she said as she packed away the remains of the platter into the refrigerator and headed down the long hallway to her bedroom to gather her attire for the celebrations.

Although Jade felt an indifference to the normality of the local town's people's way of thinking and personal tastes of their own behaviour and activities that they pursued, she had not been one to allow the displeasures of other people's opinions to subdue the spontaneousness of her nature which spurred her along different paths of controversy and excitement.

After showering and dressing into the pretty attire of the summery dress that she had saved for the special occasion, Jade gathered her things and drove back to the festival to join the many local patrons who had gathered to attend the night time festivities of the rock bands and enjoyment of the night time's scheduled entertainment. As Jade entered through the gates of the showgrounds her eyes glanced over at the many different faces that scurried up and down the long galleries of sideshows and rides and within minutes had been sighted by a group of well-known acquaintances that waved and ushered her towards their position of standing.

"Hi Jade," Tina greeted as Jade approached the circle of friends standing awaiting their turn within the long queue of sideshow riders.

"Hey Tina, how are you?" Jade replied with a polite, friendly smile. As Tina and Jade immersed themselves into a friendly conversation of a variety of subjects, Jade told her story of the dangerous liaison that she had encountered earlier that afternoon with the large poisonous brown snake.

"You're kidding," Tina replied placing her hand to her open mouth in a fearful gesture of astonishment. "I would not have known what to do if that was me."

Jade smiled as she nervously tried to change the subject quickly as an awkwardness of her own compunction began to wash over her and stutter her words.

"Believe me it wasn't something I'd ever thought I'd have to do. Or would like to have to do again. Anyway," Jade continued in her stammered speech of small talk. "Are you guys staying for the bands tonight?"

"No," Tina replied. "We've been here for most of the day now and honestly I'm ready to go home. How about you?"

"I'm not sure yet," Jade replied politely smiling. "The kids are with their father this weekend and I haven't really decided on what I might do."

After continuing with the polite small talk for a moment longer Jade said her goodbyes to Tina and her group of friends and continued venturing deeper into the showground's galleries of amusements.

As Jade moved amongst the mass of the crowd she was startled by a familiar voice calling her name from within the queue near one of the popular side show rides. She turned her head into the direction of the voice and suddenly felt the impetuous rush of avoidance as the face of the voice came into view.

Although she had not had a long-time association with Lilly and Jenna who stood calling out her name and ushering her over towards their direction she had heard the rumours of their associations with the local bikie club and had heard the many stories of their shameless provocativeness and recreational partaking in the drug scene which did not strike a favourable chord in Jade's way of thinking.

"Hey Jade," Lilly and Jenna greeted as Jade approached them with a polite wary smile.

"Hey," Jade replied as her mind quickly leapt into an acquisition of excuses to excuse herself from the displeasure of conversing with this company.

"What are you up to tonight?" Lilly asked with a smile. "Are you staying for the bands?"

"No," Jade replied politely. "I've just come here to collect my kids and then I have plans with friends tonight for dinner." Although Jade was an honest person and knew that she had just told a little white lie in order to relieve herself of the situation, she felt no remorse in her adversity to renounce the truth and continued into a short speech of her dispersion before excusing herself and walking further into the crowd.

As Jade approached one of the rides that had caught her interest and stood next to the queue of fellow riders watching while she made her decision of her inclusion upon the joy of the thrills, she was approached by one of the ride's operators who began to strike up a conversation of flirtation expressing his interest in her.

"Hello," the younger man greeted, pronouncing a unambivalent smile upon his approach. "Are you going to have a ride?" Jade smiled nervously back and dropped her head slightly, shied by the younger man's interest in her.

"Hi," Jade replied lifting her head back up into a composure of confidence. "Yes. I was thinking about it."

"Would you like a free ride?" the operator offered flashing a cheeky smile of flirtation. Jade felt the slight flush of the blush that filled the tops of her cheeks as the flattery of the younger man's flirtation with her returned her to her once youthful roots of coyness and newness.

"Okay. Thank you," Jade replied smiling and giggling in her blush.

As Jade stood within the large queue of the other riders she glanced over at the operator who had remained within his contingency of his smiling flirtation and admiration of her womanly body as he eyed her moving within the queue until it was her time to enjoy the thrill of the free ride that he had offered her.

As the ride came to the end of its last spin Jade started to unbuckle the seat belt that had held her tightly and safely within the confines of the chair but was quickly joined by the younger operator who helped her in her climb out of the ride's chair and walked her back down the galley of the walk way that led out onto the side lines of the ride and without haste conversed back into his flirtation of conversation and smiles.

"So are you a local then?" the younger man asked as Jade remained standing within his attentions.

"Yes I am," Jade replied feeling inadequately lost in the new sudden attention.

"Are you staying for the night's entertainment?" he asked inquisitively. "I'd like to spend some time with you to get to know you if you were. I knock off about."

Although Jade was flattered and engrossed in the admiration of the younger man's attentions which had evoked the young spirit of her own womanly sensuality, she had also felt the maturity of her own moral virtue which had denied her any intentions of involvement within the realms of provocativeness especially with a man of a younger standing.

"I'm sorry," Jade interrupted as the younger man continued in his intentional speech of suggestion. "I probably won't be staying tonight but."

"Well," the man interrupted in his quest. "I will be working out of town at one of the other festival locations tomorrow if you'd like to catch up tomorrow instead?"

Jade dropped her head into an embarrassed giggle at the man's enthusiastic charms of enticement before raising her head back up in a polite flattered smile.

"Maybe," Jade replied smiling and giggling flirtatiously under her breath. "I have to go now but it was really nice to meet you. Thank you for the ride. Bye."

As Jade walked away from the man's flirtatious charms she turned her head to glance over her shoulder towards the younger man's direction who had remained in his stance of eyeing her as her frame disappeared into the crowd.

"Oh my," Jade whispered and smiled to herself placing her hand to her cheek as she continued with her exploration of the festival's activities. "Well, that was something different. Time for me to go home I think," Jade continued giggling as she made her way back through the density of the crowds and through the large gates of the showground that led back out to the car park.

That night as Jade sat down in the relaxing softness of the large sofa chair alone in her loungeroom, her mind wandered back through the volume of the day's unusual events which formed a rhetorical smile to spread across her face. "Oh my, what a day," Jade giggled to herself as she sipped the chilled can of bourbon that sat on the small table next to her. "What a day."

Over the next couple of months Jade continued with her meticulous schedule of continuous studies and assignments of research within the specific field of her developing business plan within the local region of Suisania Bay whilst maintaining a vigilant approach to establishing her new life as a single woman and mother while under the strict watchful eye of her ex-husband's jealous continuous harassment.

Although her life within the confines of the family home had remained a steady structure of routine and dedication to her children and her nights were spent enticed in the provocative exotics of her surreptitious affair with Max, her life beyond the boundaries of the family home had begun to gather a momentum of change as her confidence of independence began to grow and flourish.

No longer confined to the restrictions or demands of Derek's manipulation of control and demeanour of strict guidelines of her activities, which had once confined her to a life of apprehensive solitude within the boundaries of the family home, Jade's portfolio of activities and friends within the community drew an endless bounty of everyday liaisons, parties and luncheon dates as she associated with a wide variety of new people.

One afternoon whilst enjoying the company of her long-time friend Sherri as they dined amongst the many luncheon guests of the local restaurant, Jade listened as Sherri began to explain to her of the many adventurous liaisons she had encountered while venturing out into the night time dance scene of the night clubs.

"You should come out with me one night," Sherri suggested.

"Oh, I don't know," Jade replied with a shy smile at the thought. "I haven't been out amongst that scene since I was a teenager."

"Oh C'mon, You'll have a good time," Sherri answered, cheekily smiling. "You may even meet a man."

Jade dropped her head as the apprehensive giggles left her lips and swam within the realm of her cogitative mind. "Maybe," Jade replied giggling and smiling as Sherri continued in her chatter of enticement.

The following weekend Jade accepted Sherri's invitation of joining her at the night time dance venue on the Saturday night while in the freedom of her responsibilities of her children.

That evening as Jade spent hours in the fossick of her wardrobe for clothes and makeup in her preparation for her first evening out on the town in seventeen years, she felt the undeniable tribulation of the nervousness of aberration as her conscience concerning the path that she was about to embark upon swept upon her in a shadow of doubt.

As Jade nervously watched the clock hands reach the hour of her departure from the house with Sherri she reached for the dullness of her senses that stood idle within the chilled can of bourbon that had remained in the refrigerator from the previous weekend of her entertainment in Sherri's company.

"Oh god, I don't know if I can do this," Jade muttered to herself as she paced back and forth along the loungeroom perimeters. "What if." As the words left her mouth, Jade heard the familiar sound of Sherri's car pull in along the gravel of the driveway and come to a stop.

"Oh my," Jade whispered to herself as the nervousness formed a giggle to escape her lips. "Here we go." Jade quickly placed the half-drank can of bourbon down onto the small table top next to the lounge chair and walked to the front door opening it to greet Sherri who stood smiling in her enthusiasm.

"Hey Sherri, come on in," Jade greeted her friend smiling nervously.

"Hey Jade," Sherri replied as she entered through the opening of the front door and stepped into the well-lit loungeroom. "You look nice," Sherri continued as Jade closed the front door and joined her in the room. "So are you ready for our big night?"
Jade dropped her head as she smiled and giggled trying to hide the nerves that ran up and down through her stomach in a composure of self-desideratum.

"Oh Sherri, I'm so nervous. I don't know," Jade began in her reply but was quickly interrupted by Sherri's enticement of convincing reassurance.

"Oh Jade," Sherri giggled as she stood watching Jade quiver and stutter. "You'll be fine. We'll have a few drinks and get up and dance. It's good fun."

Jade lifted her head back up to meet the smiling glance of Sherri's eyes and nodded her head in agreement before walking back down the long hallway to lock the house for the night and follow Sherri to the car.

On their arrival at the dance venue, Jade followed Sherri closely through the large open entrance doors that led to the brightly coloured dancing lights of the dance floor and continued to follow her to the bar of the venue to purchase their first round of drinks. As they stood at the bar sipping the iced bourbon amongst the mass of party dwellers that formed a line along the long wooden bar Jade found herself in the midst of feeling out of place and uncomfortable within the rhetorical glow and exhilaration of the loud pounding music and younger revellers. She leant over in an inconspicuous slant towards Sherri who had melded into the atmosphere of jubilation with a comfortable ease and raised her voice above the music in an admittance of her concernment. "Sherri, I think I want to go home," Jade exclaimed as an ashamed furrow formed within her brow. "This is not my scene at all."

Sherri turned her head to look at Jade as she continued to wave and greet the other guests who passed them by in frequent succession. "Jade, It's just something new. Relax," Sherri replied with a giggle reaching her hand out and rubbing Jade on the top of the shoulder in a gesture of reassurance. "Here, have another drink and we'll go and have a dance. You'll be okay."

Sherri turned around to face the bartender and continued in her order of a potent shot of Sambuca liqueur and handed the small shot glass of the strong sweet liquid to Jade. "Cheers," Sherri said laughing and smiling as she tapped the small shot glass against Jade's and gulped the drink down in one hit.

Jade glanced nervously at Sherri as she returned the gesture and held the small glass up to her lips.

"Oh god," Jade muttered under her breath before tipping the sweet liquor into her mouth swallowing it in full. Jade let out a slight cough as the strong liquor hit the back of her throat in a potent torrent of intoxicating aspiration. Sherri let out a loud laugh as she reached for Jade's hand and pulled her towards the perimeters of the other revellers who had conformed in rhythmic grandiose across the plain of the dance floor.

As the rhythmic sensations of the loud music began to beat louder and louder within the depths of Jade's soul which swayed her hips into a rhapsody of melody, she began to feel the calmness of her formidable confidence which waivered into a mellifluent grandiose of expression.

Jade smiled and swayed as the music lifted her back into the realms of her youthful flamboyance of exhilaration and settled her nervousness into a comfortably within the new surroundings.

As Jade was about to leave the intoxicating rhythms of the dance floor and step into the direction of the long wooden bar she was approached by a tall, blonde, muscular younger man who stood flashing a vivacious inviting smile in her direction.

"Hi," the younger man said smiling upon his approach. "I think you're absolutely stunning and I would love to take you home tonight."

Jade stood wide eyed in a startled halt of her feet as the words of the younger man took her by surprise and rendered her speechless momentarily.

As the surprise of the sexual proposition slipped away and allowed Jade to reposition her composure into one of a knowledgeable confident woman she slowly stepped towards the younger man as she played sexy flirtations with her eyes.

"How old are you?" Jade asked flashing a sexy devilish smile.

"I'm twenty one," the younger man replied stepping closer into Jade's vicinity.

"Well," Jade replied touching the younger man on the muscles that bulged and stretched the fabrics of his T-shirt. "I'm thirty five and have four children, Mummy didn't give you permission to play with this just yet," Jade continued flashing a cheeky smile in the younger man's direction before walking away with a giggle under her breath. Jade continued in a confident linger towards the direction of the long wooden bar leaving the younger man standing in his own expression of speechless rejected shock momentarily before turning around and leaving the vicinity of the dance floor.

As the night wore on into the early hours of the morning, Jade had watched as the younger man made his attracted intentions towards her noticeable in a brazen display of smiles and watchful eyes as she swayed in rhythm amongst the other revellers around the crowded dance floor.

In a an unambivalent disregard for Jade's previous rejection of his sexual intentions the young man once again approached Jade as the lights of the establishment had illuminated the room at the end of the evening and began his quest of alluring Jade into his intentions of provocativeness once more.

"Would you like to come back to my place for a party?" the younger man asked, enticing Jade with a flash of his vivacious smile. Jade stood grinning at the younger man before softly announcing her rejections of the inconceivable notion. "No I'm sorry, I can't. I have to get home to my children."

As Jade turned and went to walk away the younger man called out the details of the address of which he resided and enthused with her to change her mind and join him for a night of getting to know one another in a persistent pursue of her attentions and affections.

Jade turned her head once more and smiled at the younger man and wished him goodnight before following Sherri out of the doors of the dance venue and out into the car park of which her car had been parked for the night. Jade climbed into the front seat of Sherri's car with a flattered smile that lit up her face and touched the neglected recognition of her being of a sensual woman, something that she had been craving for so long.

"Oh my," Jade said smiling over into Sherri's direction. "Mmm wasn't he gorgeous, if only ten years older," Jade continued with a cheeky devilish giggle. "That was lots of fun. Thanks for a great night Sherri. We'll have to do this again sometime hey."

Sherri looked at Jade with a disgruntled grin but remained silent in her answer as she started the car and drove towards the direction of Jade's house of which they departed company for the night.

Over the next couple of months Jade continued with her meticulous construction of her collected research amongst the specific field of her chosen industry and had collected enough information to start the complex development and writing of her business plan.

Her relationship with Max had grown into one of exotic provocativeness as their love for each other deepened and he pushed his enticement of his erotic desires for the pleasures of her flesh further and further. No longer satisfied with the tantalisation of her promiscuous erotic photographs and stories that she had attached on a nightly basis with her letters, he enticed her down a path of producing erotic pornographic video shots of her own self-stimulation with the visual effects of a variety of sex toys and sexual outfits. Although Jade had held an innocence of the erotic pleasures that Max beckoned for, she fell into the submission of his pleasurable enticements and found herself wrapped into a world of an unconscionable surrender of her virtue and wanting to please his desires of sexual pleasure.

As Jade's confidence and recognition of her own sensual sexuality within herself grew and with the introduction of the exuberance of the night life of the dance venue Jade had developed into a frequent staple amongst the night time revellers at the local nightclub.

Although her friendship with Sherri had remained within the realm of luncheon dates and coffee venues Sherri had refused to accompany Jade at the dance venue with a contingency of fabricated excuses and the consistency of their meetings and friendship had started to waver into a stagger of separation.

Although the construction of her business plan and education had remained a tenacity of focus in Jade's life, her estranged relationship with Derek and her older children had developed into a bitter embattlement of continuous harassment and contemptuous attacks which had driven Jade into a state of anxiety.

Desperate in her bid to escape and release the constant pressures of her embattled home life Jade slid from the aberrance of her virtue and surrendered to the enticing exuberance of the night time scene when not restrained in the responsibility of her children.

With each passing weekend of alcohol induced indulgence amongst the revellers of the dance venue, Jade had formed many new associations and friends within the party scene and had developed into a well-known face of confidence and friendly joviality as she danced and moved about the night time establishments.

One Saturday night while standing at the long wooden bar of the venue enjoying the rhythmic sensations of the loud music and party revellers, Jade was confidently approached by a well-groomed man adorning the attire of the local motorcycle gang who had a well-known reputation for their notorious behaviour.

"Hey sexy," the man said on his approach leaning across close to Jade to speak above the loud music.

"Hi," Jade replied with a confident naive smile.

"You are one gorgeous lady with the sexiest little hips I have ever seen," the man continued in his flattering flirtation of seduction.

"Thank you," Jade replied turning to face the man with a giggly smile before collecting her drink from the wooden bar and continuing in her pursuit of joining with the other dance floor revellers.

As the weeks passed Jade continuously noticed the mass of the motorcycle members that grouped around the perimeters of the dance floor eyeing and complimenting her open display of rhetorical rhythm amongst the floor of the dance scene but had remained in her stance of precarious distance and avoidance of the notorious group.

After encountering and rejecting many occasions of the group's invites to join them back at their local clubhouse to continue in the celebrations of exuberance after the nightclub's closure at the end of the night, Jade finally surrendered her resistance and apprehension to one of the men in the group and was led down the path of the clubhouse's dwelling.

As Jade sat in the car that was parked on the footpath in front of the motorcycle group's clubhouse with the member that had extended her the invitation of association, Jade watched nervously as the other members and associates massed in intoxicated comradely along the stretch of the open veranda.

"Ohhh," Jade stuttered nervously as she filled with the incorrigible foreboding of trepidation.

"I'm really not sure about this," Jade said quietly in her nervousness as she turned and looked at the member sitting next to her in the front seat of the car.

"Ah you'll be alright," the member replied with a flashy smile. "I'll look after you."

Jade turned her head back towards the direction of the loud intimidating mass of members that stood across the length of the small veranda and spread out onto the plain of the front yard of the clubhouse.

"No," Jade stuttered. "No, I can't, I think I should go home. Do you mind?"

The member sat glancing at Jade laughing at her apprehension of nervousness momentarily before reaching over his hand to touch her softly on the shoulder. "It's okay.

I'll take you home. Maybe another time hey," he replied slipping the key back into the car's ignition and steering it out onto the surface of the narrow road that led back into the township of Suisania bay.

"So where do you live?" he asked turning his attention back into Jade's direction.

"Um. You can just drop me off at the shopping mall," Jade replied in a disingenuous intention of the hiding of her true location of residence. "I live just around the corner from there."

"Okay, no worries," the member replied and proceeded to drive towards the location of the local shopping mall where Jade made her departure from the car and continued the short distance to her home on foot.

Over the next two weeks Jade continued to receive harassment and threatening text messages from Derek who had compounded the pressure of his demands into one of obtaining marijuana for his pleasure. Jade had refused profusely to his demands of obtaining the drug for him, a recreational habit which she had once shared with Derek during their sixteen years of marriage but had refrained from the usage with the dissolution of their marriage and had entered into a new path of transcendent self-discipline and of upholding a solid reputation of a higher standard within the community.

With each refusal of Derek's demands Jade paid the price of his continual abuse and that of the children's abusive behaviour as he cohered them into a combative force against her until she finally surrendered her refusal of his demands and found herself on the footstep of the one place she knew where she could obtain his pleasure of the recreational drug, the local motorcycle gang's clubhouse.

That afternoon Jade climbed into her car and drove down the narrow road that led to the notorious establishment of the clubhouse dwelling and pulled her car to a stop alongside the gravel laden footpath.

"Oh god," Jade whispered to herself as she felt the waves of her trepidation fluster deep inside of the pit of her stomach. "I don't want to do this. I don't want to do this," Jade continued to repeat to herself as she slowly slid the keys from the car's ignition and climbed out from the driver's seat of her car.

Step by step Jade nervously made her way along the gravel footpath and up the stairs of the small veranda to come to a stand at the front door of the motorcycle gang's clubhouse.

Jade looked at the front door as her eyes filled with the precarious apprehension of the unknown and slowly raised her trembling curled fist to knock on the door to alert the members of her arrival.

Within seconds of announcing her arrival, the door swung open to reveal a solidly built, bearded man dressed in jeans and a black vest.

"Hey girl," the member greeted Jade with a smile as she stared nervously into his direction.

"Hi," Jade replied quickly, trying to regain a composure of confidence and friendliness.

"I didn't think that I would see you here again after last time. I'm surprised you even remembered how to get here," the bearded man continued in his greeting, laughing at his own manner of teasing. "Come in." Jade let out a nervous little giggle as she proceeded to follow the bearded man into the dark-painted walls of the clubhouse adorned with the members memorabilia and direct her to a stool that was situated at the foot of a bar that was laden with coasters and cannabis paraphernalia.

As Jade positioned herself upon the stool and placed her handbag strap over the back rest of the stool, she was greeted by another solidly built bearded man whom she knew held a high standing of rank amongst the clubhouse members.

"Hello," the man greeted her with a smile before glancing over at the other member with an inquisitive bemused expression across his face. "This is a bit of a surprise, I'm Ryan," the bearded man continued, introducing himself.

"Hi. I'm Jade," Jade greeted back as a friendly smile spread across her face, shaking Ryan's hand.

"Would you like a drink?" Ryan asked as he stood behind the perimeter of the bar.

"Um. Yes please," Jade answered and proceeded to fetch her purse from her handbag that hung over the back rest of the stool.

"Nah. This one's on the house," Ryan continued as he reached for a chilled can of bourbon from the refrigerator and placed it on the bar in front of her.

"Thank you," Jade answered and proceeded into a friendly manner of relaxed conversation with the attending members.

As the conversation continued into a friendly diversion of an openness and banter Jade suddenly announced the agenda of her unannounced arrival of venturing into the domain of the notorious clubhouse.

"Um. So I was just wondering," Jade stuttered nervously as she began to ask the question that had been harrowing within the nervous confines of her mind. "Would you guys know where I could score a twenty five?"

Ryan looked over at the other members astonished as the words left Jade's mouth before returning his attentive stare back into her glare of attention.

"So young lady. You smoke pot then," Ryan replied breaking into a bewildered chuckle.

"Well," Jade started to reply in her honesty, slightly dipping her head to one side. "I have been known to but I haven't in quite some time. It's actually for a friend." A large smile spread across Ryan's face as he looked into Jade's honest stare.

"Well, yeah. I can help you with that," Ryan replied as he stepped out from behind the bar and proceeded to walk out of the back door of the clubhouse, returning in just moments with a small bag of cannabis.

"Here you go miss," Ryan said, still smiling as he placed the small bag full of the pot into Jade's open hand.

"Brilliant. Thank you very much," Jade replied smiling. "And here you go," placing the twenty five dollars into Ryan's hand.

After remaining in the relaxed engaging conversation with Ryan and the other members of the clubhouse for another hour Jade announced here departure and was led back out through the front door of the clubhouse.

"You're welcome to come back here any time Jade," Ryan called out as Jade walked out through the opening of the front door.

"Thanks. I might just take you up on that," Jade said turning around and waving goodbye.

As Jade climbed into her car and drove away from the motorcycle gang's clubhouse, a comfortable large smile settled across her face as she reminisced over the amusing conversations that had taken place whilst in the presence of the controversial company of the clubhouse members.

"Well I must admit, that was nothing like I had expected," Jade started to say to herself laughing. "That was a whole lot of fun."

That evening after delivering the small bag of the cannabis to her estranged ex-husband, Jade drove back towards the outskirts of town and returned to the welcoming relaxed atmosphere and company of the members of the clubhouse.

On her arrival at the bikie's clubhouse, she was greeted by Ryan at the sliding gates of the tall railed fence that had been constructed that day in order to impede the intrusion of passers-by and that of any unwanted visitors to the clubhouse.

"Hey girl. You came back," Ryan greeted with a smile as he slid the key into the locked gate and slid it open along the long steel rails.

"Hey Ryan," Jade answered confidently smiling back as she walked through the open gate and in through the front door of the clubhouse.

While Jade sat at the long wooden bar surrounded by the other members of the notorious clubhouse she felt an ease of comfort surround her as she listened quietly to the many tales and humorous stories shared and swapped amongst the men.

"Would you like one of these?" Ryan asked, as he stretched out his hand in Jade's direction in an invitation to join him in the partaking of inhaling the intoxicating bending of the pot stocked bong.

"Oh, no thanks," Jade answered in her objection with a slightly coy giggle. "I haven't smoked that stuff for months now. I actually quit when I separated from my husband and haven't looked back since. But thank you," Jade continued in her explanation.

After spending the next two hours immersed in the joyous company of the clubhouse members, Jade felt an exuberance of freedom flow through her and sweep her into an aberrance of her refusal to join in the rebellious nature of which she had abstained.

"Umm, I think I would like one of those now if the offer is still there," Jade said looking at Ryan and then nodding her head towards the bong that sat on the table before him.

Ryan looked at Jade in surprise before allowing a slight giggle to escape the corners of his mouth and proceeded to pack the small cone full of the lush green substance and handed the smoking apparatus over into Jade's willing hand. "Thanks Ryan," Jade said smiling, reaching for the lighter that sat on the long wooden bar of the clubhouse. "Well it's been a while. But here goes," she continued in her rebellious enthusiasm, lifting the small rim of the plasticised bong to her lips and inhaling the intoxicating smoke of the cannabis into her lungs.

"Whoa," Jade giggled as she felt the effects of the drug wind its way into the depths of her mind and release her into a realm of confabulation.

Ryan's face lit up into a flash of grandiose and laughter as he stood close in Jade's proximity eyeing the spontaneous smile and laughter that covered her face and left her mouth in an unfettered release of drug induced joy. "Oh now I remember what this stuff does," Jade continued in her induced giggle of garrulous fashion.

After many hours of improvident garrulous banter and laughter while accompanying the acquaintance of the clubhouse members, Jade decided that it was time to end her night of insurgent acquiescent and return to the rationalisation of her own realm of civilized virtue.

"Thank you for a brilliant night," Jade said as she walked back out through the large sliding gate of the clubhouse enclosure.

"Anytime Jade," Ryan replied with a smile. "We'll see you soon hey. Take care."

Jade climbed into the front seat of her car as her face still bore the grandiose of the unfettered humorous night and drove back into town returning to the confines of her home.

"What a brilliant night," Jade giggled, still feeling the intoxicating effects of the cannabis and alcohol that she had consumed over the course of the evening as she climbed under the warm covers of her bed and lay her head restfully upon her pillow. "Hmm," she hummed pulling the blankets snugly around her shoulders before closing her eyes and falling into a deep peaceful slumber.

Over the next few months Jade became a frequent visitor of the notorious bikie clubhouse and had soon formed a special alliance with Ryan who had fallen helplessly for her charismatic quick wit and unambivalent honesty, as he welcomed her into his open arms of friendship.

Although it had taken many months of hard-learnt disciplinary measures for Jade to learn the rules and procedures associated with her association within the clubhouse, she had earnt her respect and trust amongst the hard knock rebels and had become a familiar, welcomed addition amongst the members and their families.

Even though Jade found solace and unfettered freedom of a rebellious nature whilst in the company of the bikie gang members, she had tenaciously held onto her air of lady-like virtue and an etiquette of stylish dressing and had not been subdued into the temptations of being involved in any form of sexual promiscuity or going beyond her own boundaries of insurgent derogation.

Although Jade had become a regular sight amongst the gang of rebels whilst free from her responsibilities of her children and accompanied the members frequently at the night-time venues, she had remained steadfast in her refusal to surrender to the enticement of using a higher form of drug use other than that of cannabis and alcohol or to be involved in any other form of rebellious activities or impudent behaviour towards the local residents of Suisania bay.

As Jade's acquaintance with the bikie gang grew and she spent her weekends wrapped in the joviality of rebellious partying and release of the stressful nature of her everyday life, her weekdays with Derek and her children had escalated further into a torrent of incorrigible attacks and threats that drenched her with contemptuous trepidation.

With each passing moment spent in the hands of Derek and her children's cohesion of tempestuous desolation, Jade felt the undeniable unravelling of the strength and courage that had propelled her into the exploration of her own liberation and found herself spiralling into the depths of emotional declension. Although Jade suffered the intense immensity of Derek's unashamed persecution, she had remained vigilant and meticulous in her protection of her children's knowledge and involvement in the incessant embattlement between herself and their father.

As the vile attacks of Derek's desecration against Jade's virtue and disposition escalated, Jade remained steadfast in her surreptitious silence from the residents of Suisania Bay and that of her closest friends, until the night she lost the battle and the perilousness of her silence shattered into a disclosure of inconsolable truths.

Reality

As Ryan and Jade lay silently and still in the separate beds that were positioned on each side of the clubhouse bedroom, Jade felt the overwhelming tribulation of her suppressed emotions twist and turn inside of her, cornering her into a transition of her own helplessness and grief.

Jade opened her eyes staring up at the dark ceiling that hovered above her in a desperate battle to conceal the desolation that filled her eyes and threatened to fall down her cheeks into a prolific stream of inconsolable grief.

She could feel the tightness that wrapped itself around her throat and knotted within her stomach in an emotional spiral of perilousness which had finally rendered her powerless to contain her steadfast silence of surreptitiousness and surrendered her words into a helpless whisper of hopelessness and truth.

"He's going to take my children," Jade whispered into the silence of the room, as the tears that she had hidden so well under her cover of normality fell from her eyes and covered her cheeks in a torrential stream of heartbroken sorrow and helplessness.

"What?" Ryan answered softly in a question of intangible concernment.

"It's been going on for months Ryan," Jade blurted out in a chocking, sobbing admission. "Derek's been threatening me and abusing me ever since we separated nearly twelve months ago and now he's threatening to steal the kids and run away with them and that I'll never see them again. It's been absolutely horrendous Ryan. He even asked me to have sex with him for money. He's a terrible, terrible person and I don't know what to do anymore. Oh god, it's just hopeless," Jade sobbed uncontrollably covering her face with her hands and rolling over, burying her face deeply into the pillow. "He just won't stop."

As Jade lay drenched in the misery of her inconsolable grief of hopelessness she heard the rustle of Ryan's footsteps along the small piece of wooden flooring that separated the two beds and rendered her alone on the opposite side of the small bedroom.

"Come here," Ryan said softly, touching Jade gently on the shoulder. "Come here." Jade lifted her head from off of the tear stained pillow and looked into the concernment that filled Ryan's eyes. "Ohhh Ryan," Jade wept as she crawled out from under the warmth of her blankets and fell into the comforting wrap of her friend's arms. Ryan and Jade stood in the middle of the room in a desperate embrace of sympathetic empathy as the grief-stricken tears continued to stream down Jade's cheeks and fall to the wooden floor of the small bedroom.

"What do I do Ryan? What do I do?" Jade wept lifting her head from off Ryan's shoulder and looking desperately into his eyes searching for an answer.

"C'mon, It's too cold to stand out here," Ryan said softly leading Jade over to the other bed allowing her to climb into the safety and support of his comforting embrace and under the warmth of the blankets. "I had no idea Jade," Ryan said softly. "You never said a word."

"No one knows Ryan. I haven't told anybody," Jade whispered in her sobbing reply. "It's just got worse and worse as times gone on and now this. He's been threatening this for months. Turning the kids against me. Telling them I'm a bad mother and saying the most horrible things to me," Jade continued in her sobbing admission, "It got so bad one night that I placed Monique and Cody into the car at about one o'clock in the morning and drove them to my friend's house and told her to take them to Derek's. That he could have them. I just couldn't take it anymore. The incessant threats, abuse and accusations. I just couldn't take it."

Jade dropped her face into a tearful submission of her grief and pain as she continued in her explanation of her personal embattlement. "I went home and drank two bottles of wine and loaded up my car with my belongings before heading out onto the road towards Alterro."

Jade stopped momentarily in a pause of silent compunction as she swallowed hard through the tightness within her throat and wiped at the stream of tears that continued to pour from her grief-stricken eyes, before continuing with her admission of the desperation and recklessness that Derek's incessant abuse had driven her into.

"As I approached the bend leading into Point Winifield, I fell asleep and was awoken by a truck honking its horn loudly at me. When I opened my eyes I was on the opposite side of the road and heading straight for the truck. I could have died Ryan. I could have died," Jade wept loudly. "I stopped at Point Winifield for about half an hour before turning the car around and driving back to Sherri's to collect the kids and take them home. I was so desperate Ryan. I had no one to turn to. He just wouldn't stop."

Jade buried her face back into Ryan's shoulder in an inconsolable stream of tears as the perfunctory of the immense suppressed pain of her embattlement with Derek and her children released itself in a prolific heartbreak of emotional capitulation.

After moments of laying within the depths of Jade's sorrowful weeping and the cogitative silence of words, Ryan leant over to kiss Jade gently on the forehead and pulled her closer into the warm embrace of his comforting arms.

"You know," Ryan said quietly, finally breaking the silence. "You haven't met him yet. But I have a friend who I think you would get on really well with. He's a hard worker. He doesn't play games. He doesn't do drugs. He's like a brother to me and he would treat you like a queen."

Jade felt the pricking of her cogitative thoughts as she lay silently next to Ryan listening to his suggestion of his proposal of introducing her to a new romance with a man that had held his air of respect and high regard.

Although Jade had been separated from Derek for close to twelve months now, her thoughts had not ventured into the equation of involving herself in another relationship, as her life had become one that was filled with the traumatic conflagration of Derek's oppugnation and contemptible behaviour.

She had become aware of Derek's acrimonious objection towards her involvement with another man as he had made his threatening intentions be known in the face of her business associates and the collegiate of the local education centre, which had held Jade in a precautionary abstinence from her own happiness and from placing that burden into the depths of another man's life.

Jade listened carefully in pensive depth as Ryan continued in his description and praise of his friend's reputable manner of nature, enticing her into a suasion of aspiring possibilities.

"He'll be coming here for a visit soon," Ryan continued in his suggestion. "I could introduce you to him." Jade turned her head to look at Ryan with her tear-stained, bloodshot eyes as rolling questions and thoughts continued to collaborate and swirl within her mind.

"Do you think that he would like me?" Jade finally asked coyly, dropping her head to a slight slant and allowing a small smile to lift the corners of her mouth.

"Yeaah," Ryan replied quickly in his response. "Who wouldn't."

Jade giggled at the comment, amused by the complimentary nature of the statement before continuing with her exploration of inquisitive enumeration of the leading possibilities of forming a relationship with the man that Ryan had spoken so highly of.

"What about everything that is going on with Derek? And my children?" Jade questioned, in her concern.

A large smile formed across Ryan's face before replying with amused laughter that had sent a slight blush of her naivety rushing through Jade's cheeks.

"He won't mind. He's been out of a relationship for ten years. He'll fall for you in an instant," Ryan replied looking over at Jade and smiling. "And do you really think Derek is going to mess with one of the crew," he continued in his persuasion of acquiesce, raising his eyebrows in an arch of perceptible questioning and reassurance

"Hmm," Jade hummed as a smile formed across her face. "No. I don't think he will," Jade continued in her gratitude. "Thank you Ryan. Thank you for everything."

Jade leant forward and kissed Ryan on the cheek and gave him a hug before climbing out from under the covers of his bed and climbing back in to hers on the opposite side of the small bedroom.

"Goodnight Ryan," she said softly as she pulled the blankets up tightly around her shoulders and drifted off into a peaceful sleep.

On the Friday night while her children were still spending their time in the visitation arrangement which she and Derek had come to form with an agreeable civilised collaboration, Jade headed out onto the highway and made her way towards the small town of Copper Cove to spend the night in the company of her cousin who she had not visited in quite some time.

The next afternoon after spending a night of fun and laughter with her adored cousin, as Jade was travelling the highway on her way back home to the town of Suisania Bay she heard the ring tone of her phone permeate from the inside of the car's console compartment.

"Oh," Jade said to herself as she started to deviate the cars direction off the highway and towards the dirt path of the side of the road to answer the unknown caller.

"Hello," Jade answered, picking up the phone and placing it to her ear.

"Hello," the caller's voice replied. "What are you up to?"

"Oh, Hey Ryan," Jade replied in her recognition of the voice that sounded through the speaker of the phone. "I'm actually out on the highway heading back towards Suisania Bay at the moment. I went to Copper Cove last night to visit my cousin," Jade continued.

"How far away are you from here?" Ryan asked.

"About thirty minutes. Why? What's up?" Jade asked curiously.

"Well," Ryan continued in his reply. "When you get back, come straight to the clubhouse. I have someone here I would like you to meet."

"Ohhh really," Jade replied, allowing a slight omniscient giggle to escape from her mouth. "And who may that be hmm?" Jade teased in her flirtation of revealing the instinctive knowledge of Ryan's intentions.

"Oh, just somebody," Ryan teased back permeating a smile that sounded through the tone of his voice. "I'll see you soon," he continued in his persuasion before quickly disconnecting from the conversation and leaving Jade in silence on the other end of the disconnected phone call.

"Matchmaker," Jade said with a grinning giggle as she placed the phone back into its place within the compartment of the console and steering her car back onto the highway to continue in her drive back to her home town of Suisania Bay.

As Jade drove the last stretch of the thirty-minute drive along the highway that led into the small town of Suisania Bay, her mind drifted into the cogitative depths of her curiosity and anticipation of the blind introduction with her unknown acquaintance of whom Ryan had spoken so highly about in his recommendation of compatibility.

Although Jade had met many of the members, families and associates upon her frequent visits to the clubhouse, she had not heard the mention of his name or of the association of this mysterious man from amongst the conversion of the other clubhouse members or associates.

After completing the last stretch of the thirty-minute drive back into the town of Suisania Bay, Jade arrived back at her house and parked at the end of the long gravel driveway before entering the house to amend her dishevelment of the long drive she had just embarked upon, whilst still absorbed in her incessant inquisitiveness of the man that she knew she was about to be introduced to.

"Oh god. Well, here we go," Jade said with a giggle, stepping from the confines of her bedroom and making her way out of the house and towards her car.

Within minutes of leaving her house Jade had arrived at the location of the notorious clubhouse and parked her car along the short stretch of footpath that ran parallel to the entrance of the clubhouse gates.

Although Jade had entered the clubhouse many times without a fear of hesitation, today as she stood at the gates entrance in her wait to be allowed entry, she felt the unnerving, undeniable palpitations of her apprehension of the unperceived introduction to the mysterious man of which she held no previous knowledge of.

As Jade stood nervously within the disposition of her apprehension, within moments she sighted Ryan stepping through the front door of the establishment and walk towards the large sliding gates of the clubhouse which she was standing at.

"Hey," Ryan greeted her with a large smile that spread across his face, sliding the key into the locked padlock and sliding open the large steel gate. "How was your trip?"

"He's here isn't he?" Jade blurted out in an eagerness of the omniscient, ignoring the polite question of which she had been asked.

Ryan threw his head back slightly in a glorious laugh of Jade's eagerness and nervousness before finally answering in a disingenuous teasing manner. "Maybe. Maybe not. You'll see."

"Oh you. Tell me. Come on," Jade replied, giggling in her nervous questioning as she tried to retrieve the concealed information from her friend's tight lips of surreptitious conversance.

As Jade followed Ryan across the grass-laden courtyard of the front entrance to the clubhouse, consumed by the nervous twitch that ran through her stomach and through her fidgeting fingers she paused momentarily in her pace of followed steps as she tried desperately to reposition her disposition into one of confidence and elegance. Noticing the absence of footsteps that had been following behind him, Ryan turned around to face Jade in her position of pause smiling as he noticed the unusual nervousness that had thrown her off her usual balance of composure and poise.

"Hang on a minute," Jade said, smiling with a slight giggle.

"C'mon. You'll be alright," Ryan replied, smiling back and chuckling under his breath.

As Jade entered the clubhouse and positioned herself on one of the stools situated along the long, wooden bar, she was soon accompanied by one of the clubhouse prospects whom she had come to know quite well over the six month period of her frequent visitations and had formed a friendly companionship with.

"Hey trouble. What have you been up too?" the prospect teased, in his usual joking manner.

"I'm not trouble," Jade quickly replied in playful defence, displaying a cheeky grin that spread across her face.

Although Jade had formed a reputable reputation amongst the clubhouse members for her disciplined contingency to remain within the boundaries of her own integrity, she had at times been held accountable to the austerity of Ryan's teachings, as she learnt the rules of her association with the clubhouse, which had now become an ongoing amusement amongst the other members and prospects.

The members of the clubhouse had quickly accepted Jade into their collaboration of rebelliousness and had admired her street wise smarts and quick wit but had been amused by her troublesome hard learnt paths with Ryan, which had earnt her to acquire the clubhouse nickname, "Baby."

Jade had established a place of respect and trust amongst the men of the clubhouse and had been welcomed as one of their own, an attribute not shown to other women who entered the clubhouse.

Although she was held in high regard and treated with sisterly admiration, it did not equate Jade with the same privileges as a member or a prospect within the collaboration of the clubhouse and therefore held her to a high level of acuity of her behaviour while in the presence of the men.

Over time Jade had learnt to turn a deaf ear and a blind eye to the profanity of the men's behaviour and their profound stories of rebelliousness and recklessness, which at first had struck her as an unambivalent aberration from her usual properness of conduct, but had learnt to adapt within her newfound territory and had accepted it as a form of their anti-conventional lifestyle.

While Jade sat at the long, wooden bar amused in the engaging conversation of the men's tales of adventure while sipping slowly at the cold can of bourbon that had been placed on the bar before her she noticed Ryan walking back through the office door to re-enter the setting of the men at the bar.

"Well, what do you think?" Ryan said with a smile, pointing to a shorter, well-built man that stood across from Jade at the other side of the bar.

"Is that him?" Jade replied quietly, looking over at the stranger whom on first account had struck her as possessing an awkwardness amongst the other members of the clubhouse.

"Hey," Ryan called out, raising his voice above the chatter of the massed crowd of revellers and directing the stranger towards him with a flick of his head. "Come over here."

Without showing a sign of hesitation or resistance to Ryan's command of request, the unknown associate retrieved his can of cold liquor from the wooden bar and walked around the corner of the bar's dividing doorway, where he came to stand alongside Ryan, who had situated himself on one of the bars stools next to Jade.

"This is Jade," Ryan said, flashing a precative grin as he proceeded with the introductions. "Jade. This is Shane."

"Hi Shane," Jade greeted the stranger, smiling a friendly greeting.

"Hello," Shane replied nervously, dropping his head slightly in a coy presentation of shyness.

"I've heard a lot about you," Jade confidently teased, tilting her head slightly, flashing an inconspicuous smile in Ryan's direction, who sat glowing in his blush of romantic propensity.

As Jade began her inquisitive questioning of unambivalent conversancy with the stranger which she had been introduced to, her eyes secretly darted over the fidgety nervousness of Shane's disposition that had permeated into an admiring blush that had spread across his cheeks and illuminated a spark within his eyes. Although Jade's knowledge and sexual experience with men had remained limited having been committed in her long term marriage of sixteen years, her secret explorations of provocative erotica with her online lover had enlightened her womanly sexual prowess, and now basked in the undeniable knowledge of Shane's attraction to her.

For the next two hours, Shane and Jade conversed themselves into an enjoyable exploration of each other's personal privity of self-devolution, while cocooning themselves away from the garrulousness and intrusions of the other clubhouse members, only immersed in the attraction and intrigue of each other's voices and attention.

While conversed in their private discussion of each other's personal activities, Jade discovered that Shane held a position in the sector of mining which required him to travel long distances to remote areas for a set period of time, which had answered her question of intrigue and curiosity as to why she had not known of his existence amongst the collaboration of the clubhouse revellers.

That evening Jade left the clubhouse basking in the soft glow of the unexpected glorious afternoon that she had spent in the company of the man that was once a stranger, but now knew of him as Shane.

Although Jade had remained within the testimonial duty of her own morals of rejecting the many proposals of attraction and not allowing herself to be romantically involved with any of the rebellious natures that dwelled within the confines of the bikies clubhouse, she had noticed over the next week of her visitations that Shane had not adorned the conditional attire of the members and prospects, which Jade had assumed Shane to be of a neutral association amongst the members of the clubhouse.

That week Jade spent her days swept up in the excitement of her time spent at the clubhouse indulging in Shane's attentiveness and advances of the beginnings of forming a new romantic connection. Even though Shane and Jade drew from different forms of character and moral affirmation, Jade's exhibition of her extrovert open nature had swirled a level of excitement and openness within the reservations of Shane's hesitant and reserved nature of a quelled persona, and fuelled his allurement of pursuing a romantic pursuit towards her.

On the Friday afternoon as Ryan escorted Jade towards the large, steel, sliding gates of the clubhouse entrance, on her departure from visiting with Shane, he suddenly came to a pause in his step and turned around to face Jade with an omniscient smile that spread across his face.

"Whaat?" Jade replied giggling, facing the dubious smile.

"We're having a party back here tonight if you would like to come?" Ryan announced with the invitation. "It's Shane's birthday."

"Ohhh. Well, in that case, I'd love to come," Jade replied, smiling eloquently.

Ryan stood paused momentarily as he watched the undeniable glow of excitement that radiated from within the depths of Jade's enthusiasm, before slightly dropping his head into an omniscient grin of approval.

"Now when you come back tonight, dress as a girl," Ryan continued in his speech of suggestive suasion. "You know, a skirt. Shane likes a lady you know."

An illuminated smile flashed across Jade's face before escaping into a coy giggle that slipped from between her smiling lips.

"Yes sir," she cheekily joked in her reply, standing to attention.

"He likes you Jade," Ryan divulged, grinning at her cheekiness.

"Ohhh," Jade teased again before leaning forward to close the distance that stood between them. "I like him too." Jade stood paused in a girlie giggle of a squirming blush that spread across the top of her cheeks and hid her face under the shadow of the tilt of her head before quickly regaining her composure of a confident woman of eloquence and astuteness.

"Okay," Jade finally replied, recovering from her blushing admission. "I'll be back later on tonight around nine o'clock. I'll see you then okay."

"See you then," Ryan replied smiling and carefully slid the key into the gate lock before sliding it open to allow Jade to depart from within the confines of the clubhouse grounds and the position of their surreptitious conversation.

That night Jade fossicked through the many different alluring outfits that hung neatly pressed within the length of her wardrobe searching for the appropriate attire that would strike an impressive attraction to Shane's desires of the woman he sought.

After finally settling on a tightly cut knee length pencil skirt, matched with an eloquent silk top and high heels, Jade dropped James and Nick off at their friend's house for their arranged sleepovers and headed towards the outskirts of the small town and parked her car on the footpath that ran parallel to the notorious clubhouse.

"Okay. Here we go," Jade whispered to herself, looking at her reflection in the rear view mirror of her car before climbing out of the front door of her car and walking in the direction of the large steel gates of the clubhouse surrounds.

As Jade stood at the foot of the sliding gates awaiting entry into the confines of the clubhouse, she felt an impetuous rush of nervousness and agitation undermine her usual confident demeanour.

"Oh god," Jade whispered giggling, looking down at the ground. "Get it together girl."

Within moments of ringing the gate's horn to alert the members of her arrival Jade spotted a familiar face walking towards the gates to where she stood patiently waiting.

"Hello pretty lady," Eric greeted her with a complimenting, welcoming smile.

"Hey Eric. How are you?" Jade greeted back as she entered the gate and stood to await her escort into the clubhouse.

Upon her entry into the clubhouse, Jade noticed Ryan who stood profusely smiling in the pathway of the doorway that led into the associates of the club's un-permissible members' side of the long wooden bar.

"Hey Ryan," Jade greeted, flashing a cheeky grin. But Ryan stood silent, glowing in his permissible grin as he eyed the outfit that Jade had worn from top to bottom.

"What?" Jade questioned with a giggle. But still Ryan said nothing and remained in his silence of his approval of admiration.

"Ohhh," Jade said smiling, "I look like a girl." Jade giggled in amusement as she hung her handbag over the back of one of the bars stools and slid upon the tall padded chair.

As Jade turned to face the bar to order herself a can of the chilled bourbon that sat in the clubhouse bar's refrigerator and reach for her purse from within her handbag, she was greeted by one of the members that had placed a can of the chilled liquor on the bar in front of her.

"All paid for love," the member informed her with a rhetorical smile.

"Umm. Who?" Jade questioned, dropping her brows into a questionable frown of the unexpected sweet gesture of surprise. But the member remained in only his smile as he motioned his head towards the man that stood smiling shyly at her on the other side of the bar.

"Ahh," Jade sighed in acknowledgement as she raised her eyes to meet the admiring stare of Shane's smile. "Thank you," Jade whispered in a silent gesture of the words that formed upon her lips.

As Jade sat at the long wooden bar immersed in the garrulousness of the clubhouse revellers whilst sipping slowly at the alcoholic beverage of which had been bought for her, she felt a nudge of her shoulder from a shadow that stood behind her.

"Hey," Ryan said positioning himself on the bar stool beside her.

"Hey," Jade greeted back smiling precariously at the intentions that surrounded her. "Shane bought me this," she explained, questioning the gesture once more. But Ryan sat silent in his smile of amusement of the undisclosed knowledge that he was holding closed in his surreptitious comradeship while in Jade's absence.

Within moments of Ryan having positioned himself on the bar stool next to Jade, Jade watched as Shane slowly made his way through the mass of the crowd and around the long wooden bar to position himself on the empty stool that sat on the opposite side of Jade.

"Hey Shane. Happy birthday," Jade greeted, leaning over into the gap that sat between them and placed a gentle birthday kiss upon his cheek. "Thank you for the drink."

Shane smiled back dropping his head slightly in shyness as his admiring eyes lingered over the depth of Jade's alluring smile before finally regaining his composure and lifting his eyes to meet hers.

"So, can I ask? How old are you today?" Jade questioned carefully as not to cause a feeling of intrusion into a personal revelation.

"I'm thirty nine," Shane answered without hesitation.

"Ohhh. So you're not that much older than me," Jade replied with a flirtatious smile. "I'll be thirty six soon, next month. You'll have to come celebrate mine with me," Jade continued, bumping Shane playfully.

As the hours passed and the clubhouse began to fill with the joviality of the atmosphere of the gathered crowd, Jade began to relax into the rhythmic sensations of the loud music and celebrations that surrounded her and filled her with exhilaration. Although Jade had always been a woman who had paid her own way throughout her life, Shane had offered to spoil her with a night of freedom and splendour from the usual misgivings and expenditure of the men she had known before him. Jade had refused Shane's offer to begin with but had fallen to the persuasion of his sweet charms and accepted his offer gracefully, pushing aside the strong liberated womanly pride that had held her to a tenacious refusal of his gentlemanly qualities and succumbed to the free flow of the alcoholic beverages that were placed before her in succession.

While Shane and Jade sat at the bar emerged in their garrulous conversation whilst surrounded by the exuberance of the loud music and party revellers that gathered within the confines of the club house, Shane suddenly turned his head, as he noticed Ryan's gesture of distraction as he directed Shane towards the members meeting room that was situated at the back of the club house.

"I'll be back in a minute okay," Shane whispered quietly, turning his attentions back towards Jade's positioning on the bar stool next to him. "Don't go anywhere," he continued, smiling as he stood up off the bar stool and followed Ryan out of the bar area and into the members' room.

"I'll be here when you get back, I promise," Jade replied, flashing a precative smile of reassurance as she watched Shane walk away.

As Jade returned her attentions back towards the other members and associates that gathered around the length of the long wooden bar, she was met by an array of knowledgeable acquiescent smiles.

"What?" Jade giggled cheekily, dipping her slightly blushed cheeks down towards the floor.

Over the six month period of Jade having spent many hours fraternizing with the members and associates as they gathered within the walls of the clubhouse, swapping garrulous tales of adventures and life's excitements, Jade's relationships with the notorious rebellions had grown into a tight bond of friendship whom had lent an ear to her poignant woes of her personal attacks in the hands of Derek and her children's acrimonious behaviour towards her.

They were quick to notice the alluring enchantment that danced along Jade's lips and caused a smile to form across her face whilst in the presence of Shane's attentiveness, which brought them much joy to watch as the new relationship started to blossom before them.

Within moments of Shane excusing his presence while sitting at Jade's side and following Ryan into the members' room, he once again returned to sit on the bar stool next to her, that had remained empty in his absence awaiting his return.

"I have something for you," Shane announced quietly, turning to Jade and slipping a small, white circular pill into the palm of her hand.

A bemused frown formed upon Jade's brow as she eyed the little white pill in dubious naivety.

"What is this?" Jade whispered, leaning over closer towards Shane as to conceal her naive question.

"Haven't you done them before?" Shane replied, retuning the look of bemusement before revealing an explanation of what he had placed into her hand. "It's Ecstasy."

"Oh," Jade replied, dropping her head slightly to hide the naive blush that entered the tops of her cheeks. "No, I haven't. What do they do?" Jade continued to ask, feeling slightly embarrassed in her line of questioning.

"They just make you feel good," Shane replied, smiling and allowing a slight giggle to escape from his lips. "Don't worry. I'll look after you. You'll have a good time. Celebrate with me, it's my birthday," he continued in his explanation and suasion before quickly placing two of the little white pills into his own mouth and swallowing them without hesitation.

Although Jade had a history of partaking in the scene of party revellers and held a knowledgeable awareness of drugs on a theoretical sense, she had not succumbed to the temptation of going beyond her own set boundaries of remaining in the permissible use of cannabis, and was now unprepared in the face of the impetuous circumstances of Shane's suasion and temptation.

Jade sat motionless in her pensive thought as she stared at the little white pill that sat enticingly within the palm of her nervous hand, before finally swaying her eyes back into the direction of Shane's smile of persuasion.

"Ohhh. Okay," Jade whispered to herself, before nervously raising the pill to her mouth and placing the hallucinatory bitterness against her tongue and swallowing the pill through the apprehensive reflection of the nervousness that ran through the muscles of her throat.

Jade anxiously sipped at the continuous flow of the chilled alcohol that sat before her on the long wooden bar, surrounded by the protective correlation of Shane and Ryan's watchful eyes, as they awaited the intoxication of the ecstasy to flow through Jade's system and rush through the depths of her mind.

"Are you doing okay?" Shane asked, glancing his eyes towards the hands of the clock as they ticked towards the duration of the twenty minutes that had passed since the moment Jade had consumed the little white pill.

"Yes," Jade replied, smiling and touching Shane gently on the hand. "I'm doing fine."

As Jade continued to sit at the bar listening to the incessant chatter of the clubhouse revellers she suddenly felt an impetuous intoxicating influence rush through her mind and senses as the pills hallucinating effect permeated and melded into her system.

"Whoa. Oh my," Jade stated out loud, reaching her hand up towards her forehead and touching the illuminated tantalisation that danced in tingles across the contours of her face and perception.

"Oh wow," Jade giggled, dropping her glance towards the wooden floor beams of the clubhouse. Jade lifted her head and precariously eyed her surroundings as she heard the sound of the mellifluent laughter of the crowd and the melodious music that surrounded her suddenly raise in volume and momentum.

"Oh god," Jade whispered quietly into the direction of the floor as she awkwardly squirmed her body off the bar stool and slid onto Ryan's lap, who had remained in a steadfast stance of protection by her side.

"Please don't let me do anything silly," Jade said quietly, trying to steady her hallucinatory focus that danced and swayed in bright succession around the room through the glaze of her sight.

"You'll be alright, just go with it," Ryan said, reassuringly, emitting a laughter of amusement into the room, as he reached down under the bend of Jade's knees and lifted her from his lap, placing her securely onto Shane's lap who had remained firmly seated by her side.

Jade started to giggle in an uninhibited transition of her disposition as she placed her arm around Shane's shoulder and lifted the gaze of her eyes to meet the admiring acquiesce of the smile that formed rhetorically across his face. "Don't worry, I've got you. I'll look after you," Shane said reassuringly, smiling before reaching his hand down to the dishevelled length of her skirt and pulling it down into a respectable position just above her knees.

"Thank you," Jade whispered, looking at Shane and fluttering her long eye lashes admiringly as the unexpected gesture of Shane's chivalry touched a sweet chord within her attraction.

Although Jade tried to conceal and suppress the chemically induced grandiose that surged and danced throughout her senses, propelling her into a world of surreal transcendence, she was powerless to suppress the incessant flow of words that leapt from her mouth in unambivalent conversation.

In his experienced awareness of the induced intoxication of the effects of the ecstasy pill that had now surged through Jade's system, Shane laughed affectionately with amusement as he listened to the garrulousness of Jade's exuberance and unfettered abound of energy.

"Time to go," Ryan announced out into the room to the other members and revellers who consorted around the confines of the clubhouse. "Let's do the rounds."

"Yes," Jade said, enthusiastically leaping off the bar stool and collecting her handbag from the chair's back rest.

"Ohh," she giggled as her feet reached the floor in an emulated stumble of balance and loss of coordination that had been affected by the grandiose of the hallucinatory drug.

"Come here you," Shane laughed, reaching his hand out to steady her offset balance and guide her towards the door that led out to the waiting cars.

"Are you alright?" he asked once more, flashing her an omniscient smile and opening the car door for Jade to climb into the back seat.

"Yes. Don't worry," Jade continued to giggle as Shane slid into the back seat next to her, grasping her hand in a tight embrace of entwined affection.

Jade had become well-accustomed to the familiar routine of the clubhouse's Friday night gatherings amongst the local town's nightclub venues, which had formed into a regular tantalising staple of fun, dancing and excitement during her absence from the responsibilities of her children.

Although the cars were filled with the occupants' indulgence of alcohol and drug fuelled intoxication, the assigned drivers who were derived of new additions of hangabouts or prospects from the clubhouse, had been conditioned by the compulsion of their clubhouse responsibilities to remain in a state of soberness, as to prove their worthiness to Ryan and devotion to their duties and the club.

Within minutes of departing from the enclosure of the situated clubhouse the members and the associates arrived at the vicinity of one of the town's local nightclub venues and proceeded to vacate the cars to join the revelling scene of live music and crowds that gathered within the walls of the premise.

But Shane and Jade had remained sitting in the back seat of the car transfixed in each other's company of admiration and affection as they continued, locked in their own world of provocative transcendence.

As Jade's starry, glazed eyes stared into the warmth of his affections, Shane lent forward and placed a passionate kiss against the warmth of Jade's parted soft lips. "Mmm," Jade moaned as the passion of their first kiss lingered between them and aroused the lustful fires of desire that enveloped them and swept through their senses. The kiss grew deeper and deeper as their hands began to roam from the complacency of their own laps and explore the contours of each other's neatly dressed bodies.

"Ohh. Mmm," Jade moaned in pleasure as Shane's fingers ran along the smoothness of her inner thigh under her skirt to touch the moist heat that radiated from her desire.

"Yes," Jade whispered against Shane's cheek as his fingers lifted the moist satin fabric of her panties to touch and probe the wetness of her desire and lust.

Although Jade had remained in the moral virtue of abstaining from the pleasures of sexual temptation up until now, she felt helpless against the insatiable desire that ignited and surged throughout her body and tantalised her senses into a frenzy of lustful promiscuity in Shanes presence and under the influence of the little white pill. "Ohh yes," Jade lustfully moaned as she felt the tips of Shane's finger enter the inner layers of her yearning and entice her legs to open wider, allowing his finger to probe deeper and deeper into her wet desire.

"Hey you two. Get a room," a voice echoed from the pavement that ran under the coverings of the nightclubs veranda.

"Oh god," Jade whispered, parting her lips from the warmth and lust of Shane's and returned her hands to the virtue of her own lap. Shane and Jade sat motionless in the back seat of the car staring at each other as they realised the vulnerability of their lustful actions had caused a visual scene amongst the nightclub revellers that paved the outside surroundings.

"Oh my," Jade said softly, dropping her head into a covered giggle of embarrassment and apperception.

"Don't worry about them," Shane replied, smiling and laughing as he fixed his dishevelled clothes and lit up a cigarette, blowing the smoke out of the open car window.

Jade giggled and sighed as she set her dishevelled clothes back into the respectable place which they had sat and reached for the cigarettes that lay untouched in her handbag.

Realising that Shane and Jade had not entered the nightclub venue with the other members and associates of the group upon their arrival, Ryan suddenly appeared from out of the nightclub venue and stood glaringly out on the front pavement searching for Shane and Jade's whereabouts.

"Come on you two," Ryan called out, laughing and grinning in joyous disbelief as he sighted Shane and Jade still sitting astutely in the back seat of the car.

On Ryan's motion of command Shane and Jade simultaneously flicked their cigarettes out of the car's open window onto the asphalt of the car park, giggling as they gathered their belongings and climbed from out of the back seat and followed Ryan inside to join the other members who were gathered and interacting with the venue's revellers.

On entering the premise Jade hastily walked over in the direction of Rebecca who had positioned herself on one of the nightclub's bar stools in her wait for Jade's appearance.

"Where have you been?" Rebecca asked smiling and diverting her glance into Shane's direction.

"I, ummm," Jade replied, dropping her head slightly unable to conceal the giggle and the blush that radiated from the top of her cheeks.

"Oh my god. Look at me," Rebecca requested, reaching her hand out to lift up the edge of Jade's chin. "You popped a pill didn't you?" she continued to proclaim as she viewed the glaze of the drug that danced through Jade's eyes.

"Yes," Jade admitted, throwing her head back in stupendous laughter.

"Oh god Rebecca," Jade continued in her grandiose of confession. "We had our first kiss and it was on. I've never been kissed like that before. Not ever. I just wanted to 'hmm mmm' right there and then," Jade boasted naughtily, giggling and dropping her eyes into a provocative glance of her sexual arousal.

"Ohh you naughty girl," Rebecca teased, throwing Jade a glance of wickedness. "And here I am thinking you are so innocent. You little tease."

Within moments of her revealing her confession to Rebecca, Shane returned to the position of the bar where Jade and Rebecca were converged in their conversation of elicit secrets and tales of sexual desire.

As he placed the alcoholic beverage that he had purchased for Jade on the bar in front of her, Shane wrapped his arms around either side of Jade's position in a protective stance of ownership.

Although Jade had remained silence in her knowledge of the omniscient truth of the gesture she reciprocated the knowledge with an affectionate reassurance of touch upon Shane's hand that had been placed on the bar close to her whilst she continued with her conversion with Rebecca.

After enjoying many hours of uninhibited interaction at the nightclub with the venue's revellers, Ryan announced that it was time for the members to leave and head back to the clubhouse to continue with the night's festivities.

"Ohh not yet," Jade complained, her body and mind still fuelled by the intoxication of the drug. "I want to dance. Let's go dancing. Please?" Jade asked, dropping her face into a cute grin of persuasion.

"It's time to stop girl," Ryan replied, laughing at Jade's eagerness and anticipation.

"Nooo," Jade pleaded, "Please?" diverting her glazed glance of persuasion into Shane's direction. Shane stood speechless in the momentary acquisitiveness of persuasion before throwing his head back into a laugh of precarious bemusement.

"She's your girl," Ryan pronounced, raising his eyebrows into a questioning arch and turning his attention into Shane's direction.

"Okay," Shane finally agreed, smirking and laughing. "I'll take you to the night club."

"Yesss," Jade called out in glee and excitement, kissing Shane on the cheek. "Thank you."

As the other members collected themselves, gathered their belongings and dispersed from the doors of the establishment to continue with their grandiose of entertainment back at the rebellions clubhouse, Jade remained standing in the presence of Shane, Ryan and three prospects of the club, who remained in their escort of duty to accompany the request of entering the contrasting nightclub at the opposite end of the small town. Upon entering through the large glass doors of the usually crowded dance venue, Jade's lips dropped into a scour of disappointment as the rationalization of the empty dance floor and scantly scattered revellers that lined the length of the bar dawned upon her of the night's ending.

"Ohhh," Jade moaned in her disappointment. "I wanted to dance."

Shane returned Jade's moan of objection with an admiring laugh before leading her to the end of the bar and positioning himself in a stance of protection around her.

"We can stay for one drink," Shane stated, before gesturing to the bartender for the requirement of his services and placing the chilled glass of alcohol on the bar in front of Jade.

Although Jade had remained in her state of the intoxicating fabricated high joviality of the little white pill which had deemed her helpless against her usual resistance of the tantalisation of the continuation of the evening's compulsion of revelling, Ryan announced that it was time to leave the establishment and bring the long night to a standstill.

"Really?" Jade questioned, smiling and giggling in her uninhibited state. Ryan stood still in his disciplinarian state of command flashing a mellifluent smile, as he eyed the drug-fuelled glaze that danced through Jade's eyes and enhanced her vivacious spirit into a frenzy of energy.

"Come on girl. It's time to go," Ryan stated with a smirk, before gesturing to Shane and the clubhouse prospects that it was time for the group's departure.

As Jade collected herself and slung her handbag over her shoulder in preparation for her departure from the dance venue, an impetuous disconcertment of aberrance rushed through her hallucinogenic mind.

"Would you like to come back to my place for drinks?" Jade asked, turning her attentions to Shane in a smile of suggestive provocativeness.

"Yes. I'd love to," Shane replied without haste, wrapping his arm around her shoulders as he led her out of the large glass doors of the venue and helped place her into the back seat of the car.

"Can you please drop us off at my place?" Jade asked in her request, as the clubhouse's designated driver started the car and steered out of the nightclub's car park towards the road.

Within minutes of leaving the nightclub venue, the car full of dutiful rebellions parked momentarily along the gravel-paved footpath that ran adjacent to Jade's home in their escort of delivering Shane and Jade to their desired destination.

"Have fun you two," Ryan called out of the open car window in audacious recognition of Shane and Jade's potential embarkation. In a turn of their heads in spontaneous unison, Shane and Jade flashed an unconscionable smile of their intentions in the direction of the car's occupants as they walked and giggled their way towards the front entrance of the house.

"Make yourself comfortable. I'll be right back," Jade invited, gesturing Shane towards the queen bed positioned against the wall in the middle of her bedroom before walking down the long hallway to enter the bathroom situated at the opposite end of the house.

"Hmm. Oh my," Jade whispered quietly to herself giggling, viewing the reflection of her drug induced glazed eyes staring back at her in the bathroom mirror. "Oh well girl. Time to get comfortable," Jade continued in her solitary slurred speech, reaching her hands underneath the seam of her knee length skirt and sliding her panties down the length of her legs, allowing the scantly silky fabric to fall from her ankles to the tiled bathroom floor.

As Jade re-entered the bedroom door, she provocatively glanced her view into Shane's position as he lay fully splayed on top of the comforts of the bed's décor.

"So now that I have you all to myself. Cheers birthday boy," Jade whispered, laying down on the bed next to him and grasping the chilled can of alcohol from the offering of his hand.

"Hmm. I think it's time for some music," she said quietly, raising to her feet off the bed and walking over to the stereo, placing a compact disc into the player.

"Now it's time to dance," Jade continued, swaying her hips into a hallucinogenic soft rhythm of provocative conceptual enticement of Shane's attention of visual stimulation.

"Mmmm," Jade seductively moaned, running her hands down the soft curvaceous length of her womanly body until her fingertips grasped the hem of her knee length skirt and slowly, seductively raised the tight fabric to the top of her smooth, firm thighs. "Mmm," Jade moaned softly again, climbing onto the foot of the bed in a crawl of seductive allurement, placing herself in an erotic pose within the warmth of his lap. "I want you," Jade whispered softly into Shane's ear, as she lent her body forward against his and placed her soft, warm lips into a passionate, lustful embrace of sensuality against his.

As the passion that emblazed between their lips lit the erotic lust of the sexual desire that escalated between them, Shane slowly ran his fingertips up the back of her open thighs, unabashedly touching the smoothness of her bareness until he came to the moist crevice that lay uncovered against his lap.

"Ohh. Mmm," Shane moaned, allowing his fingers to caress the moist nakedness of the desire aroused between Jade's thighs.

"Ohh yes," Jade seductively whispered between her lustful breaths of desire as their sexual motions of movement began to quicken and their hands began to explore every inch of their nakedness. "Oh god," Jade whispered huskily again as her fingers slid under the covers of Shane's T-shirt before lustfully removing it and throwing it to the floor to reveal the warm muscular structure of his naked contours.

Jade glanced provocatively into Shane's eyes as her body slowly crawled down the length of his nakedness until she reached the pinnacle of his lustful excitement.

"Mmm," Jade moaned, undoing the fastening of Shane's jeans and sliding the fabric off his body to reveal his arousal.

"Ohh," escaped from Jade's lips in a moan of seductive pleasure as she took his arousal deep into the moist warmth of her mouth.

After continuously applying the seductive pleasuring of the warm wet pleasures of her mouth and tongue, Shane conceded into an admission of disdainful disappointment as he reached his hand down to touch the soft lengths of Jade's long blond hair.

"Fuck," Shane said in a raised voice of his own displeasure. "It's the drugs hey. Fuck."

"What's wrong?" Jade asked gently, concerned with Shane's shift in disposition. "Has this happened before?"

"Yeah," Shane replied. "But only when I do those bloody things."

"Oh," Jade replied carefully, as not to cause tension within the situation.

Jade felt awkward in the objected emasculated function of Shane's disappointment which had brought their foreplay of love making to an abrupt halt. She had not been placed in the experience of objection before with her past lovers but quickly set her mind in motion to ease the discomfort of Shane's disappointment and frustration.

Jade crawled back up the length of Shane's body placing kisses along her path as she closed the gap between the distance that separated their lips.

"It's okay," Jade whispered softly in Shane's ear, leaning forward and kissing him gently on the lips. "I have toys. Would you like to play?"

Shane quickly shrugged aside the frustrated momentary pause of the situation and returned Jade's question with a rhetorical smile of acceptance and willingness to pursue the art of foreplay through the means of a woman's technique of self-masturbation.

Jade smiled seductively as she reached into her bedside cupboard draw and produced the small pink vibrator from within the cupboard draw's concealed confinements. "Mmm. Let's play with this," Jade hummed in a sexy voice of enticement, as she placed the small sex toy into Shane's open palm.

Shane sat motionless in his curiosity, eyeing the sexual apparatus that sat in his hand as Jade raised the hem line of her skirt back into the position of her thighs and laid back onto the mattress, resting up on one elbow.

"Come and play with me. I want you to," Jade invited in a sexy tone, biting her bottom lip gently and curling her finger erotically as she opened her legs to reveal the wanton desire of her pleasure. An excited hum escaped from the tight corners of Shane's smile as he laid himself down on the mattress between Jade's open legs and gently placed the erotic sensations of the vibrating toy against the moist pink pinnacle of Jade's lustful arousal.

"Mmm," Jade moaned through her lustful breath, as the vibrating toy began to entice and excite the heightening sensations that stirred deep within her wet pleasures of desire and harden her clitoris.

"Ohhh yes. More, oh more. I want it inside of me," Jade moaned in a whisper, diverting her eyes into a seductive expression of lust in Shane's direction. "I want you to."

Jade arched her back as she felt the vibrating sensations of the sexual toy shift from her aroused clitoris and slide provocatively into the depths of her moistening pleasure.

"Mmmm. Ohh yes. Oh god. Yes," Jade moaned louder through her breaths of pleasure as the toy stroked and satisfied the inner lust that ignited inside of her, edging her closer and closer to her climax. "Oh god. Yes. Right there. Don't stop," Jade gasped in pleasure, rising her hips in an upward motion to meet the sliding thrusts of the small vibrating toy. "Yes. Yes. Ohhh yes," Jade moaned loudly one last time, as she felt the intense pleasurable pulsations of her orgasm rush throughout her body and satisfy the burning desires of her sexual lust.

"Ohh, mmm," Jade hummed as she lay motionless in her satisfaction on top of the bed catching her breath.

As Jade lay still in her satisfaction of pleasure, Shane slowly moved himself from the erotic position of watching the sensual indulgence from between her legs and slid the length of his body against hers to lay in the distance of space that had separated them and placed a passionate deep kiss on the warmth of her lips.

"You sexy little bitch," Shane commended, his eyes looking deep into the satisfaction that blazed through Jade's eyes.

"I've never done that before. Not with someone," Jade confessed, releasing an enlightened sexy giggle from within. "But I'd like to do it again," she continued with a devilish little smile.

"Mmm. Me too," Shane replied in a rhapsody of pleasurable affirmation as he pulled her into his circle of embrace where they both closed their eyes and drifted off into a slumber of contentment.

Shane and Jade had not stirred in their slumber and slept motionless in each other's embrace until the late hours of the afternoon the next day. Although their duration of sleep had been enough to suffice and be defined as a good night of sleeping, Shane and Jade had both awoken exhausted and lethargic, a repercussion of their indulgence of the hallucinogenic drug that they had both ingested the night before. Jade lay motionless looking over the man lying next to her in her bed, as her mind drifted off into the pensive moments of the erotic sexual lust and attraction that they had shared so unabashedly the night before. She had not known nor was experienced in the world of erotica which had forsaken her desires with her past lovers, except within the surreptitious erotic confines of her alluring fantasia with her online lover, Max.

"Would you like a coffee?" Jade finally asked, her mind shifting from the moments of her pensiveness and refocusing on the reality that lay next to her in her bed.

"Yes Please," Shane answered, yawning and rubbing away the sleep from within his tired eyes.

Within minutes of making her way down the long hallway to the kitchen area of the house, Jade returned to the comfort of the bedroom, placing a cup of piping hot coffee on the bedside cupboard next to Shane, before slipping back under the warmth of the bed's covers at Shane's side.

"I have to head back to the clubhouse soon," Shane started to explain. "I'm on shift today, umm. Could I have your phone number though?" he continued in his tentative questioning, flashing a cheeky smile in Jade's direction.

"Yeah, sure," Jade answered disconcertingly, concealing the true nature of her thoughts. "I can drive you back to the club after our coffee if you would like."

"Yes please," Shane replied, reaching for the hot cup of coffee sitting next to him on the bedside cupboard. "I want to thank you for a great birthday Jade. It was the best fucken birthday I've ever had," Shane blurted out in an unambivalent confession, laughing in his unashamed blatancy. "It was unreal."

Jade placed her hands in a cover over her face as the glow of the aberrant blush started to fill the top of her cheeks. "Well. It was the best orgasm I've ever had too," Jade replied laughing, in her unambivalent quick wit of humour.

After spending their last minutes of moments engaged in garrulous laughter of the events that had taken place the night before, whilst captivated in the hallucinogenic high of the fantasy love drug which they had both indulged in, Shane and Jade got dressed and returned to the dwellings of the rebellious clubhouse of which Shane held a responsibility to his commitment of duty. But Jade did not reveal the secrecy of her hidden phone number and remained silent in the affirmation of her devolvement of the private number as Shane left her presence and she returned to her home.

Although Jade had formed an appealing liking for Shane, she still harboured within her the sense of freedom that she had fought for and chosen to pursue in her liberation from her former marriage of commitment and control and kept a safe distance within her emotions and attraction for Shane that remained under her own control.

That evening as Jade busied herself preparing her evening meal she heard the familiar tone of her mobile phone as it received a delivered message. As Jade opened the setting to the newly delivered message she had received, she noticed the digits of the unknown number that was attached to the message which had left her in a momentary pause of bewilderment, until she read the unmistakable, recognizable words of enticement. "Miss me yet sexy."

"Ohh," Jade whispered to herself before allowing an amusing giggle to escape through her lips. "How did he get my number?" she continued to question, studying the unknown number before lifting her glance into a look of astuteness.

"Aha. Ryan. Ryan gave it to him I bet," Jade continued in her amused giggle.

"Yes. I do," Jade began to type on the keypad of her phone in her seductive reply, "When are you coming back? I want you again."

Jade cheekily giggled as she sent the reply to the unknown number in her bid to provoke the enticement of Shane's presence back into the erotic pleasures of her bedroom. Within minutes, Jade received another message on her phone and proceeded to read the reply.

"I'm on my way sexy." "Don't waste any time, do you," Jade said out loud, throwing her head back into mellifluence of laugher as she placed the phone down onto the kitchen bench and proceeded to make her way down the long hallway that led into the confines of her bedroom.

Within minutes of having received the text message on her phone, Jade heard a knock coming from the direction of the front door of her house and walked to her bedroom window to peer at the presence of the announced sound. "He's here," Jade whispered to herself, smiling coyly down at the ground before straightening her knee length skirt as she walked to the position of her front door to welcome the unexpected presence of her arouser.

"Weit wil," Shane whistled through the mesh of the security screen door, as Jade stood enclosed on the other side. "You are one sexy woman."

As Jade unlocked the screen door allowing Shane entrance into her home, he scooped her up into the strength of his muscled arms and carried her the short distance down the long hallway and into the confines of his lustful admiration atop of the soft covers of Jade's bed.

Although their first erotic encounter had been filled with the misgivings of Shane's drug-fuelled emasculation of his own self disappointment, their lustful anticipation of their sexual yearnings erupted into an evening of provocative splendour and lustful satisfaction that lasted for hours.

While Shane and Jade lay next to each other catching their breaths in the afterglow of their vigorous love making, Shane turned his head to glance his eyes into Jade's direction.

"I have to go back to work tomorrow," Shane explained with a slight disappointment in his voice.

"That's okay," Jade replied, smiling and rolling onto her side to kiss him gently on the cheek. "My children come back home tomorrow as well for their week with me. So it's perfect timing really."

"I would like to see you again though Jade," Shane admitted, flashing a welcoming smile that spread across his sexually flushed cheeks. "When I come back in four weeks' time."

Jade dropped her eyes towards the bed as her face lit up into a smile of admired coyness and conceded to the formulism of venturing into a developing relationship rather than enveloping upon a lustful adventure.

"Yeah sure. I'd like to see you again too," Jade finally answered, leaning over and kissing him sweetly on the lips.

That night as Shane was leaving, he stood holding Jade in his warm tight embrace as he spoke quietly into her ear. "Wait for me. I will be back. I promise you Jade."

Jade lifted her head from out of the warmth of Shane's embrace and looked deep into the softness of his brown eyes that sparkled in their glow at her, before answering softly with sincerity.

"Yes Shane. I'll wait for you. I promise."

As their arms reached out to embrace each other once more and the warmth of their lips met, their promise to each other was sealed.

Over the next week, Jade continued with her tenacious commitments to her studies and the establishment of her business plan while indulging in the exuberant pleasures of her lifestyle of luncheon dates, social gatherings and the rebellious revelling amongst her clubhouse associates at the local towns nightclub venues in Shane's absence. She revelled in the freedom of living between the two worlds of her fantasy and her reality, as Shane's absence allowed her to frolic without restriction of conviction as she continued to indulge in her erotic surreptitious fanciful exploitations with her online lover while waiting for Shane to return to the lustful warmth of her bed.

Shane had explained to her of his inability to remain in contact with her whilst working away at the remote location of the mines site, which Jade was led to believe inhibited the use of any kind of phone reception or contact from the regions of the world outside of the area, until the Friday night of which Jade received an unexpected phone call.

"Hey sexy," came the excited voice down the line of the phone.

"Shane," Jade replied in her astonishment. "Hey, I thought that I wouldn't hear from you for a few weeks. Where are you calling from?" she continued in her questioning of curiosity.

"Well," Shane started to explain with a slight giggle. "I sort of missed my plane, I'm still here."

Jade's face spread into a well-lit smile as a giggle of omniscient enthusiasm escaped from her lips. "You sort of missed your plane huh," Jade continued in her recitation of Shane's explanation.

"Yeah I did," Shane replied, nervously laughing. "So I thought that I would come back there to see you if that's alright with you?"

"Yes, of course you can," Jade replied, giggling under her breath. "But I have my twins at home this week, soo. We'll have to catch up while they're at school that's all. I hope you don't mind?"

"Of course that's alright," Shane replied cheerfully. "That's fine with me. I just want to see you and touch that sexy body of yours," he unabashedly teased in his compliment of declaration of his own desires.

Jade felt the warmth of the blush that spread across the tops of her cheeks, as her face formed into a complimented smile which momentarily silenced her words as she stood listening on the other end of the phone.

"Okay," Jade finally answered with a coy giggle. "So when are you coming back?"

"Tomorrow," Shane quickly replied.

"Ohhh," Jade unashamedly teased, tantalising her voice into a tone of sexiness. "Then tomorrow it's on. Text me when you get into town okay. I'll see you tomorrow."

Although Jade felt the enthusiasm of her desires to spend her time with her newly found love interest, the compaction of her responsibilities and love in the role of motherhood to her children compelled her to remain in a continuation of abstaining from deviating into a world of aberrant behaviour that would disrupt their routine or her visitations with them.

Jade had felt responsible for turning their world into a spiral of contemptuous bickering and the precariousness of the circumstances that surrounded them as a result of her decision to separate from their father, which had escalated into an enumeration of animosity and the segregation of their loyalty and love between their two worlds.

Shane had shown Jade the understanding of her position as a mother and the circumstances that had now shrouded her in a deep spiral of concernment and agitation when in her dealings with Derek.

He had applauded Jade's constant efforts and dedication to pertain the stability and well-being of her children, which was a quality he had found to be impressive and admired, having had come from the background of parents that had separated when he was a child.

That evening Jade sat down in her small home office in front of her computer and composed an intimate detailed account within the surreptitious boundaries of their written letters, of the new found love interest that had entered into her life and sent it to Max. Although Jade had held onto the divine secrecy of her exoticness with her online lover from the boundaries of the outside world, she had abandoned her morals of secrecy with Max, who lavished in the erotic tales of her sexual adventures that she shared while in her secrecy of masturbation and of that of which she had shared with her new found love interest, Shane.

Max had become a harbour of intimacy, safety and security of which she had not known before which had formed into a beautiful picture of perfection of which no other man had or could measure up to.

Their unique bond of friendship and sexual intimacy within their relationship had given Jade a sense of belonging and of love which she had not encountered within the realms of her own world and emblazoned a yearning within her of the hope that one day she would be graced with his presence in person and know his love and passion in the flesh.

That night Jade sat in baited breath for her online lovers reply to the intimate admission of her letter.

Max had always shown Jade her importance to him and had always answered her letters of affection which had abated her fears of doubt or bewilderment of confusion, of assiduity.

As Jade awaited the longed-for answers to her intimate letter that she had sent to Max, she continued in her usual routine of the construction and research of her intricate business plan as her eyes played a continuous flicker towards the screen of her email inbox. Jade continued to wait as the email inbox on her computer screen lay empty of all inclusions and notifications throughout the long evening, but Max did not answer, he did not send a reply and his words fell into silence.

The next morning Jade busied herself preparing the school lunches for Nick and James and once delivered at their destination of the school grounds for the day sent a text message of enticement to Shane.

"The house is all ours for the day. I am waiting on the bed for you, touching myself. I want you now."

Within minutes Jade heard a knock on the large wooden frame of her front door which sparked a smile of promiscuity to spread across her face as she walked to the front door to welcome Shane into the confines of her bedroom walls.

Over the next four hours Shane and Jade did not leave the intimacy of the bedroom and spent the day entwined in their sexual lust of provocativeness and erotic pleasures as they explored their insatiable desires for one another, that grew more and more with every touch of their warm skin and kiss of their passionate lips.

Jade was unable to hold any resistance against the growing lustful appetite of Shane's flesh that excited her and took her to heights of unmeasurable ecstasy of sexual pleasure and blinded her perception to her awareness of Shane's reputable rebellious disposition of anarchistic behaviour. Jade had been seduced by the constant flow of the grandiose of excitement and found herself in the grips of perpetual aberration, as she was introduced to the world of lustful passion and partaking in the hypnotic hallucinatory world of the drug scene.

All that week within moments of having delivered her children to their place of education on a daily basis, Shane arrived at Jade's doorstep, lured by the seductive prowess of her bedroom walls.

With each kiss, touch of their skin and lustful embrace of their sexual adventures, they were swept further and further into a world of uncontrollable insatiability of desire and rebelliousness as their time spent together formed a tightening bond of connection between their bodies and provoked their hearts.

As their week together drew to an end and it came time for Shane to return to his place of employment in the remote location of the mines, while they stood together on the cement path that led to the driveway of Jade's home, Shane turned to Jade and embraced her up into his arms for one last time and kissed her deeply on her warm lips.

"You're my girl baby. If I open my heart to you, don't you break it girl," Shane said as he looked deep into Jade's eyes. A soft smile of warmth spread across Jade's mouth as she leant forward to kiss Shane's lips once more before whispering softly into his ear, "Don't break mine either. I'm all yours."

Over the next three months while Shane worked away at the remote mines site and returned to the small town of Suisania Bay to Jade's waiting arms at the end of each of his designated rosters of work hours, Jade continued with her tenacious study and research as she drew closer and closer to the establishment of the development of her business plan. Although Jade had made her promise of commitment to Shane and they had developed their once lustful affair into the committed boundaries of a relationship, Jade could not eradicate or resist the ever growing lure of the exuberant night time scene which was now filled with the interaction of the hallucinogenic fantasia of the little white pill in Shane's absence.

Alone in her home, Jade continued in her exploration of surreptitious arousable provocativeness with Max, her online lover, which had increased in intensity and promiscuity as Max's awareness of Shane's presence within Jade's life fuelled his attraction into a transcendence of seductive suasion of the attention of sexual demands. Max did answer Jade's letter of her pronounced inclusion of Shane's presence into her life until late the next evening, which spelt out a confession of his overwhelming jealousy and fear of an imminent loss of Jade's erotic affections, that had engulfed him and rendered him speechless and silent in the face of the written announcement. Even though Max was aware that the day would eventually come of Jade's inclusion of a new love into her life, he had not been prepared for the overwhelming feelings that had swept through him in a wave of jealousy and fear of sharing or losing the tantalising treat of the other woman, Jade, who had become his online mistress and whom he had also fallen deeply in love with. Although Max had been engulfed with his jealousy and struggled in the loosening of the reins, he had offered Jade sweet words of encouragement, wishing Jade happiness and hoped for the best for her within the new boundaries of her relationship with Shane.

An illuminated smile of affection spread across Jade's face as she read the sweet written words of the man whom had captured her affections of admiration and had been placed within the loving depths of her beating heart. That night Jade replied a letter of reassurance to Max, with the written declaration of her undying devotion to his love and of his position of importance within her heart and life, something that would last a lifetime. Never to be together but also never to be apart, Jade's life revolved around her online infatuation, love and admiration that she shared with Max on a nightly basis, and had kept her sworn promise of secrecy to him to never reveal his presence in her life which she had tenaciously upheld, even from Shane, and continued in her surreptitious love affair in Shane's absence which had offered Max a pride of place within her heart and reassured him of her devotion to his love.

Over the next week of the children's absence from Jade, while they were in the visitational transition with their father, Jade awaited for Shane's return from the remote site of his work position, of which he had asked the imminent question of his inclusion within the setting of the domestication of the house for his week of rest and relaxation. Jade agreed to allow Shane to spend the week with her within the confines of her home and looked forward to his return when they could indulge in the desires of their exoticness of sexual pleasures, that had been exemplified in her fantasia of provocative role playing with Max in Shane's absence.

On Friday evening Shane arrived at Jade's house prepared to spend the week-long period within the settings of the home's domestication.

Jade listened as she heard the familiar sound of Shane's car engine and the car's tyres ground along the long gravel driveway of her house and come to a stop behind her own parked car.

"He's here," Jade shrilled, in her joyous moment of anticipation and excitement before quickly checking her appearance in the large mirror of her dressing table and without haste ran to the front door and out into the driveway to greet his long awaited return.

"Hey. There's my sexy lady," Shane greeted with a joyous smile, as he sighted Jade rushing towards his direction before leaping into his open arms of affection.

"I missed you," Shane said, placing a passionate deep kiss against the warmth of her lips.

"I missed you too baby," Jade replied, her smile glowing across her face as her arms embraced the presence of his form even tighter.

As Jade's body lay wrapped within the tight warmth of Shane's embrace, he whisked her off towards the opening of the front door entrance of the house and entered the confines of the office walls, clearing the office desk with one hand and placing her gently down on top of the office desk as he slid the tightness of her knee length skirt to the position of her exposed thighs.

"I've missed your beautiful little, Mmm," Shane hummed, opening her thighs wide and diving his tongue deep into the warm moist heat that lay untouched in his absence between her legs.

"Ohhh. Mmm," Jade moaned, arching her back against the hardness of the table top, gripping at the sides of the wooden desk with her long fingers, as each deep stroke and touch of Shane's warm moist tongue provoked and emblazed the inner lust of her wanting desires.

As Jade lay absorbed in the seductive beautiful pleasures of Shane's mouth and tongue that teased and stroked at the moist pleasure between her legs, she was oblivious to the sound of the lowering of his jeans zipper and the heavy fabric of his jeans that fell from his legs and onto the carpeted flooring of the office.

"Mmm. Roll over sexy," Shane ordered, as he lifted his head up from between her thighs and rolled her body over to position her on her stomach on top of the office desk. "Mmm," he hummed, spreading her legs open to expose the moist pleasure between her legs before quickly thrusting the full length of his hardness deep inside of her. "Ohhh," Jade moaned out loud, reaching her hands out above her head to place them firmly against the wall of the office.

"Oh god. Yes, yes, oh god. Oh god. Oh yes, just like that," Jade moaned loudly the thrill of the lustful pleasure leaving her lips in words she never thought would leave her mouth as he thrust faster and faster and deeper inside of her.

In one quick motion Shane lustfully reached for the curves of Jade's narrow waist, rolling her back over as he placed himself in the office chair, sliding her down from off of the table and onto his hardened lap of sexual desire. "Ohh god," Jade moaned releasing her sounds of pure pleasure from between her lips, as she wrapped her long legs around the back of the office chair and began to raise herself up and down within the tight grip of Shane's strong hands wrapped around the curves of her small waist.

"Ohhh, ohhh yes, I'm going to cum," Jade moaned loudly, as she felt the peak of her climax tighten within the moist heat of her loins. "Oh god yes, yes. Ohhh," her moans sounding loudly through her parted lips as the sensations of her orgasm released itself in a pulsating rush of moistened pleasure all around the hardened length of Shane's lap. A pulsating arousal of sexual excitement rushed through Shane's body taking him beyond the peak of his control as his own climax dawned upon the edge within the moistened grip of the lustful sensations of Jade's pulsations.

"Oh fuck, Me too baby, I'm gonna cum," Shane moaned, looking into the erotic arousal of Jade's blazing eyes. As the lustful words swept through Jade's hearing, and with one quick motion she lifted herself off the hardened length of Shane's excitement and quickly dropped to her knees in front of him, taking his swollen member all the way into her mouth and swallowed the warm sweet juices of Shane's orgasm that flowed over her tongue and down her throat.

"Mmm," Jade hummed, resting down onto the smalls of her feet, wiping the sweet glistening moisture from off her lips, smiling up at Shane's satisfied stare.

"You fucken sexy little thing," Shane said, looking down at Jade shaking his head in disbelief. "You're gonna do me in girl, you are," releasing a small giggle from his astonished opened mouth.

Jade looked back into Shane's eyes as the spread of her giggle swept across her sexually flushed cheeks before raising to her feet and gathering the loosely strewn clothes that lay scattered across the office floor.

"Would you like a drink baby? I bought some bourbons," Jade offered, slipping her body back into the layers of her clothing. Although Shane did not have a tendency towards the consumption of alcohol, he agreed politely to the enjoyment of consuming just one of the chilled cans of bourbon out of the six pack of which Jade had specially purchased in the anticipation of his arrival.

As they both sat together in the afterglow of their erotic pleasures of their sexual insatiability, sipping at the chilled cans of the sweet bourbon mix, Shane reached his hand forward towards his luggage that lay dropped to the floor upon his arrival.

"I have brought something with me for us to enjoy over our time together this week," Shane announced with a devilish grin that spread across his face, as he bent forward unzipping his luggage and revealing a plastic bag filled with an assortment of intoxicating choices.

"Oh," Jade said, widening her eyes in disbelief at the array of drugs that lay piled inside of the plastic bag in front of her. "You are planning on having a good week aren't you," she continued, spreading a smiling giggle across her face. "How many is in there? And what is that?" Jade questioned in her curiosity of naivety as she eyed the little bag filled with a white powdery substance.

"Yes I am girl," Shane quickly replied with a smile. "These are for us," holding up the bag filled with the little white pills of ecstasy.

"Oh fuck girl, where have you been?" Shane continued picking up the bag filled with the white powdery substance as a laugh escaped from his mouth. "It's coke you know, cocaine. This will get you hot girl, you'll love it."

The rush of hesitance ran through Jade's mind as she sat eyeing the bag of cocaine that was held in front of her in Shane's grinning stare. Although she had not seen nor tried the mind stimulation of the illegal white powder before, her mind wandered into the intriguing fascination of the allurement, but had still been held in the hesitant tight grip of her intransigent morality of principles.

"I'll have to think about that one," Jade finally replied with an uncertain smile.

"Are we going to the club tonight?" Jade asked, quickly shifting the conversation from the subject of her own slide into aberrant behaviour.

"If you would like to," Shane replied, allowing Jade the option to choose the course of their entertainment of the night.

"I'd like to," Jade quickly replied without any hesitation. "This is my week off from my responsibilities. And you do know how I like to party," she continued, flashing a mischievous glint across her eyes in Shane's direction. Shane laughed out loud as he nodded his head in knowledgeable compliance, before sifting through the clean clothing of his luggage and heading down the long hallway of the house towards the shower cubicle of the bathroom. "Mmm. I might join you in there," Jade hummed wickedly, following Shane down the long hallway giggling.

As the couple applied the finishing touches to their attire for the anticipated night's entertainment, Shane reached into his luggage and fetched the bag that was filled with the little white ecstasy pills.

"Here you go sexy," Shane announced, placing one of the little white pills into Jade's open palm.

"Thank you baby," Jade replied, kissing him on the cheek and placing the pill in her mouth upon her tongue. This time Jade did not hesitate to consume the intoxicating, hallucinatory effects of the little white pill as it sat within the confinements of her consumption, this time, Jade swallowed without question or a hesitant moment of delay and patiently waited the twenty minutes for the pills effects to take place.

After enjoying the consumption of another two chilled cans of bourbon whilst still within the privacy of their own company, Shane and Jade decided that it was time to make their way to the exuberance entertainment of the rebelliousness of the notorious clubhouse dwellings.

By the time they had arrived at the gates of the clubhouse the other members and associates of the club had swung the night's entertainment into a full swing of loud music and high spirits of intoxicated mischievousness.

Although the members had been privy to Jade's exploitations of her wild, mischievous behaviour whilst under the influence of alcohol and the laughing joviality of cannabis, they had not experienced the uninhibited brashness of her transcendence into the fabricated ebullient world of her pill indulgence.

"You naughty girl," the members jokingly teased and laughed, looking into the glazed efficacious roll of the little white pill that danced through the blue of Jade's eyes and sent her into a rhapsodically ball of energy and an incessant chatter of a surrealistic nature.

The nature of the member's sporadic teasing of her mischievous antics throughout the course of the evening had not set any source of effect on Jade, as she continued in her unfazed fantasy of playfulness prancing and pacing around the clubhouse's eight ball table and mingling with the other women who joined in her antics of gestural fun and exhilaration.

As the night wore on into the late evening hours, Jade's energy was still running at a fanatical pace as she swept around the room in rhythmic fashion to the loudness of the beat of the music that played over the speakers situated throughout the length of the clubhouse.

"Let's go dancing," Jade called out in prompting joyous fashion to the other women who sat in groups around the large wooden wine barrels that had been transformed and utilised as tables of which to sit to enjoy the company of the establishments gathered revellers.

"Yesss. Let's go," Rebecca replied joyously in her enthusiasm, jumping to her feet off the wooden stall that surrounded the make shift tables. As the other women within the group collected their handbags and things that they needed for their venture out into the fun-filled world of the night-time venues, Jade and Rebecca informed the designated drivers and their partners of their plans to join the other revellers at the local night-time dance venues and proceeded to vacate the clubhouse in a joyous exuberance of loudness and laughter.

Within minutes the large group of the rebellious revellers arrived at the doors of the local night-time dance venue and flooded the colourfully lit dance floor in an unambivalent sway of rhythmic vigorousness amongst the large crowd that had already gathered within the walls of the establishment.

The men of the clubhouse who had escorted their women to the night club stood protectively around the perimeters of the dance floor watching on in smiling laughter as the intoxication of the pills of which their partners had consumed that evening drew them into a fanaticism of invigorating correlation with the rhythm of the music that beat loudly throughout the speakers splayed around the dance establishment.

Although Jade had always enjoyed the rhythm of dance and music the rush of the ecstasy pill had taken her to new heights of excitement and invigoration as she danced around the dance floor in an unstoppable ebullience of rhythmic exploitation until the last minutes of the night-time venue's closing.

As the night drew to a close the men gathered the women and returned to the private confines of the clubhouse where they continued with their ecstasy-fuelled revelling until they had to leave with the closure of the gates.

Still invigorated and fuelled by the effects of the strong fantasia of the drug of which she had consumed, Jade was not prepared for the night to come to a halt and enticed Shane's enthusiasm to continue in an alluring seductive proposition of sexual provocativeness in the confines of her bedroom and the household walls which continued until the late morning sunrise of the next day.

Shane stayed with Jade all that week as they had arranged before his arrival from the remote setting of his work at the mines site, which had compelled their connection beyond one of a sexual lustful desire and compounded the forming of their desires to develop their interlude into one of a solid commitment to each other. As the days drew close to the end of the week Shane received an unexpected phone call from the mines site requesting his early return as one of his colleagues had fallen ill and could not return until the following week. Shane accepted the request of his return and prepared for his departure back to Alterro to catch the next available flight to deliver him to the remote setting of the mines site. Although Jade felt slightly disappointed that their time together had been cut short due to the unexpected request, she understood the reasons and spent the last hours of their togetherness in lavished attention. As the couple stood in the long gravel driveway of Jade's home in a tight embrace of farewell, Jade felt the overwhelming emotion of the departure from within herself rise throughout her until the words left her lips in a soft whisper.

"I'm going to miss you," Jade gently whispered against Shane's ear as his arms held her tightly against him.

"I'm going to miss you too baby," Shane said softly back before kissing her deeply upon the lips and releasing her from within his tight embrace and walking around to the driver's side of the car.

"Bye baby. I'll see you soon," Shane called from out of the open car window, as Jade watched him drive away and disappear around the bend of the road.

Two hours after Shane's departure from her home, in Jade's business of returning her household to its regular organised cleanliness after spending the week with Shane, she unexpectedly received a message on her mobile phone from Shane.

"Hey sexy. I left a surprise for you. Look under your bed. I'll be back as soon as I can. I miss you already."

Jade's eyes furrowed into a bewildered stare as she read the message and her mind puzzled over the interpretation of his surprise, which was hiding under the confines of her bed.

"Hmm. Under my bed," Jade hummed to herself, puzzled. "What have you placed there?" Jade was stumped by the unusual message which she had received and quickly ran to the confines of her bedroom and lifted up the covers to reveal the underlining boundaries of her bed.

"What is this?" Jade said quietly to herself as she eyed the large cloth shopping bag that lay hidden on the floor underneath the covers of the queen size bed. Jade reached her hand out to grasp the cloth lined strapping of the shopping bag and dragged the heavy bag out from underneath the bed and placed it at her knees in front of her.

"Oh my," Jade said again to herself, opening the top of the bag to reveal the contents that lay hidden inside. "Oh my god. You're kidding," escaped from within an astonished gasp from her opened mouth, as she stared at the contents within the bag.

Jade sat silently stunned in a moment of speechlessness as she eyed the large bag filled with gold and silver coins which Shane had been collecting over the course of the year and had left for in her weight of struggle, poverty and debt that had been left in her hands by the actions of her separation to Derek.

Although Jade had not informed Shane of her impoverishment of which she faced as a result of Derek's unwillingness to accept his part in the responsibility of the debts that they had shared while still within the commitment of their marriage, she had many times in-depth conversations with Ryan, who had offered a compassionate shoulder on which to unburden her worries and sorrows. Jade knew that this is where Shane had been informed of her impoverished state of the dilemma she faced with Derek and had compassionately offered his generosity as a sign of his devotion and feelings that had arisen from within himself towards her. Jade rushed to the side of her mobile phone and quickly started to type a sincere message of thankfulness and admiration of his generosity and sent the message to Shane.

"Baby. I can't believe you did that. I'm absolutely speechless. Thank you so much. You're the best."

Within moments of sending the sincere message to Shane, Jade's message tone displayed a received message of reply.

"That's alright baby. I want you to look after yourself and be alright. I'm not sure how much is in there but it should help pay some of your bills. Please stay safe. I'll see you soon."

Jade felt the warm glow of benevolence flow through her in a soft wrap of nurture as she read the words displayed within the reply that she had received from Shane, and gently placed her phone against the warmth of her chest as her eyes filled with the overwhelming joyous tears of his generosity and kindness. "No one has ever cared about me before," Jade whispered to herself. "Helped me."

Jade lifted the heavy-clothed shopping bag onto the softness of her bed covers and emptied the contents of the ample amount of gold and silver coins onto the soft fabric and sat silently staring for a moment before starting to separate the coins into divisions of counting.

"Oh god," Jade whispered again as her mouth opened in her disbelief. "There's over three hundred dollars here. I can't believe you just gave this to me. I can't take this," Jade continued in her hesitance to accept such an enumeration of generosity. Although Shane had been in a position of employment for most of his life, Jade had been in a position of a marriage to an ungenerous man who did not enrich her with the spoils of kindness or of a monetary value and had found herself now in a position of an unskilled woman who had spent the younger years of her life raising her four children and had found employment to be one of an impossible task. Even though Shane had not seen his generosity as one of an enormous value, to Jade the proportion of the enumerated amount was a contradistinction of enormous proportions which would amply suffice her past the financial hurdles which she had been facing alone, but felt a moral conscience of accepting his generous contribution.

Jade reached for her phone once more and began to type a message to Shane of refusal to accept the money of which he had so selflessly left for her in his absence.

"Baby, there's over three hundred dollars here. I cannot accept your money. I don't feel right about it. I'll save it for when you get back okay. But thank you for thinking of me. I'm really touched by your generosity and thoughtfulness. I'll see you when you get back okay."

Within seconds of sending the message Jade received another reply from Shane, a stern reply of sweetness. Jade opened the message on her phone and began to read as she sat on her bed surrounded by the coins that sat neatly stacked into piles of enumeration.

"Jade. I gave it to you to help you and because I love you. Please look after yourself while I am gone. I'll be mad with you if you don't."

Jade just shook her head in sweet mellifluous of disbelief as she read Shane's words of stern tenderness, before finally expressing the gratitude that swept through her within a replying message.

"You are a wonderful man. Okay, I will. Thank you so much. I love you too, take care baby."

Jade placed her phone back onto the dresser within her bedroom and proceeded to walk through the wide hallway and into the confines of her office, where she collected a large, fully laden folder of unpaid billing accounts from the filing cabinet draw.

"Well which one first?" Jade said quietly to herself, taking a deep breath and sighing as she laid the array of unpaid billing account documents in a circle around her upon the office floor.

Jade began to shuffle through the substantial amount of unpaid bills, segregating them into groups of importance and of first priority. "Well," Jade sighed, looking over at the amounts of the unpaid credit card statements which had enumerated to an astronomical amount of $50,000, a debt that had accumulated over the course of her marriage with Derek.

Derek had been persistent in his pursuit of establishing a home-based business in the small town of Suisania Bay and had required the purchase of a variety of expensive tooling equipment and machinery, in order to perform a professional level of functionality within the business.

Although Jade had disagreed with the establishment of the small business after conducting a variety of viability studies and conducting market research throughout the small town of Suisania Bay, she showed her husband the support that he needed and relented to his suasion of applying for the credit cards necessary for the establishment of the business, in her name. During their many discussions in regards to the financial requirements necessary to establish the business, Derek had informed her of his past bad credit rating of which he accumulated over the course of his previous marriage.

The credit cards had also incurred debts of Derek's excessive gambling habits which had been acquired by the use of cash advances on the credit cards and also the establishment of furniture and household goods for Derek's new residence upon their separation. Derek had sworn that he would take full responsibility for his part in the debts that had been incurred during their marriage and of that upon their separation, which persuaded Jade to relent against her best judgement and agree to the charges being placed into her name.

Jade had put her faith in Derek's statement of acquisition, a statement that had proven to be false on the application and approval of his acquiring of credit cards after the separation of their marriage, and the abandonment of his financial obligations and responsibilities, once he had been established within his new place of residence.

The matrimonial home, which Derek and Jade had resided during the course of the marriage whilst in the region of Suisania Bay, had been placed on the market for sale upon their separation. Even though Jade had held onto the hope of acquiring a quick sale of the property in accordance to rid herself of the accumulated immense debt of the mortgage, credit card debts, utility accounts and the store accounts that had been established in the duration of the home based business, Derek had served as a hindrance to the sale, refusing to accept any of the generous offers that had been made towards the sale of the home, as a defiant stance against releasing Jade into the world of liberation and freedom from the tight grip of which he still held.

"Well hopefully the house will pay these off when it eventually sells," Jade said quietly to herself, pushing aside the pile of accumulated credit card account statements and grasping at the next pile of accounts and placing them in a splayed out fashion of importance in front of herself.

"Hmm," Jade hummed, as she paused momentarily briefing the amounts of the account of which she held to her eyes. "Maybe this one." Jade eyed the amount of the fine of which she had foolishly brought upon herself in an aberrance of her usual moral behaviour, whilst enjoying the celebrations of her father's seventieth birthday within her childhood hometown of Copper Cove.

Jade had not celebrated her father's birthday with the other members of her family for a period of ten years due to the factors that had surrounded her father and mother's disapproval of the behaviour of Derek's mistreatment towards their only daughter, whilst in the boundaries of their matrimonial bond.

But the family had also harboured a dark secret of Jade's suffering as a young child while in the hands of her incestuous older brother, which had driven an impregnable wedge between the relations of the children and formed the outcast of Jade amongst the other family members, who could not accept the truth of her innocence and deal with the misfortune and shame that it had brought to the family's circle.

But upon this invitation Jade had decided to push aside the animosity and antipathy that she had harboured for twenty one years in subsequence towards her older brother's vulgarity of her innocence and accept the invitation to her father's celebration, at the consequence of facing her older brother, who would also be in attendance.

Jade arrived at the hotel that evening at 6.30 pm, as she arranged a week beforehand with her parents blessing and excitement of her acceptance of the invitation to her father's birthday celebrations. The celebrations had gathered quite a large gathering, which had been an efficacious re-acquaintance of Jade's brothers and their families, immediate relatives and friends and acquaintances of the family.

The night's occasion had proven to be a joyous night of celebrations with the servings of deliciously succulent meals and the incessant chatter of joyous company.

Even though Jade had faced the battle of being seated within the company of her older brother, Peter, she had not allowed the permissibility of his presence to interfere with the joviality of the evenings celebrations and avoided his contact with a precision of eloquence and fine etiquette.

Over the course of the evening, Jade had reacquainted with a group of her past gatherings of party revellers of whom she had not seen for a number of years, who enticed her into a continual evening of celebrations at the ending of her father's occasion, of which Jade accepted in their jubilation of unity.

Jade had enjoyed the celebrations of her father's seventieth birthday, sipping the wine responsibly of which had been provided throughout the night, as she had been restrained to the responsibility of the safety of driving of her vehicle from the designated venue to her parent's home and had not wanted to place herself or anybody else on the night's roads within the risk of harm's way.

Jade paced the alcohol beverages evenly throughout the evening, dousing the effects and potency of the alcohol with a mixing of soft drinks between the glasses of the wine of which she had been offered, as she continued in her celebrations with the group of acquaintances escorting them from venue to venue. Throughout the fast-paced, action-packed, fun-filled evening Jade had stumbled across many of the night-time revellers which she had once spent the time of her youth converging with throughout the venues of the night-time dance clubs and parties, who had joined in the celebrations and exhilarated the gathering into a concourse of excessive mischievousness of laughter, effusion of garrulousness and loud music. Although the mass of revelling acquaintances accompanying Jade were enjoying the excessiveness of their continual alcohol consumption whilst in her presence, Jade had remained vigilant in her indefectible astuteness to her responsibility of designated driver, as she ferried them from place to place enjoying the night-time entertainments of eight ball and dancing. As the evening wore on into the early hours of the morning, Jade's friends had suggested that they visit one of their favourite venues within the vicinity of the next town that was situated within a ten-minute drive from Copper Cove, which they had reminisced over the course of the evening about the many fond memories which they had shared together so many years earlier in their younger years.

The large group of party revellers composed of Jade's acquaintances and their accompanying friends, began to vacate the night-time venue located in Copper Cove in a drove of laughter and loudness, as they climbed into groups within the confines of Jade's vehicle in their process to make the short journey towards the location of the next town. As the group began the short distance of the drive, a roll of clouds dispersed across the night sky in a thunderous array of stormy weather that scattered rainfall across the small towns and down onto the bitumen roads on which Jade and her accompanying group of revellers were travelling. Although the thunderous storm had drenched the roads with the treacherous downfall of rain and blew wind in all directions of the towns water's edge, it had not dampened the joyous spirits of the party as they continued in there mischievous descendent of disconformity into the streets of the next town.

Within minutes of having left the site of the venue in Copper Cove, the loud group arrived at the next nightclub of which they had held a reputable requisition of mischievous behaviour, and had soon caught the view of the familiar faces of the accomplices that had partaken in the aberrant behaviour of the many wild nights of their youthful days.

Jade revelled in the vigorousness of the exhilarating joviality of the crowd of which had accompanied her in her vehicle and stood in gatherings along the long pavement that ran parallel to the night club establishment, and had soon slipped into an aberration of her astute responsible disposition under the suasion of encouragement from the crowd that surrounded her.

"Woohoo Jade! Hey girl! You're back. Come party with us girl," the voices called loudly from the sidewalk, as Jade and her vehicle full of garrulous laughter came into view of the gathered crowd.

"Let's go Jade. Park the car," called a voice from within her vehicle. "We're coming," yelled another voice to the gathered crowd from out of the open car window.

"Stop Jade, stop. Let us out," the continuous calls of the loud invigorated voices echoed from within the car. Jade pulled the car to a halt next to the sidewalk of the establishment, as the large crowd of revellers vacated the car and ran over to the crowd of voices who had encouraged them to join them in their night-time entertainment of jovial exuberance.

"I'll just park the car around the corner okay," Jade called out to her friends, her voice carrying out pass the passenger who had remained seated in the front seat, winding down the car window in order for Jade to call through her instructions.

As Jade began her descend back out onto the path of the road and headed towards the corner of the adjoining intersection that ran parallel to the establishment, she heard the loud voices of the mischievous rebelliousness of the crowd that lined the length of the establishments sidewalk.

"Spin it around the corner Jade. Go on. Give it to it," yelled out the loud voices in their mischievous encouragement.

In the younger years of Jade's youth, her friends had been well-equipped with the knowledgeable recognition to her spirit of adventurous rebelliousness, recklessness and disregard of the careful consideration of the legalities of the road rules, that disallowed the reckless behaviour of speeding and the spinning of a vehicles tyres upon the streets and the open plains of the mud fields that surrounded the white sands of the local beach foreshores. In Jade's temperament of cheekiness and her natural flare of chasing the wildness within her spirit of adventure, she had unconscionably partaken in the disrespectful nature of blatancy towards these rules whilst in the company of her spirited accomplices, in her aversion towards the law.

Jade threw her head back in a reminiscence of laughter and excitement as the stimulation of the invigorated crowd cheered her into an enticement of reckless exhibitionism, and placed her foot down harder against the accelerator, increasing the revs of the motor and accelerating the car into a squealing, sweeping, slide across the bitumen road of the adjoining intersection and rounding the corner in one quick motion. Jade and her passenger laughed with joyous wickedness as the crowd behind them roared into an extravaganza of exhilarated laughter, cheers and whistles of applaud, until the

157

site of the red and blue flashing lights of the police vehicle that had been parked around the corner brought the inappropriate unlawful spectacle to a standstill.

On an unblemished record of cheeky invasiveness within the twenty years of her driving history of conducting a behaviour of insolent exhibitionism, for the first time Jade faced the incriminating infringement of the laws consequence, as she sat nervously waiting in the driver's seat, watching as the police officer sternly approached her.

"Oh no," Jade winced, placing her face into her hands in an embarrassed expression of foolishness.

As Jade watched the officer take his last steps towards her stationary vehicle in her revision mirror she quickly but calmly wound down the car window and inhaled the deep breath that clung tightly within her throat.

"Can I see your licence please miss?" the police officer sternly asked, staring at Jade through the opening of her car window.

"Yes," Jade said nervously, reaching her hand out to fetch her licence from within her handbag that sat on the floor of the position of the passenger seat.

"Thank you miss," the officer politely said, opening the wallet of the licence which Jade had handed to him.

"So I think you realise why I have asked you to pull your car over tonight," the officer continued in a tone of sternness.

"Yes I do," Jade replied, looking shamefully into her lap. "I'm very sorry officer. I didn't realise that the roads had become so slippery with the fall of the rain and I had placed my foot down too heavily onto the accelerator as I rounded the corner. And. Well," Jade stuttered, nervously abating the truth. The officer looked down at Jade through the car window, raising one eye brow in his disbelief of the fabricated excuse of which Jade had tried to explain.

"Mmm," he hummed, raising his radio to his mouth and requesting a licence check to be conducted on Jade's history of driving.

"Have you been drinking at all tonight Jade?" the officer continued.

"A little," Jade confessed. "But not enough to be over the limit."

"I will have to ask you to blow into the breathalyser to test your blood alcohol level Jade," the officer said, placing the long tubular mouth piece onto the breathalyser unit.

Jade humbly agreed and did not feel the nervousness of the request, as she had deliberately paced the limits of her alcohol intake throughout the evenings celebrations and had no reservations about the test displaying a negative result.

"Just keep blowing into the mouth piece until I tell you to stop," the officer explained, placing the mouth piece against Jade's lips.

Jade calmly blew into the long tubular mouth piece of the breathalyser as the police officer watched vigilantly over the indicators of the testing apparatus, before removing the mouth piece from between her lips upon the completion of the specified time.

"I'm sorry Jade," the officer said, looking down at Jade once more. "But you have shown a high reading of alcohol in your system. You will have to come to the police station with us to conduct further testing."

"What," Jade replied in a high note of astonishment. "No. No, that can't be right," Jade contested. "I've been pacing myself all night. I haven't drunk that much at all. Not enough to be over officer. Truly."

"I'm sorry Jade but you will have to come with us. My partner will drive your vehicle back to the station in Copper Cove and you can either passenger with her or be escorted in the police car. Can I have the keys please?" the officer explained, reaching out his opened palm as he opened the car door with his other hand.

"Oh god no," Jade winced, as the thick swallow of the incrimination tightly slid to the back of her throat and knotted within her stomach.

"I can't believe this is happening," Jade said, placing her hand to her forehead before sliding the keys from out of the car's ignition and swinging her legs out of the opened car door to walk to the passenger side of her car. "This is the worst thing that could happen right now. Oh god," Jade cried out, opening the passenger side door and staring at her startled passenger still sitting in the confines of her car.

Jade had not known of the passenger before this night and who had accompanied one of her friends during their rampage of mischievous revelling, and had remained seated within her car during her foolish act of exhibitionism and while the police proceedings were in progress.

"I'll come with you Jade," the young man replied in a kind voice as Jade opened the passenger side car door.

"Really. You don't have to. Are you sure?" Jade replied, looking sheepishly down at the man.

"Yes. It's okay. I'll come," the young man replied, climbing out from the opened car door and situating himself into the back seat of the car. Jade hung her head in shame, looking down at the floor of the passenger seat while the female officer escorted her and her passenger back to the vicinity of the Copper Cove police station and placed her in one of the questioning rooms for further alcohol breath testing.

Three hours later Jade was charged with the incriminating offence of her reckless driving while under the influence of the intoxication of alcohol and was required to appear in front of the magistrate at the Copper Cove court house on a later date. The officers had agreed to allow Jade the use of her car within a twenty four hour time period in order to return to her place of residence the next day, but impounded her vehicle until the next morning until the effects of the alcohol had dissipated from her system.

The passenger who had accompanied Jade back to the police station had remained in a humble vigilant stance of gallantry and offered Jade the escorted safe return in her long walk back to her younger brother's house which she had arranged to stay that night after her father's birthday celebrations.

That night Jade felt the hard slap of the misconduct of her reckless behaviour and the derogation of the hell that she was about to encounter in the face of Derek's disapproval of her misdemeanour.

The next morning Jade awoke early and made the long walk back to the police station to collect her impounded car before wishing her family well upon her departure back to the small town of Suisania Bay. Jade left that day in a silence of surreptitiousness and had never mentioned a word of what had transpired the night before to her parents or her brother, and had remained silently ashamed in her admissions upon her return to Suisania Bay. Jade never saw the young man again whom had so selflessly stayed with her that night during her time spent in the Copper Cove police station and had showed her the kindness of protectively escorting her back into the safe confines of her brother's home. But Jade had never forgotten the young man's act of kindness and had always wished the best for him throughout the journeys of his life.

Three months later Jade returned to Copper Cove to appear before the magistrate in the local court house of Copper Cove, accompanied by her father who she had shamefully confessed the misconduct to one month earlier. Although the misconduct was one of Jade's first offence within the history of her driving, the magistrate proceeded to suspend Jade's licence for a period of seven months and charged her with a one thousand dollar fine, which could be paid in fortnightly instalments in accordance to the unemployment income of which she was receiving.

Upon her admission of the seven-month suspension of her licence to Derek, she faced the derogatory reprobation of his disapproval and his tenacious refusal to collect the children each morning and deliver them safely to their daily place of education, even though he held a place of employment within the education department as a groundsman within the children's attending school.

Derek had offered Jade a conditional monetary proposition to offer his services of the collection of his own children and taking them to their place of education, a proposition which Jade had refused to consider and refuted his offer as an insult and lack of support to the children.

Although she felt the weight of the magnitude of Derek's disdainful manipulation of contempt, Jade remained vigilant in her refusal to give in to his despicable conduct towards her, and continued in her determination of remaining standing on her own two feet and re-building a new life of her own without him and enrolled her two youngest children at another school of which they could catch the bus to attend instead of giving into his demands.

Jade placed the document of the drink driving infringement notice on the carpet next to her, as the memories of that night replayed in a rhetorical vision within the depths of her mind.

"Silly girl," she whispered to herself, shaking her head slowly. "Silly girl."

The next morning Jade placed the numerated coins into the designated money bags and drove to the local banking institution to convert the coins into an amount of monetary dollar bills, which she paid towards the amount of the fine that she had received as a result of that reckless foolish night.

Over the course of the next month Jade received a surprise long distance phone call in the hot summer evening of a Friday night.

"Hey baby," came the voice down the phone line. "I miss you."

"Shane. It's you," Jade replied in her excitement of surprise, as a smile spread across her face. "Oh baby, I miss you too."

"I'm thinking about coming home baby," Shane continued, in an admission of his explanation. "I'm thinking about getting a job in the city and living back at Mum's. I don't want to be away from you for so long and thought that that way I could come and see you every weekend. I need to be closer to you baby."

A mellifluous smile spread across Jade's face as the words she had longed to hear settled beneath her skin and touched a chord within her heart, producing a sweet glow of ebullience to swirl throughout her and release the truth from within, that she had been truly touched by Shane's presence in her life.

"I think that's a brilliant idea," Jade finally answered, as the excitement mingled in the chords of her voice. "If that's what you would like to do, yes, I need to see you more too baby."

"Okay then baby, It's settled," Shane replied in his own excitement. "I'm coming home."

That night after they spent many hours transfixed in the sound of the sweet intertwinement of their affections and the plans and hopes that they held for their future together, Shane and Jade finally said goodnight to each other and slid into the comforts of their solitaire beds.

As Jade lay awake under the warmth of her blankets staring at the lights that flickered through her curtained bedroom window that cast shadows across the white of her ceiling, her mind wandered over the many details of Shane's return and the personal transition that was about to enter into her life.

Although Jade had divulged her explanation to her children of her involvement with Shane, she had not allowed their involvement in the meeting of the man that had captured her interests and had remained in a steadfast stance of discretion of her indulgence into the life of the rebellious behaviour, whilst not serving in her role as a responsible parent and while not in their presence.

As the notion of Shane's permanent return from the remote setting of his work at the mines site loomed, Jade knew that she now had to find the courage to express her desires to her children and introduce them to the man that she had been meeting under the privacy of the immiscible separation of her double lives.

Over the course of their separation Jade had suffered the perpetuation of Derek's tempestuous oppugnancy of contemptible inflictions which had escalated into the systematic manipulation of the children's minds and a direct contingency of Nick's involvement in the conflagration towards his mother.

Jade was aware of the emotional suffering that had raged through her son as a subsequence of the adverse effects of the dissolution of his parents' marriage, and watched helplessly as his young mind twisted under the weight of his father's contemptible manipulation of negativity, which had rendered him into a violent attack of abusive behaviour towards his mother and Cody whilst in the visitation of the family home.

"Hmm," Jade hummed to herself as the pensive thoughts tangled within the cores of her mind. "Well I guess that it's time that I introduced Shane to the children. I can't hide this any longer. But how do I do this?" Jade placed her hand to the worrying furrow that had started to form within her brows under the weight of the precariousness of her thoughts, and her mind darted into a concentration of concern of the effects that the introduction would have on her son, Nick.

"I'm just going to have to be honest," Jade continued, in her conclusion of the situation. "And nurture them through the best I can. I'll talk to Max about it tomorrow night. He'll be able to help me."

After hours of staring at the bedroom ceiling lost in her thoughts of apprehension, Jade finally closed her eyes and fell into a deep peaceful sleep until the early hours of the next morning.

Whilst in the visitation of her father Jade received a text message from her daughter explaining that she had been invited to the birthday party of her best friend, but had faced the hesitation of her father's approval and willingness to drive her to the designated residence of the celebrations.

Although Jade had continuously refrained from making contact with Derek as a result of his continuous contemptible behaviour of retaliation, she reciprocated Monique's suasion of pleading with a dubitative capitulation and with strict specifications of arrangements that she would make with her father upon the specified date of the celebrations.

That night Jade wrote a message to Derek on her mobile phone explaining that Monique had spoken to her about the anticipated birthday celebrations and had offered her willingness to escort her daughter to the birthday party if he was able to drive her to her home by 4 pm on the Wednesday night on commencement to the party, and that she would bring her back to his residence on completion of the celebrations.

Jade received an immediate positive response from Derek, whom had agreed to the specified details of the arrangement with grace and had not succumbed to a conception of a premeditation of conspiracy being formed against him with Monique's contact with her mother of her desire to join the celebrations.

161

On the Tuesday afternoon Jade spent the day rushing two and fro between her commitments of her full time study at the local education centre and that of the research that she had been conducting in order to establish the development of her intricate business plan within her chosen field.

Although Jade had been spending her time involved in the rebellious nature of her secondary life that she had embarked upon with the members of the clubhouse and the friends that she had made through her associations at the night clubs, she had intentionally informed them that this week she had to devote her full concentrations to that of her work commitments, whilst her children were still within their visitation with their father to which she received their full understanding. As the day drew to a close in the late afternoon Jade sat silently in her office as her mind reflected over the day's hours of productiveness and drifted into a space of her own leisurely agape of daydreams but was suddenly disturbed by a loud knock coming from the direction of her front door. Startled by the sudden noise Jade's mind quickly returned to the reality of her surroundings that raised her to her feet to walk through the long hallway towards the locked front door of her house.

"Who could that be?" flashed through Jade's mind, reaching her hand out to unlock the door and open it to reveal the source of the sound. "Oh," Jade said, the site of Derek, Monique and Cody standing on her front porch spilling from her mouth in a bewilderment of surprise. "What are you doing here?"

"I've brought Monique in for the birthday party that we had arranged," Derek answered in a gruffly voice.

"Ohh," Jade replied, rolling her eyes sideways into a glance of trepidation. "But the party is not until tomorrow night."

Jade stood precariously silent in her apprehension as she watched the formation on Derek's face change into a transition of an indignation of dissension and the words flew from his mouth in a loud roar.

"You stupid bitch. You told me it was tonight. I've got fuck all petrol and now I've just wasted it getting here. Why can't you get anything right? That's fucked," hurling the accusations at Jade in a vicious verbal attack.

"No," Jade replied sternly, placing her hands on her hips in a stance of strength and staring back into Derek's face. "I told you tomorrow night. Check your phone Derek."

Jade stood firm in her knowledge of the truth of the arrangements that she had made with Derek on the night that her daughter had contacted her regarding her plead of being able to attend the birthday celebrations, and stood in her appeal for Derek to check the details that had been written in the message bank of his phone as conformation.

"You're wrong you stupid bitch," Derek yelled back in his own defence, reaching his hand into the depths of his front pocket, sliding his phone out into full view and tossing it at Jade in his rage.

"This is all your fault. You bloody bitch. Were you off chasing some bloke instead of thinking of your kids huh?" Derek roared, hurling the abusive verbal attack in a continuum of irrational derogatory contention, as the children looked on in fearful vulnerability.

As the abusive words cut through the civil perfunctory of her disposition that she had been upholding whilst in the children's presence, Jade felt the strength of the veil of her eloquence fall to the ground and unleash a sudden rush of the suppressed retaliation of the victimisation that she had suffered in the hands of Derek over the abusive duration of their marriage.

"You're the one who got it wrong," Jade yelled back in contemptuous fury.

Vicious words of contemptuous vindication hurled back and forth through the evening air in a loud fury of hostile animosity, raging Derek into a volatile attack of a physical assault targeted at Jade's vulnerable small frame.

"Get your hands off me," Jade roared, prying at Derek's hands that had pinned her tightly against the cold hard stone of the house walls. "Let me go Derek," Jade yelled loudly again, pulling at his fingers to gain a release from the hard abusive pressure of which he had applied to her body.

As Jade struggled with Derek against the pinned pressure of his attack her eyes glanced over at Monique and Cody, who stood frozen and petrified in their terror of watching their parents animosity towards each other. "Get in the house kids," Jade called out desperately trying to remove her children from the abusive scene of which they had not beared witness to before. "Please, get in the house."

"No. You shut your fucken mouth," Derek roared in his tempestuous contempt, pressing his finger firmly against Jade's cheek. "Get in the car kids. Now," Derek yelled loudly at the children. Confused and terrified at what they were witnessing Monique and Cody stood motionless and silent in their terror and of their loyalties to their parents as they huddled together behind the large steel railings of the veranda pole. As Derek released the firm pressure of his attack towards Jade he hastily ran towards the children swiping them along with the ushering of his arms towards the direction of the parked car that sat at the end of the long gravel driveway next to the house.

"No kids, no," Jade yelled out, standing herself defensively protective between Derek and the direction of the parked car, in a desperate attempt to stop Derek from placing the children in the vehicle after previously witnessing her son's endangerment in the hands of Derek's tempestuous rage.

"No Derek," Jade yelled again, directing her protective intentions in Derek's direction. "You're not taking them. You're too angry."

"Get out of my way you bloody bitch," Derek roared, punching the back of the air conditioner unit that sat in the window of the office walls before rushing his hands out to grab Jade by the fabric of her shirt.

"Derek no," escaped from Jade's mouth in a loud sound of trepidation, her feet leaving the solid footing of the verandas cement floor as Derek flung her violently into the air landing her within the hard rocky flower beds of the front garden.

A loud noisy gasp left Jade's mouth as the magnitude of the unconscionable attack landed her hard upon the ground on the side of her small frame, forcing the air to rush out from within her lungs and rolling her battered body over on to its side in a tight ball. As the air began to flow again filling the empty casings of her lungs, Jade's eyes lifted into a transitional oppugnant glare of animosity in Derek's direction, raising her hastily to her feet and rushing her towards him into a tackle of furious retaliation.

"Please kids, get in the house. Now," Jade yelled out, struggling against the weight of Derek's attacking furiousness of force.

"Get in the bloody car, Now," Derek roared at the children, sending them into a precarious motionless huddle on the pavement running parallel to the front of the house.

As Derek and Jade continued to struggle in their wrestling of excessive furious animosity towards one another and the torrent of contemptible words cut through the air in vicious velocity, Monique and Cody made a dash towards the direction of the parked car at the end of the gravel driveway in a flood of frightful tears.

"I hate you," Jade roared, losing her footing against the cement pavement as Derek's impetuous force slammed her back against the stone walls of the house, falling her to the ground upon her knees.

163

"You're not taking them," Jade yelled out, raising once more to her feet and dashing furiously towards Derek who had ceased the opportunity to make a hasty scramble towards the open car door, of which the children had climbed through and formed a terrified tight huddle in the front seat.

"Nooo," Jade yelled loudly in a tempestuous roar, climbing into the front seat on top of Derek who had produced the vehicles keys from out of his jeans pocket and proceeded to jam them into the car's ignition in a struggling force.

"Get off of me you bloody bitch," Derek roared, in lashings of his hands and arms against her face and body, sending Jade into an impertinent daze of perturbation.

"Ahhh… You bastard," roared from Jade's mouth in an unassailable objection of repugnance, as the harsh sting of the violent attack reddened her cheek and sent a rage of indignation rushing through her veins. "That's it. You bastard, I bloody hate you," Jade roared in a furious tone of her indignation, reaching her arm around the perimeter of Derek's neck, encasing it in a tight lock of her rounded arm. "You're not taking them," Jade roared again, viciously yanking Derek from the front seat of the car with all her strength and slamming his head into the hard metal sheeting of the driveway fencing. Rendered defenceless and powerless against the brutality of the attack, Derek fell hard to the gravel-laden ground in a dishevelled daze of trepidation, rolling himself into a tight ball of his own protectiveness, as the retaliated blows of Jade's shoes landed furiously upon the length of his body.

"You fucken crazy bitch, get off me. Get off me. Jade stop," yelled from Derek's mouth in his desperation to escape from the vicious attack.

"Ahhh," Jade roared, diverting her furious attack towards the panes of the metal fencing, denting the railings with the brutal blow of the force of her shoe covered foot.

As the escalated commotion of the vicious tangle began to unwind, Derek and Jade's struggle was suddenly disturbed by the sound of a rushing police vehicle that quickly pulled to a halt at the front of the house, of which two police officers hastily climbed out from the vehicle and ran to site of the commotion, separating the tangle of disorderly ferocity.

"Calm down miss. Please," the female officer said in a calming voice, leading Jade away from the commotion to stand within the boundaries on the opposite side of the front yard. "What is this all about? Tell me what has happened."

While the two officers quickly led Derek and Jade away to separate corners of the front yard's perimeter, a second police vehicle halted in a rush upon the subdued scene of the altercation, in an aid to the officers and a comforting support to Monique and Cody, who had remained fearfully huddled in a stream of tears in the front seat of Derek's car.

Calmed and subdued in a disposition of rationalization by the police officer's presence, in a compliance of the officer's request Jade began the explanation of the tempestuous tattered tale of the abuse and indignation of which she had suffered while in the hands of Derek's control and demoralising crucifixion within the duration of their marriage and separation.

As the female officer studied the marks and bruises that had started to form upon the cheek bones and jaw line of Jade's facial regions a transitional frown of her concernment spread across her face and buried itself within her eyes. "I think you need a restraining order Jade," the officer replied, in a concerned suggestion of Jade's safety and wellbeing.

Jade dropped her eyes momentarily to the cement flooring of the front veranda before raising the tentative stare that had filled her eyes back into the direction of the officer's concern.

"Yes, I think it's time I did," Jade agreed, hanging her head in a disappointment of silence.

Although Jade had held onto the hope of the dissolution of Derek's contemptible rampage of her demise, and had not wanted to surrender to the ramifications of seeking a legal order that would render them beyond that of a civilised affiliation for the sake of the children, his incessant acrimonious behaviour had enforced the irrevocability of the couples segregation.

After speaking with Derek on the opposite side of the front yard's boundaries, the male police officer approached Jade and the accompanying female officer, in a union of collaboration regarding the proceedings of the separated couples' precarious situation.

"I have spoken with Derek Jade, and I have a clear understanding of the situation here," the male officer stated upon his approach.

"No, I don't think you do," Jade snapped back, raising her eyes to meet the male officer's glare. "I have been advised to apply for a restraining order by this officer, which is exactly what I intend to do," Jade continued, turning the bruising of her face into the direction of the male officer's view.

"Can I talk to you a minute," the female officer said, directing the male officer over to the site of an isolated corner of the veranda.

Within minutes of the officer's conducting in their affair of a private collaboration they re-approached Jade, who had remained anxiously standing alone on the site of which she had been separated from Derek upon the officer's arrival to the violent domestic scene.

"Okay, I think that obtaining a restraining order would be an appropriate idea in this situation," the male officer stated, looking at Jade with the same concern that she had received from the accompanying female officer. "Under the severity of the circumstances we can put an urgent rush on that for you Jade. I will put in the recommendation with our report as soon as we have returned to the station."

"It's going to be alright Jade," the female officer continued in her reassurance and support before allowing the accompanying officer to continue with his line of questioning.

"Derek has informed me that when he came here the children were within his care under your own arrangements. I can assure you that he has now calmed down and is thinking rationally and has requested the right to return with the children back to his place of residency, until the arranged time of next week," the male officer continued.

Jade's eyes darted a glance of apprehension straight at Derek who stood anxiously waiting for the officer's return before dropping her pensive stare to the cement floor of the veranda.

"Okay. Yes," Jade finally agreed, raising her eyes up to meet the questioning view of the officer's eyes.

"Alright. I will go and inform Derek that you have given him permission to take the children with him and I will return in a moment okay," the officer explained before calmly returning to Derek's waiting position.

Within minutes of their discussion, Derek returned to the seating of his vehicle and reversed out of the driveway and left the site of the house where he and Jade had so furiously fought.

Over the next hour Jade stood with the accompanying female officer revealing the contents of the abusive threatening text messages that she had received from Derek over the duration of their separation, which she had saved within the message bank of her mobile phone in proof of her innocence, and explained in detail of the full intensity of the reprehensible events that had led to the couple's violent altercation on that particular day.

Satisfied with the evidence of which Jade had supplied, the female officer left the scene of the altercation and returned to the station to file the report in support of the restraining order, which Jade had been advised to get and now desperately sought.

Bruised and shaken from the intense violent struggle of her battering with Derek, Jade returned to the safety of the locked confines of her home and laid her aching body down upon her bed in a tearful emotional recollection of the unimaginable inescapable nightmare which her life had become.

Upon her return from the police station early the next morning, Jade was greeted on her front door step by the neighbours whom she had grown close to over the period of living in the house that she had purchased with Derek, and had remained in close contact with her over the course of their separation.

"We saw everything Jade. I'm so sorry. Are you alright?" the neighbours asked, sympathetically wrapping Jade in a warming embrace. "We are the ones who called the police for you. We were so scared for your safety."

Jade embraced the warmth of their concern with open arms of gratitude, and explained that with the help of their involvement she was now able to put a stop to the endless abuse that had become a treacherous tessellation of sleepless nights of trepidation.

That day Jade nursed the wounds of her battered, bruised body in a restfulness of relaxation and solitude, as she reflected upon the pensiveness that held her in a state of quandary and equivocation.

Should she tell Shane the truth?

In the early hours of the Wednesday evening, Jade received a phone call from Shane from the remote mines site of his employment, as she sat in her office working tirelessly on the intricate details of her business plan.

"Hey baby," Shane replied joyfully, as Jade answered the phone.

"Shane. Ohh, it's so good to hear your voice," Jade answered, tentatively turning her head towards the carpeted floorings of the office space. "I've missed you."

"Baby, I'm coming home. This is my last week of work then I'll be home for good," Shane announced in an elated anticipation of excitement.

Jade held her breath as she listened to the ebullience of Shane's voice, holding down the secrets that lay buried within the dark bruises that lay upon her skin, covering the length of her battered body and face.

Although Jade had pondered many times within her own pensiveness over the course of that week of how she would offer an explanation to Shane of the vicious day which she had suffered in the hands of Derek's abuse, she abated the revelation of the truth in her fears of facing another volatile reaction, from the man whom was about to meet her children.

Over the next two nights Jade tossed and turned in a restless slumber, as she tussled with the compunction of the emotional denouement of her decision to remain vigilant in her equivocation, as she awaited the last final hours of Shane's permanent return from the remote mines site of which had held them apart.

As Jade heard the familiar sound of the vehicle that slowly entered the long gravel driveway that ran down the side of her house and pull to a stop, she felt the compaction of her breath tangle in a convergence of relief and agitation, as she rose to her feet and ventured towards the outside path that led to the driveway.

"Oh Shane. You're home. You're finally home," Jade cried out, rushing towards him and falling heavily into his arms in a declension of vulnerability and tears, burying her face deeply into the comforting safety of his warm chest.

"What's wrong baby, what's is it?" Shane questioned, in a concernment of the tears that ran down the carefully concealed bruising of her face.

"I'm just so happy to see you baby, that's all," Jade sobbed, in a perfunctory cover of the truth that lay hidden deep inside of her. Shane cast his eyes into the evasiveness that shadowed through the downward slant of Jade's disconcerted expression, as he placed his hands gently against the softness of her cheeks and raised her eyes to meet his.

"No Jade. There's something you're not telling me," Shane continued, in his gentle suasion of questioning. "Please baby. Tell me what's wrong."

"Ohh We," Jade replied, dropping her head slightly in her explanation as she stammered over the words of the unassailable truth that had remained buried within her.

"Derek and I had a disagreement and things got very heated and, well, I, I have to get a restraining order against him," spilt tentatively from her lips in an exposure of truthful disclosure, "I have to attend court next week."

"What," Shane replied in a raised voiced.

"Please, please, don't get mad Shane," Jade pleaded. "I really don't need to be around anymore anger right now. Please," Jade continued, raising the perilous sadness that had filled her eyes to meet his glare. Shane stood momentarily silent in his glare as he absorbed the emotional turmoil that permeated and surrounded the vulnerability of Jade's disposition, before turning his glare towards the gravel laden driveway in a surrender of his own comradely of protectiveness.

"Alright, alright," Shane finally replied, shifting his disposition into a stance of concernment. "What happened Jade? Tell me. What did Derek do to you?"

Jade lifted her tentative stare from off the direction of the ground of which it had held her and sat down on the edge of the cement wall fencing that surrounded the edge of the front garden beds as she reached for Shane's hand to guide him to sit down with her.

"You're not going to like what I have to say," Jade started in her admission, dropping her eyes once again towards the ground. "Maybe it's best if I just show you. You're going to see anyway. Come inside baby. I'll show you."

Jade placed her hand gently into the openness of Shane's palm and slowly led him along the cement path that led towards the front door of her house and into the confines of the closed doors of her bedroom walls, where she carefully removed the covering sleek fabric of her silky top.

Jade watched as the vision of the horrific bruising and grazes that covered the length of the side of her torso shocked and alarmed Shane's subdued disposition into an apperception of realisation and protective animosity.

"Get fucked," leapt loudly from Shane's mouth, jumping to his feet from off the end of the bed.

"You tell me right now Jade. You tell me everything that has been going on," Shane sternly demanded, shaking his head back and forth as he paced around the room, glancing over at the bruises that covered Jade's body. Jade felt the tightness of her apprehension wind its way up and down the confines of her clenched stomach, as she carefully slipped the silky fabric back over the soreness of her battered body, before slowly taking a step towards the steps of Shane's pacing.

"Please Shane. I can see you're upset," Jade said softly, reaching her hand out towards Shane's tight clenched fists.

"You bet I am. That bloody bastard," Shane angrily snapped back, his mouth forming into a thin tightness of his anger as his eyes filled with the fiery indignation of his contempt.

"Please listen to me Shane," Jade pleaded, placing the concernment of her stance directly into the path of Shane's anger. "Okay, yes. Derek did do this. We had an argument and things got out of hand but I also was to blame Shane," Jade continued in her plight of explanation.

"Bullshit Jade," Shane replied angrily.

Jade dropped her head in a surrender of her equivocacy as she proceeded cautiously with her explanation of revealing the truthful details of her volatile relationship of which she had shared with Derek.

"Please sit down Shane. Please. I'll tell you everything okay," Jade pleaded, placing herself in a sitting position upon the end of the queen size bed.

Shane looked over at Jade sitting on the end of the bed as her eyes filled with the sorrow of her story, beckoning him to calm the anger that raged inside of him and to sit down alongside of her.

As Shane slowly lowered his body to the space next to her upon the end of the bed, Jade placed her hand gently into his and began in her confession of the truth of which she had kept hidden for the duration of her marriage.

"You know when you asked me how the holes and dents that are scattered throughout the length of the walls and door of this room had got there, and I told you that they had been caused by accidents. Well, I lied Shane. I didn't want you to know. I didn't want anyone to know," Jade began in her explanation of the truth, as she struggled in her delivery of the right words. "The holes and dents were caused by Derek's temper Shane. It has been going on for a very long time, ever since I fell pregnant with the twins. But he's gone now. I've left him and started a new life without him. With you." Shane's face dropped into a transitional stare that looked straight through Jade's soul, as the horrific truth of the words seeped beneath his skin and into the depths of his own perspectives in a conflicting protectiveness of the woman that he had grown to love.

"But please Shane. Please stay out of it," Jade pleaded repeatedly, dropping to her knees in front of him. "This is not your battle okay. He'll take my kids away from me if you get involved, he's already threatened to do so. He'll use anything he can to stay in control. I know him Shane. Please promise me you'll leave this alone. Please Shane," Jade continued to plead.

Shane momentarily lowered the silent stare of the contemplative expression that had formed within his eyes, as Jade's discretionary plea recapitulated throughout his mind.

"Alright. Alright baby. I promise I won't interfere," Shane finally replied, lifting his eyes up to meet the concernment that apprehensively stared back at him. "We will do it your way."

"Thank you," Jade whispered softly, wrapping her arms around him in a tight embrace of insouciant gratitude. "I just need you to be there for me baby. Trust me, I know what I'm doing okay."

"Okay baby," Shane gently replied, as he held Jade closely to him in a supportive reassuring embrace of his promise.

"Let's go out hey?" Jade solemnly suggested, allowing a small smile to curl the edges of her lips. "Let's just enjoy our weekend together okay baby."

"Okay baby. Yes, I agree," Shane replied, returning an efficacious smile as he reached into the concealment of his suitcase and produced a bag filled with the remnants of the ecstasy pills, of which he had brought with him upon his previous return from the remote mines site of his employment.

"Would you like one of these?" he continued, holding the bag up inside Jade's line of view.

"Yeah, why not," Jade replied without hesitation, giggling as she held out her open palm to the little white pill, placing it upon her tongue and swallowing down the anticipated intoxication of the substance. "Time to forget for a little while hey."

In their collaboration to shed the continual dissension of which Jade was enduring in her battle with Derek, that weekend Shane and Jade wrapped themselves into a galvanic ebulliency of drugs, alcohol and the erotic lust of their sexual provocativeness, as they revelled amongst the crowds of the notorious clubhouse and night-time scenes within the local town of Suisania Bay.

On the Sunday evening as the weekend drew to a close, Shane and Jade spent the last few hours of their togetherness locked in their discussion of the forward direction of their relationship of which they were about to embark upon and had both reached an acquiesce of retaining a level of discrepancy and caution.

Although they had spoken many times about the revelation of their relationship and Shane's introduction to the children, Jade had remained tenacious in her stance of retaining the disclosure of the new life of which she had been building, and had kept her children in a veil of protective obliviousness, as she waited for the timing to be right.

"I'm going to miss you," Jade whispered in Shane's ear, as they lay on the bed together embraced in the last hours of their intimacy.

"I'll miss you too baby," Shane replied, lowering his head to place a gentle kiss upon her lips. "But I'll be back next weekend okay. I'm not that far away now."

"I know baby, I know," Jade replied, raising her eyes to meet the reassuring glimmer that sparkled in the depths of Shane's eyes, before resting her head back into the warmth of his chest.

"I want you to call me if you need me though Jade. I don't care if it's in the middle of the day or night. If you need me, I'm here for you okay," Shane continued in a gentle stern disclosure of his devotion and support. "I love you baby. You have me now," wrapping his arms tighter around her, pulling Jade into the depths of his devoted protectiveness.

"I love you too baby," Jade replied, lifting her head off his chest and placing a soft kiss gently against his. "And I promise I will call you if anything happens okay. I will."

Shane had become aware of Jade's stance of independence and ambition to remain standing in a position of her own strengths, as she battled against all the obstacles and trilogies that she had been faced with in the complexity of her life, but had reached out his arms of support in a noble stance of gallantry and reassurance that she had not need to face it alone anymore. Although she had found it hard to conform to the surrender of her independence within the realms of the plights of which she was facing, Jade found comfort in Shane's words of support and the unity of their stance together within the tempestuous circumstances that surrounded them due to her separation from Derek.

While Shane and Jade stood in their last moments of companionship in the gravel driveway that ran down the side of the house as Shane prepared for his departure and return to the residence of his mother's home in Alterro, Jade heard the sound of the message alert tone on her mobile phone that sat on the table within the confines of her office. "Oh, just a minute okay," Jade said in surprise, pointing her finger towards the office space window. "That was my phone. It might be from Derek. I'll just go and check it okay baby."

Jade quickly walked the narrow cement path that led along the edge of the front garden beds and entered the front door of the house to collect her phone from within the office walls.

As Jade opened the message storage bank of her phone and began to read, she felt the disturbing tightness that wrapped itself around her throat and swirled within the depths of her stomach, as the divulgence of the senders name stood her on an edge of tentativeness.

"Hmm. It's Derek," Jade said nervously to herself, as she stood glaring at the phone's screen. "What does he want this time?"

"Hey. I just want to apologise for the way I behaved towards you the other day. I'm sorry Jade, I didn't mean to hurt you."

Jade rolled her eyes in apathy as she read the words of which had now lost their meaning of a manipulatory surrender to extend a stance of understanding and to accept Derek's constant apologies for his impudent behaviour. "Yeah yeah," Jade muttered under her breath as she skipped her eyes along the meaningless frame of the words and continued to read to the next paragraph.

"And I realise that I scared the kids and that was very wrong of me to do. I am trying to make it up to them so I am taking them to Alterro for a couple of days to have some fun. Is it okay if I bring them back on Tuesday instead of today. Please?"

A spark of suspicious paranoia curled its way through Jade's mind as she stood in the middle of the office space floor staring at the words, her mind swirled around in deep thought of the truthful intentions behind Derek's apology and change of behavioural stance towards herself and the children's wellbeing.

"What are you up to now Derek?" Jade said quietly to herself, raising her hand to touch the tentative frown that had formed between her eyes. Although Jade still held a level of trust in Derek in concern with the nurturing of the children's needs, the actions of his tempestuous contemptible behaviour towards herself and his thoughtless selfish tendency to involve the children in his calculated debasement of her had placed her on an edge of mistrust and apperception.

"Maybe he's really realised that he has been wrong," Jade said quietly to herself, slowly stepping along the length of the carpeted floor. "Maybe I should just give him a chance to prove himself."

After minutes of standing in a moment of procrastination Jade finally surrendered to the decision of allowing Derek the benefit of the doubt and relented in her suspicion of him of behaving under a layer of false intentions. "Okay," Jade said, picking up her phone off the office room desk and started to type her reply of compliance. "But please Derek. Please do the right thing by the children."

As Jade pushed the message send button on her phone a wave of compunction swept over her in a questioning of her own decision and judgement of Derek's intentions and clung to her in a veil of hopefulness that she had made the right choice in her decision.

"Oh god Derek. Please don't be foolish this time," Jade whispered, raising the tentativeness that sat in the depths of her eyes towards the ceiling.

"Well," Jade announced walking from the house towards the direction of the driveway of which Shane had remained standing patiently waiting for her return. "That was Derek. He has asked if he can have some extra time with the kids, so they won't be coming home until Tuesday."

"Oh okay," Shane replied. "Well, is it alright with you if I stay until then?"

A joyous smile spread across Jade's cheeks and giggled from between her lips, as the joyful coyness in her eyes flashed a welcoming glance in Shane's direction.

"Yes, of course you can baby. I would like that very much," Jade replied, leaning forward and lovingly wrapping her arms around him.

In the early hours of the following morning Jade was awoken by the unexpected sudden sound of a loud knock on her front door. "Hmm. Who could that be?" Jade questioned, pulling herself out from under the soft warmness of the quilt covers and quickly slipping into her clothes.

As Jade opened the front door to the house she was greeted by two police officers who stood waiting under the front veranda equipped with a handful of undisclosed documents.

"Hello," the policeman said as Jade appeared in the doorway view. "Are you Jade?"

"Yes," Jade answered inquisitively.

"We are here to serve you with the court documents for the restraining order that you have recently applied for," the policeman continued, reaching his hand forward and placing the worded documents into Jade's hand.

"Thank you," Jade replied, skimming her eyes quickly over the documents contents.

"Ohh. The court date is tomorrow. That was fast," Jade continued, her eyes lifting from the printed documents and meeting the officer's view with a friendly smile.

"Thank you," Jade replied once again, excusing herself from the officer's presence as they departed into their vehicles and she returned to the confines of her bedroom to where she had left Shane sleeping peacefully in the warmth of her bed.

"Why were the cops here?" Shane inquisitively asked with a worried expression that filled the crevasses of his face, as Jade re-entered the bedroom.

"Don't worry," Jade reassured him. "They came to serve me the documents in regards to the restraining order that I had filed for. The court date is set for tomorrow morning. This is what I had been waiting for," Jade continued in her explanation, flashing a reassuring smile in Shane's direction as she continued to look over the legal documents. "Now it ends baby. Now it ends."

Although Jade had known of the ordeals and tribulations of the abuse that she had suffered in the hands of Derek's contemptible abusive behaviour, obtaining the official documents had still not offered her a source of comfort, as the overwhelming feeling of the outcome of the deliberation played a havoc of speculation within the depths of her mind.

"It's going to be alright baby, you'll get it. You've shown them the messages, they've seen the bruises. They're not bloody idiots. It will go through," Shane replied, reassuring Jade's restless mind as he pulled her down to rest within the warmth of his supportive loving embrace. "I'll come with you." Although Jade tried to allow the comforting words to absorb into the perspectival confines of her conscience, she could not escape the pensiveness within her mind as she lay in bed next to Shane that night in a sleepless toss of anguish.

The next morning Shane and Jade awoke early and wandered briskly through the house in their preparation for Jade's court appearance, which had been scheduled for 10 am.

As Shane and Jade drove the short distance from Jade's house to the court house's location, the couple sat in the nervous deafening silence of Jade's equivocality until they finally arrived at the doors fronts of the court house and entered in their wait to be called into the court room before the deciding judge.

The period of the hour-long wait as Jade sat with Shane in the waiting area of the court house, held Jade in a constant state of silent nervousness as the outcome of the deliberation played over and over within the depths of her mind until finally she heard the calling of her name to enter the court room to stand before the judge.

"Good luck," Shane said quietly in Jade's ear, kissing her gently on the cheek as she rose to her feet and walked the short passage way that led to the room of the court house . "I'll be here when you get out okay. You'll be fine."

Although Jade felt the reassurance of Shane's selfless support, she still carried a nervousness within the pit of her stomach that had wound itself tightly around her breath and knotted in the desperation of her apprehension of the judges final decision.

The judge sat quietly in the examination of the abusive, contemptible evidence of Derek's behaviour that had been conducted within the period of their separation, which he had been provided by Jade and the witnessing officers of that horrific day of their brutal physical battle whilst in the presence of the children. Jade's breath knotted and held within the tightness of her throat and dangled in the twiddling of her fingers as she awaited for the judges impending official statement to be spoken.

Within minutes, that to Jade had felt like anxious hours of perturbation, the judge finally lifted his eyes off the provided documents of evidence and moved his eyes of a sympathetic view into the direction of Jade's standing, as he pronounced the decision of his deliberation.

"Granted," the judge pronounced. "On the grounds of the evidence which I have been provided here today, I give my approval of the restraining order being ordered against Mr Derek Jones and to be effective immediately."

Jade inhaled a deep breath of relief as the judge's words of compliance rose up within her and unknotted the tight anxiousness of her disposition in a replacement of hopefulness and gratefulness.

"Thank you," Jade replied, tears of relief swelling in the brims of her eyes. "Thank you."

Jade did not utter another word but instead allowed the softened view of her face to shine through and speak the thousand words of her relief and appreciation as she walked from the lawyer's bench and out of the court room and into the arms of Shane who had been waiting patiently outside for the outcome of the court proceedings.

"I got it. Baby I got it," Jade announced smiling, as she placed her lips upon Shane's in a kiss of victorious joyfulness. "Take me home baby. Let's celebrate."

As the couple drove the short distance through the streets of Suisania Bay that led back to the location of Jade's home , Jade allowed her mind to delve into the depths of the imaginary vision of a new life without the trepidation of Derek's contemptible rage of heartbroken vengeance, which sparked a smile of abreaction to spread across the corners of her mouth and warm through to the depths of her soul.

That day Shane and Jade spent their time together wrapped in the joyous celebrations of their new beginnings as they consumed the intoxication of their alcohol beverages and erotic sexual desires in the serene comforts of the confines of Jade's home.

Jade had not heard from Derek nor knew when to expect the children back home, but she had decided today was the day that her new life would begin.

As the couple sat together upon the edge of Jade's queen size bed within the walls of Jade's bedroom, a smile formed upon her face and softly emitted a radiant glow of emancipation.

"Stay," Jade whispered in Shane's ear, turning her head and leaning into the small space that sat in the separation of their positioning.

"What?" Shane answered, a frown of bewilderment forming upon his face.

"I want you to stay. Meet my children. I would like them to meet you. Could you stay. Please," Jade asked, a gentle smile spreading across her lips.

Shane raised his hand to touch the smallness of Jade's soft cheek before placing his lips upon hers in a kiss of acquiesce. "Yes baby. I'll stay. Of course I will," Shane replied without hesitation or deliberation.

"But I don't want you to mention anything about the clubhouse to my children okay. No one knows that I go there and I would prefer to keep it that way," Jade explained, in her decision of her mothering authority. "I do not want my children to be involved with the clubhouse in anyway."

"Okay baby. I won't say a word," Shane replied with a reassuring smile.

"Thank you baby," Jade whispered, leaning her body over against his and placing a kiss upon his cheek as Shane's arms of comfort wrapped tightly around her.

Although Jade had made the aberrant decision of her venture into the confines of the notorious clubhouse on that day of Derek's constant demands to relieve him of his craving for his drug addiction to cannabis, Jade had remained steadfast in her aversion of allowing her children to gain the knowledge of her activities within the clubhouse or their involvement within the gang of rebels. "I better send Derek a message and find out what time to expect the children home," Jade finally said, lifting her head up from Shane's comforting shoulder and reaching for her mobile phone that sat nearby on the bedroom dressing table.

"Hmm," Jade hummed, looking down at the screen of her mobile phone as she awaited a reply from Derek before raising her glance up into Shane's view. "That's strange, he normally answers straight away. Maybe they're still on the road heading for home."

"That means we've got a couple of hours to spare," Jade continued in a giggly fashion as a sexy glint cast sexual sparks of desire across her eyes. "Mmm, come with me."

Jade reached her hand forward and placed it into the palm of Shane's open hand, standing him to his feet in an embrace of a lustful kiss before laying him down onto the soft coverings of the strewn bed covers and slowly lowered her body down upon his.

"Let's put some music on hey," Jade whispered in Shane's ear, before once again raising to her feet and switching on the power to the stereo that sat on the bedroom cabinet.

"Mmm," Jade hummed and smiled provocatively, swaying her hips rhythmically to the beat of the slow sounds of the music as she slowly started to remove each piece of her clothing and dropping them down upon the carpeted floor of her bedroom.

"Mmm," Jade hummed again, placing her knees upon the end of the mattress and seductively crawling along the length of the bed until her body lay above the clothed excited posture of Shane's body.

Shane raised his head slightly off the soft pillow that cradled his head to meet the soft sweetness of Jade's parted lips in a gentle embrace of intimacy that quickly dispersed into a kiss of fiery passion and sexual lust. As the passionate embrace rose and rushed through their bodies in a lustful heat of sexual seduction, Jade's hands quickly reached down the contours of Shane's body, pulling the coverings of his clothing off his body to reveal the excitement of his naked flesh, before lowering her wet parted lips down upon the excitement of his hardness that beckoned her to touch.

Shane reached his hands down and pulled Jade up to meet the warmth of his passionate kiss as his hands slid down the curves of her naked body and up the softness of her inner thigh, touching the moist heat that radiated from within the depths of her lustful desire.

"Ohh," Jade moaned softly, as she felt the tips of Shane's fingers stroke and push into the depths of her wanton pleasure, beckoning to be caressed and touched.

"Mmm," Jade moaned louder, as she felt the warm moist touch of Shane's tongue swirl around the contours of her hardened nipples as he continued to stroke the depths of her desire.

"Ohh, I want you now baby," Jade moaned loudly, wrapping her long legs around the contours of Shane's naked body and pulling him down upon her body between the opening of her parted thighs.

"Ohh," Jade gasped, raising her hips as she felt the hardness of his manhood push deeply into her and start to stroke the moist pleasures of her wanton desires. "Ohh yes baby. Mmm harder," moaned from Jade's lips, with each hard stroke intensifying the hot passion within her.

"Oh god yes. Yes," Jade gasped, raising her hips and arching her back against the soft firm mattress of their lovemaking to meet his every thrust. Jade lifted her head slightly off the mattress and placed her parted lips upon his in a passionate kiss of lust, as she wrapped her long smooth legs around Shane's body and rolled him over onto his back and lustfully straddled his lap, grinding her hips down as she felt the rush of his hardened excitement push up deeply inside of her once more. Shane moaned as he heard the soft gasps of Jade's pleasure fill his ears with the wild passions of her lust as he watched her hands between her legs touching herself and stimulating herself closer to the pleasures of her orgasm.

"Mmm. Ohh," Jade moaned, raising her hips up and down in rhythm with the pleasurable sensations of his excitement. "Oh god baby. Yes. Yes," escaped from Jade's lips, as their rhythm quickened and the touch of her own fingers against her hardened clitoris stimulated the moist heat between her legs in a tightened sensation of lustful pleasure. "Oh god baby. Yes. Oh god," Jade moaned again, gasping as the rush of the pulsating sensations deep inside of her releasing into a multiple rhythm of pleasurable moisture that flowed from the depths of her orgasm in a rush of pleasure that permeated in a flow upon Shane's lap, thighs and the sheeting below them.

"Oh baby fuck. Don't stop. Don't stop," Shane gasped, as the sensation of Jade's pleasure pushed him into the insatiable heights of his own orgasm.

"Oh god," Jade gasped trying to catch her breath, laying her naked body down into the depths of Shane's embrace. "What just happened?"

Shane raised his body into a wrap of affection around Jade's, as he tenderly stroked the soft skin upon her back and kissed her gently upon the length of her shoulders.

"Hasn't that ever happened to you before baby?" Shane asked, a soft loving smile spreading across his face.

"No baby, it hasn't," Jade replied, dropping her head slightly into a coy little smile. "You had a multiple orgasm baby which made you squirt," Shane answered, smiling and placing soft kisses along Jade's shoulder blades.

"Really. Oh god," Jade replied once more, lifting her eyes to meet his in a slightly embarrassed giggle as she slowly lifted herself off the wetness of the sheeting and stood by the side of the bed.

"Well I better place these in the wash," Jade continued, giggling as she slipped back into the fabrics of her clothing and pulled off the bed's sheeting before carrying them down the long hallway to the laundry.

As Jade wandered slowly back down the long hallway towards the confines of the bedroom, she heard the unexpected tone of the message alert notification sound out from within the loungeroom walls.

"Hmm," Jade hummed to herself, her eyes falling into a glance of bewilderment towards the sound of her mobile phone. "I wonder if that's Derek and the kids on their way back home."

Jade walked into the loungeroom picking up her phone from off the coffee table and began to read the unexpected message that she had just received.

174

"Hey. We have only just got back into town and the kids have asked me if they would be able to stay with me for another night. Is that okay with you? I can bring them back tomorrow before lunch if it's okay."

Jade's eyes drifted towards the ceiling in an exemplified unmistakable stare, as the waves of the disappointment of her planned introduction of Shane's meeting with them for the first time mingled with the fear that sat within her, of Derek's true intentions of asking for the extension of his time with the children. Although Jade had always accommodated for the deviation of her children's wishes to spend time with their father, she felt the underlying uneasiness of her cogitative precautionary reservations of her own intuition that ran through her in a swirl of questionable suspicion.

"Ohh well. We can do this tomorrow if that is what the kids would like to do," Jade said quietly to herself, re-reading the unexpected message of Derek's request, before replying with her own compliance to the request.

"Guess what?" Jade called out, raising her voice to permeate through the thick stone walls of the large family home as she walked back towards Shane who was waiting in the bedroom. "That was Derek. The kids aren't coming home until tomorrow so we have another night together. Just you and I," Jade continued to explain, flashing a cheeky sexy smile in Shane's direction, as her eyes filled with the wicked glint of her provocative intentions.

"Ohh girl," Shane giggled back at her, as Jade leapt onto the bed in a playful pounce of seduction.

The next morning, Shane and Jade awoke early from their peaceful night of slumber and rushed around the home returning the house to a dwelling of the children's accommodation, in their preparation for the children's return from their overnight stay with their father. As Jade stood at the kitchen sink in her rush of tidying the accumulated dishes of the days of which she had spent in indulgence with Shane the telephone that had sat idle on the hallway stand began to ring in an alertness of a caller.

"Ohh. I wonder who that is?" Jade said to herself, slipping her hands out from the protective rubber gloves and hastily walking to the phone to answer the call.

"Hello," Jade answered, placing the phone receiver to her ear. "I know you're seeing someone Jade. I know he's there right now," the acrimonious scowl came through the receiver of the phone.

"Derek. Please don't do this," Jade calmly replied, closing her eyes as her hand reached for the frown of trepidation that began to form within her forehead.

"You're nothing but a bloody little bitch. I hate you, I bloody hate you. I'm not bringing the kids back. They're staying with me and I'm taking them to Meltona. You will never see the kids again," Derek's scowl of treacherous contemptuous poignant of threats filled Jade's ears, before the sound of the circuit of communication was slammed shut in a gestural expression of Derek's hatred.

"No. Derek No. This can't be happening," Jade cried out, falling to her knees at the base of the phone stand, as the perilousness of Derek's words sank under her skin in a stream of tears that soaked her whitened cheeks. "No, no. He's not taking my kids. He's not taking them. What do I do?" Jade cried out again, covering her tear-soaked face with the shakiness of her hands.

Jade believed Derek's threats of revenge of which he had threatened in the previous months, and felt the magnitude of the situation of which had fallen her to her knees and sent her into a state of overwhelming panic. The inconsolable tears of anguish fell from Jade's eyes and ran through the cracks of her fingers as she faced the reality of not being able to see her beloved children, which tore through her in a desperation of incomprehensible despair.

"Baby. What's wrong?" Shane cried out in concern, rushing to her side from out of the bedroom door, falling to his knees beside her and placing his arms around her in a desperate attempt to console the uncontrollable despair of emotions that had gripped her in panic on the hallway floor.

"He's going to take my children. Oh god Shane. He's going to take my children," Jade cried out uncontrollably, through the flood of tears that streamed down her face.

"Derek. Oh god. You've got to go to the police Jade. Now. Look at me baby," Shane replied, looking into Jade's blank swollen eyes awash with the emotions that had rendered her inconsolably incoherent to the world around her. "Jade. Baby. Listen to me please. The police can help you but I can't go with you. I'm sorry but they know me, who I associate with," Shane pleaded, trying desperately to comfort her grief and despair.

But Jade did not respond and sat silently staring and motionless, lost as the panic gripped her mind in its tight tangle of overwhelming precariousness. "Jade. Are you listening?" Shane said again, placing his hands upon her tightly shrugged shoulders in a desperate bid to awaken her from the blankness of her emotional state. "I… Yes… Yes, okay," Jade mumbled back, lifting her tear-soaked stare to meet the concern that had filled Shane's eyes. "Ok, I'll go now. I'll go to the police."

Jade slowly lifted herself off the hallway floor and rose to her feet in a shaken state of uncertainty and began to wipe at the tears that trickled from her swollen eyes and down her flushed cheeks, in a desperate attempt to extinguish the grief that had settled heavily upon her face.

"What do I tell them Shane?" Jade said quietly, raising her swollen eyes to look into his.

"The truth baby. Tell them the truth about what has been happening. They have the text messages that he had sent you threatening this," Shane replied gently, wrapping his arms around her in a tight embrace of comfort.

"Okay. Okay," Jade sobbed, her face buried protectively into Shane's chest.

Without haste Jade rushed to the bathroom and began to wash her face and fix her clothes as Shane walked through the house locking the doors and windows, before both climbing into Shane's car and headed towards the police station that was situated in the centre of Suisania Bay's main shopping centre.

"Jade," Shane called out, as Jade stepped from the doorway of the car. "It's going to be alright, just tell them the truth okay. Give me a call when you are finished and I'll come and pick you up."

Jade just nodded her head in silent compliance as she held onto the tightness that had swollen in her throat and threatened to fall in tears from her eyes once more, before turning around and walking towards the large sliding glass doors of the local police station and approached the long counter at the rear of the front entrance.

"I need to speak to someone please. I need help. My ex-husband," Jade began to explain, but could no longer hold onto the emotional pain that had tightened within her throat and bent her composure into a stream of tears that ran down her cheeks once more.

"Hey, hey," the officer replied in a comforting voice. "It's okay, come through there where we can talk in private," pointing to the locked security door that led towards the privacy of the interrogation rooms situated within the rear of the police station.

Jade stood anxiously waiting at the entrance to the locked security door before being met by the police officer who then guided her towards one of the rooms and sat her at the large office desk in her wait to be questioned by the attending officers.

"I'll be back in a moment okay. It's going to be alright," the officer reassured her, leaving the room and closing the heavy wooden door behind her.

Within minutes of situating Jade at the desk within the safety of the interrogation room, two officers re-entered the room and sat themselves on either side of the desk in their preparation to hear Jade's plea of concern.

"So what is the problem Jade? You seem very upset," one of the officers asked gently, in his suasion of revealing the cause of Jade's anxious, emotional state.

"My ex-husband, Derek is going to run away with my children," leapt out from Jade's mouth, in an emotional outburst of tears, as she covered the display of anxiety with the anguish that ran through the shakiness of her hands.

"He was supposed to bring them home yesterday but he rang me today, abusing me and telling me that he is going to take them away to Meltona and I'll never see them again."

Concern filled the officer's eyes as Jade's words filled his ears and questioned his mind of the legalities and capabilities that surrounded the cause of the discussion, before finally asking Jade the questioning cause of his concern.

"And you think that Derek is capable of this? That he would take the children with him?"

"Yes," Jade answered without haste, dropping her head into the palms of her hands, as the tears continued to flow heavily from her eyes. "I have only just been to court and applied for a restraining order against him which was approved by the judge, but he has already threatened to do this previously within the text messages that he had sent to my mobile phone. It's all written within your reports. It's on your files," Jade continued to explain to the onlooking officer.

Equipped with the required information the officer began to search the legal file banks of the computer that sat on the large office desk within the interrogation room, while Jade awaited anxiously wiping the tears that had swollen her eyes and flushed her cheeks with the softness of the tissues that had been handed to her by the accompanying officer.

"Yes I see. It's all here on file," the investigating officer replied in a calm voice, raising his eyes in concernment once more to meet Jade's, before asking the next line of questioning. "Who has custody of the children Jade?"

"No one. It has all been by our own arrangements. No one has custody," Jade quickly replied, as the questioning fear tangled within the pit of her stomach and sent waves of trepidation through the depths of her mind. "Why?"

Jade's eyes followed the questioning officers eyes across the room as he turned his attention of concernment towards the accompanying officer, who's face had filled with the same look of helplessness and desideratum before returning their attentions back to Jade, who sat anxiously waiting for their reply.

"We can't make him give them back to you Jade. I'm very sorry. But the law states that without a custody order being put in place we do not have the legal power to have the children returned back into your custody. There's not a lot that we can do," the officer explained, reaching his hand across the desk to touch Jade's in a comforting gesture of compassion.

"What. No. Oh god no," Jade sobbed, closing her eyes as the tears of devastation spilt from her eyes and rolled down her whitened cheeks. "He can't take my kids. Please help me, please," Jade pleaded desperately, grasping at the officer's hand that wrapped around hers.

"Okay, okay," the officer replied, rubbing the tension of Jade's tightly gripped fingers that grasped at his in a desperate plea of oppressive disconcertment. "I know you're upset, but calm down okay. Just listen to me Jade. The only thing that we can do is what is called a police stand by. We can come with you to Derek's home and serve the

177

restraining order upon him and ask him to willingly allow the children to be returned back into your custody for the visitation of which you have both agreed upon. But please understand that we cannot forcefully make him comply or remove the children physically from his place of residence. That is our only option without a custody order Jade," the officer continued in his stipulation of the legal ramifications of the precarious situation.

Jade lifted the shakiness of her hand to cover the gasp of trepidation that escaped from her opened mouth, as the hope of retrieving her children from Derek's tight insidious grip drained from her heart and sat heavily in a tangled web of foreboding denouement within the depths of her mind.

Although the police officers had offered a solution in retrieving the children safely back into her custody, Jade knew of the battle that she was about to face, as Derek escalated his revengeful rage of contemptible derogation and inflicted the attack of his damnation upon the vulnerability that lay within her heart, the love of her children.

"Yes. Okay. I am willing to try that," Jade replied in agreement, holding down the apprehension that tightened within her throat. "When?" raising the questioning concernment that swept through her eyes towards the affiliated officers.

"This afternoon. We can get everything organised this morning. What's the time now?" the police officer replied, glancing a look down towards the ticking hands of his watch. "It's 11 am. We will meet you at the address which you have informed us of at 3 pm. That will give us time to put everything in place."

Jade sat anxiously motionless except for the correlation of the nod of her head, as the precariousness of her stare filled the room with an apprehension of silence before shifting her eyes towards the ceiling in a gesture of tentative hopefulness.

"Thank you," Jade replied through the emotional quiver that had filled her voice, rising to her feet from off of the chair and following the accompanying officer back through the corridor towards the locked security door and into the foyer of the police station.

Jade looked tentatively back at the police officer who stood silently behind the counter of the foyer as she felt the tight grip of her apprehension knot within the pit of her stomach and form within the tightness of her throat as she walked out through the large sliding doors of the police station and onto the adjoining footpath in her wait for Shane's arrival.

That afternoon Jade waited patiently alone sitting at the dining room table as she watched the ticking hands of the clock that hang on the kitchen wall, while the unconscionable impact of Derek's words played over and over throughout the depths of her mind and cut deep into the despair that filled her heart, until she could no longer remain still in the overwhelming anxiousness that engulfed her.

"I can't believe you're doing this Derek," Jade said quietly to herself, pacing slowly down the long hallway as the flow of the anxious words spilt from her mouth and filled her eyes with a tentative anguish of despair. "How did it get this bad? Oh god please Derek. Please give them back to me. Don't do this. Oh god Shane, I wish you were here."

Although Jade struggled in the tentative silence of her solitude and longed for the comforting support of Shane standing by her side through the traumatic ordeal, their conversation that morning had bared the true facts of Shane's involvement with the notorious bikie club, which would discredit her position to having her beloved children back in her loving arms and bring harm to her reputation within the small community of Suisania Bay.

After anxiously waiting in a pacing array of fear and dubiousness for what had seemed like an eternity to Jade, the designated taxi driver pulled to a stop along the long narrow footpath that ran adjacent to her house and awaited for her departure to the outskirts of town, to which Derek had set up his new place of residency and was holding her children in his contemptible ransom of threats.

"Oh god. Here we go," Jade muttered under her breath, clutching at her handbag and walking the long hallway to the front door of the family home. "Please god, let my children come home to me," as she closed the front door of her home and climbed into the back seat of the taxi in a stifling slump of silence.

The drive, although only ten minutes away had seemed like the longest distance to travel, as Jade held her heart in her throat and the tension of apprehension in her tightly gripped fists that sat nervously within the tenseness of her lap. Jade did not know what to expect and dreadfully feared Derek's reaction to the involvement of the police, as he had refused and forewarned her in the past of her suggestion of their meeting within the protective cover of the police station on their interchanging of the children's visitations, as their interaction with each other escalated into a warning of confrontational tempestuous rage.

As the taxi driver pulled to a stop alongside the gravel footpath that ran adjacent to Derek's place of residency, Jade sat in breathless silence, as her heart anxiously raced and her mind tangled in its own torment and despair as she glanced towards the front yard of the home of which she knew her children were being held against their will, in her wait for the arrival of the police officer's assistance.

Jade dropped her glance from the anxious fixated stare of the front door of Derek's home and turned her focus back into the confines of the taxi of which she sat anxiously waiting.

She had felt terrible to have to involve the taxi driver, an innocent person in her pursuit to retrieve her children from the acrimonious clutches of Derek's revenge, but had been left in a position of not having a choice or another option, as she had been hampered with the loss of her licence and the ability to allow Shane to show his support during the harrowing incident of which she now faced.

"We have to wait for the police to arrive," finally left the silence of Jade's lips, in a quiet explanation of the desperate situation to the taxi driver. "I am really sorry to have to involve you in this but I'm in a bad situation with my ex-husband and the police are coming to assist me in retrieving my children from his care. They should be here any moment now."

The taxi driver turned his head in acknowledgement and offered Jade a comforting smile of benevolence as he reached his hand forward and switched off the ignition of the car and removed the safety of his seat belt.

"It's okay miss. I can wait with you," the taxi driver replied, reaching for the clip board that sat beside him on the front seat of the vehicle.

"Thank you," Jade replied, mustering a small smile of her appreciation in the taxi driver's direction, as her eyes darted back in a vigilant stare towards the length of the long outskirts road that led to their position in their wait for the police officers to arrive.

"Here they come," Jade nervously announced, as the sight of the oncoming police vehicle came into her view from within the distance and came to a stop along the footpath directly in front of the parked taxi. Jade's eyes darted nervously back towards the direction of Derek's front door as she slowly opened the back door of the taxi and climbed tentatively out from the back seat and onto the footpath to meet the authority of the accompanying police officers.

She could feel the contemptible stare of Derek's eyes permeating from behind the windows within the confines of the locked house and knew the oncoming battle of the uproar of which was about to come, as she followed in the police officer's footsteps along the winding garden path towards the front door of the house.

"Oh god," whispered from the tremble that had filled Jade's lips, the rush of anxiety filling her stomach, tightening in her throat and filling her mind with the daze of foreboding surreality, as her hand reached forward to place a loud knock on the frame of the wooden front door.

Jade lifted her eyes to meet the authoritativeness of the officer's glare that fixated upon the front door of the premise, as the first knock of their arrival had been left unanswered before reaching her hand forward to place another loud knock upon the frame of the wooden door. But still the sound of their arrival had remained unanswered.

"What do we do now?" Jade questioned the officers, her voice trembling with the apprehensive fear of her despair. "It's okay Jade," the male officer replied in a calm stern voice. "We'll take it from here."

Jade's breath held a tight pause within her throat as the police officer approached the door and knocked loudly upon the wooden frame. "Open up sir, it's the police. We're here to see Mr Derek Jones."

As the last words left the male officer's mouth the unlocked click of the wooden front door sounded and the door flew open, slamming against the side wall of the house as Derek charged out in a tempestuous fury towards Jade and the accompanying officers, as the words of his contemptible nature flew from his mouth in a rage of uncontrolled abandonment of disrespect.

"What the fuck are you doing? You little bitch, you bring the cops to my house now," flew from Derek's mouth in a stand over of his pointed finger in Jade's direction.

"Calm down sir," the officer calmly replied, standing his body between Derek's rage and the position of which Jade had remained motionless in her anxious stance. "We're here to serve a restraining order on you. I have the papers here and I believe that you have your wife's children here. Your wife has come to collect them for her time of visitation with them," the officer continued, reaching his hand forward to place the papers of the restraining order into Derek's hand.

"She's not my wife," Derek roared back at the officer, pacing back and forth along the cement of the front path that ran along the perimeter of the front garden of the house. "She's a bloody useless woman who hangs with bikers. She's an unfit mother. She's not getting the bloody kids back."

The flushed colour of Jade's trepidation of despair drained from her face into a ghostly white shade, as the horror of Derek's abusive words and her worst fear unfolded before her in a momentum of tempestuous fury and incomprehensible unambiguity of Derek's refusal to release the children from his tight grip.

"Oh god," Jade cried, placing her hand to her open mouth, as the children came into her view from within the openness of the door. "Oh god, Monique, Cody, boys, come here. Come on, it's time to go home. Come to me please," trembled from her lips in a frightful plea, reaching out her open arms into their direction.

The children stood motionless, unable to move as their faces filled with the stricken confusion and fear of the overwhelming situation of which had caught them in the middle of their loyalty's and love for their parents and fathers tempestuous rage of conflagration.

"Don't you bloody move, kids. You're staying here with me," Derek roared in raging anger, tearing up the papers of the restraining order which he had been handed by the male police officer and throwing the shreds back into the officer's face. "I can't bloody read. This is of no use to me," roaring his lies of denial straight to the officer's face.

"It's a restraining order, sir," the officer replied, holding a stance of stern calmness. "I can read them to you if you have trouble with reading."

The accompanying female officer stood firmly alongside the male officer in disbelief of what she was witnessing in a gesture of silent disgust as she shook her head from side to side before placing her body towards the direction of Jade's standing, which had remained closely guarded by the two officers.

"Come to me please. Monique, Cody, boys, come on," Jade pleaded to her children with open outstretched arms, coaxing them from the frightening standstill of their terrified disposition. "Please kids, come to me." Cody raised his tear-soaked face up to look into his mother's outstretched arms as his small feet stepped backwards and forwards in trepidation within the frame of the open front door, before suddenly dashing past his father through the openness of the door and falling into his mother's arms in a tearful tremble of his tight grasp, quickly followed by the fast tearful dash of his sister.

Tears spilt from Jade's eyes and rolled down her cheeks in an unstoppable flow, as her arms wrapped around her children in a tight embrace of the tremble that ran through their small bodies, as she held them securely against her.

"Get in the taxi okay, it's going to be okay," Jade said to them softly, dropping to one knee and looking up at the fearful confusion that had filled their small faces.

"It's going to be okay. We're going home," Jade said once more, placing a reassuring touch of her hand upon their flushed, tear-stained cheeks. Monique and Cody unlocked their tight grasp from around their mother's waist and without haste ran to the back door of the awaiting taxi and climbed into the back seat in a tight tearful huddle as they awaited for their mother's return.

Jade turned back around to face the sight of her two older boys who's feet danced in fearful agitation along the carpet at the edge of the open doorway while Derek held a vicious stare of oppugnation in her direction as the accompanying officers looked on in a protective stance of authority.

"Boys, come on," Jade pleaded desperately. It's okay. It's okay. It's time to go home."

But James and Nick stood motionless and pale as their tears rolled from their eyes and down their cheeks in a fearful stare of confusion, before returning their glance back into the vicious stare of their father.

"We're staying with dad," finally spilt from Nick's mouth, dropping his tear stained eyes towards the floor. "We're staying Mum. I'm sorry Mum," James and Nick announced in unison, as the heavy flow of tears continued to fall from their eyes.

Jade stood frozen in her stance as her heart sank into her chest and ripped at the unassailable protectiveness with which she had shielded the vulnerability of her children's wellbeing during the continuous onslaught of Derek's oppressive contingency of contemptible revenge. She knew she had lost her boys to the cruelty of Derek's words and were held in the fear of his rage and their decision had not been one of their own to which she had held them to no blame.

Jade dropped her head in a capitulation of conceded sadness before raising her tear-filled eyes back into the view of her despaired children. "It's okay boys, shhh, don't cry okay, don't cry, it's going to be okay," she said desperately, reaching her hand out towards their tear-stained, flushed faces in a gesture of her compassionate consolation. "Oh boys. I'm here for you okay. I'm always here for you," Jade continued through her uncontrollable sobbing of the horrendous grief that tore through her heart as she turned away and focused on the officer that stood alongside of her.

"You can go now Jade. We've got it from here, you can go. Take your children home," the officer informed her, comforting her with a compassionate touch on her shoulder.

"Thank you," Jade replied, her voice filled with the trembling anguish and sadness of the ordeal.

Jade slowly glanced her eyes back into the direction of where James and Nick stood still crying within the entrapment of the open front door. "I love you boys. Don't forget that okay. I love you," before dropping her tear-filled eyes towards the ground and walked away towards the awaiting taxi, climbing into the back seat to place herself between Monique and Cody as her comforting arms formed a tight embrace around their trembling distress of tears.

"We can go now. Please take us home," Jade whimpered to the taxi driver in a quiet, saddened voice, glancing one more time at her distressed children standing in the doorway of their father's home, as the taxi driver turned on the ignition and drove away leaving her two children behind.

On their arrival back home Jade led Monique and Cody outside to sit with her at the large wooden outdoor setting positioned underneath the veranda that ran the length of the home at the back of the house, where they all sat together in motionless tearful silence.

"Come here," Jade said softly, pulling her children into her arms as the tears rolled from their eyes and flowed down their cheeks.

"It's going to be okay," she whispered softly into their ears, wiping away the tears that fell from their eyes. "It's going to be okay."

As they sat silently wrapped in their consolation of their distressed discretion of grief and sorrow Jade heard a car suddenly pull into the long gravel driveway of her home and park at the entrance to the large steel gates at the end of the driveway.

"Oh no," Jade gasped, unwrapping her arms from around her grieving children and jumping to her feet from off the wooden bench setting, as the thought of Derek's returning rampage of dissention rushed through her mind. "Stay here kids," she ordered, hastily walking around to the side of the house in a confrontational stance of courage. Jade's heart thumped hard within her chest as she quickly approached the height of the closed steel gates at the end of the driveway and poked her head over the top to bring into view the sound of the unexpected visitor.

"Ohhh, Shane. It's you," Jade cried out in an apperception of relief, opening the lock of the large steel gates and rushing towards the vehicle that had parked at the end of driveway, falling into the compassion of Shane's arms in a flood of tears as he climbed out from the front seat of his car.

"Oh god Shane. It was terrible. Derek went ballistic. He lost it, right there and then in front of the officers, pacing back and forth as he ripped up the restraining order and threw it back in their faces," Jade explained, the words flying from her mouth in a quick recapitulation of the awful truth.

"And I. I couldn't get James and Nick back. They wouldn't come with me. Derek wouldn't let them go," Jade wept, falling back into Shane's arms, burying her tear-stained face into the comfort of his chest.

"It's over now baby, it's all over," Shane said quietly, wrapping his arms tightly around her and kissing her softly upon the top of her head. "Baby I'm here. I'm here."

That day Jade introduced Shane to her daughter and her youngest son but it had remained in an introduction of an uncomfortable silence and blank stares as the day's horrific events held them in a disposition of shock and despair, a situation of which Shane had held no previous experience as he had remained childless throughout his years.

Over the following weeks, although Shane's lack of experience with being within a family unit of children had rendered him ill-equipped to the orientations of a family life, he had adjusted and adapted well into the role of providing a home of stability and support as he whole-heartedly embraced the children into his life and showed them love as if they were of his own.

182

A week after the horrific distress of that unconscionable day of Derek's vindictive tribulation of rage, Jade received an unexpected distressing phone call from her son, Nick.

"Mum, Dad has decided to move to Meltona and we are going to go with him. We're moving there in one week's time."

Jade placed her hand to her forehead as she felt the foreboding sadness of the realisation of her son's words as they rushed through her mind and sank her heart into her chest in a momentary speechless silence of heartbreak.

"Is that what you really want to do sweetheart?" finally left Jade's lips, in a quietened quiver of the sadness that had filled her heart. "You can always stay here with me you know."

"Yes Mum, I know," Nick replied in a soft voice. "But James and I are going with dad okay. Dad will bring us in on Wednesday so that we can spend the day with you, Monique and Cody and to collect our things and to say goodbye. Dad would like to see Monique and Cody to say goodbye as well when he comes to pick us back up."

Jade stood silent in a momentary pause before finally answering, as she felt the apprehension rush through her and wrap around her in tight grip of trepidation, as the protectiveness of her two remaining children reeled in a mistrust of Derek's true intentions of being within the company of her two youngest children. Although she agreed to Derek's wishes of being able to say goodbye to his children, she was wracked in the overwhelming fear of her doubts and did not trust that he would possess the integrity to not take the children with him and could not take the risk of allowing him access to Monique and Cody on the imminence of that foreboding day.

That Wednesday Derek arrived at the front of Jade's house at the designated time of the arrangement of which she had made with Nick on the day of the phone call, and kept a comfortable distance sitting out in the parked car along the footpath as James and Nick climbed out of the car and entered the front door of the family home.

Although Jade had hidden her sorrow and heartbreak well under her persona of perfunctory as she spent her time that day in the mellifluous flow of their laughter and smiles, deep inside of her soul she knew that this time would not be their last time together and that their return home into her loving embrace would be imminent. Jade had not allowed Monique and Cody to remain in the presence of the family home that day and had hidden the truth from them that their father and brothers had made the decision to move to another state which they would not be permitted to visit until she had required the legal rights of gaining custody of her two youngest children out of her fear of Derek's vengeful contemptible tactics of provocation. Although she had felt the ramifications of the magnitude of the guilt of her decision to not allow her children to say goodbye to their father and brothers, Jade had felt that her over-protectiveness was warranted and justified in the height of the conflict that had surrounded itself around the tumultuous situation that had raged out of control between herself and their father.

That evening Jade held her two sons within the loving embrace of her arms in a statable immensity as her tear-filled eyes absorbed their smiles and the warmth and smell of their skin imprinted upon her memory and sunk deep within her soul as she kissed them goodbye for the last time.

Jade felt the tears that had welled within her eyes fall and run down her cheeks in sorrowful pain that cut deep into her heart as she watched her two sons walk from her arms and disappear into the distance with their father, not knowing when or if she would ever see them again.

She had not wanted to allow her two sons to leave the vicinity of Suisania Bay or her loving embrace but had been rendered helpless by their decision as they were now deemed of age within the legalities of the custody orders which had made the choice to leave the township with their father one of their own.

That night once Monique and Cody had been tucked snugly into their beds and the house had fallen into solitary silence, Jade lay down upon the covers of her bed and released the sorrow that had been held within her strengths in front of the children and cried until her tears could fall no more and she finally fell into a heartbroken slumber.

Within the next two months in the absence of her two eldest children, Jade's heart had started to once again feel the warmth of her healing as she settled into her new life with Shane and her two remaining children whom she had been deemed custody of which had offered her a comfort of relief and stability within the family unit. Jade had sincerely apologised profusely and explained to Monique and Cody of the circumstances that had surrounded her decision in keeping them safe within the secrecy of her knowledge of their father and brothers' departure from the small township of which they had called home, which had been received with understanding and returned them to their innocent state of joyful, playful children within the family home. Although Jade had remained in constant contact with James and Nick and rang to hear their voices which sung a beautiful tone to her heart, she also suffered the heart-wrenching sorrow of her longing to once again hold her children in the loving embrace of her mother's love, which drowned her in tears with each phone call. The restraining order which she had sought after the tempestuous abusive events which she had suffered on that day of Derek's unannounced arrival on her doorstep, had stood to be one of a blessing as his constant abuse and demands faded into a subsequence of silence and peacefulness within her new life.

Her relationship with Shane had blossomed and grown into a commitment of love and affection as his decision to leave the remoteness of his employment at the mines site enabled them to remain close to one another and form their union of commitment upon his return to the township of Suisania Bay every weekend. Jade longed for the weekends when she could return to the affections of Shane's loving embrace and had admired his ability to adjust to the conformity of living life with her two small children and provide love and stability within the family which he now called his home. Jade watched on in joy as Shane and Cody formed a special connection with one another and lavished in the quality time spent together on Shane's return to the family home.

Although Jade had continued with her tenacious drive of ambition with her continual research into the field of her business, enrolling in courses to acquire the adequate skills required to bring her business plan into one of a developed and established business within the township, she had been accepted into the field of dentistry as a dental assistant and was committed to a four day roster where she had been placed into the responsible role of opening and closing of the busy dental clinic.

Although Shane had continued with his devotion of returning to the family home every weekend the couple had not made plans for their time spent together until the weekend when Jade had received a surprise phone call from Shane during the week announcing that he had made special arrangements for their union, which required the assistance of her parents to have her two youngest children within their care.

Jade's excitement and curiosity of intrigue grew with Shane's surreptitious silence of the planned details which he had gone to elaborate lengths to conceal and plan without her knowledge and had left her with an anticipated enthusiasm as the weekend drew near. Although Jade's parents had informed her that they no longer had the desire to care for small children in their denial of her previous requests of accepting her children into their lives along with their acceptance of her siblings' children of whom they had regular contact with she made the phone call of request to her mother with baited breath.

"Hey mum," Jade greeted merrily, as her mother answered the phone. "I was just wondering if you were able to look after the kids this weekend? Shane wants to take me away somewhere special and."

Before the last words had left her mouth, she was quickly interrupted by her mother's voice of congruity. "Yeah sweetheart, we're not busy this weekend. I'd love to have the kids."

Jade's mouth dropped open slightly in surprise before forming into a shimmering smile that spread across her face as the unexpected words of agreement sank in and rendered her momentarily speechless in her appreciation. "Really. Brilliant, thanks so much Mum," Jade finally answered gratefully.

As Jade continued in her arrangement of details with her mother for the weekend of Shane's surprise getaway together, she could feel the excitement build inside of her and shine through her eyes in permeated exuberance of anticipation.

That night as they talked on the phone Jade informed Shane of her mother's approval of having the children for the weekend which took them to an exuberant level of anticipated excitement as they went about making the final details for the surprise weekend getaway.

As the busy days of the end of the week slowly trickled past in Jade's anticipation of the weekend, finally the day came. Jade busied herself packing her suitcase and organising the children's belongings to pack for their weekend with their grandparents before sitting down to patiently wait in her eagerness for Shane's arrival that evening. While Jade waited patiently sitting on the patio setting that sat under the covers of the back veranda sipping at a can of pre-mixed bourbon, her mind wandered into the questioning thoughts of Shane's secrecy of surprise.

"Where are you taking me Mr, hmm?" Jade whispered to herself, as a questioning giggle escaped from between her lips.

At five pm Jade finally heard the familiar sound of Shane's car pull to a halt at the end of her driveway and leapt to her feet off the patio setting chair with an excited smile that spread across her face and danced through the movement of her hurried steps as she rushed through the house to the front door in her greeting of the man she had fallen in love with.

"Baby," Jade greeted with excitement as she opened the front door and wrapped herself around Shane who stood on the other side of the opened door. "Okay where are you taking me?" Jade continued with bubbly jubilation, placing her soft moist lips against his in a kiss of affection and excitement.

Shane giggled, placing his forehead against hers looking deep into her eyes with a smile. "Ah ha. You'll just have to wait my beautiful girl. It's a surprise," placing his lips against hers in a teasing soft kiss. Jade smiled cheekily as her inquisitive mind ran circles in thought and threw questions of suggestions into her vocabulary to entice the concealed secret out from under Shane's tightly shut lips.

"Shane. Shane's here Monique," Cody called out from within the confines of the loungeroom walls, his feet flying to the floor in an eagerness of excitement as he ran to greet Shane who had entered through the opened front door of the house.

"Hey Cody," Shane greeted back enthusiastically with a smile, as Cody wrapped his arms around him in an affectionate hug.

"We're going to nanna and pops for the weekend," Cody continued in his excitement, his mouth spilling the words at a fast pace.

"I know mate. I know," Shane replied, giggling at the youngster's joviality.

"Where are you and Mum going?" Cody continued to question.

"Ahh. Well that's a surprise mate. Not even your Mum knows that," Shane answered, smiling down at the young face staring up at him.

Within minutes of Shane's arrival, Jade gathered the suitcases and her belongings that sat waiting on the loungeroom floor and handed them to Shane who neatly packed them into the space within the back section of his four-wheel-drive and they were soon on the highway heading towards the township of Copper Cove of which Jade's parents resided.

After allowing enough time to stay to enjoy a coffee and a quick chat with Jade's parents, Shane and Jade said their farewells, climbed back into the car and headed for the highway that led out of the township towards Alterro and the undisclosed destination of Shane's surprise.

"Okay, come on. You've got to tell me Shane. Where are we going?" Jade continued in her inquisitive line of questioning, flashing him an enticing smile as the suspense of the surprise ran circles of curiosity within her mind. Shane grinned a cheeky grin as a giggle escaped from his lips before finally answering the question that kept leaping from Jade's mouth.

"I'm taking you to Vincent Point. You've always said you really like it there and wanted to go again someday. So this weekend, we're going," he finally revealed in his concealment of his conception.

"Ohh yesss," Jade applauded in her excitement, clapping her hands playfully and lurching sideways to kiss Shane on the lips. "You're brilliant. Mmm I love you."

A flashy smile spread across Shane's face as he joyfully watched the childish enthusiasm of excitement which he had evoked within his woman and sat proud in his achievement of placing a smile on the face of the woman that he had fallen in love with, after she had suffered such a horrendous ordeal with the aftermath of the separation of her marriage and the segregation of her children.

"I love you too baby," Shane replied, touching her gently on the hand in a gestural expression of affection.

As the couple drove the four-hour drive along the highways towards their destination of Vincent Point they continued in their garrulousness of swapping funny stories and laughter at their inappropriate behaviour of the past times with their friends and places of which they had been throughout their years.

As the couple entered the town, situated only two hours from Vincent Point they deviated off the highway to come to a stop at the local bottle drive-thru where they purchased a bottle of red wine for Jade to enjoy whilst they continued on their travels along the highway to their final destination.

Jade popped the cork from the bottle of wine and poured the beverage into the plastic wine tumblers that they had purchased in the local town in an excitement of enjoyment and giggles as they pulled the car into a secluded landing to enjoy the freshly packed cone piece of marijuana of which they joyfully shared together.

"Look. Fit for a queen," Jade joked and laughed, holding the plastic wine tumbler in the air in Shane's direction. Shane's face broke into a large smile as the laughter left his mouth at the playful uninhibited antics that they conversed upon. With each separating mile along the vast highway that sent waves of calmness and tranquillity blowing through the winds of the open car window which sailed through the lengths of Jade's long blond hair and swept along the soft contours of her cheeks, Jade could feel the accumulation of the acrimonious treachery of Derek's rampage slide out from within the depths of her disposition as her natural ebullience flowed through her in a wave of giggles and smiles.

Jade could feel the excitement illuminate her face as the car steered off the highway and drove into the vicinity of the township of Vincent Point and followed the populated winding streets of the town to the secluded parking bay that was situated behind the hotel, of which Shane had booked their stay for the special weekend which he had secretly planned.

"So this is what you had planned hey," Jade said, smiling at Shane as they gathered their luggage from out of the back section of the four-wheel-drive and walked towards the entrance of the reception area of the hotel. After signing into the reception desk and collecting the keys to their room, Shane and Jade hurried back to the secluded parking bay area behind the hotel and climbed the long, narrow staircase that led to the upstairs area of the hotel rooms.

"Ohhh, this is nice," Jade said, smiling as they entered the vicinity of their hotel suite and started to explore the basic layout of the amenities. "Oooo. A spa bath," Jade cooed, giggling as she flashed the twinkle that had entered her eyes into the direction of Shane's standing. Jade walked out from the bathroom and headed towards the large sliding glass doors which led to the outside area of the room and slid them open to reveal the surprise which Shane had kept hidden from her. "Ohhh. Yesss. Oh Shane, this is awesome," Jade cooed back through the room, standing on the wooden decking of the rooms private balcony overlooking the swirling waves of the open sea that spread along the distance of the surrounding foreshore.

"You like," Shane replied smiling, as he stepped out onto the wooden decking of the balcony and placed his arms affectionately around her waist.

"Yes I do. Very much," Jade answered in an affectionate whisper, as the couple stood together in each other's arms admiring the glistening views of the sun-soaked ocean.

"It's perfect," Jade smiled and giggled, placing a soft kiss against the warmth of Shane's cheek. "I can't believe you did this for me. You're the best baby. I love you," wrapping her arms tighter around Shane's waist and placing a soft kiss against his lips.

"I love you too baby. Let's just enjoy our weekend together hey. Let's just relax," Shane replied, reciprocating the softness of Jade's affections. Jade smiled in her moment of joyous contentment before turning to face Shane in her suggestion of the night's adventure of pleasurable indulgences.

"What do you say to us going for a walk down to the local restaurant to get some dinner and a nice bottle of wine then coming back here to enjoy? Then if you would like, we could do a little of that," Jade suggested flashing a cheeky sexual grin as she pointed to the small bag of the drugs that lay displayed upon the bedside cupboard that had been removed from within the concealment of Shane's luggage. "Then we could have a spa together and well," Jade continued, tipping her head slightly, covering the devilish giggle that had escaped from her mouth with her hand.

"Yesss," Shane giggled in his reply, "Good suggestion baby," before gathering their things and heading out of the hotel door and towards the location of the local restaurant.

Although Shane and Jade enjoyed the socialization of their friends within the notorious bikie clubhouse, their connection within their relationship had transcended them into a realm of isolated pleasures and enjoyment of each other's company, with the exception of the nights of which Jade had chosen to venture into the night-time venues of the local township to enjoy the invigorating loud music and dancing amongst the mass of revellers. But this weekend Shane and Jade's focus had become about them and the pleasurable solidarity that they had created within their own world of familiarity with each other and had chosen to isolate themselves away from the prying eyes and attentions of the outside world.

On returning from the local township's restaurant that was situated within walking distance from the hotel room the couple returned and positioned themselves at the small table and chairs that adorned the small balcony, and began to enjoy the meal and the chilled bottle of wine that they had purchased, before indulging in the intoxicating pleasures of the ecstasy pills that had remained untouched upon the bedside cupboard.

"Oh Shane this is just brilliant," Jade said smiling in her joyful admittance, turning her face away from the beautiful sunset that sat above the rolling waves that crashed softly against the white line of the sandy foreshore to look into Shane's eyes.

"It is baby. I just want you to be happy," Shane replied, standing from the chair and placing a kiss upon her lips before gathering the empty plates and wine glasses and disappearing back inside the hotel room.

"Here baby," Shane said upon his return to the balcony where Jade had remained seated, reaching his out-stretched hand towards hers and placing one of the little white pills into her open palm.

"Oooo, thanks baby," Jade replied, flashing a cheeky smile at Shane before placing the little white pill upon her tongue and swallowing as she sat back against the back rest of the chair to continue in her momentary delight of absorbing the breathtaking view of the night's setting skies.

As Shane and Jade continued in their delight of enjoying the fabulous views of the open rolling sea and the sounds of the township springing to life beneath them, Jade felt the intoxication of the illicit drug flow through the depths of her mind and sweep her up in to a world of fabricated beauty and bright lights that lined the townships cliff edges and danced and swayed in her vision in the gentle sea breeze.

Intoxicated and brimmed with joyous exhilaration Jade's garrulousness of laughter, energy and cheekiness escalated into an impetuous display of suggestive provocative affection.

"Mmm. Come here you," slipped from Jade's mouth with a confidence of desire, placing a deep passionate kiss against Shane's lips. "Mm. I want you baby," Jade whispered. "Right here on the balcony."

Jade positioned her chair next to Shane's and slowly, provocatively started to raise the hem line of the sheer weighted fabric of her little summer dress up the length of her tanned, smooth thighs, stopping just below the little white triangle of the silk of her panties, as her eyes ablaze with the enticement of her desires flashed in temptation in Shane's direction. "Come here baby," she tempted, smiling and raising her hand towards Shane, curling one finger in a seduction of her demands.

"Ohh. You naughty girl," Shane replied, smiling and giggling at her temptation as he slowly raised from his chair to nestle snugly on his knees between her smooth opened thighs.

Shane slid his hands down the length of the sheer fabric that sat tightly against the soft curves of Jade's body, until his fingertips had reached the silky laced fabric of Jade's panties and slid his fingers under the fabric to pull them aside to reveal the soft protruding lips of her wanton desire.

"Mmm," Jade moaned softly, placing her hand upon the top of Shane's head and slowly pushing him down towards the place of her pleasuring. "Ohh, yes," Jade moaned again, tilting her head back slowly and closing her eyes as she felt the first thrust of his warm moist tongue touch against the wanton heat between her legs. "Mmm more," raising her long smooth legs to wrap them around his shoulders as she enjoyed the exotic sensations of the pleasures of his tongue that thrust and lapped at her erect clitoris.

"Yes, like that, oh god more, yes," Jade moaned, as she felt the pleasurable sensations of Shane's fingers move slowly in and out of the moist depths of her desire.

As the erotic sensations sent an uncontrollable desire of sexual wickedness throughout Jade's body and mind, she slowly reached her hands down to lift Shane's face up from between the moist pleasures of the heat that rose from between her legs and pulled him to a standing position behind her against the railings of the small wooden balcony. "Let's go all the way baby. Right here, right now," Jade demanded, through the huskiness of the sexiness that had a blazed within the tone of her voice.

"You are so bad girl," Shane said quietly against her cheek, undoing the fastenings to his jeans and sliding the heavy fabric down his thighs to reveal the height of his arousal.

Jade grasped the balcony railings tightly, closing her eyes as a pleasurable moan escaped from her mouth with the first slow push of Shane's hardened desire until he had nestled his length deep inside her moist wanton erotica of sexual exploration.

"Ohhh, yes, yes," Jade gasped, as Shane's sexual pleasure intensified into a lustful hard rhythmic motion, gripping her hips tighter and thrusting faster and faster with every moan that escaped from her lips. "Ohh yesss. That's it, fuck me, fuck me hard," Jade moaned louder from the depths of her insatiable lustful desire as her eyes looked down upon the populated laden streets below. "Ohh, that's it, more, more," escaped through the loud deep breaths of her sexual lust, as her fingers reached down between her legs, stroking and touching the erectness of her excitement through the silky fabric of her panties. "Oh god. Yes. Yes," Jade moaned louder in an emancipated expression of the wild sexual excitement of their lust as she watched the oblivious crowds walk the long-paved streets below them. "Oh god yes. Ohhh," Jade moaned again, as the rush of her orgasm sent waves of pulsating moistened pleasure throughout the length of her body and down her opened inner thighs.

"Oh god, me too baby," Shane moaned in a subsequence of heightened sexual ecstasy, his hands gripping her hips tighter, as the intensity of his orgasm pulsated in a rhythmic saturation over the firm roundness of her buttocks and trickled down the length of her naked thighs.

"Mmm," Jade moaned softly, smiling in her satisfaction, as their half-naked bodies pressed together in a momentary mould of satisfied sexual pleasure.

"I'm going to have a shower baby," Jade whispered, turning her face towards Shane and placing a soft kiss upon his moist lips before lowering the hem line of her dress and stepping back through the large sliding glass doors into the private confinement of the hotel bathroom.

The next morning Shane and Jade arose from their deep slumber in an excited eagerness to explore the small township's various attractions of entertainment, and quickly consumed the assorted delectable flavours of their morning meal before rushing from the solidarity concealment of their hotel room to join the crowds that had gathered upon the streets below.

As the couple wandered the streets weaving in and out through the mass of the gathered crowds in their enjoyment of the many different sites and sounds of the populated beachside township and the many sideshows and rides of the assorted entertainments of the local amusement park and attractions, Jade had noticed the enticing lights of the local night-time venues.

"Oooo baby. Can we go there tonight?" Jade questioned excitedly in her suggestion. "I can go dancing," she continued with a cheeky smile and a wiggle of her hips.

"Hmm. I don't think that would be a good idea baby," Shane answered apprehensively.

"Why?" Jade asked, dropping her eyebrows into a small frown of bewilderment.

Shane explained that although he held an understanding of Jade's excitement to join the exhilarating exuberance of the brightly coloured extravaganza of loud music and rhythmic dance, his hesitance had been drawn from the unfamiliarity of the locals population and held fear that they may step into troubled waters from the threat of a rival motorcycle gang, which would render him defenceless against an attack without the backing of his allied members from within the well-known establishment of their own local clubhouse in Suisania Bay.

"Oh, I understand," Jade replied, smiling and placing a soft kiss upon his cheek. "It's okay. I'm sure we can find something to do back in the hotel room. We do have a spa," Jade continued, flashing a little devilish smile in his direction, softly nudging up against him and placing her hand in his as they continued in their wander through the township's attractions.

That night upon their return to the hotel room after enjoying the succulence of their evening meal at the township's local restaurant, Shane retrieved the small bag of the white powdery substance that had laid untouched within the concealment of his luggage and proceeded to prepare the white powder upon the glass top fixture of the bedside cupboard.

That night Jade had her first taste of the bitter sweet rush of the hardened narcotic of cocaine, a rush that hit her senses in a tantalising enticement of an emancipated elevation of arousable delight.

Over the next two weeks, Shane had remained with Jade in the township of Suisania Bay as his new employment which he had obtained within the vicinity of Alterro, which had been contracted as a seasonal position, had drawn to a close with the completion of the job's specifications.

Jade had wholeheartedly welcomed Shane's stay as her responsibilities with her employment within the dental profession had held her in the responsible position of long hours and had found the reversed order of Shane's involvement and willingness within her home and with her children to be that of a godsend.

One night Jade arrived home exhausted from the long busy hours that she had spent upon her feet rushing to and fro from patient to patient within the popular local dental clinic, and sat upon the end of her bed with Shane as the days business washed away with a chilled can of bourbon in the arms of her lover.

"Baby, I've been thinking," Shane said, dropping his head slightly and turning to face Jade in a questionable discretion. "I might throw my job in in the city and move here permanently. What do you think?"

Jade's eyes stared into Shane's as her mind slipped into a momentary pause of appealing questionable definition.

"Where would you live baby?" she finally asked, reaching her hand out in a comforting assurance upon his shoulder.

"Well," Shane began in his reply. "I was thinking that maybe we could live together or if."

"Live together?" Jade abruptly interrupted, pausing for a moment in her denouement.

"Well. Umm. Yes. If it would be alright with you?" Shane replied, studying the questionable pause that had spilled out from Jade's mind and showed upon her face.

"Well. Yes. Of course that would be okay," she finally answered, the dubious thoughts dissenting from within her mind and from the gesticulation of her face and being replaced with a smile of a welcoming reciprocation.

Jade looked on in smiling excitement as she watched Shane's face fill with the smile of ebullience of her acceptance of his permanent presence within the family home. "Excellent baby. Excellent," Shane finally said through his smile, reaching his strong arms out to wrap tightly around her in an embrace of joviality. "When would you like to do this?" Jade questioned, pulling herself back from out of his tight embrace to look into Shane eyes.

"Well I was thinking that maybe I could move in this weekend. What do you think?" Shane asked.

"Yes. I think yes," she replied with a smile.

Although Jade had agreed to the transitional shift within the boundaries of their long distant relationship, the surreptitious nights of the erotic sexual fantasia of intimacy that she shared with her online lover flowed into her mind in a guilty array of subsequence. Jade knew that the her involvement in the intimate affair that she shared with Max was of a sinful consequence if the truth had ever been revealed, and now faced the contemplation of the written words of her world of fantasy and that of the reality that she now shared within her relationship with Shane, and felt torn in her commitments between the two men of whom she had fallen deeply in love with.

On the Friday morning, Shane and Jade awoke early in their excitement of their transition into the new aspects of the consummation of their relationship, and eagerly drove the long distance along the vast highway to collect Shane's belongings and in the introduction of Jade and her children to the extension of her prospective new family of in-laws.

Jade smiled in her anticipated excitement of meeting Shane's mother and stepfather for the first time as the family made its way along the open highway towards the outskirts of Shane's family home.

Jade had listened intently many times to Shane's many words of expressed admiration for his mother, which had held a high appeal of impressive comfort within herself of Shane's love and dedication to the welfare and care of his mother.

Upon their arrival Jade and her children followed Shane nervously along the narrow concrete path that led to the back door of the house and into the confines of the home's kitchen where they were greeted by Beverly and Dylan with a welcoming smile and a warm embrace.

"Hi," Jade replied, smiling, placing herself in the kitchen chair directly across from the direction of Shane's mother. As Shane rummaged through the family home gathering the contents of his belongings, Jade, Monique and Cody happily engaged in the joyful conversant of the small talk that gathered between them at the kitchen table, which held an air of comfortable reciprocation and an impressive warmth as the introduction changed into a welcoming flow of laughter and acceptance of their presence within the family. As the day drew upon the early hours of the evening, Shane packed his collected belongings into the open section of the back of the vehicle before returning to the kitchen in the gathering of farewells to his parents before the family began the long journey back along the open highway in their return to the small town of Suisania Bay in the anticipated exaltation of their new life together.

As the new formation of the families convergence shifted into a smooth transition of happiness and joyful togetherness over the beginning days that quickly turned into weeks, Shane and Jade flourished in their roles of responsibility to Monique and Cody and revelled in their un-disciplinary rebellious activities of their insatiable appetite of the fast thrills and excitement of their sexual lust and partaking in the excessive consumption of alcohol and illicit drugs, behind the secrecy of their closed doors whilst not in the presence of the children.

Although Shane's presence within the family home had altered the assiduity of the intimate predisposition that she had been sharing with her online lover, the intensity of the love and the infatuation that she had felt in the depths of her heart had driven her to an alteration of secrecy and had begun to secretly write to Max within the hours of the day whilst Shane was absent from the family home.

One morning upon his return from his obligational designated shift of his role as a prospect to the clubhouse of the motorcycle gang , Jade was gently awoken in the early hours of the morning from her night of peaceful slumber, greeted with a warm smile and a freshly brewed cup of coffee as Shane sat down upon the bed beside her.

"Good morning baby," Jade said softly, stretching her arms out from beneath the warmth of the blankets and placing her sleepy head against the comforting warmth of Shane's chest. "How was your night?"

"Good baby, yeah good. Much better now that I am home with you though," Shane replied, placing a gentle kiss upon her forehead. "But"

Jade's eyes furrowed into a questioning stare as she heard the dubitative tone of Shane's words which sparked a level of concern within her mind.

"What's wrong baby, what's happened?" Jade questioned, raising from her rested position upon his chest in her attentive omniscient of inquisitive concern.

"No, no, nothing's happened. Everything is alright. It's just that," Shane replied, pausing momentarily as he placed a comforting hand upon her shoulder before continuing in his explanation. "I think that I may have had enough of my obligation to the club that's all. I need to concentrate on finding a job and it's too much working all hours and then having to fill my shift at the club. It's just not for me."

Jade sat up straight in her concerned listening, as she remembered the conversations of which they had shared upon the early days of their introduction to each other. As the words swept in in a flow of remembrance of his concerns of the time restraints that the club had placed upon his devotion to his working life and that of his personal preferences of forming a life for himself outside of the club's obligations, her eyes darted back and forth in questioning detail in her comprehension of his decision.

"I remember baby. I remember us talking about this when we had only just met," Jade replied. "You had mentioned then that the work load had been too much for you which had made you feel as if you could not fill your obligation and that you would let down the other members, Ryan. So you still feel the same?" she continued in her questioning, placing her hands into the soft warmth of his.

Although Jade had understood Shane's concerns at the time of their first conversation she had persuaded him in a suasion of her loyalty to Ryan and that of the clubhouse to remain within the role of his obligation in a temporal transition of the changes of which had occurred within the spaces of his working and personal life.

"Well baby, if that's what you really want to do, the choice is yours," Jade replied, offering a reassuring view of her support to his decision.

"But we can still go there, can't we?" she asked, questioning the onset of the outcome of his decision.

"Yeah, of course we can," Shane replied quickly in a return of reassurance to Jade's concerns. "That's not going to change."

"When are you thinking of doing this?" Jade questioned once more, placing the empty coffee cup upon the bedside cupboard and quickly focusing her attentions back into the direction of the discussion.

"In a few months, I'll get my job first," Shane replied. "That way I'll have an excuse. It will be easier that way," Shane replied in a confident conversance of affirmation.

Jade's face flowed into a smile of unconcerned relief as Shane's words assured her that it would not impact upon them in a compromising position of their loyalty to the club and compromise the friendships of importance of which they had made, as their life unfolded into a conformity of normality within the boundaries of the new life of which they had begun to form together.

Over the next coming weeks Shane and Jade basked in the transitional joy of the change of conformity of which they had formed within the family home and found contentment in the enjoyment of each other's company, as their relationship flourished into a tight bond of commitment and the imminence of Shane's decision drew upon them in a compaction of concealed secrecy.

One weekend whilst sitting in the dispersion of the massed crowd amongst the members of the clubhouse in the early hours of the quite morning's sun, Jade suddenly felt the unexpected intangible consciousness of a shift in Shane's disposition of which she had held a trusting obliviousness to, as she watched over the interaction of which he was immersed in with a younger woman that frequented the clubhouse.

Upon her return from the entertaining laughter of the interaction that she had been sharing with Ryan outside of the confines of the clubhouse, whilst Shane had remained seated at the long wooden bar of which they had been enjoying the last few hours of the uninhibited freedom of their personal indulgence, Jade stopped frozen in her step as her eyes drew upon the inappropriate behaviour that portrayed itself within the view of her unexpected return.

"You have beautiful eyes," Shane whispered quietly across the bar to the young woman who sat closely, flattered in the flirtation of his forbidden attention.

Jade's mouth dropped open in astonishment as the whispered words entered her mind and glared her eyes into a stance of disgust and anger, before placing her hands upon her hips in a prominence of confrontation.

"What's going on Shane?" Jade questioned unambivalently, stepping sternly in her glare towards them. "Oh hey baby," Shane answered quickly, as the unexpected exposure of their flirtation darted their eyes into a parting of their forbidden seduction.

"Don't hey baby me," Jade snapped back angrily in disgust. "I heard what you said to her. So that's your pick up line huh? You said that to me when we first met."

"Calm down," Shane snapped back at her, raising to his feet in his defence from off of the bar stool. "Nothing's going on for fuck's sake girl. I'm just talking."

Jade stood furious in her silent glare, engulfed in the shocked disappointment of the man that she had believed had held her heart on a pedestal and intentions of loyalty and devotion to her and her children had been placed upon a level of the highest importance.

As Jade placed herself upon the stool at the bar beside Shane's side she fell into the deafening silence of the awakening of her own awareness as the events of the night played a role of alarmism of his womanising ways within the depths of her mind. She had heard the whispers of the seduction and had seen the guilt held within the compunction of expression upon the young woman, Tracey, as her eyes had lifted from the isolated indulgence of their flirtation as Jade had entered the bar.

That night as Jade followed Shane from the doors of the notorious clubhouse dwellings her mind swirled and tangled with the questioning deceptions of Shane's disingenuous behaviour that had been displayed before her over the period of their fast whirlwind of romance and drug-fuelled excitement of their unconscionable sexual appetite, as the seduction of her vulnerable naiveness of gullibility led her into a world of the oblivious and obscurity.

As Jade lay down beneath the covers of her bed with Shane that night she heard the ring tone of her mobile phone as a message entered the surreptitious data banks of her private number.

"Hmm, who could that be at this time of night?" Jade questioned, reaching for her phone off the bedside cupboard next to her. "It's Tracey. Oh my," Jade mumbled quietly, arching her brows into a furrow and placing her hand to her mouth as she read the message out aloud and watched as a wave of emasculated jealousy spread across Shane's face, as Tracey, her friend of whom had joined ranks amongst her group of party followers of the local night time dance venue chased for the phone number of another member of the clubhouse.

"She's asking for Jarred's phone number," Jade whispered. "I can't give her that, I'm not allowed to. And what about Katie. She'd be furious. Oh my," Jade whispered again, before silencing in the bewildering ambiguousness of the moment.

Jade's mind darted back and forth, racing between the unconscionable question of Tracey's request and of that of which she had seen held within the reaction of Shane's expression as the words of the message left her mouth. "What is going on here?" Jade whispered silently within the concealed depths of her mind.

That night Jade refused Tracey the discloser of the phone number as she had known of Jarred's relationship which he had formed with Katie and the law of secrecy that surrounded the clubhouse's forbiddance to disclose any of the member's phone numbers to anyone without their permission, and closed her eyes in a whirl of unguarded mistrust.

Over the next couple of weeks, Jade had remained unsettled and puzzled in her startling attentions towards the revelation of Shane's unusual behaviour, which now had become prominent and pronounced in the many phone calls and text messages of which he had regularly received from many different woman. Although Shane had revealed within his confession that the phone calls and messages that he had been receiving had been from only woman, he had informed her and assured her that it was of a upstanding behaviour of innocence, as the woman had been that of close family relations and that of a friend of whom he had grown close to whilst living within the confines of seclusion within another state, but still Jade had remained suspicious and dubious and had begun to question his intentions.

Jade sat still and silent day after day in her remembrance of the conversations of which she had shared with Ryan of Shane's previous involvement with a woman of whom he had been engaged to and adored in the midst of his younger years, which had held the destruction of betrayal and the damage to his faith in love. She had listened to Shane's stories of numerous lovers and involvement with prostitutes which had offered him the physical contact of which he had sexually desired and released him from the commitment of an emotional connection of which he had held subsequent incessant fear.

She had listened to his tale of the one night stand of which he had had with a woman of which until the night of their second meeting had remained a secret quiet affair of a night of lust, which held the suspicions of a pregnancy wrapped in surreptitious speculation upon his sight of the roundness that protruded from the loose fitting top that hung over her stomach of the unborn child. Shane had stood motionless in a state of shock and equivocal questioning as he stood in the face of his sinful night of passion until finally the words left his lips.

"Is that mine?"

Although the woman had explained that whilst in the midst of a separation from her then fiancé she had ran into the arms of a lover on that sinful night, she had assured Shane that the child that she was now carrying had been that of her fiancé's as they had impassioned their relationship once more and had now become husband and wife and were expecting the birth of their first child.

But Jade had found the story to carry an air of speculation as the last comments on Shane's lips ran through her mind in an inconclusive subsequence of suspicion.

"But who knows, there could be a little Shane junior out there. I just have not been told about it." Jade had found the comment humorous and had giggled at the time of the admission, but now hung in the balance of remaining in a state of suspicion and dubiousness and had begun to question his motives of intention, as she watched him gain the trust of the members of the clubhouse and squeeze closer and closer to their wives and girlfriends.

Each day whilst in the company of her own seclusion Jade's mind wandered into the depths of the retraced steps of Shane's stories and confessions of behaviour as she meticulously searched for the truth that surrounded her in a veil of secrecy and lies. Although Jade's suspicions tangled her in a web of mistrust and dubiousness she could hold no judgement within the sweet loving kindness of her heart, which held a naive reservation of leniency and forgiveness as each passing moment of deception unfolded, and remained silent and secluded in her questioning disapprobation.

In the following weeks, Shane's plans of establishing himself within the small town of Suisania Bay and finding full time employment escalated into a tactical array of a continual search pattern of scouring the town's local newspapers, searching the employment boards and an endless inquisition of internet job applications, whilst Jade attended her responsibility within the town's dental clinic.

As the long, gruelling week neared the weekend after completing a busy morning's schedule, Jade waited patiently on the footpath for Shane to arrive to enjoy the short break of her lunch hour together which they had incorporated into their days as a joyful interlude of spending time together, whilst the children attended their education at the local school.

As Shane arrived and parked his car along the long strip of the footpath's parking bays, Jade noticed an unusual scowl that sat upon his face and tightened his lips from the usual welcoming smile of his arrival.

"Hey baby," Jade greeted, climbing up into the four-wheel-drive's front passenger seat.

"Hey," Shane replied, turning his head to a slanted drop towards the window.

Jade's mind fell into a bewildering inquisitiveness as the couple drove silently in Shane's distant and silent disposition to the spot of their usual dining area within the small town, before parking the car and engaging in a conversation of inconsequent perfunctory.

"What is wrong with you today?" Jade finally asked, puzzled by the lack of Shane's response to her attentions.

"Nothing," Shane snapped back, dropping his head to the side in a refrained expression of his moodiness.

"Okay," Jade answered, bewildered and dubious within the cold silence that surrounded her within the car. "Um. Maybe you should take me back to the clinic now as my lunch break is almost finished anyway and we can talk some more tonight."

As Shane parked the car in the parking bay along the dental clinic's footpath, Jade leant across as she had always done to place a kiss upon Shane's lips, but was met by an abrupt aversion as he turned his face away in an unambivalent avoidance of her affections. "Ohh," Jade said silently within her own mind, climbing from the front seat to stand upon the footpath as the questioning foreboding sent shivers along her spine. Jade stood silent in a bewildering daze as she stood on the footpath watching as Shane quickly reversed the car out from within the car parking space in a hurried perturbation of avoidance, before speeding down the road and into the distance.

That night as Jade left the dental clinic and climbed into the front seat of Shane's four wheel drive she was greeted with an angry sullenness of silence, as they drove the short distance back to the family home.

As Jade attended to the families responsibilities in a hurried array of nervousness, her mind raced with the inquisitive perturbation of Shane's unusual temperament of a distant disposition before finally joining him within the concealed confinement of their bedroom, once the children had been placed into the quiet comforts of their beds.

"So are you going to tell me what is going on now," Jade asked nervously. "You've been silent all day."

Shane's face quickly dropped into an expression of extreme abhorrence as he raised to his feet off the foot of the bed and stood over her in a confrontational stance of interrogation.

"So are you going to tell me who the fuck Max is? And why the fuck you have been sending him filthy pictures of yourself," flew from Shane's mouth in an angered scowl of disappointment and disapproval. Jade's face flushed white as the bottom of her jaw dropped open and the nervousness raced up her spine in a tightened obsequiousness, as she stood in the face of the indignant glare of questioning of the surreptitious seduction of the love affair of erotic fantasia with her online lover, of which she had been involved in since the breakdown of her marriage.

"I. I. How did you find that Shane?" Jade stuttered, in her nervous prosecution of shame.

"I went online to look for employment using your computer as you had told me I could and I needed to send an email to an employment agency so I opened up your email account to contact them," Shane snapped back angrily.

"But how did you get my password?" Jade stuttered, placing her hand upon her forehead.

"Your details where sitting in the top draw of your filing cabinet. I didn't want to miss out on the job and I had to get in quick so I searched your office for your email address," snapped the quick angry reply. Jade dropped her face towards the floor as a tight gulp swallowed down her throat and knotted within her stomach as a foreboding guilt of shame and embarrassment wracked itself through the tightened knot that sat deep within the pit of her stomach.

"Oh god Shane, I'm so sorry. I'm so sorry," Jade cried, her hands cradling the sides of her whitened cheeks.

"How bloody long has this been going on for?" Shane questioned angrily, pacing back and forth along the bedroom floor, shaking his head at the unconscionable indignation of which he was suffering, before scornfully dragging his bags out from under the cover of the bed and throwing his belongings into it in a dishevelled disarray.

Heavy tears welled in Jade's eyes and fell down the pale contours of her cheeks as her mouth searched desperately for the right words of explanation through the guilt that knotted deep within her stomach, dropping her to her knees in front of him in a sorrowful apologetic atonement of her impertinent betrayal.

"Oh god Shane, I don't know what to say," Jade wept, dropping her head upon his knees before raising her tear soaked eyes up to meet the poignant dishonourable glare that stared straight through her. "I'm so sorry Shane. Oh god, I'm so sorry. It has been going on for a while. Before I even knew you. It just got out of hand and I couldn't stop. Please baby, oh god please forgive me. I will stop. I will. I will tell him goodbye and I won't speak to him again. Please baby, please don't leave," Jade begged, tears streaming down her cheeks.

"Oh baby. Why. Why did you do this?" Shane sobbed, placing his head into the palms of his hands as the tears rolled down his cheeks and fell upon the wooden boards of the bedroom floor in a moment of deafening silence.

Jade's tear-stained eyes fell to the floor as the impregnable silence and the grief of which she had caused plunged her into a submission of an irreparable shame of consequence.

"I understand if you want to leave," Jade sobbed quietly, looking into Shane's eyes as he slowly raised his head from within the sorrowful protectiveness of his hands.

Shane's mouth quivered within the sorrow as his hollow grief stricken eyes stared back at her before the transitional slant of his stern demand narrowed his eyes into a tightened glare.

"You get on the internet right now and tell that bloody bastard goodbye. Right now, here in front of me. I mean it Jade. If you ever speak to him again it will be over between us. I won't ever forgive you again."

"Oh god. Yes, yes. Thank you. Oh god, thank you," Jade sobbed, swallowing down a deep breath of an intense gratefulness of relief, raising to her feet and wrapping her arms around Shane who stood cold and still in his response.

Without hesitation Jade hastily walked out of the bedroom door and entered the office where her computer had remained refrained from use and carried it back into the bedroom, placing it upon the end of the bed and waited for the start-up of the settings to commence before composing the demand of Shane's wishes into a letter upon the screen, as Shane sternly watched on and sent it to Max.

That night Shane remained quiet and distant as Jade sat beside him at the top of the bed within the silent shame of guilt that had surrounded her before they both succumbed to the sleepiness of the events of anguish that had engulfed them throughout that day and nestled under the warmth of the beds blankets and fell into a slumber of restless abandonment of their affections.

The next day whilst Shane had been absent from the family home, Jade quickly logged into her email account in an inconspicuous aberrance of her desperate attempt to hold onto the man of which she had fallen in love with. As Jade entered into the message bank of her email account a letter sat waiting in its reply of the stern demands of which she had written the night before.

My dearest Jade,

I am sorry that you have been placed in this position with your partner and I can assure you that if what you have written if at all true and sincere that I will solemnly respect your wishes and depart from your life.

But can I just state that having read your letter numerous times, I do believe that you had written it in front of Shane, as the words you have written do not ring true. Those are not your words of choice.

I wish nothing but the best for you Jade, as you have become a very important part of my life and I love you very much. Take care my beautiful sweet girl.

Goodbye. I love you. Love always

Max
xxxxx

"Oh Max," Jade whispered, tears welling in her eyes, as her heart sank into a depth of devastation and sorrow, raising her feet off the office chair to turn her eyes away from the painful magnitude of the sweet words. Jade wandered back and forth along the carpeted office floor with her head hung low towards the ground as her heart wrenched with the devastating pain of letting go of the man she had come to know so well and whom had inspired her and loved her in a way like no other. "Oh god Max. What do I do? I love you with all my heart. How do I let you go?" Jade sobbed, feeling the tears fall from her eyes and run down her cheeks in sorrow. "I can't let go Max. I just can't."

That day Jade replied to Max's letter with an explanation of what had occurred within the day of the arrival of the unanticipated written letter of the dissolution of their interaction and intimate secret affair.

She had explained that it was within Shane's presence and at Shane's demand of disapproval and heartbroken grief of finding the intimate letters of which she had shared with him that she had written the letter of dissolution that she had sent that night. But within her heart she held a spot for the two men in her life whom had captured her heart and whom she had fallen deeply in love with, and now felt torn between her two commitments of loyalty and love. Jade continued to explain that although she loved Max very much and had gained great pleasure from the intimacy of their erotic tales and pictures she could no longer enter into a deceitful indulgence of provocativeness as her physical pleasures belonged to the man of whom shared her life and home, but requested a correlation of a deep and meaningful friendship of which would remain within the boundaries of their secrecy.

The next day, Jade received a joyous reply from Max and had admitted that whilst reading the words of the letter of dissolution of which she had sent he had felt the anguish of the painful separation within his heart which had reduced him to tears of sorrow and grief and struggled with the thought of having to let her go. He had confessed that it was selfish of him to ask her to continue to explore and involve herself in an exposure of a physical erotic nature as she was now committed within a relationship with Shane, but had wholeheartedly agreed to remain within the boundaries of Jade's request of friendship.

That night whilst Shane was absent from the family home while he attended his duties at the clubhouse she secretly spent the night with Max locked behind a secret password within a new hidden email address.

Over the following weeks, Jade no longer questioned Shane on his behaviour of phone calls and text messages nor questioned his conduct whilst in the concealed dwellings of the clubhouse and remained patient and compassionate within his forgiveness and the mending of his heart and their relationship, which had once again begun to flourish and heal from the devastation of which it had suffered.

She turned a blind eye to his remarks of insult and words of mistrusted abuse and heavily carried the responsibility of the damage of which she had caused through the secrecy of her online affair.

The family home which had been placed on the market for sale had received many high offers upon the proposal of appraisal and although Derek had refused his acceptance on the previous offers of a higher sale price, he finally agreed to the sale and the family home was sold.

Jade was ecstatic with the sale of the house and viewed it as a blessing which would ease the financial burden which she had been left to carry upon the dissolution of their marriage, which had contributed to the many debts incurred whilst still in the midst of her marriage vows.

One month after the sale of the family home had reached its completion, Shane and Jade moved from out of the family home and into a new rental home situated on the outskirts of the small town of Suisania Bay, where they began the journey of the fresh start that they had longed for, and within a month had settled into a sweet routine of companionship and family life.

Jade tirelessly continued in her responsibility of the gruelling training of the local dental clinic, which required her attentions four days of the week and continued with her passionate devotion and dedication to the development of the business plan, of which she wished to propel herself into a long lasting career of managing director of the much anticipated business.

As the drawings of the business plan drew to a completion, Jade began the strategic process of sourcing the required qualified specialists to join her in the new business venture, and had begun the gruelling task of conducting a thorough search of the local business premises to source an establishment of suitability in which to commence the opening of the business.

Shane had found the much sought after employment within a small local business within the community of Suisania Bay, and although he held an aversion towards his new boss he felt the pleasing satisfaction of being able to support and contribute to the running and responsibilities of the family home, of which Jade had held sole responsibility for over the long period of time of which they had begun to reside together within the commitment of their relationship.

Within the month of the family moving into the new premise of their rental property, the longing to be reunited with his mother and siblings had reached its pinnacle of compelling imminence, as Jade awaited with open arms for James eager return amongst the settled environment of the family unit.

Jade was ecstatic to have her son reunited into the loving embrace of his mother's arms, as she had grieved her son's absence terribly with each passing day of his departure from the small town to reside with his father miles away in another state, and longed to hear his voice and capture his smile once more amongst the loving confines of the family home.

Now separated from his mother and also his siblings, within the month of James having departed from his father's care and returning to the loving embrace of his family, Nick had followed in his footsteps and returned to his mother's open arms within the peaceful structured environment of the family home.

Jade welcomed her sons' return with extreme jubilation and a mother's ebullience of seeing her children reunited within the family home once more, and lavished in their smiles of joyous innocence and playful togetherness of each passing day. Although she had held the hope that the devastation and heartbreak which her son had suffered in the duration of the separation of the marriage had pacified within himself, Nick's rage still remained and Jade continued to suffer the wrath of Derek's contemptuous damnation, which had been placed within the distraught heart of her son, who portrayed a behaviour of tempestuous consequence amongst the other family members and within the family home.

With the sale of the house now in completion, Jade had anticipated the financial settlement of the debts that had been incurred in the duration of the marriage and held an excited air of anticipation for the excess funds to be used to propel her developed business plan into one of establishment within the small town.

But Derek had refuted the claims of his responsibility to the outstanding debts and had constantly refused to take any responsibility towards any of the payments required to settle the debts, which he had left in the responsibility of Jade, whom struggled with each payment and as a subsequence suffered the infliction of the incessant phone calls and letters of demand by the company's debt collectors on a daily basis.

With Derek's intransigent refusal to take any responsibility for the outstanding debts, Jade was left without a choice and had sought the legal expertise of a lawyer to fight in her defence.

Month after month Jade travelled the distant highway to Alterro for the incessant court appearances which she had found herself locked in a gruelling legal battle of inequitable proportions, as Derek continued to refuse her request of accepting his part of the responsibility for the outstanding debts that had occurred within the duration of their marriage.

As an agreement could not be met between the separated couple, the considered amount acquired from the sale of the family home had been deemed untouchable and had been placed under a judge's order of being placed within the safeguarding of a lawyer's trust fund, until a settlement could be met between the feuding couple. With each passing month the tension intensified under the strain of the incessant acrimonious ramifications of which she faced with Derek each month within the courthouse, and of that of the battles which she faced within the obliteration of the once peacefulness of the family home under Nick's assault and the tensions within her relationship with Shane that had begun to grow.

Although Jade felt the enormous compaction of the arduous task of the strenuous emotional struggles she faced with the disconcertment of her troubled relationship with Shane, the incessant battles with her children, work commitments and the continual court appearances, she refused to concede and fought tirelessly and tenaciously.

With each passing month the tension between her children escalated into a bitter battle of sibling rivalry and an inconsolable heartbreak of turmoil caused by the separation of the marriage, which Shane found increasingly hard to contain his objectiveness of emotional disconcertment, which had placed Jade within the middle of her love for her children and that of Shane. And within three months of having her beloved children back in her loving arms, the once peaceful family home had transcended into a declension of bitter violent endless battles and tears.

As James emotional state spiralled into one of tumultuous rebelliousness, his education declined into a constant stream of absences and misdemeanours which resulted in Jade's incessant attendance of meetings with the secondary school's principle and expulsion from the school grounds.

Unable to cope with the irreversible heartbreaking emotional circumstances of the dissolution of the marriage, James dove into a world of excessive drinking and drug use and staying out until early hours of the morning in an aberrant of destruction and thievery.

Jade searched endlessly through the streets of the small town for her son and paced the house night after night in an engulfment of desperate concern, as she frantically tried to pull her once happy child away from the rebellious trail of bad company and crime and back into a consoled state of mind.

Unable to no longer cope with the emotional suffering that tore at his heart and sent his mind into a twist of conflagration. Nick and James became embattled in a vicious attack of rivalry ending in vicious words and fists being thrown, as Nick's tumultuous attacks turned towards that of Jade and his youngest brother. Each night Nick escaped into the peacefulness of his girlfriend's home but returned in a bitter state of agitation and anticipation of a confrontation with the escalated tensions that incessantly grew within the family home.

With his only focus being that of his education but his adamant refusal to ride the school bus provided to attend his daily routine of his education and Shane's refusal to allow or provide Jade with the means to take her son to his place of education, Jade felt the tremendous struggle between that of her responsibility and love of her son and the commitment she had formed with the man that she loved, and secretly arranged transport for her son's travels to the secondary school of his enrolment.

Although Jade had made the supportive commitment of the arrangement for Nick's attendance of his education, his refusal to co-operate within these terms of arrangement brought about constant morning battles of will and determined refusal, which resulted in

Nick storming off from the house on foot to walk the long road into town, as Jade quickly followed in a chase in her car.

Unwilling to enter into any more mornings of tempestuous proportions and having to remain under the strict demands of Shane's disapproval to support her son's education, Jade set about her own refusal until Nick conceded into a state of co-operation, of which he held firm in his determination of refusal.

Day after day Nick stormed from the house on foot to travel the long road into town as Jade wrestled with the guilt that sat within the pit of her stomach, as Shane's refusal to show support or love towards her older children mounted into bitter arguments of contempt within their relationship and between that of her relationship with her two older children.

The mounted tension within the structure of the family home grew into a guard of protection as she continuously watched for the signs of the imminence of animosity and confrontation between her children and an unwarranted attack of her son from the man that she had formed a relationship with.

Although Jade had exhausted every avenue available to her through the use of counsellors and children services, Derek's contemptible rage which he had filled into the hearts of her children in a vengeful bitterness of damnation towards her, placed her into a position of helplessness, as Nick's heartbroken rage escalated into an irrevocable extreme of violence and hatred towards her and the family members.

Unable to no longer contain the tempestuous tension that grew within the family home, Shane and Jade began to turn on each other, as Shane withdrew his emotional support and distanced himself into a world of solidarity within the concealed privacy of the clubhouse.

As Shane's distance grew with his frequency of attending to matters at the clubhouse he withdrew his invitation of inclusion, and excluded Jade from attending any functions at the clubhouse, leaving her in a state of anguished solidarity within the family home, as he continued to attend the many parties and social engagements in which Jade was not welcomed on his behalf.

Although Jade had questioned the change in his behaviour and his willingness to include her in his nights of exclusion, Shane had not offered a reason of explanation and had remained silent in his refusal to include her in the celebrations but instead had ordered her to remain at home in a seclusion of unsupported loneliness and grief, as the tension within the family wrapped her in a tight knot of anguish and desperation.

Over the next few weeks of Shane's exclusion of her presence within the clubhouse, whilst trapped within the isolated anguish of her helplessness, as Jade walked sullenly along the carpeted floor of the long narrow hallway past her daughter's bedroom that led towards the kitchen entrance, she heard the familiar sound of the sweet giggles of Monique's laughter coming from behind the walls.

Jade smiled as the sweetness of her giggles brought a welcomed glow of unexpected happiness to spread across her face and flow within her saddened heart.

Each night as Jade walked past her daughter's bedroom door she listened as the giggles intensified and grew with frequency and lateness and ventured into the late hours of the nights quietness, as the children had been placed to bed in preparation for their early starts of their schooling the next morning.

Night after night Jade heard the familiar sounds of the giggles coming from within the concealed confinement of Monique's bedroom walls late into the nights evenings, as she strolled along the long carpeted hallway.

"Who are you speaking to?" Jade asked one night, knocking on her bedroom door, curious as to whom it was keeping her daughter awake until the late hours of the evening.

"I'm talking to dad, Mum," came the sweet soft voice from within the walls of the bedroom.

Jade stood still in a momentary pause of concern as her heart leapt up into her throat and the concern tied knots within the pit of her stomach. "Oh no," Jade whispered to herself, before finally answering in a voice of calmness. "Okay sweetheart. But don't stay on there too long as you have school in the morning okay. You need to get your sleep."

"Okay Mum," came the quietened reply from behind the bedroom walls.

Each morning Jade listened as Monique excitedly talked about the conversations of which she had shared with her father the night before, of the excitement and glamour of which the city had to offer in a tempting coaxing of his manipulation to lure her precious daughter out from within her loving arms and into the life of which he was promising to provide for her.

With each passing day Jade's concern of anguish grew within her mind, as she felt her daughter's loyalty and love slipping out from within her loving arms in a sweet enticement of her father's lure.

Jade knew that the end was inevitable and treasured each moment of which she got to share with her precious only daughter, as each passing day drew closer and closer to the day of which she would have to face the reality of losing her to Derek's vindictive systematic revengeful enticement.

As the escalating court cases increased with frequency and the intransigent furiousness of Derek's refusal to accept his responsibility of the debts that were incurred in the duration of their marriage, combined with the enumeration of the escalating court cases of which she was required to attend with James, Jade's employment within the dental clinic fell into a position of precariousness which eventuated in the loss of her employment in the final stages of the dental assistant training.

As Jade continued in her struggles of juggling the incessant court cases with Derek and mastering the requirements necessary to build her career within her chosen field , her personal life had hit a period of extreme deterioration as the succession of tempestuous events unfolded in a declension of contentiousness. The tumultuous tension that had remained firmly wedged between them with each interaction grew into an impetuous force of magnitude, as Jade and Nick battled it out in a uncompromising clash of determination, until it hit the pinnacle of irreparable discretion.

In an attack of tempestuous abuse of words and the acrimonious destruction of the dishevelled furniture that lay strewn across the bedroom floor, Jade stood standing within the shattered splinters of the punched broken glass mirror that scattered upon the floor around her, and the trickle of blood that ran down her cheeks from the flown splintered shards that pierced the delicate skin upon her face.

"Oh god. Nick," Jade cried out, raising her hand to the blood that trickled from the small open wounds on her face. "Please stop. Please Nick, stop."

As the rain of tempestuousness continued in a rage of contemptible damnation and destruction as Nick stormed through the room yelling his rain of abuse, Jade placed her face into the palms of her hands, sobbing and faced the painful heartbreaking truth of the decision that had just been placed upon her shoulders. "Oh god Nick. I'm so sorry," Jade whispered to herself, hanging her head towards the floor in a defeatism of heartbreak, walking out of the room, down the long narrow hallway to the phone stand that stood in the loungeroom near the front door entrance.

"Sherri. Is that you?" Jade replied, sobbing to the voice that came down the line of the phone. "Please, please Sherri, I need your help."

202

"What's wrong Jade? What has happened?" Sherri questioned, concernment filling her voice.

"I don't know what to do Sherri. He just won't stop," Jade answered, tears streaming down her face. "Can Nick please come stay with you for a while? He's so angry with me. He just can't stay here anymore. Please Sherri. Please," Jade continued to ask, her muffled voice breaking through the tears that streamed down her cheeks and tightened within her throat.

"Jade. Jade. Stop crying. Stop crying," Sherri replied, trying to soothe the grief-stricken tears that flooded the sounds of Jade's voice.

Even though Sherri's words were of a comforting support, Jade could not hold back the tears or contain the tightening within her stomach that knotted and turned within the depths of her, as she slowly slid down the length of the wall and placed her head into her hands. She felt the overwhelming sorrow engulf her in a heartbreaking distress of helplessness that swallowed her in a compunction of failure and guilt, of having to remove her child from within the loving embrace of the family home.

That night Sherri agreed to the heartbreaking request of taking Nick into the safe retreat of her home, until the painful grief that had filled his heart and changed him into one of extreme animosity towards his family subsided and healed within him.

Jade stood motionless at the large glass sliding doors of the entertainment room that faced the back veranda watching in heart wrenching sorrow and tears, as Nick sat at the outdoor setting stricken with heartbreak and grief that poured out in tears upon his flushed cheeks and over his hands that had covered his face.

As Jade departed the house and walked over to place a comforting arm around her son she was met with an abruptness of perturbation, as he flung his arm away from the comfort of her embrace and stormed off towards the front of the house to stand upon the unpaved footpath in his waiting for Sherri's arrival. Emotionally distressed and overwhelmed with sorrow, Jade returned in a flood of tears to the confinement of Nick's bedroom to collect the packed bags of his belongings that sat neatly against the wooden door frame, before quickly carrying them out of the house to join Nick who stood upon the footpath in his wait. As Jade approached the unpaved footpath her eyes began to dart along the length of the narrow strip of the house lined street in a desperate search for her sons location, as her eyes viewed the vacant open space of the abandoned footpath.

"Nick. Nick where are you?" Jade cried out in desperation, as she paced the long narrow footpath past the houses that lined the streets.

"Oh my god Nick, where are you? she cried out again, placing her hand to the anguished bewilderment that had filled the contours of her tear-stained face.

Jade grabbed at the handles of the packed bags and rushed them towards her car that sat under the carport located along the side of the house, throwing them into the back seat of the car, before reversing out from the driveway and driving down the road towards the location of Sherri's home in a rush of concerned anguish.

"Sherri. Oh god. I left Nick on the footpath at the front of the house but when I came back he was gone. I can't find him anywhere," Jade cried, placing her hand to her forehead and closing her eyes from the anguish that engulfed her.

"He's here sweetie. Calm down, he's here," Sherri explained, placing her arms around her in a comforting embrace of assurance. "Oh thank god. Thank you Sherri. Thank you," Jade wept, pressing her face into the comfort of Sherri's shoulder.

That night Jade left her son in the safety of her friend's home and returned to the isolation of her heartbreaking sorrow within the concealment of her bedroom walls and wept endlessly until her swollen reddened eyes closed into a sleep of silent sobbing. Nick was only fifteen years old.

Over the next few weeks Jade felt the strength from within herself, which had held her in a stance of intransigent unassailability, fading and spiralling her down into the depths of despair as the excessive traumatic events unfolded and erupted in an incessantness of heartbreak and tension.

Unable to contain the emotional spiral that had tangled itself within her mind, within the quietness of her children's slumber, Jade escaped each night into her solace of the intoxication held within the bottom of the bourbon cans that lay scattered around the bedroom furniture.

Each day Jade found herself in a struggle of rising to the day in the face of the adversity that surrounded her, but drew strength day after day from the love of her children and her determination to bring her business plan to success, as she dragged herself from under the sheltered comforting warmth of her bed covers.

As the school holidays approached, James informed his mother of Derek's proposed plans of his invitation to obtain the children for the two week period of the holidays.

Although Jade had not denied Derek contact with the children and had paid the thousands of dollars to support his relationship with them, she had been unaware of the legal implications that had surrounded such an arrangement, which had deemed Derek liable for the costs of his visitation, as he had moved away from the region of the family's residence. After raising the concern within the legal battle of their court hearings surrounding the monies paid by Jade to support her children's relationship with their father, Derek was informed by the attending judge of his legal responsibilities and had honoured his responsibility of paying the full costs of the children's flights over that period of the school holidays.

The following weekend, on the Friday night, as Jade waved to her children as they boarded the plane for their arranged visit to spend time with their father, she turned to face Shane with a devious cheeky smile, whom had remained standing sullen in a slight silent distance from her positioning against the boarding walkway.

"So baby. We've got the whole weekend to ourselves," Jade said, a sexy glint flashing across her eyes. "What shall we do?"

"Well," Shane replied, glancing his eyes towards the flooring of the airport before raising them again in a slant of aberration. "I have plans with the clubhouse tomorrow to go to Alterro, but I'll be back by 7 pm. We can go out if you want to. We haven't been for a while?"

"Yesss. Yes, I'd love to," Jade replied, as the morale of her spirits lifted and spread a joyous smile across her face. "We could go out for dinner, then wait until the nightclub venue opened and go dancing. I'd like to do that," she suggested, waiting eagerly for his reply.

"Yeah okay baby, that sounds good to me. You book the table and get it all organised alright," Shane replied, as they continued in their departure from the airport terminal towards the position of their parked vehicle.

Early the next morning, Shane and Jade were awoken by the ringing alarm clock which had been set in Shane's preparation for the day's events, of his role of responsibility to drive the highway in delivering the other clubhouse members to their desired locations within the city limits of Alterro. Although he had made previous plans with the clubhouse and was committed to his responsibility to the other members, he had assured Jade that he would return within the set time which he had specified and would announce the time of his returning with a text message sent to her mobile phone as he was leaving. At nine am Shane climbed into the driver's seat of his four-wheel-drive, leaning his head out from the open car window and placed a soft warm kiss upon Jade's lips as she stretched her height up to meet the tenderness of his kiss.

"I'll see you tonight okay? I love you," Jade said quietly, a warm smile spreading across her lips.

"See you tonight sexy," Shane called out through the open window, backing his car out from under the shade of the carport and heading down the long narrow road towards the township.

That day in Shane's absence Jade lavished in the joyous excitement of the nights plans as she played with the numerous different styles of her outfits, makeup and hair, until she had found the perfect style of which she had hoped would capture Shane's attention and heal the rift that had formed between them.

Although Jade had been caught in the desolation of her isolated state of the spiralling emotional tension and the heartbreak of losing her son, today held an air of exhilaration as she prepared in her wait for Shane's return and the night's plans of their special occasion.

5 pm: Jade decided it was time to prepare for their big night of the plans of which they had arranged the day before and showered before dressing in the special outfit of which she had chosen that day.

After checking her appearance numerous times in front of the long bedroom mirror attached to the bedroom wardrobe, glowing in her satisfaction and excitement, Jade's eyes glanced over at the clock radio that sat beside the bed on the bedside cupboard. "Ohh, it's nearly seven o'clock," Jade whispered to herself. "I better check my phone to see if Shane's sent a message yet."

Jade walked over to her mobile phone that sat motionless upon the dressing table and picked it up in an anticipation of having received a message from Shane informing her of his close return.

Jade's eyes dropped into a slant of inquisitive bewilderment as she viewed the empty space of the message bank before carefully placing her phone back down upon the top shelving of the dressing table. "Hmm. He can't be that far away," Jade said quietly to herself, tapping her fingers upon the dressing table top in her inquisitiveness.

8 pm: Jade's phone had remained in a silent state of inactiveness, as she sat in her wait for Shane's message to arrive and had decided to cancel the reservations of the dinner arrangements of which she had made at the townships local Chinese restaurant that morning.

"Hmm," Jade hummed, twitching her mouth from side to side in her bewilderment. "Maybe he's just got caught up and hasn't been able to get a message through to me."

Jade had known of Shane's role within the clubhouse which held an air of prospective subsequence to his role of prospect within the local motorcycle clubhouse, and held an air of understanding for his role of responsibility to the other clubhouse members, to which he held a position of proving his loyalty and worthiness.

Jade walked the house stepping through the long hallway and weaving in and out of the empty rooms in a stance of uncomfortable fiddling within the inquisitiveness of her wandering mind, as she tried patiently to whittle away at the solidarity of her long wait, whilst her eyes remained on the ticking hands of the clock that hung on the kitchen wall. "Where are you Shane?" Jade questioned, placing her hand to her forehead in a reconditeness of concern.

9 pm: Jade's bewilderment of concern had started to turn to irritation as the impertinence of Shane's silence began to sink beneath her skin and settle into a burn of disconcertment.

Jade's mind raced through the possibilities of Shane's absence from his return as she tossed her mobile phone back and forth between the palms of her hands in a pondering of silence.

"What's going on Shane? I hope you are alright," she whispered to herself, rubbing her fingers over the keys of her mobile phone.

But Jade could not wait any longer within the irritation of her bewilderment as her fingers that slowly glided over the keys of her phone pressed down into a typed message of questioning.

"Hey. What's going on? Are you nearly home?"

Jade pushed her lean off the kitchen bench in a stance of irritation as she awaited for Shane's polite reply of explanation.

But Jade's phone remained silent and motionless in Shane's ignoble behaviour of silence, as she placed her phone down upon the bedside cupboard and walked through the long hallway towards the kitchen to collect a can of the chilled bourbon that had remained untouched within the refrigerator.

10 pm: Jade's irritation had flared into one of disrespected contempt as her mind raced and surged with the irrational temper of her over stretched emotions.

"That's it," Jade said out loud, placing the can of bourbon down hard on the bedside cupboard and reaching for her phone. "I'm ringing him."

Jade paced back and forth along the carpeted flooring of the bedroom as she listened to the endless ringtone of her phone, while she awaited Shane to answer in an explanation of his silent absence.

"Hey baby," Shane finally answered.

"Shane. What's going on, where are you?" Jade questioned sternly, demanding an explanation.

"I'm sorry baby but I haven't been able to leave. The boys decided to stay longer than expected and I've been stuck here until they're ready. I should be coming home soon though. Give me a couple of hours alright," Shane quickly explained.

Jade's eyes rolled towards the bedroom ceiling in an unimpressed expression of her disapproval of his incorrigible behaviour of insensitivity, as he had kept her in a state of silence as she awaited for his return.

"Please baby, don't be mad. I'm really sorry," Shane pleaded, offering his apology for his discrepancy.

Although Jade had remained unimpressed by the explanation of which she had received she accepted Shane's explanation and apology but had remained within the emotional knotted tightness of her irritation as she hung up the phone and placed it back upon the bedside table.

"Wanker," she muttered under her breath through the tightness of her lips, opening the fresh can of the chilled bourbon that soothed her emotions as she quickly gulped at the chilled liquor.

"I bet he knew all along," Jade muttered to herself in her disappointment and disapproval, as her feet began to pace back and forth once more along the carpeted floor of her bedroom.

As the hands of the clock struck midnight Jade's disappointment had flared into an acrimonious pace of rage, as she continued to walk the house in an expression of profanity while the act of Shane's disingenuous behaviour played over and over throughout her mind.

Jade had trusted Shane's words of sincerity as they walked from the airport in the midst of their plans for the weekend, and had felt that they had both reached the point of understanding within their relationship of having to place the shattered pieces of their love back together and form a place of unity within the boundaries of the family home. But Shane had remained within the silence of his impudent behaviour as Jade sat alone waiting for his call and arrival which did not come.

"I can't believe you did this to me Shane. How dare you," Jade growled, pacing back and forth down the long hallway. "I will never forgive you."

Jade gulped at the chilled bourbon that sat tightly squeezed within the palm of her hand, slumping herself down into the lounge chair as she kicked her high heels off, flinging them across the flooring of the loungeroom.

"You wait until you get home. You just wait," she growled, staring angrily at the loungeroom wall. "How dare you disrespect me in this way."

Jade grabbed at the can of bourbon which she had placed on the small coffee table and stormed off into the bedroom where she picked up her mobile phone once more and rang Shane's number, her eyes ablaze with the anger that surged throughout her. As she sat on the edge of the bed, angrily swinging her crossed leg back and forth listening for the ringtone to the dialled number, her face contorted into a transition of contentiousness as she listened to the recorded message of the phones disconnection of contact.

"What? You switched your phone off? You bloody bastard," Jade yelled, slamming the phone down onto the surface of the bed covers and rushing towards the kitchen refrigerator to collect another can of the chilled liquor.

Holding the can of alcohol tightly within the tension of her gripped hand, Jade picked up her phone off the bed and dialled the number once more to which the connection was rejected with a recording of the same message of disconnection.

"Grrr," Jade growled loudly, slamming the phone down in a tumultuous state of agitation and rage.

"You arsehole. You took off and just left me here after making plans with me. How dare you," Jade roared, gulping down the remnants of the can of bourbon.

Emblazoned into a rage of furiousness, Jade reached into the draw of the bedside cupboard and pulled out the contents of the hidden small bag of the white powdery substance that had remained untouched in preparation for their weekend together, and began to prepare it upon the small glass panel upon the top of the dressing table shelving.

That night Jade's furious rampage of profanity and pacing of the house continued in an unconscionable aberrance of self-destruction, as she excessively gulped down the contents of the bourbon cans in quick succession and indulged in the bag of cocaine that lay scattered in white powdery residue over the top of the dressing table shelving.

Even though she had wanted to believe in Shane's story of sincerity the answers laid within the silence as Jade continuously periodically rang Shane's number throughout the night, to which she received no reply and the phone had remained switched off permanently.

In the early hours of the next morning Jade continued in her tenacious pursuit of contacting Shane but was met by the same answer of the recorded message. Jade's furiousness grew into a abhorrent rage of coldness as Shane remained in his elusive absence of silence while she busied herself completing the household chores and continued to indulge in the solidarity of her own self-destruction.

Jade continued in her wait until the hours of the late afternoon to which she had not received any word from Shane regarding his location or if he was to return.

At four pm, as Jade sat silently upon the outdoor setting engulfed in the cold contemptible rage that surged throughout her, she heard a voice call out to her from behind the perimeter of the side gates that led towards the carport at the side of the house.

"Hey Jade," Trent called out in a meek quiet voice.

Jade's eyes flashed in a glare of avertable furiousness towards the voice that came from behind the gate's railings, before raising to her feet in a stance of confrontation but remained within the silence of her rage, holding her tongue from the vicious words that circled and rose within her throat.

"Hey," Jade finally spoke, glaring her eyes at Shane's brother, who stood waiting for her reply.

"Umm," Trent stammered, confronted by the cold reply of the shortened greeting. "Shane will be back soon okay. He's just finishing up."

"Yep," Jade replied, short and sharply, glaring at Trent as she raised the can of bourbon to her lips and continued to consume the alcohol.

"Okay, I'll see you later then," Trent answered gingerly, before turning from the position of the gates and leaving as Jade continued in her aberrance of impoliteness.

At six pm Jade heard the familiar sound of Shane's car as it pulled to a stop underneath the cover of the carport at the side of the house.

"Hey baby," Shane called out, bouncing innocently through the gate and walking towards her, placing a soft kiss upon her cheek.

But Jade showed no response to Shane's greeting and sat silent within the cold rage that surged through her, as she furiously tapped the end of the lighter against the hard wooden grain of the outdoor setting table top.

Shane stood back precariously as he viewed the silent glare that stared straight through him in a furious abreaction of contempt, as Jade remained sitting at the outdoor setting tapping the lighter hard against the surface.

"Umm. I'm going inside to get cleaned up okay," Shane said hesitantly, fiddling nervously with his car keys as he slowly walked away towards the back door.

Jade raised to her feet quickly following Shane inside into the confinement of their bedroom, as her eyes narrowed and her tightened lips gripped back the furiousness of the words that threatened to leap from her mouth in a disgust of profanity.

"Well, looks like you had a good night hey," Shane sniggered and smiled nervously, viewing the remnants of the white powdery substance that lay upon the glass panel on the dressing table and the numerous emptied cans of bourbon scattered upon each surface of the furniture.

"What," leapt from Jade's mouth, as her eyes narrowed and her hands raised to the contours of her hips in a furious stance. "I had a bloody good night did I."

Shane's eyes widened in a state of shock as he conceded into a silent slump upon the bed, whilst Jade paced furiously from end to end along the foot of the bed in a harsh venomous lashing of contemptible words that continuously spilt in an unrestrained precise attack of disrespect.

Shane sat motionless and silent in his defence and denial as the tears rolled slowly from his eyes and down the contours of his cheeks, as the sting of the harsh venomous words continued in layers of contemptible lashings, until the last breath of Jade's words fell into a silence of her own tears at the foot of the bed. Although the couple had quarrelled before over the trivial matters that had arisen, their arguments had remained within a calm state of respect and understanding, as they worked through the problems of their disagreements. Pushed beyond the limits of her emotional capabilities Jade had reached a point of irreversible conflagration and emotional declension, as she struggled with the heartbreak of losing her son and the pressures of the incessant tensions that surrounded her and engulfed her in an ambivalence of frustration.

That night Shane and Jade shared the house in separated corners of silence in an abstinence of affection or acknowledgement as the events of the last two days settled beneath their skins in a burn of disrespected prides. For two days Shane and Jade walked the house in separation and silence unable to break the contemptible silence that had fallen between them, until finally Jade conceded in a swallowing of her pride and approached Shane.

"I'm so sorry baby. I'm so sorry I said those nasty things to you," dropping her head slightly at her own act of shameful behaviour. Shane's mouth quivered with emotion as his eyes began to fill with tears, before reaching his arms out to wrap around her in an embrace of forgiveness.

"I'm sorry too baby. I'm so sorry," he whispered softly, as they held each other in empathy.

Although they had reached a state of forgiveness for each other's actions of disrespect they had remained within the state of insoluble inconsonance, as the distance left between them fell into a permanent correlation of contentiousness.

Over the next month, Shane's behaviour deviated into one of a distant contradistinction as his involvement with the clubhouse intensified and his visits and overnight stays increased, leaving Jade in a solitary state of suspicion and questioning. Although she had tried to forgive him and erase the emotional damage which he had inflicted over the duration of his silent absence from the family home over that weekend, her mind had remained in a state of cogitative disconcertment.

Jade tried desperately to keep her mind in a clear focus of composure and strength as the events replayed in a repercussion of recapitulation each night, as she walked the lonely walls of the home in his absence.

Night after night her mind helplessly wandered into the discern of imagery as she questioned his faithfulness and honesty, plunging her into a depth of suspicion and conflict of an irrational frenzy within herself. Jade had to know the truth.

That day as Shane left for work Jade rushed to the bedroom in a frenzied state of suspicion and picked up her mobile phone off the bedside cupboard and searched through the apps of the GPS locator researching the terms and conditions required to link Shane's phone to hers in a desperate attempt to track his every move.

After thoroughly reading through the terms and conditions of the activation of the services of the GPS application, Jade sent Shane a playful message in her desperate determination of manipulating the situation in order to obtain Shane's acceptance of agreeing to the terms of linking their phones through the use of the application. Within minutes of sending the message to Shane's phone, Jade received a reply with an acceptance of the terms of the application without a suspicion of curiosity or of a questionable nature.

"Yes. Now let's see what you're up to Shane," Jade said softly to herself, a smile of wickedness forming upon her lips.

That evening as Shane prepared for his departure from the family home to fulfil his duties at the motorcycle clubhouse, Jade busied herself within her usual routine of housework and preparing the children for their bed times, as her mind raced through the details of the disingenuous plan that she had devised throughout the week, whilst Shane was busied at his place of employment.

"I've got to go now," Shane called out from within the kitchen area.

"Okay," Jade answered, wandering slowly back through the kitchen door smiling. "You have a great night. I'll see you in the morning," and placed an elaborate kiss upon his lips, before heading back into the confines of the bedroom, as Shane left through the back door of the house.

As Shane reversed from underneath the carport at the side of the house and drove down the long narrow stretch of road towards the township, Jade placed her mobile phone into the palm of her hand and set the application of the GPS tracking device to activation, and watched as the device cleverly tracked Shane's movements along the lines of the maps as he drove into town.

"Hmm," Jade hummed to herself, placing her finger in a tapping motion upon her chin, as the details of Shane's location filtered through the GPS application.

"So you do go where you say you are going? But what are you doing there I wonder?"

After carefully monitoring Shane's movements of the night through the use of the GPS application on her phone, Jade placed her youngest child, Cody, in bed and explained to James that she had an errand to run at the local shopping facilities and that she would return shortly.

As Jade drove down the narrow stretch of road towards the township, her mind raced with the possibilities of the surreptitious indiscreetness of Shane's actions, as she secretly wove her way through the different routes around the perimeter of the camera monitored clubhouse, in her frenzied pursuit to gain the knowledge of which she was seeking.

Jade's face dropped into a contorted furrow of impudence as her eyes viewed the scene of the road that stood in front of her, as she rounded the sweeping bend that led towards the parallel road of the clubhouse's footpath.

"What. You've got to be kidding," quivered out of Jade's opened mouth in disgust. "Jenna. You're cheating on me with her," Jade continued, placing her hand to her forehead as she secretly viewed her friend's parked car on the side of the footpath in front of the clubhouse.

Jade's heart froze into a state of disgust and coldness as the toil of the betrayal settled beneath her skin in an inflicted turmoil of tempestuousness.

"You bastard," Jade growled to herself, her mind rushing into a perplexing state of tactical calculation, as she turned on the ignition of the car's engine and drove back out of the township towards the solidarity of her dwellings.

That night as Jade lay awake beneath the warmth of her bed covers, concealed in her own impassioned bruising of the indignation, her mind remained in a state of subsequent recapitulation of the uncovered truth of Shane's ignoble behaviour. Although the revealed truth had formed a state of contemptibleness to settle beneath her skin, Jade did not shed one tear or feel the bruising within her heart of Shane's incorrigible infidelity, but instead remained in a state of coldness and calculation, as she awaited for Shane's return in the early hours of the next morning.

"Good morning baby," Shane said softly, leaning down above Jade to place a kiss upon her cheek, stirring her from the peacefulness of her slumber.

"Good morning," Jade replied, casting her eyes into a sleepy slant of her disgruntled disapproval and disgust in the facts of the knowledge of which she had uncovered the night before.

Each time as Shane left the house for his routine of fulfilling his duties amongst the dwellings of the motorcycle clubhouse, Jade followed in a systematic calculation of pursuit, as she strategically positioned her car in a location of hidden view, and sat and watched the movements of Jenna's arrival or departure from the clubhouse surrounds. Many nights passed as Jade watched in abhorrence as Jenna's parked car at the front of the clubhouse remained in a parked state of standstill, whilst Shane's phone remained silent and inactive, rendering Jade no contact with him during the long hours of his shift.

With each passing day Jade's faith in Shane declined further and further into a declension of isolated desolation, as she struggled with the double betrayal of her friend's affair with the man that she loved and shared her home with.

In a frenzied affliction of suspicion and mistrust, each night as Shane left the presence of the bedroom and retired to the peacefulness of the bathroom's shower recess, Jade quickly scurried through the contents of the message data banks and phone calls lists held within the concealed privacy of his mobile phone.

Day by day their relationship tattered and tapered into a declension of abstinence, as their interaction of conversation filtered out into just a few words in passing in a silent battle of prides.

Although Jade had uncovered the shocking truth that lay behind the lies of Shanes surreptitious behaviour, she remained silent in her admission of revealing the knowledge which she had acquired through the use of her plan of strategical precision.

Wracked and tangled within the solitude of her desolation, Jade fell into an unbalanced state of temperamental coldness, as the extremity of the anguish and tension rose around her and surrounded her in a veil of irreparable debasement.

Although Jade suffered the enormous weight of the tension and the conflict that surrounded her and struggled each day with the battles that she faced, she leant on her strength from within and stood tenaciously firm in her retainment of normality within the ambience of the infliction and battled on.

During the week Shane had explained that he was considering the sale of his car in order to obtain an upgraded model and that a man who was situated in Alterro had put in an offer but had asked to view the car first in order to make his final decision. Shane had accepted the offer with eagerness and had arranged with the man to drive the car to Alterro on the weekend to meet with the potential buyer and that he would return on the Saturday afternoon. Although Jade had listened to Shane's reasons of having to make the trip to Alterro for the weekend, she held great doubt that the elaborate story of the sale of the car drew any form of truth, but accepted Shane's story with grace, as her mind gathered into a interrogatory secrecy of incrimination.

Early Friday evening upon his return from his day of employment Shane gathered a small overnight bag of his belongings and placed them into the back section of his car before kissing Jade on the lips and leaving for the drive along the open highway that led towards the city of Alterro.

On the Saturday morning Jade received a text from Shane explaining that the potential buyer of his car had been in contact with him but was unable to meet with him to view the car until the early hours of the afternoon, due to his work commitments and would not be returning home until the early hours of the evening. Once again Jade accepted Shane's explanation with a dubious smile but remained within her silence of secrecy as she continued to track his movements by the use of the GPS tracking application activated on her mobile phone.

Within the early hours of the afternoon Jade started to receive numerous text messages from Shane offering an explanation of his lateness, as the potential buyer had not yet arrived and had not offered him an explanation as to his late arrival or a time of his viewing of the car, and that Shane had decided to stay in Alterro until the arrival of the potential buyer. Jade giggled at the message as the words flowed through the knowledgeable antipathy of her mind before replying in a sweet toned message of cunningness, as she continued to track his movements across the streets of Alterro.

That evening as Jade continued in her dubious exploration of uncovering the truth of Shanes disingenuous explanation of having to leave for the weekend, she received another text message from Shane explaining that the man had not arrived that day as he had arranged and that he had decided to stay in Alterro another night as it was now too late for the long drive back home to Suisania Bay.

Although Shane had explained that he had no intention of leaving from his mother's house in his wait for the potential buyer to arrive, Jade had doubted the truthfulness of his story and swept it away from entering into a truthful form within her mind. Once again Jade secretly giggled at the contents of the message of Shane's explanation, but remained tenaciously firm in her contingency of attack or to reveal the truthful knowledge of which she had acquired through the use of the GPS tracking application, or what she had seen whilst watching from afar at the local motorcycle clubhouse.

Jade sat and watched as the GPS tracking application weaved in and out along the paths of the maps as Shane's location moved within the streets of the city and came to a long standstill on the other side of the town.

"Hmm," Jade hummed to herself, smiling satisfactorily in her deviousness. "Maybe it's time to give this a little shake up." Jade opened the saved contacts section of her phone and dialled Shane's number and smiled wickedly within her wait as the number continued in its ringtone of calling.

"Hey baby," Shane answered joyfully.

"Hey baby," Jade replied, remaining within the normal tones of her response. "What are you up to?"

"Oh, I'm just at Mum's. We're just watching a movie at the moment. I'm a little bored actually," Shane answered, a giggle of perfunctory leaving his lips.

"Ohh. Really," Jade replied, a lie forming within the depths of her mind and spreading across her lips in an omniscient smile. "Well that's funny. I just rang your Mum and she said that you were not at home and that she didn't know where you were."

"Ohh, umm. Oh. Well," Shane stammered, searching for his words of disingenuous manipulation. "We only just left Mum's. Trent and I are at the carwash getting the car ready for tomorrow."

"Oh, okay. But I thought the buyer was coming today?" Jade questioned, smiling to herself as she held the phone to her ear.

"No no, he changed his mind. He is coming tomorrow instead," Shane explained, clearing his throat of the tightened lump that had formed through his lies.

"Oh, okay. Well. I'll let you go then okay. Have a good night," Jade replied, smiling deviously through the sweet tone of her voice, before hanging up the phone and reactivating the GPS tracking application on her phone.

Within minutes Shane's car started to move from the place of which it had been parked for the previous four hours and began its weave through the streets of the city, until it came to a standstill at the address of his mother's residence, where it had remained for the rest of the entire evening.

A loud devious laugh leapt out from Jade's mouth as she watched the movements of Shane's car scurry back through the street maps of the GPS tracking application on her phone and come to a standstill at his mother's house.

"That will teach you. Think you can lie to me you bastard," Jade growled, sipping at the chilled can of bourbon that sat tightly in the grip of her palm.

Caught within the web of Jade's precision of strategical attack, Shane returned to the small town of Suisania Bay within the early hours of the afternoon the next day composed of his disingenuous story of lies, as he parked his car underneath the carport at the side of the house, unsold.

Derek had remained within his manipulation of suasion as he continued in his relentless pursuit of drawing Monique away from the loving comforts of her family home with a sweet enticement to the bright city lights of a better life with him.

Night after night his phone calls continued in an endless conspiracy of promises of falsified intentions, as Jade secretly listened in on the happy giggles that escaped through the grain of the closed bedroom door.

"Oh god," Jade whispered to herself, placing her hand against her forehead, as she closed her eyes in the formidable desolation that gripped her and sent waves of immanence running through her heart.

One month later whilst Jade sat with her daughter happily engaged in their daily talks at the dining table within the early hours of the morning, Monique announced a statement that dropped Jade to her knees within herself and swelled tears in her eyes of imminent bereavement.

"Mum. I want to go to Meltona to live with Dad."

Jade froze momentarily within the moment, as the impact of the formidable words ran an oppression of tentativeness throughout her mind and settled in overwhelming sorrow within her heart.

Finally, Jade's mouth opened in a silent stammer, as her mind searched for the right words to say to her daughter, as she sat and waited for her mother's words of approval.

"I don't want you to go."

Jade swallowed hard at the devastation that rose within her throat, as the words of which she had not wanted to say slipped from between her lips and lowered her eyes to the floor.

Monique's eyes followed her mother's to the lowered level of the floor as they both sat their together within the silence of the tentative moment.

"I, I," Jade stammered, struggling to allow the right words to fall from her mouth. "Yes. Okay sweetheart. If that's what you really want to do. Yes you can go."

Monique's face lit up with magniloquent delight as the veil of uncertainty lifted from within her eyes, raising her to her feet from off the kitchen chair and rushing her into her mother's arms.

"Thank you Mum. I love you. I love you," Monique replied, nestling tightly against her mother's chest, whilst Jade held back the sorrow that threatened to fall from her eyes and spill from her heart.

"I'm going to miss you my sweet girl," Jade whispered, placing a soft kiss upon her daughters head, as she held her tightly within the warmth of her mother's arms.

"I'll miss you too Mum," Monique whispered.

Over the course of the next week Jade spent her every waking hour attentively absorbed in the playfulness of her only daughter's joy as they enveloped each other in their favourite activities.

"Let's get some ice cream," Jade suggested, placing the lid upon the open bottle of nail polish that sat on the table before them. "Then let's watch a movie hey."

"Yes," Monique replied, a joyous smile spreading across her young face. As Jade drove her daughter through the roads of the small town of Suisania Bay towards the shopping mall to collect the supplies for their special day, a smile of everlasting memories spread across her face, as they both sang in tune to their favourite song that played upon the local radio station and filled the car with mellifluous melody.

That week Jade absorbed every moment of her daughter deep into the depths of her heart and soul as she silently sat and watched Monique and Cody play amongst the gardens of the large back yard, engrossed in their playfulness of giggles and laughter. Every sound, every smile, every hug entrenched deeply within her memory as she looked into her daughter's big brown eyes, her glowing soft cheeks and watched as her long brown hair swirled around her small slender shoulders in soft wisps within the airs breeze.

Jade could feel the sorrow growing within her heart, engulfing her into a world of irrevocable darkness as the truth of her awareness grew deeper within her soul.

Although Jade had suffered the loss of her sons as they moved away to live with their father, her heart had always known that one day they would return to her loving arms once more, but this time her heart was irreparably breaking within the knowledgeable truth of her intuition that Monique would not return.

213

The following week Derek arranged the day of Monique's departure, which had allowed Jade and the children one more week of togetherness as a loving family unit until the imminent segregation of her children and of that from her mother. Derek had suggested as a supportive gesture in order for Monique to settle and to become accustomed to the newness of her environment that Jade allow the other children to join Monique in her travel and to stay with him for the two week period of the school holidays.

A suggestion of which Jade had found to be imperative for her daughter's settling into her new environment and to allow the children more time together as a family, before they were segregated into a form of separation from the togetherness of which they had always known.

As the weekend of Monique's departure drew closer and closer Jade could feel the darkness that clouded the judgement within her mind and tore shattered pain within the depths of her heart engulfing her into a world of perfunctory measures. The smile that once glowed upon her face became a tight lipped curve upon her lips and the joyous banter that once flowed freely from her mouth became a sullen distance memory, as she slipped into a silence of heartbreak and tension.

On the Thursday afternoon, Jade sat with Shane on the end of the bed within the secluded confinement of their bedroom, locked within the cold silence of which their life had become until the words of formidableness trickled from her mouth in a quiet sigh. "Well I guess I better make a start on packing up Monique's room. I'm going out to the storage shed to gather the boxes and suitcases okay."

"Alright," Shane replied, glancing his eyes up at Jade as she rose from the bed and walked from the confines of the bedroom. Within minutes Jade returned from the storage shed armed with the many boxes and suitcases which she had gathered in her preparation for the poignant weekend of Monique's departure.

"It's time to pack up all your things sweetheart," Jade said, knocking and entering into her daughter's room, holding down the sorrow within her heart with a smile of hidden subsequence.

"Okay Mum," Monique replied, a glowing smile spreading across her young face, placing the computer game of her attention down beside herself and slipped down from the top bedding of her bunk bed.

"I love you baby girl," Jade whispered, holding her daughter tightly within her loving arms and placing a motherly kiss upon the top of her head.

One by one, Jade and Monique began to disassemble the array of posters on the bedroom walls and the carefully placed ornaments that adorned the shelving of the bedroom unit and wrapped them into a protection of bubble wrap, before carefully packing them into the opened cardboard boxes.

As the pair continued with the systematic packing of Monique's possessions into the many cardboard boxes whilst lavishing in the chitchat of their mother daughter bond, a knock came from the other side of the closed bedroom door.

"Come in," Jade said, placing the wrapped ornament she held within her hand into the cardboard box.

"Jade. I'm just going over to the clubhouse for a couple of hours okay," Shane announced, poking his head through the gap of the opened door.

"Oh, okay," Jade answered, stepping towards him with a worried look of disconcertment.

"Spend some time with your daughter. I'll be back soon okay," Shane replied, assuring her of his imminent return, before closing the door and leaving.

Jade flashed a loving smile in Monique's direction as she walked towards her and placed her warm hand upon her slender young shoulder before turning to the opened boxes in the continuous packing of her daughters possessions.

"Well. I think that is enough for today," Jade said, turning to her daughter and embracing her into her arms. "I'm going to cook your favourite meal tonight, then we can relax together with a movie. What do you think?"

"Yes mum. That will be good. Can I help?" Monique answered, raising her cheeky glowing smile into the loving look of her mother's eyes.

"Yes, of course you can," Jade replied, giggling at her daughter's enthusiasm.

As Jade and Monique entered the kitchen through the hallway door Jade glanced her eyes towards the hands of the clock that hung on the kitchen wall above the doorway. "Okay, it's five o'clock, that gives us an hour to get it all cooked before the boys arrive back home," Jade said, pulling the pots and pans from out of the kitchen cupboards. Whilst Jade and Monique continued in their preparation of the evening meal, Jade stood at the frypan in a silent reminiscence of the many times of which they had shared the joyous experience of their weekends of baking sweet treats and cakes together, before devouring the sweetness of their days efforts. "I'm going to miss you my baby girl," Jade whispered to herself, dropping her eyes down upon the floor in a disappointment of sorrow.

At six pm, James and Nick came bouncing through the back door of the house in their excited obedience of their mother's wishes, and placed themselves at the kitchen table in their wait to enjoy the special dinner which their mother and sister had prepared one last time together.

"It's almost ready," Jade called out through the large open doorway that separated the kitchen from the dining area. "Can you please go and tell your brother to wash his hands and come to the table."

"James will," Nick called out, poking at his brother's arm. "You do it," James replied, poking his brother's arm back and screwing his face into a disgruntled tease.

Jade giggled and shook her head from side to side as her eyes glanced at the hands of the clock that hang on the kitchen wall once more. "Come on boys, behave. James, go and get your brother please," Jade commanded, lifting the cooked items from out of the pans and serving them onto the prepared dinner plates. "I thought Shane would be back by now," she said to herself, scratching at the top of her head.

Jade glanced at the hands of the clock one last time as she placed the full dinner plates upon the setting of the table and sat down in the dining seat with her children as they began to enjoy the succulent feast of which she had prepared with her daughter. "I'm just going to place Shane's meal into the warm oven okay," Jade said, raising herself off the dining table chair and placing the covered full plate into the warmth of the oven. "Where are you Shane? she whispered to herself, a glaze of annoyance spreading across her face.

At seven thirty pm Jade began the nightly ritual of clearing the kitchen of the dishes and preparing the house for the next day's activities before driving Cody to his arranged sleepover at his friend's house. Upon her return Jade continued in the cleanliness of the household chores, whilst the children bathed and sat within the warmth of the loungeroom chairs in their enjoyment of the movies of which Jade had especially hired for their last nights of togetherness.

Jade could feel the overwhelming agitation sweeping through her senses as her eyes continuously glanced at the lateness of the evening, as she patiently awaited within the silence of Shane's arrival and notification of his lack of presence within the family home. "You could have at least let me know," she snapped at his blatant disregard of courtesy and care, pulling his waiting plate of food from out of the warm oven and placing it into the concealed unit of the microwave to cool down. "I think I'll send him a message."

Jade picked up her phone off the top of the kitchen bench and typed a message of questionable importance to Shane and sent it before placing her phone back upon the top of the kitchen bench, as she continued in her nightly ritual of cleanliness. Jade waited patiently for Shane's reply of explanation whilst sitting amongst her children's joy of the movies entertainments, as the ripples of agitation and anxiety surged through her senses, sending her mind and emotions into a questionable disconcertment.

"I can't believe you would be so thoughtless," Jade muttered under her breath, the grips of the agitated state rising within her in a growl of disapproval.

An hour later Jade heard the familiar tone of the message notification come through on her phone and rushed to the kitchen bench top of which she had placed it down in an agitated state.

"Hey babe. The boys have roped me into partying with them. Can you pick me up at 11 pm?"

"You're kidding," leapt from Jade's mouth in a growl of aversion, as she viewed the indecency of Shane's request. "How dare you do this today," Jade growled, slamming down the phone upon the small side table situated at the side of the loungeroom chair and raising to her feet in a disgruntled stance of disapproval.

"I'm just going outside kids okay," she announced, stomping through the dining room doorway and out of the back door to sit upon the outdoor setting chair to light a cigarette.

Jade anxiously tapped the lighter against the hard grain of the wooden tabletop, as her mind surged with the angry agitation of Shane's lack of empathy and consideration amongst the heartbreaking situation of her daughter's departure from her life.

"I needed you Shane. I needed you to be here," Jade cried, the tears of frustration falling in streams upon her flushed cheeks.

Jade paced the narrow pathways of the gardened area wiping at the tears that fell continuously from the frustration that had formed a tight knot of disappointment and disapproval within the pit of her stomach.

"How could you do this to me. Fuuck," she growled, stomping her feet back and forth along the narrow, gardened pathways in a desperate attempt to relieve the tempestuousness that swirled and knotted within herself. "Ahhh. I can't take this anymore," Jade growled out loud, pouring the wine into the glass that sat untouched on the outdoor setting. "That is it. That is it Shane," she yelled, marching towards the back door and up the hallway into the privacy of her bedroom.

Driven to the point of extreme frustration and overwhelmed within the acrimonious state of her emotions, Jade slammed open the doors of the tall cupboard which contained the contents of Shane's belongings and ripped them off clothes' hangers in bundled armfuls, before marching them through the house, dropping them in piles upon the back doorstep entrance.

"I hate you Shane. I hate you," Jade cried out, wiping away the tears that kept falling from her eyes.

"Mum, Mum. What's going on, what are you doing?" Monique called out, running from the peaceful confines of her bedroom into the chaos that lay at the back doorstep of the house.

Flustered in her agitated state of emotional declension, Jade kept stomping through in her stride of desecration, as the armfuls of Shane's belongings fell to the ground in a stream of frustration.

"That bastard has taken off again. I've had it with him. I've bloody had it," Jade yelled, tears streaming down her flushed cheeks. "He can get out."

Monique looked at her mother shocked and startled in the site of her mother's actions and words of frustration and bitterness, before running back into the safeness of her bedroom.

Although the children had bared witness to the horrific actions and words of their fathers' animosity towards the separation of the marriage, Jade had kept them in a concealed world of obliviousness to the onslaught of desolation and tempestuousness, as she faced each arising battle within the family home, but tonight she didn't.

As the last armful of Shane's belongings fell to the ground in a dishevelled pile of abandonment, Jade pulled her mobile phone from out of her jacket pocket and began a relentless attack of abusive ruthlessness, as she continuously typed messages of abuse and disappointment of which she sent to Shane's phone until she finally heard the call of his answer.

"What the fuck is going on?" Shane yelled as Jade answered the phone. Get in your fucken car and come and get me now," yelling his demands of confrontational profanity down the line of the phone. Jade let out a growl of contempt as she hung up the phone and harshly slid it back into her jacket pocket, as she walked back into the house and gathered her car keys from off the key hook situated on the kitchen wall.

"Monique get in the car," Jade said loudly, knocking on her bedroom door of where she had hidden herself away from the emotional chaos that surrounded them.

"Where are we going Mum?" Monique sobbed, wiping at the fearful tears that trickled down her young cheeks.

"I have to go and pick up Shane," Jade answered, mumbling continuous words of frustrated abuse under her breath. As Jade placed the cars gear lever into the reverse position Nick and James came running out from the confines of the house in a hurried state of question.

"Mum," they called out, running through the gate that led towards the undercover carport. "Can you give us a lift to our friend's house please."

"Yes alright," she answered, placing the car's gear lever back into the parked position, as the two boys climbed into the seats of the car.

Jade could feel the tension tightening throughout her senses which contorted her face into a tight lipped frown as she drove through the streets of Suisania Bay under the confrontational demands of Shane's request, until she came to a standstill on the opposite side of the footpath that ran down the length of the motorcycle gang's clubhouse. Jade pressed at the cars horn in her attempt to attract Shane's attention and to avoid exposing the confrontation of their dispute in the view of the other clubhouse members, and to not place Shane in a position of embarrassment in the eyes of his peers.

Frustrated in her agitation at the ignorance of Shane's attention to the cars horn, Jade climbed from out of the car door, followed by her daughter who walked sobbing in a terrified state to the locked gates of the clubhouse perimeter and pressed the horn to notify the members of her arrival.

"Hey Jade," the member greeted, opening the locked gate allowing her access to the concealed clubhouse.

"Hey," she replied tight lipped, walking through the gates and into through the door of the clubhouse followed by her daughter who stood huddled and sobbing behind her mother's legs.

"Is Shane here?" Jade abruptly asked, looking around the room of the clubhouse, searching for Shane's whereabouts.

"He'll be out in a minute," Ryan called out through the doorway that led to the privacy of the members room.

As Jade stood at the end of her bar in her wait for Shane's arrival within the presence of the other member who proceeded to console the terrified tears that ran down her daughter's cheeks with an essence of humour and empathy, Jade reached out her hand in an innocent playful tap of his shoulder and watched in unbelievable horror as he fell to the floor in an intoxicated tumble.

"Oh no. Oh my god," Jade gasped, covering her mouth with the cusps of her hands, trembling as she looked around the room for help of the members rise to his feet. Jade stood frozen in her confusion of what to do as her instincts told her to quickly leap to the other side of the forbidden space of the bar and help the fallen member back up to the stability of his feet, without the recognition of embarrassment or crucifixion of her innocent action of playfulness with the other members. Within moments of the member's tumble one of the members who stood behind the bar rushed to the scene of the fallen member and lifted his intoxicated state back into a standing position against the end of the bar, as Jade looked on in apologetic nervousness.

"Oh god, I'm so sorry. I'm so sorry. I didn't mean to. I just," Jade profusely apologised nervously, placing her hand to her forehead in disbelief of the event.

As the member stood stable in a slurred giggle of his swaggering intoxication, Shane entered the bar area from the hidden concealment of the members' room in an angry glance of agitation that looked straight through Jade in a conflagration of bitterness.

"Let's go," he demanded, shaking the hands of the other members and leading Jade and her sobbing daughter out through the doorway of the clubhouse.

As Jade placed her daughter into the back seat of the car she could feel the angry tension radiating from the agitated stance of Shane as he stood above her with his hands on his hips.

"You stupid bloody bitch. What do you think you're doing having a bloody go at me? Get over there," Shane growled, pointing Jade towards the direction of the passenger front seat of the car.

"No Shane. You're drunk. You're not driving the car with my daughter in the car in your state," Jade argued back, standing her ground in a moral defiance of his demands as they stood upon the gravel footpath next to the car.

"Get in the bloody car," Shane yelled, grabbing Jade with force by the top of her arm and marching her around to the passenger seat door before firmly shoving her down into the seat of the car and slamming the car door shut.

In a stance of drunken aberrance, Shane stomped back around to the other side of the car, climbing into the driver's seat and accelerated dangerously down the narrow streets of Suisania bay towards the outskirts of the town, enraged in the animosity of the continued quarrelling, as the tears fell in terrified streams down the face of her child in the back seat. Within minutes of leaving from the clubhouse situated on the other side of town, Shane sped the accelerated car into the covered driveway of the carport at the side of the family home and placed it into the parked position, as Monique scrambled from out of the back seat of the car in a state of inconsolable tears and hid herself behind the safety of their mother's legs.

"You stupid bloody bitch. You're gone," Shane yelled angrily through the open window of the driver's seat, slamming the gear lever into reverse and speeding out of the covered carport, leaving Jade and Monique standing helplessly in their distressed state.

"Shane. Come back Shane," Jade cried out, tears streaming down her flushed cheeks, as her mind twisted and crumbled under the emotional torment into a darkened world of helplessness.

"Ahhhhhhh," Jade screamed, dropping to her hands and knees on the carport pavement, looking helplessly into the darkened evening sky, as Monique fled from the conflict that surrounded them into the safe confines of her bedroom walls.

"Come back," Jade sobbed helplessly, the tormented tears flowing down the hollows of her cheeks.

Jade felt the torment closing in on her in a darkened blanket of helplessness as her world fell into a hypnotic silence of desperation, lifting the heavy weight held within her tiny frame to the steps of her footing as she slowly wandered blankly back in through the back door entrance and in through the kitchen door.

Leaning helplessly against the kitchen cupboard she reached her hand out towards the kitchen draw and gripped the handle of the sharpened knife and pulled it out from the draw, placing it hard against the soft skin of her wrist in a downward motion, closing her tear-stained eyes as she drew in the last breaths of her life. Within the darkness of the blackened trance Jade heard a soft whimpering cry of distress coming from within the confines of her daughter's bedroom walls.

"Ohh god," Jade cried out, the sound of her daughter's distress snapping her mind back from the darkened spell of her helplessness, her eyes falling towards the sharpened edge of the knife that pressed hard into the soft tissue of her skin.

"Ohh god. What am I doing?" her hand loosening from the tightened grip of the sharpened knife, dropping it to the hard tiles of the kitchen floor as she fell to her knees, placing her tear stained face into the palms of her hands.

"Oh god, help me, please help me," she cried, praying within the depths of her tormented mind, sliding her back down against the kitchen cupboard, looking out into the emptiness of the kitchen as the sharpened knife sat beside her on the kitchen floor.

Broken and shattered into a world of despair, Jade desperately searched for the strength to pull herself out from within the blackened spell of her own demise, as the whimpers of her distressed child's voice called louder and louder in her ears, rising her back to the standing of her feet.

"I'm coming. Oh god, I'm coming," Jade sobbed, wiping at the desperation that fell in a stream of tears down her flushed cheeks. Alone and shattered within her distress Jade walked from the solitude of her darkened world into the long hallway placing her head against the wooden grain of her daughter's bedroom door, her shaking hand reaching for the door knob as her hand turned the handle to open the bedroom door.

"Mum," her daughter cried out, running into the warmth of her mother's arms as she wrapped her distressed daughter into a comfort of her love.

"I'm sorry baby girl. I'm so sorry. I will never leave you. Never," Jade cried, holding her sobbing daughter tightly against the warmth of her heartbeat, as the heavy flow of tears fell in a continuous stream of heartbreak down her face.

That night Jade wandered the house alone within the blackened trance of her despair and tears as the sharpened knife of her near death lay still upon the tiled kitchen floor, until she finally came to rest upon the carpeted flooring of the hallway outside of her daughter's bedroom door, placing her head into the fold of her arms upon her knees.

In the early hours of the morning Jade heard the familiar click of the back door as she sat in the hallway outside of her daughter's bedroom, where she had stayed shattered and crying in the overwhelming torment of her heartbreak all night.

"Shane," she whispered, lifting her tear-stained face slowly from the folds of her arms upon her knees, turning her head towards the sound of the footsteps that stepped upon the tiled kitchen floor.

"What are you doing?" Shane said, startled by the shattered site of Jade's despair that sat silently sobbing against the wall of the carpeted hallway.

219

"Oh Shane," Jade sobbed, frozen into a state of emotional immobility. Shane rushed to Jade's side, lifting her tiny shaking frame up into his arms, carrying her along the long hallway to their bedroom and gently placed her down upon their bed, as he held her tightly against his chest.

"Oh god girl. Your daughter needs you," Shane said quietly, gently touching the side of her tear-stained cheeks.

"I don't know what to do. I don't want her to go," Jade sobbed, the inconsolable tears flowing in streams down her face.

"She needs you baby. She needs you," Shane replied, looking into the despair of sorrow within her eyes. Jade wiped at the tears that ran down her cheeks, pressing her forehead into the comforting warmth of Shane's chest as she grasped at her composure of strength to pull her from the blackened world of her emotional desperate state.

"I know. I know. Oh god, my baby girl," she sobbed, slowly climbing out from the comfort of Shane's arms and walking along the hallway to her daughter's bedroom, knocking quietly on the wooden door. "Oh sweetheart. Come here," she whispered, falling to one knee upon the bedroom floor and wrapping her daughter up into the comfort of her loving arms, as her daughter cried against the beating of her chest. "Come with me," Jade whispered, placing her finger gently under the down-tipped slant of her daughter's chin and raising her eyes into her own. "I love you baby girl. I love you." Jade wrapped her arms around her daughter and led her to the comforting warmth of her bed and lay her down in her arms next to her, as Shane curled himself around her, placing his arm around the two in an embrace of empathy, until the sounds of their sobbing became a silence of slumber.

Jade awoke within the early hours of the Saturday morning with her heart in her chest filled with the grieving sorrow of the impending sadness of the day's events.

As she crawled out from under the warmth of the covers of the bed and placed her feet upon the carpeted flooring of her bedroom she came to a standstill, as she sat motionless in a momentary of silence on the edge of the bed, placing her face into the cover of her palms. "I'm going to miss you sweet girl," Jade whispered to herself, raising to her feet from the side of the bed and walking down the long hallway to the children's bedrooms. One by one, she knocked on the children's bedroom doors, poking her head in between the crack of the opened door, waking them from their peaceful slumber in the preparation of her daughter's departure to move to Meltona to live with her father.

As she stood within the open crack of her daughter's bedroom she listened quietly to her daughter's breathing, as she watched the peacefulness of her slumber and breathed in the final moments of her light that filled the room with joy but was soon to be empty. "It's time to wake up sweetie girl," Jade whispered, kneeling down at the side of her bed, gently brushing her long brown hair from the small of her soft round cheek. "I'll miss you every day, my beautiful sweet girl."

Jade could feel the tears welling within her eyes as she watched her daughter's eyes open and a smile form upon her tiny lips with the sight of her mother's love sitting over her on the side of the bed.

"Good morning sweet girl," Jade said softly, smiling, sweeping the wisp of hair away from out of her eyes that lay upon her forehead.

"Good morning Mum," Monique replied quietly, stretching her arms out from under the warmth of her blankets, raising herself into a sitting position to place herself into the warm embrace of her mother's arms.

Jade could feel the pain within her heart grow within her in an overwhelming grip of emotional despair, but quickly composed herself into a state of supportive strength in her bravery and love to support her only daughter's decision of starting a new life with her father.

"We've got to get ready now okay? We've got to leave soon."

Jade walked back into the kitchen, where she sat to have her morning coffee, contemplating the moment of change that was about to occur. "Oh my sweet girl," Jade whispered to herself, her head falling heavily into the disconcerting sadness that covered her face and quivered her lips into a sadness of tears that ran freely down her soft cheeks. "What will I do without my sunshine."

Jade and Shane steadily packed Monique's belongings into the car and by seven thirty am, Jade called the words she had dreaded. "It's time to go kids."

As the weeks passed into only days until Monique's departure Jade spent the moments wrapped in sullen solitary as she hesitantly made the arrangements with Derek for the final day.

Derek had reciprocated the arrangements of the meeting at the police Station situated near the hills of Alterro, the restraining order posing no problem in their restraint of vicious attacks towards one another.

They had arranged to unhinge the packed trailer at the police station in order for Derek to hitch the heavy load of belongings and continue the hourly distance across the states to Meltona.

Jade swallowed hard at her emotions, pushing them down into the pit of her stomach were it ached with heartbreak as the family made their way down the long distance highway towards the city.

Each word that fell from her mouth hid in a cover of laughter but swallowed in a tear-stained formidableness. Jade soaked up each smile that spread across her children's faces, she adored each giggle, each word that lingered in her ears and tugged at her heart strings, the last moments of her family's togetherness.

The only silent moment sat between Jade and Shane as her attentions attentively lingered on her children.

Three hours later, they arrived at the designated police station that Jade had arranged with Derek, bringing the car to a halt and backing the trailer into the vacant parking bay.

Jade's heart pounded hard, tilting her face towards the ground in a dishevelled arrangement of her heart.

She rubbed at the pain that flowed through her chest, the pit of her stomach in an incessant flow of pain. "Oh, this is so hard," Jade whispered to herself, wiping at the tear that trickled from behind her dark sunglasses. "Ohh. Come here my sweet girl," Jade said, a smile lifting the tilted arches of her lips.

"Oh Mum, I am going to miss you," Monique said, raising her tiny face towards her mother, a quivering smile reaching the peaks of her mouth and reddening her cheeks in anxious sadness.

"Oh my sweet girl," wrapping her arms tightly around her young daughter in an embrace that swore it would never let go. Jade absorbed each moment, each sweet smell of her daughter's innocence and sweetness, their fingertips stroking each other, finger tips that would soon depart and let go into a world of perceptual heartbreak and longing.

"Everything's going to be okay," Jade said quietly, looking down at her daughter's beautiful little face. "You stay happy okay. I'm always with you, even though I'm not there okay, I'm right here," Jade whispered, holding down her emotions, pointing to Monique's heart. Jade could see the tears forming in Monique's eyes the emotions straining in her tiny face.

"You'll be fine sweetheart," Jade whispered again, wrapping her daughter in a tight embrace. "Don't you worry okay," Jade reassured her, kissing her warm cheeks. "I'm only a phone call away. Remember that okay."

Monique nodded her head and in a quiet, little voice, whispered to her mother, "I love you Mum."

Jade's heart nearly burst out of her chest, her embrace gripping tighter around her young daughter as her eyes filled with the immense pain of the solemn moment of sadness. Jade could feel the sadness grip her all the way through as she looked over at her boys, resting her chin upon her daughter's head.

Jade tried desperately to stop her tears from falling but lost the battle hearing those words from her little girl's lips, broke down the last bit of strength and composure she had and the tears flowed down her cheeks in a wash of heartbreak.

"Ohh, my girl," Jade sobbed, holding Monique even tighter. "I love you with all my heart. I'll miss you every day," Jade sobbed as they both stood there, holding onto one another, tears flowing down their cheeks as the time ticked over into a distant memory.

"Jade. It's time to go," Shane said, his face showing the emotional strain of the moment as he stood silently waiting and watching.

Jade placed herself into a selfless state of abandonment from her own emotional transition as her heart broke in front of his eyes. She had wanted to fall into the depths of her misery but held herself in a state of inconsolable silence.

Jade reached into her handbag and pulled out the tissues, handing one to Monique, with a slight, covering smile and giggle. "Look what you've done to me," she giggled pointing to her top. "I'm all wet."

Monique stood back, a small smile forming on her tiny mouth and giggled too. "Look what you've done to me," Monique said back, pointing to where her mother's tears lay on the shoulders of her top.

Jade and Monique nudged each other in a playful giggle. "Okay sweet girl, you take care of yourself okay. I'll give you a call in a couple of weeks when the boys get back okay. I love you," and Jade hugged and kissed her daughter one last time. "Bye sweetheart."

Jade slowly walked over to where her boys were standing stretching out her arms in a warm embrace and hugged and kissed them goodbye.

"Enjoy your time with your father okay," Jade said. "I love you. See you when you get back okay."

Jade slowly started to walk back to the front of the car, each step a painful acknowledgement of her children's departure.

Jade looked back at Monique as she opened the car door smiled at her and waved goodbye as she climbed into the car. Shane started the car and slowly started to drive away.

Jade turned her head, facing into the backseat to peer out of the back window, her hand waving at her children, at Monique, staring blankly in her solitary pain, holding painfully to the precious view that sat before her eyes until finally they drifted from view and Monique was gone.

Jade turned back to face the front of the car, her eyes falling heavily into her empty lap as the strained tears welling in her eyes fell into a solemn dryness. She knew in her heart that this was it, the last time her family would be together, the last time she would ever hold all her children at once in her arms. She knew her daughter's departure would be a final blow. Nothing would ever be the same.

A silent foreboding filled the front seat and covered Jade in a darkness of her broken heart as she closed her eyes behind the darkness of her sunglasses. A attentive numbness filled Jade's body and ached within the pit of her stomach as she sat in the front seat in silence, unable to mutter a word of her painful affliction as they drove towards the outskirts of the parking bay and away from her children. She did not cry, she did not speak as her hands wound into a tight balls into her lap before falling heavily by the side of her legs.

"I miss you already," Jade whispered into the seat of her lap, her eyes closing as the tears trickled down her cheeks from behind her dark sunglasses.

Parked within the perimeter of sight, Shane and Jade sat silently as they watched a blue car drive up the lane way and into the parking bay of the police station and reverse into the parking bay next to the abandoned trailer of which the children hoovered around in their wait.

"He's here," Jade said softly, watching as Derek quickly unloaded the trailer of Monique's belongings and filled the empty trailer attached to his car before the children finally got into the vehicle and they drove out from the perimeter of the police station's parking bay and headed towards the outskirts of Alterro and disappeared from view.

"Okay, I'm going back to get the trailer," Shane announced. "Then were going to Simon and Kay's house for the night. I told them we would stay the night with them and have a few drinks."

"Thoughtless," ran through Jade's mind as she listened to the announcement. "That's the last thing that I want to do. I just want to go home."

"Okay," Jade finally muttered, suppressing the tender emotions welling up within her.

Jade sat in silence looking out of the car's window as Shane drove back into the parking bay of the police station and hitched the empty trailer to the car before heading back towards the highway.

The thirty-minute drive felt like an eternity as Jade stared blankly out of the car window, her eyes avoiding the contact of the other passing vehicles and oblivious to the people that surrounded her in their travels. Her mind raged with the sadness that overwhelmed her senses and tugged at the tears that welled continuously in her eyes and tightened within her throat.

Shane pulled the car to a stop at the end of the narrow cement driveway and exited the vehicle and walked towards the rundown entrance of his friend's house, leaving Jade sitting alone in her isolated state of emotions. "Come on," Shane called out, directing his attention back in the parked car's direction.

Jade swallowed hard, the sullenness of her emotions written all over her face and weighing heavily in her slumped shoulders as she exited the vehicle and came to join Shane on the front door step.

"Have you told them why we came down today?" Jade asked, her lips quivering with emotion.

"No, no I didn't," Shane replied quickly, as the front door of the house burst open and they were greeted with a smile.

Jade sat down at the outdoor setting, the family utilised as a dinning suite, staring at the stained concrete floor and the paraphernalia of drugs that lay strewn across the kitchen benches and the alcohol laden table in view of the babies and toddlers that lay oblivious across the laps of the mothers sitting around the outdoor setting.

"God," Jade whispered to herself, dropping her face into the direction of her lap out of view. Although Jade had always accepted Shane's friends and conducted herself in a precise manner of friendship she had not condoned the ill-moral behaviour of the setting within view of the numerous children and babies that suckled at the breast of their alcoholic and drug induced mothers. Jade hid her angst well behind a mask of a smile or words of friendship but did not approve of Shane's friends whom she felt were below the normal standards of which she was accustomed.

Jade sat silent, sipping the tea from the smeared tea cup as she watched the pot smoke bellow through the atmosphere of the kitchen and loungeroom filling the lungs of the toddlers that wandered in dirty nappies through the small house, while their mothers refilled their plastic cups with the cheap wine and beer and merrily drank without restraint or moral aversion.

The foul-spiked words of the men's chatter filled the room without scrupulousness or refrain of the children's presence which sat in Jade like an ill-moral bad seed, this was not her scene of preference and kept her in a state of pretending past the obvious.

"I just want to go home," ran through her mind and traced through the lost sparkle in her eyes until she could stand no more.

Jade rose from the make shift table setting and walked over to join Shane at the kitchen bench who had just emptied a little clear bag of cocaine onto the kitchen bench and started to arrange the lines of their pleasure into an assortment of usage.

"I'm going to bed okay," Jade said quietly in Shane's ear. "I'm not feeling very well."

Shane looked at Jade, studying the blankness that filled her eyes and lay across the bleakness of her face in a cold shoulder of disgust.

"Yeah, okay. I'll be there soon, give me about an hour and I'll be with you okay."

A small polite smile tilted the corners of Jade's mouth as she said goodnight to Shane's friends and vacated the kitchen to the small, dishevelled, clothes-strewn bedroom which they had been allocated for the evening, and climbed into the dirty, stale sheets of the beds covers and rolled into a tight ball of her own lonely sobbing. "How could he be so cold and so indifferent to my emotions. My only daughter has just moved away and I don't know if she'll ever come home again," Jade sobbed to herself, the tears rolling down her makeup and staining the soiled pillow case that lay softly under her cheek.

In a house so full of people, she had never felt so alone and could find no comfort.

The next morning, Jade awoke early, tired and emotionally weary from the constant tossing and turning of her emotional sleep. She had not felt Shane come to bed that night as she sobbed silently in her own melancholic state of sadness until she finally feel asleep and was sure that it was a late night until he finally slipped between the sheets to join her.

"Shane," Jade whispered gently nudging his shoulder. "Are you awake?"

"Hmm, what?" Shane stirred, muttering in a sleepy tone, his eyes, bloodshot and glassy a picture of the night he had spent with his friends.

"Yeah, I'm awake, now," Shane replied, his voice grumpy at the disturbance of his sleep.

"Can we go soon? I want to go home," Jade asked gently, careful to not cause a commotion between them. "I really want to go home," she told him, her voice filled with sadness and hollowness.

"Yeah, okay," Shane answered, as he rolled over onto his back, wiping the sleep from his weary eyes.

Jade climbed out of the bed, grabbing her overnight bag on the way out and headed for the bathroom. She opened the bathroom door.

"Oh my god," she whispered to herself, as she viewed the site before her, raising the palm of her hand to cover her open mouth in disbelief.

Black, thick mould and mildew covered the once-white tiles within the shower cubicle and followed the tiles around to the basin and bath that smelt of mould and filth.

The white enamel of the bath a putrid grey of soap scum and dirt of which the toddlers had once bathed and left their mould-stained toys in the bottom of the sentiment that clung to the bottom of the bath.

Dirty clothes and towelling covered the floor in a strewn disarray of dirtiness, discarded by the many bathers whom had been before.

"You've got to be kidding. I cannot shower in here," Jade said to herself clinging tightly to the clothing strewn over her arm and walked back towards the bedroom where Shane continue to lay. "Ohhh. Those poor kids," the thought running through her head at the site.

Jade stopped and stood in front of the basin situated outside of the bathroom cubicle and quickly washed her face and tidied her hair into a neat pony tail before venturing down the hallway to join Shane in the bedroom. "I'll have a shower when I get home," Jade said upon entry into the bedroom.

Within moments of Jade's return Simon knocked on the door of the bedroom and announced himself, the sequential signs of the night before written in a vindication across his face.

"You guys off hey," Simon asked.

"Yeah, we've got to get back mate," Shane answered, the reason for their early departure not explained in words.

Shane and Jade continued to place their belongings into their overnight bags and packed them neatly into the back seat of the car as Simon followed them to the vehicle heavy-footed.

"We'll see you again soon then," he said, waving, as Shane backed the car out of the driveway and wound down the window.

"Say goodbye to the others for us and just explain that we had to leave early mate will ya."

"No worries mate, will do," Simon replied, raising his hand in a waving gesture as the car left down the road.

Over the next three hours of the long drive back to Suisania Bay Jade sat sullen and silent in the front seat, her face shielded from Shane's view with a turn of her head towards the closed car window.

The sights around her had disappeared into a distant blur of emptiness and subdued withdrawal from Shane's knowledge, as the tears of anguish overwhelmed her and fell heavily down her sallow, pale face from behind her dark sunglasses.

"Are you crying?" Shane snapped at her angrily, Jade's silence a deafening ignorance to the comment.

"Hey," Shane said again, his voice now irritated.

Jade motioned her head in a response without a word leaving her lips and wiped at the tears that ran in a continuous stream down her cheeks.

"Fuck girl, get the fuck over it and toughen the fuck up for fuck's sake," Shane yelled at her, his voice angry in annoyance at her display of emotion.

Jade drew a deep breath as her breath wavered with the tears she now held so tightly within the depth of her throat and wiped at her tear soaked cheeks as she turned her head away from the neglect of sympathy.

"How could you be so cruel to me, lack so much empathy. You know how much I love my children," ran through Jade's mind as she consoled the raising sediment within the pit of her stomach and curled her hands into a tight ball within the depths of her lap.

Jade went numb, a hollow formed in her heart as the world around her turned a dark shade of grey and her words stuck within her throat before she could speak.

When they arrived back in Suisania Bay an uncomfortable silence travelled through the house as Shane pulled the queen size mattress off the bed base and dragged it onto the loungeroom floor in preparation for his planned time without the children's presence.

"I've got these," he announced, pulling a secret little bag from out of his jeans pocket filled with the little white pills of their hallucinogenic pleasure.

"Want one Jade? Want a drink?"

But Jade did not want to drink nor did she want to escape the overwhelming grief of devastation that filled her stomach and ached within her heart and curled herself into a solemn ball upon the empty mattress and cried.

That week, powerless to stop the dark cloud that engulfed her and drained her soul of life, Jade fell into a deep, dark depression and stayed within the comforting confines of the warm bed covers that lay upon her body and covered her face with a cloak of closure to the outside world.

Her hands remained in tight balls by her side as her posture turned from the warmth of Shanes presence and touch and stared at the blank wall that stood before her in the kitchen doorway. She did not eat, she did not sleep, nor speak and stayed within the tight coil of her depressed state for two days as her mind willed her body to give up in helplessness and heartbreak as she slowly lost her grip on the reality that surrounded her. On the third day, Jade finally moved, crawling from the bed that had been her prison for two days, a spot that had wrapped her in a coffin blanket and beckoned her to stay.

Shane had left that morning, Jade's inability to console the inconsolable grief and venture into a hallucinogenic world of fun and sex pushing away at their relationship and separating the two into reciprocated solidarity.

"Fuck ya. I'm out of here," Shane said, grabbing his jacket off the kitchen table and leaving through the back door.

The cruel words ran over Jade's shoulders and fell to the floor in a voice of familiarity, as her mind disconnected from the abusive condemnation and held no meaning to her.

"Oh Max, I need you, I really need you now," Jade whispered to herself from under the shadow of the bedcovers. You're the only one I can trust to help me."

Although Jade had stopped the affair with Max while she was in a relationship with Shane, her infatuation and love had not wavered. She had felt the guilty shame of their pleasures when she had informed Max of her relationship and the true fact that she had fallen in love with both of them.

She had no longer felt comfortable to indulge in such guilty pleasures of secrecy with Max and had stopped the sexual affair which had been deviated into a strong bond of friendship and played in the background of her life without the knowledge of the outside world.

That night in Shane's absence, Jade sat down in front of her computer screen and typed a letter to Max.

Hey Max,

Things are not going well here at all. I had a terrible weekend. My daughter has now moved to Meltona to live with her father. I'm devastated. I don't know what I'll do without her; she was my little angel. Every day I wake up, I can't see her, I can't hold her. I miss her so much already. It broke my heart to let her go. I'm so worried about her. She's moved to live in a big city, leaving primary school and heading straight into high school with the older children she's only twelve years old and I'm not there to protect her and I'm worried that I won't see her again I'm just so sad. Shane has been of no support at all; his words on the day, "Toughen the fuck up and get the fuck over it. Yeah, I know, cruel hey."

He used to be so nice to me when we first met but now he's just so mean and nasty and I think he's cheating on me and has been since we first met.

My life is a mess and I just don't know how to fix it. Everything is going so wrong with the kids, Shane, my life. I can't stop crying this has been the final blow and I don't know how I will go on without my little girl. I wish you were here I need a hug so badly right now. I love you.

Love always Jade
Xxx

Within an hour Max replied, his sweet words of comfort reaching a level of consolability of which she so desperately needed. "Oh Max, my sweet Max," Jade muttered, tears rolling down her face.

Jade read the sweet words of comfort over and over again until they deeply entrenched themselves into her heart. Each word wrapped her in a reputable state of stupendousness and slowly curled the corner of her lips to the smile of which returned and soothed her soul and brought clarity to her mind.

"Oh my sweet Max," Jade whispered, holding her palm against her chest as the clarity of his words worked their way into her heart and mind. "I knew I could trust you to be there for me."

That night Jade and Max exchanged words until 3 am in the morning, each letter a soothing reminder of their close bond of friendship and the special connection which they shared.

Jade sat back in her office chair reading Max's letters over and over, allowing the words to sink into her mind, letting them restore her battered emotions, her confidence which had suffered the momentous blow of failure to her children. Shane's cruel words that although had fallen off her shoulders, at the time wreaked havoc to her venerable state and the ordeal which she had just suffered.

That night in Shanes absence from the family home Jade did not crawl back into the isolated helplessness that had held her within the covers of her bed and instead remained within the warm comfort of her best friends words until the early hours of the morning.

In that moment with Max Jade felt she could go on although the loss of her children still rang over and over in the depths of her mind.

Could she rebuild her fractured life? Could she let Max's encouragement, his sweet, sweet words restore her back to the person she was? Would it be enough?

Jade walked the long hallway, down to the kitchen, each step, a confident reminder of her best friend's support as she allowed herself to absorb the kindness and warmth of his words.

"Max believes in me. He thinks I'm somebody of worth," Jade found herself softly whispering, trying to assure herself, raise herself from the hellish torment of emotions that had sunk her into a deep, isolated state of helplessness within the covers of her bed.

Jade pulled the coffee cup down from out of the kitchen cupboard and placed it in front of the boiled kettle, as she looked at the mattress that lay on the floor, the mattress she had found so hard to leave, to crawl from, to raise herself from and find a small piece of hope, hope to live again and go on.

Jade had not spoken to Max in a long time, they had agreed to keep their interaction to a minimal, Jade had needed to loosen the tight grip of her infatuation he had had on her as she had loved him too deeply, she needed to let him go but now, Jade needed him again more than ever. Jade needed the man that she had come to know so deeply and had loved for two years.

This night belonged to them, their world of fantasy, their world of the forbidden love.

Shane returned the next day, unaware and oblivious to the night's adultery of companionship and deception of which Jade had spent in the arms of her online lover.

"Hey," Shane said as he walked through the door.

"Hey," Jade replied, a small smile lighting her face for a moment.

"Damien has invited us over to his place on the weekend, he's going to do a tattoo for me. Do you want to come?" Shane asked.

"Yeah, I'll go," Jade replied. "What tattoo are you having done?"

"I'm getting a tattoo for us. The one I've been working on," Shane told her.

Jade had not believed Shane when he had told her about getting the tattoo, she had not believed that the words were the truth of their relationship, but rather, his devotion to the clubhouse, although he had said he had wanted to leave the club his actions spoke more to her than his words.

Jade stopped and thought about it for a moment before answering.

"Oh, okay, yeah cool," she eventually said. "I'm going for a shower okay, then we can catch up."

Jade felt the coldness of her avoidance creep up her spine as she walked away from Shane and entered the bathroom. She had felt the abandonment deeply in her hour of need and felt let down by his decision to walk out on her and go to the clubhouse to socialise because of her refusal to partake in the party drugs of his choice. To her this was not their time to celebrate but a time to reflect and morn her loss, the grief of her sadness a lonely reminder of what was to come without her little girl present and in her arms each day.

Jade wanted to leave Shane but did not have the strength to walk away and felt isolated in her own decisions as she slowly showered and groomed herself. She could not say the words and spent the night avoiding the subjects of the reflected days before when she said goodbye to her little girl.

Jade felt trapped, between her own ruins and her loyalty to Ryan whom had introduced her to Shane and felt so proud of his accomplishment of making two people happy, she no longer knew what she should do, nor which way to turn and fell into a cautious perfunctory of being.

Jade returned from the shower and joined Shane in the loungeroom, placing herself in the chair beside him. "What do you want to do tonight?" she asked quietly.

"I don't know, maybe get some movies and just hang out here," Shane suggested.

"Yeah, okay, that sounds good," smiling back at him. "How about we get some takeaway on the way home as well? I don't really feel like cooking," Jade suggested, a slight guilt covering her face at the non interest she was showing towards the kitchen.

"Yeah, we can do that," Shane agreed. "Let's go now hey."

"I'll just get my purse," Jade called back, walking towards the bedroom before returning. "Let's go."

The following weekend Shane and Jade went to Damien's house. As they started to get ready, Jade stood still in front of the mirror staring at the woman that reflected back at her, at the mask that hid her devastation so well. Although a week had passed Jade still felt the effects of the emotional collapse that had rendered her helpless and had laid her in the solitary confinement of the mattress on the floor. No longer did she feel the bubbles of excitement that had raged within her, no longer did she feel like leaving the house or socialising with her friends or Shane. Jade's emotional wellbeing suffered an endless bout of depression that harboured itself around her like a heavy black cloud of sadness and debilitating helplessness.

As Shane walked past her slowly he noticed her fixated stare into the mirror and with a slight movement of his shoulder he nudged her softly from her trance.

"What are you doing? C'mon girl, let's go," urging Jade to move from the spot she was entranced.

Jade's stare broke as her sense of reality returned from the brink of her venerability, grabbing her handbag and throwing it over her shoulder.

"I'm ready," she smiled. "I was waiting for you," Jade teased as they walked from the room and left for the day.

Moments later, they arrived at Damien's house and walked around to the back of the house to the large steel shed situated at the back of the small garden area.

Shane and Jade entered the shed and was soon greeted by Damien who stood in his waiting, sipping an ice cold beer. "Hey, how you going mate," Damien greeted them, shaking Shane's hand and nodding his head in Jade's direction.

Jade had never been to Damien's home before and although he was a member of the clubhouse, his personal socialising had remained a secret to Jade. Jade felt honoured and privileged to be invited to the privacy of his personal life and soon felt comfortable in the welcomed greeting.

"Hey mate," Shane greeted back. "We ready to do this today?"

"All set," Damien answered, motioning towards the barber chair that sat in the middle of the large shed, a make shift tattoo bed that served its purpose well.

Jade looked around at the many posters and pictures that adorned the steel walls of the large shed, pictures of club outings, motorbikes and many tattoo designs.

"Did you draw these Damien?" Jade asked smiling.

"Yes," Damien answered quickly, opening the refrigerator, and offering them a drink.

"Wow. I'm impressed, I had no idea you were so talented."

Jade sat on the old lounge settee as she watched the men's preparations for the tattoo, which Shane had come to have applied, and sipped at the chilled bourbon of which she had been handed.

Within moments of their arrival Jade heard a voice coming from behind them. "Hey, how are you?"

Jade turned around to acknowledge the voice coming from the opened door of the shed and stood in her greeting of Damien's wife, Michelle.

"Oh hi," Jade replied, smiling at Michelle. "I'm good, How are you?"

"Yeah good thanks," Michelle answered back, entering the shed to join the party of three.

"Do you want a drink babe?" Damien asked, pointing to the half-filled glasses sitting on the shed bench.

"Yeah sure," Michelle answered, giving Jade a cheeky smile.

Damien continued to make the drinks as Shane removed his T-shirt and lay down on the tattoo chair in preparation for his masterpiece to be drawn.

"Cheers," Damien said, handing them their drinks.

"Cheers," they all said together, sipping the chilled liquor. Jade and Michelle were accustomed to each other, having been introduced to each other upon her relationship with Shane and although they had not known each other that long, had found no trouble in engaging in conversation and soon the shed was full of music and a constant flow of chit chat.

Michelle and Jade sat down on the lounge that had been placed by the refrigerator in line with the tattoo chair, locked in their conversation, both eager to watch the tattoo come to life on Shane's torso.

"Okay mate, how do you want me to lay?" Shane asked Damien.

"Just straight down on your back, just like you are mate," Damien replied as he pulled the already prepared stencil from the bench draw.

Shane had decided to situate the tattoo on his stomach, three words that read Respect Trust Honour that ran down the middle of his torso in a circular arched design.

Jade and Michelle looked at each other as Damien placed the first stencil, the first word against Shane's skin. "Oh, this is going to hurt," Jade and Michelle giggled playfully at each other.

Michelle stood up and walked to the other side of the room. "I think we need some music for this occasion," she suggested, switching on the stereo and placing a compact disc into the player and adjusting the volume to a level loud enough to enjoy but soft enough to still be able to talk to one another.

"Michelle," Damien called to his wife. "Get out the gear hey."

Michelle smiled at her husband and walked over to the cupboard that was situated above the long bench of the large shed wall.

She pulled out a clear bag filled with the white powder and placed it on the bench where she proceeded to line up eight lines of the drug equivalenting to two lines each.

"Jade," Michelle called out, flicking her long brown hair sideways, motioning Jade over to the bench.

Jade giggled, dropping her head slightly in a cheeky grin, and stood to walk over to join Michelle standing at the bench. Michelle handed her the rolled up fifty dollar note. "Ladies first," Michelle teased. "Might as well party while the boys are busy hey," she said laughing.

Jade laughed back as she bent over the bench and inhaled the fine white powder then proceeded to pull the bag of pot from out of her handbag.

"Ok, let's do it," Jade laughed, as she packed the first cone into the bong sitting on the bench.

As the intoxication of the sweet, chilled liquor and the white powder of the cocaine swept upon them in a rush of exuberance and a mellifluous flow of laughter and movement, the women's chatter became louder and louder, while the men, continued to remain calm and focused on Shane's tattoo .

Once drawn in place Michelle and Jade sat back down on the lounge ready to hear the first prick of the colour-loaded cold needle of the tattoo gun infuse into Shanes skin.

"He he he," the girls giggled at each other, their eyes fixated on the gun as the tip of the needle was lowered towards Shanes skin in line with the first penetration of the needle tip.

Shane's face went still, forming a tight grimace, his body, a slight flinch as he felt the needle break his skin and lay the first coloured bead of the first permanent word.

"Oh, is that it," Jade teased, nudging Michelle's shoulder playfully. "I wanted to hear a squeal," she laughed, as Michelle joined in on the tease.

Michelle and Jade continued in their playful venture as the men continued with the concentrated design of the tattoo application.

Hours passed as the two women enjoyed each other's company, chatting, drinking and dancing to what had now become, loud music as the men continued with the application of the tattoo, that was now halfway completed.

"We should go get some munchies," Michelle suggested to Jade while the men just laughed at the now giddy girls that played around them.

"Yes," Jade giggled back jumping to her feet quickly out of her sitting position on the lounge. "I'm starving."

Michelle grabbed the car keys that hung on the hook on the shed wall and directed Jade towards the car that was parked under the carports veranda.

"Back in a minute boys," she said, as Jade and Michelle walked from the shed and out to the car.

Jade jumped into the passenger seat still giggling and chatting, enjoying the fun and the intoxication of the day with her friends.

Jade and Michelle's chatter continued as they hurried down the back streets of Suisania Bay, heading for the nearest opened bottle shop drive thru, seeking to purchase more alcohol and food supplies for the fun indulgence of the day's events.

As they pulled into the drive thru of the local bottle shop they were soon greeted by a familiar smile.

"Hey Paul," they greeted, the dark-haired tall man standing in waiting to serve them, the smiles on their faces, speaking a thousand unspoken words.

"Hey girls," Paul greeted them back with a smile. "What can I get for you?"

Michelle and Jade, chatted and laughed with him as they placed their order for the alcohol and quickly gathered the supplies from the limited choices of snack foods that the drive through had to offer before continuing the drive back to their home along the outskirts of Suisania Bay.

Within minutes, Jade and Michelle pulled up in the driveway of the house and headed back into the shed at the back of the home, waving the snacks and alcohol they had just purchased at Shane and Damien.

"We're back," the girls smiled at the men who flashed a cheeky grin at their playful antics.

Michelle and Jade continued, joking and dancing as the intoxication of the cocaine fuelled their antics into a flirtation of words and dance as they teased the men with their womanly bisexual charms. As the music slowed, so did the movements between Jade and Michelle, the gap between them shortened, as they stepped into one another and their hips swayed, pushing up against one another into a slow embrace of affection.

Michelle and Jade looked over at the men as they stroked each other's bare shoulders and slowly ran their fingertips up and down the curves of each other's womanly bodies smiling seductively at each other.

Damien and Shane looked on with amusement, the entertainment of their women playing together, thrilling them and sending them into laughter.

Suddenly Michelle seductively moved forward, closer and closer, until she meet the warm embrace of Jade's soft lips and kissed her passionately on the make shift dance floor, the tantalising sensation of another woman's lips upon hers sending quivers down Jade's spine.

Jade had known of Michelle's fascination with other women, also of the couple's adventurous indulgence in threesomes, an adventure they had tried to entice Jade into joining with them many times before she had met Shane, but Jade had refused continuously.

At the time Jade had seen it as trouble waiting to happen although she felt a connection and womanly attraction towards Michelle she worried their relationship would not withstand a capitulation into voyeurism and she would be blamed for the cataclysm of their relationship.

But Jade did not refuse, not tonight and as the intoxication of the cocaine and alcohol lowered her defences and inhibitions into an intoxicated state of surrender and slowly and passionately kissed Michelle back right in front of Shane.

"Hey! Whoa! What the fuck are you doing?" Shane yelled, leaping up from the position in which he lay, Damien quickly removing the tattoo gun from out of his way. Shane rushed towards the two women as Michelle giggled at the antics.

Jade's face dropped to a quick gasp at her own lack of inhabitations as she stepped away from Michelle quickly in the realisation of her own naughtiness.

"Oh my," Jade gasped, holding her hand to her open mouth, her feet moving one more step backwards.

Jade dropped her head in instant guilt and took a step back from Shane's angry glare that pierced straight through her, driving home the anger of his disapproval.

"You fucken bitch," Shane yelled at her, looking Jade straight in the eyes, pushing her shoulder, knocking her slightly off balance.

"Aw, chill out," Michelle piped up. "We were just playing, teasing you guys, it was nothing," Michelle explained.

"Fuck off, it was nothing. You're coming onto my girlfriend. And you. You fucken bitch. You let her," Shane yelled back pointing his finger straight at Jade. Jade stood motionless, silenced, not a word left her mouth.

"C'mon mate, calm down, they were just playing," Damien's voice came from behind the angry scene.

Shane turned his head to look back at Damien. "C'mon, let's finish here," Damien said, trying to calm the situation. Shane turned back towards Jade to face her directly, who was still standing frozen in the spot, fearing the cold glare pointing straight at her.

"That's it for the night. You're lucky I don't slap you," Shane said sternly, his voice filled with anger. "Get over there, sit the fuck down and shut the fuck up. Night's over for you," Shane yelled, pointing Jade towards the lounge.

Jade sat down on the lounge in a guilty suppression of her boyfriend's fury.

Damien smiled at Michelle and nodded his head towards the house, to which she nodded back.

"Ok, I'm going to bed," Michelle said, saying goodnight as she walked from the shed and towards the backdoor of the house.

Jade didn't dare say a word to Michelle as she left but gave her a little wave of her hand out of Shane's glare. Jade lay her head down on the lounge and curled into a tight ball of guilt, hiding from Shane's glare of disapproval, as the men continued with the art of completing the tattoo.

The next morning, Jade was awoken by a nudge to her shoulder. She slowly opened her eyes and stretched her arms out in front of her as Shane stood over her in his waiting.

"C'mon girl," Shane said. "It's time to go."

Jade rubbed her eyes as she viewed her surroundings and soon realised she had slept the night away on the lounge, the lounge in Damien's shed with their cat curled up in a ball on top of her, her blanket for the night. She reached her hand down to the sleeping cat. "Hey kitty," she whispered, as she picked it up from its sleeping position and placed it on the lounge next to her.

Jade looked up at Shane, still standing there, waiting for her to move from her sleepy spot.

"Is it done, did you get it finished?" she asked softly, unsure of the response she would receive that day.

"Yeah," Shane replied lifting up his T-shirt to reveal the raw tattooed stained skin that lay underneath.

"What ya think?" he asked. Jade looked at the fresh tattoo, studying the lines and colours of the design.

"I like it, it looks good," she said, smiling up at Shane. Shane flashed a quick smile back at her in Jade's relief. Jade quickly rose from off the lounge and gathered her belongings and followed Shane out of the shed and towards the car.

A gentle chatter filled the car as they drove home.

That night Jade and Shane relaxed and indulged in the intoxication of the little white pills as their playfulness turned into a tantalising pleasure of erotic sexual lust and passion fuelled by the intoxication.

That night Jade experienced her first touch of another pleasure as Shane pushed her past her inhibitions and into a world of erotica, as he introduced her to her first sexual pleasure of anal sex. Jade had never allowed a man to touch her so sensually or erotically, and Jade liked it.

As the week drew to an end, now sober Jade's depressive state hit her hard and she spent her days alone while Shane was at work, locked in a depressed stare out of her bedroom window, sitting on the side of her bed, alone, unable to function, unable to think or feel, engulfed in the emotional devastation of her own torment and heartbreak.

"Oh I miss you already my sweet girl," Jade cried in despair, the tears that welled in her eyes falling in a heavy cloud as they rolled down her pale, shallow cheeks.

At night, in the evenings when Shane returned from work, Jade placed on her mask, the human disguise of her heart-wrenching helplessness and joined him in a drug fuelled frenzy of the pills and cocaine.

The intoxicating world of the little white pills and the fine white powder that she once was offered, now had become her hand that asked, her mind that begged for the fantasia of the sensations of her way out of her everyday hell on earth, as she craved to stay within the fantasy of her drug-fuelled states.

Jade had fallen victim to a depressed state as the drug addiction grew in momentous proportions and held her entrapped in the world of fantasy and seduction to which she knew no way out.

The following week James, Nick and Cody returned from their vacation with their father and Jade's mornings were once again filled with the hectic school routine. Each morning Jade faked a smile as she kissed Shane goodbye as he left for work and made her way through the rush of getting her children to their place of education before returning to her bedside prison of depression within her isolation.

Jade avoided the confrontation of her daughter's bedroom, a heartbreak of which she was unable to face as she walked through the family home in her family's absence.

Within a month, her once healthy, bright disposition disappeared under a cloak of sleep deprivation, she had lost her will to concentrate or eat and her weight plummeted leaving her already petite frame a hollowed, pale version of her once curvaceous, rosy self. Jade's hair began to suffer and began to change colour as the dull, lifeless darker shade fell in matted clumps that lay in the bottom of the bathtub as she showered. Jade felt she could take no more, she felt she had nowhere to turn and one by one her dreams disappeared enslaving her hope with them.

Jade struggled through each day, locked in her emotional state of devastation as she sat alone on the side of her bed, her empty eyes lost in her battle of condemnation. She could not escape the longing in her mind to escape the reality of her shattered life by the hands of the little white pill and cocaine that she consumed on the weekends with Shane, when the children would stay at their friends' houses.

Her battle with Derek continued, and seemed never-ending as she perilously travelled to Alterro and attended endless meetings with her lawyer, month after month that had escalated to week after week. Jade had been battling Derek in court for two years now, restraining orders, custody orders, divorce proceedings and now the last battle, to which Derek had fought the hardest, refusing point blank to pay his side of the debts.

James continued in a downward spiral of bad behaviour as he slid into a world of criminal activity and drugs which Jade had lost all hope of turning around in the state of which she had plummeted.

"Something's gotta give before it's too late," Jade whispered to herself as she sat on the edge of the bed.

Derek and Jade refused to retract and stood locked in their confrontation as each court date rolled into another, neither one willing to budge, neither one willing to come to an agreement; there seemed no end in sight until under the strain, Jade finally gave in.

Jade went to court that day already defeated; she stood alongside her lawyer, her eyes grey, her face drawn and pale, blank, unable to raise any emotions, she did not care anymore and helplessly agreed to Derek's demands. The court had decided that Derek was responsible for the credit card debts that while in the marriage had accumulated to fifty thousand dollars, to which he was responsible for paying half.

"I just want this over. Pay your half of the credit cards and take half of what's left of the house settlement and I'll walk away," Jade stood up in anguish and disgust.

The court house fell silent, all eyes fell on Jade, she knew that was not the right decision, she knew she had stopped fighting for what should have been fair but this had to stop, she had lost the will to fight for her rights, a never ending battle.

Jade no longer cared for what was fair, it was just money; it couldn't replace her daughter. The case was closed.

The credit card debts were paid, the mortgage was paid and the remaining amount of twelve thousand dollars, split between Derek and Jade. But Jade did not see any of the money, her lawyers had been paid out, with a debt of two thousand dollars still owing, the store accounts and utilities were left in the responsibility of Jade and she never received a cent for the continuous flight expenses she had paid for in order to send her children to see their father on the school holidays.

But Jade did not care, she could no longer fight with Derek and needed her life to move forward past the pettiness of Derek's oppugnation.

Through the turbulence of the trials, Jade no longer held the position of her employment and had now been plunged into debt, a weight she was willing to bear and struggle through as her mind weakened in the devastation of losing her daughter.

That day Jade walked away from court relieved and closed the chapter, the battle finally over after a two year period; Derek had won.

Over the next couple of weeks, Jade's mind started to spark again day by day, bit by bit; she slowly left her prison bed seat and had started to sit outside of her daughter's bedroom door, just sitting there, staring at the pictures still stuck on the door, the pictures her daughter had drawn, her hand-drawn name tag still stuck there that burned deep into Jade's heart but now the tears that had been sunk deep within her to hide the pain, rose to the top in a gushing flood of endless tears.

Then the day came when finally, Jade opened the bedroom door and took a step behind and faced the devastation of her own heartbreak. "Oh my sweetie girl, I miss you so much," she whispered holding a hand to her forehead as she looked around the bedroom.

Jade walked to the side of her daughter's bed, still made up with the pink sheets and her daughter's favourite quilt, a reminder of her once sleeping beauty that adorned the room and shone in Jade's heart like gold. Jade sat on the side of the bed, her hand reaching to stroke the pretty pink pillow, a place where her daughter's head had rested in peaceful slumber, a place where they had laid together many times.

"I miss you baby girl," Jade whispered as the overwhelming emotions filled her soul and rushed from her eyes in a torrent of tears, dropping streams upon the empty pillow.

Day after day, when Jade's children left for school and Shane had left for work and she was all alone, Jade entered Monique's room, sitting on the side of Monique's bed, stroking at her daughter's pillow, looking at the walls still adorned with memories of the life that was once there, the precious little girl that had lit up her world, the smile that had warmed her heart every day, the life she missed so much.

Jade sat on the side of the bed feeling every moment of the short time she had got to spend with her daughter her mind going over every memory, every smile, every laughter, the little girl's birthday parties filled with balloons and giggles, the music and dancing, the drawings and colourings, the ice cream and cooking, the walks and talks, the hugs and kisses and their special words they had only for each other at the end of every day, but now it was time to let it go, now it was time.

Jade looked around at the little pieces of her daughter's memories still in the room, the pieces of furniture that were still there, the empty draws where her clothes once were placed, the pictures on the walls and the teddy bears she had left behind.

"Oh, my sweet girl," Jade cried out as she fell to her knees in the middle of the room, placing her face into her hands as the tears fell in a constant stream of admissible sadness until they finally stopped falling from her eyes and she could not cry anymore.

The next day Jade walked outside to the shed and fetched a large crate and took it back inside of the house. She stood holding it tightly in her grip standing outside of her daughter's room then she opened the door and stepped inside.

Jade started to pack her daughter's things, placing them into the large crates one by one, unmade her bed and removed the furniture and closed the bedroom door.

Slowly, Jade lifted herself off the side of the bed and wandered through the family home, past her little girl's bedroom and into the arms of her computer screen to read the lingering words of her online friend, Max. Jade could no longer mix with the associations outside of the house and only chose to associate with the outside world in the intoxicated state of the little white pill while visiting the notorious motorcycle club house. Although Jade's depression had started to lift, her relationship with Shane had suffered the consequences of the devastation of losing her little girl to Derek and they no longer felt comfortable in each other's presence as they avoided each other in the family home and spent more and more time apart.

No longer did Shane come straight home from work, choosing to visit the motorcycle clubhouse regularly without Jade.

The smile they once had for each other at the end of the day had turned to a thin line of tight lips and blank stares.

As Shane's love disappeared and he pulled away, Jade felt more and more alone, still not able to pull herself completely from the dark shadows of her depression which plagued her continuously.

With each passing day and night of Shane's absence from the family home, Jade's relationship with Max ignited into a continuous reflection of charming, comforting letters.

Jade spent her lonely nights in the arms of the computer screen, pouring out her heart and crying alone in isolation.

"Oh Max. I wish you were here. I love you so much," Jade whispered, as she shut down the computer at the end of every night and slipped beneath the covers of her cold lonely bed.

Two weeks later, Jade received a phone call in the middle of the day, it was Shane, calling from work.

"Hey Shane," Jade said as she answered the call.

"Hey," Shane replied. "Listen, I've had enough of this job. I'm going to throw it in, today."

Jade stood on the other end of the phone, a little surprised by Shane's statement.

"Huh, why, I mean it's up to you. What's going on Shane?" Jade asked.

Shane paused for a moment, silent on the other end of the phone then replied, "I don't know, nothing's wrong, I'm just sick of being stuffed around, the boss is a wanker. I'll be home in a couple of hours okay. I'm just finishing up then I'm walking out."

Jade didn't know what to say, she didn't really care either if that's what he wanted to do, it was his choice; the words ran through her mind but did not leave her lips.

"Okay then, do what you have to do, I'll see you soon," Jade answered and hung up the phone. "Hmm," Jade hummed to herself, still a little surprised by Shane's decision, he hadn't said a word to her about his work or his dissatisfaction with it or his plans to throw it in. "What's going on?" Jade said to herself, placing herself in the kitchen chair positioned at the kitchen table.

But the tight knot in the pit of her stomach would not subside and she could no longer shy away from the instincts that pulsed through her veins. Jade picked up her mobile phone off the kitchen table and went through the settings until she found what she was looking for. "I'll track his movements," rushed into Jade's mind as she set her mobile phone into the tracking device linked to Shane's phone and waited for the information to come through.

"Oh my god, I knew it," Jade said, holding it under her breath.

Jade quickly checked the location again but it came back with the same location of Shane's phone.

"He hasn't even been on the work site," Jade mumbled to herself. "I knew it. He lied to me."

Jade dropped her head in disappointment as the cold hard facts slid beneath her skin and grew a frown upon her face. "You lied to me Shane. So where have you been? And who with?"

The clock ticked continuously on the wall in the deafening silence of the family home as Jade sat alone at the kitchen table. Four hours passed.

Jade arose from the kitchen table and walked outside under the veranda to sit at the long wooden table setting in her wait for Shane's arrival.

She checked her phone, there were no missed calls there were no messages and she had not heard from Shane since lunchtime. "Where is he?" Jade wondered, holding her palm to her forehead. "I'm going to call him," her mind racing with the devious secrecy of Shane's disappearance.

"Hey," Jade said. "What's going on? I thought you'd be home by now?" she questioned.

"Yeah, they're stuffing me around," Shane explained. "They're bloody wankers. I told the boss I'm leaving, but I'm waiting for them to come pick me up from site so I can go. I should be home soon though okay."

"Oh, okay," Jade replied." I was just wondering, that's all, we'll talk when you get home okay, bye."

Jade placed the phone down on the table next to her in disbelief, something to her within the pit of her stomach sat stubbornly deep within and caused questions to mount within her mind.

"What are you up to Shane?" she said, rising to her feet, walking from the house gripping tightly to her mobile phone and positioning herself on the chair at the outdoor setting underneath the veranda.

As Jade sat down upon the outdoor setting's chair, she heard the familiar ring of her phone's message bank. "That must be Shane now," Jade said, raising her eyebrows just a tad.

Jade flipped open the phone and began to read.

"Hi. Are you and Shane on your way to Lyonsworth. I just passed you by on the highway and you didn't even wave, snob! Natasha."

Jade looked at the message in disbelief.

"Hmm," she thought, "No, couldn't have been, it must have been the wrong car;" but the tracking device also tracked his phone to that location."

Jade typed a message back. "No, I'm at home and Shanes at work, wrong car."

Natasha answered the message straight away, "Really, I'm positive it was Shane's car and you were in the passenger seat, sorry, must have got it wrong."

Jade slumped back into the chair as she blew air out of her mouth in disbelief, holding the phone out in front of her face, as her mind whirled with possibilities.

Jade raised her eyes from her phone, she had not been noticing Shane's movements nor cared about his disappearances over to the clubhouse she had been consumed in her isolated grief and thought nothing of his everyday absence at work.

"Had Shane been lying all this time? Had he been going elsewhere every day? And who was this other woman with him?"

Jade's mind raced and her heart thumped a million beats, as the anxiety filled her body and her thoughts hit there mark within the pit of her stomach. She had to know the truth.

Two hours later, Shane arrived home, walking through the back gate, a smile on his face one that he had not had for Jade for a while, adding fuel instantly to her suspicions.

"Hey baby," Shane greeted her as he walked towards her.

"Hey," Jade replied." So what's going on?" Jade asked.

Shane sat down at the table next to her and began to explain.

"Basically," he started. "I told him he can stick his job up his arse, and I walked out, I quit."

Jade looked at Shane, trying to catch her glare in his eyes, a look that Shane kept dodging, darting his glance from left to right, avoiding eye contact.

Jade's stomach clenched up into a tight fisted ball, she knew right then and there Shane was lying.

She dropped her head in a sigh before raising to her feet to face him. "So when did this happen, today, last week, start of the year?"

Jade could not hold her tongue, she had lost the strength for tactics, and the words flew from her mouth in accusations.

"What" Shane snapped back, angrily in defence. "What the fuck are you talking about today stupid." Jade's face tightened, anger was her only emotion, she knew he was lying.

"Bullshit," Jade snapped back bitterly. "You're lying to me. My friend saw you on the highway with another woman in your car. Where have you been Shane?"

"What the fuck, fuck off," Shane snapped back again, screwing his face up at the accusation. "Your friend's a bloody liar. She's just trying to cause trouble between us. I've been at bloody work. Get your facts straight before you have a go at me. I'm sick of this shit," grabbing his keys off the table and storming out of the back gate and jumped in his car, slamming the door and sped off down the road leaving Jade sitting at the table once again on her own.

Shane had not known that Jade had tracked him also and his reaction told her all she needed to know; he was hiding something.

Jade slumped back against the cold wooden chair of the outdoor setting, her hands fell to her sides in a defeated slump; her battles were just beginning.

Two days later, Shane came back home.

Shane ambled through the back gate, cautious, treading slowly, unsure of the reception he would receive from Jade. Jade had heard the click of the back gate, the slow roar of the car engine, as it ambled up into the driveway. She rushed to the kitchen window and watched as he crept inside. Jade stood at the entrance of the kitchen door as Shane entered the house.

"So now what?" left her mouth as their eyes connected in the small tiled room.

"I've received a phone call," Shane replied. "I'm going back to the mines. I've been offered my old job back, I'm leaving in a week's time."

Jade was speechless, she had nothing to say, this was out of her hands and felt, in her time of need, abandoned.

One week later, Shane left, heading back to the mines absent for four weeks at a time and Jade was now on her own left to deal with the pieces of her life that had been torn apart, left to deal with missing her children and now the man she loved, with no one to turn to but herself.

Jade sat in front of the tall glass mirror of her dressing table day after day, staring at the woman looking back at her the cold, hard stare reflection of her eyes that once glowed with life now, filled with emptiness, sadness and Shane's lies.

"This is not how it's meant to be," Jade whispered back at herself. "Where have you gone?"

Jade reached out her hand to touch the cold glass, the image that sat before her, staring back at her she did not want this to be the end. She knew she had to do something.

That weekend, Jade didn't allow Cody to go to his friend's house, she didn't allow herself to crave the escape of the life she had so desperately fallen into, the little white pills. This time Jade searched deep within herself, to find the strength and courage to carry on and put things back together, this time to search for her lost soul.

Over the next two weeks, in Shane's absence and now with the court cases behind her having let go of the emotional turmoil of Nick's and Monique's departure from the family home, Jade started to rebuild her life.

Everyday Jade forced herself from the motionless, she forced herself from the confinements of the isolated brick walls around her and stepped back into her dreams, her goals and started again.

Jade's health started to improve, as she forced herself back into her usual routine of organic cooking and exercise, strengthening her confidence within herself step by step.

She returned to her studies, striving to complete the business plan she was once so passionate about, her goal, the vision she once had of herself, her place in life.

With each passing day of her vigorous self-discipline, Jade's former self started to emerge piece by piece as she embraced each passing day, her life, her family, her future.

The month seemed to pass quickly and it wasn't long before Shane's shift at the mines was over and it was time for him to come home. Jade looked forward to his return, although she had felt abandoned by his sudden decision at the time, the distance between them had allowed her to reflect on all the events of her inner destruction, her behaviour and their relationship.

The peacefulness of his departure had given her a new lease on life, no longer compacted by his whereabouts, his lies and deceits, Jade was now able to think again, feel again and stand back up and she hoped this would be a new start.

That weekend Shane came home to Jade's smile.

The following week, Monique contacted her mother, wanting to come home for a visit. The news filled Jade with pure joy and excitement, it was the news Jade had hoped to hear and longed to have her daughter back in her arms. Shane, Jade and Cody, drove to the city on the Friday night, a constant chatter spilling from Jade's mouth in anticipation of her daughter's arrival as they headed to the airport to collect her. Jade watched as Monique stepped from the plane, walked the long terminal dock and fell into her arms once more. Her daughter was home.

All that week, while Monique was home, the family was surrounded in constant joy, giggles and excitement, wrapping Jade in pure delight but it was all to end too soon and it was time for Monique to return back home. Shane was due to return to the mines on the Friday night and left Friday morning to catch his plane which meant that Jade had to get Monique back to the airport Saturday afternoon by herself. Jade had not done the trip before and Shane had warned her not to push her tired car too hard and had advised her to stay the night at his parents' house, as not to be on the road at night with Cody; an advice Jade should have listened to.

Saturday morning came and Jade rushed around getting the children ready to leave for the airport.

She gathered the directions Shane had prepared for her and she set out for the long highway leading to Alterro.

Three hours later, they arrived at the airport and walked the long isles to the baggage departments before coming to a rest on the airport seats.

"I will miss you sweetie girl," Jade said quietly into her daughter's ear, as a tear welled in the pockets of her eyes.

"I will miss you too Mum," Monique whispered back as she leant over to hug her mother. Before long, Monique's flight was called and Jade watched breathlessly holding back the tears as her daughter drifted out of site on the loading run way again.

"Oh my sweet girl, I'm going to miss you every time you leave," Jade whispered to herself, as she waved her last wave and left the airport.

Within minutes Jade and Cody arrived at the front of Shane's parents' house.

Within the hour Cody had started to act up in an intrusive whinge that incessantly rang in Jade's ears. "Please Mum, can't we just go home. It's Easter."

"How will Easter bunny come if I'm not there. Can we please go home," Cody whined at his mother continuously.

Two hours later, Jade made the decision to go home and headed back towards the highway leading to the township of Suisania Bay.

The trip seemed effortless and the car was running smooth, the highway was clear of traffic and they were only twenty minutes away from home.

Jade suddenly heard an unusual noise come from the direction of the car's engine. She turned down the volume of the radio to listen but the noise had disappeared she checked the dashboard of the car nothing seemed a miss. All of a sudden the car started to lose power and the engine started to stutter then finally it came to a stop on the side of the highway.

Jade turned the key in the ignition, trying to restart the car's engine it would not start. "Oh no," Jade whispered to herself, raising her hand to cover her mouth.

Jade picked up her phone she wasn't sure of what to do, this had never happened to her before and Shane was out of reach for help.

She knew it was late now outside; skies darkened by the night with only a soft glow of the moonlight shadows.

Jade searched the numbers in her phone she only knew of one person who would come to her aid, who was within reach. "Ryan," Jade whispered. Jade dialled the number and waited anxiously for an answer.

Ryan did not answer. She tried again but he did not answer.

Jade looked around at the darkened highway, the lights that flickered over the hill from her hometown only twenty minutes away unable to drive the car any further to reach her destination she was stuck, stopped, sitting on the highway, surrounded by only the night with her young son.

"Mum, I'll try calling Mum," Jade said to herself, turning a soothing smile into the back seat at Cody.

Jade called her mother, who, although was away on holidays, miles and miles away and unable to assist her in anyway may know someone that could.

"Hey Mum," Jade said down the phone to her mother. "I'm in a bit of a dilemma," Jade started to explain. On her mother's suggestion, Jade rang the motor assistance company her mother was a part of and asked for assistance.

At first the operator of the motor assistance company did not believe Jade's story, and had accused her of lying to them playing a prank call and had refused to offer her any kind of assistance.

Jade tried desperately to convince the operator that she was genuine, explaining over and over that she was stranded on the highway with her young son and that anything could happen to them and pleaded for their assistance.

One hour later, the operator finally listened to Jade's pleas but had insisted that the only way they could offer their assistance was by becoming a member. Jade was forced into entering a membership with the company a debt she had no way of paying and her car would be impounded with a release fee attached adding to her already amounting debts from the divorce.

Jade sat back deep into the driver's seat and placed her head into her hands.

"I should have listened," Jade whispered to herself, turning her head into the back seat where Cody had curled himself up and had fallen to sleep.

Jade waited patiently for the tow truck to arrive as she listened to the music on the radio.

Each set of lights was an anticipation of the tow truck's arrival met by disappointment as the lights continued to pass her by hour after hour.

Three hours passed by before the tow truck finally arrived and Jade's fear of their safety started to diminish.

Within minutes, Jade's car was hooked up to the tow truck and Jade and Cody were on their way back into the township of Suisania Bay and finally arrived home, three am in the morning, safe again.

The next morning, Jade received a phone call, it was Ryan he had noticed her missed call on his phone from the previous night and contacted Jade to find out why she had rang so late.

"Hey Ryan," Jade answered, picking up her phone.

"What's going on?" Ryan asked, a concerned tone in his voice.

"Oh, my car broke down last night. I was stranded on the highway," Jade explained, then continued to tell Ryan of the whole night's dilemma.

"Could you please take me into the depot, I need my car?" Jade asked.

Minutes later, Ryan arrived at Jade's house and drove her back into town to where her car had been impounded.

The onsite mechanic had gone over Jade's car but the outcome was not good news; it was not what she had hoped for. He started to explain. "The noise you had heard just before the engine had stopped was the water pump belt that had jumped off from the pulley, leaving the engine starving of water, coolant and now the engine had ceased, cooking the engine beyond repair; it is unfixable."

"No," Jade said in disbelief, shaking her head. "Great."

Jade's mother had agreed to pay the fees in order for her car to be released and had made arrangements that morning, allowing her to remove her car from the depot of the impoundment.

Ryan hooked the car up to his car and they towed it back to Jade's house before leaving again. Jade stood looking at the car in her back yard, her only transport from the out of town home she was now situated in and Shane now not there.

That night Shane rang from the mines to check on Jade as he knew she was travelling to the city to return Monique to the airport.

"Hey Shane," Jade answered. "Ummm. I have a slight problem. We made it home safe, but well," and Jade continued to tell Shane of the night's events.

"What," Shane replied. "I told you to stay the night at Mums," his voice irritated and stern. "What were you thinking, anything could have happened, is Cody okay?"

"Yes, we're safe, nothing happened, but the car's engine is cooked, it's off the road," Jade explained, her voice filled with guilt, her conscience knowing she had not followed Shane's instructions.

"I'm sorry Shane, I really am. I let Cody talk me into it. I should have stuck to my guns I know, I know. I'm too soft with him I'm sorry."

Shanes voice calmed down and returned to the concern for the two stranded on the side of the road.

"We'll figure this out when I get home okay," Shane assured her. "Just stay safe okay."

Four weeks later, Shane returned, rushing home from the mines on the Friday night.

Shane and Jade sat down at the kitchen table, sipping the cold bourbon as they started to discuss the dilemma of the car.

"I've saved up all the pay from this month and with what I have already put away from last month, we will have enough to head to the city tomorrow and buy another one," Shane told her.

Jade's face dropped in surprise, then she felt her conscience. "No, no Shane. I can't let you buy me a car, I can't let you do that, it's my fault, it's my responsibility. I just can't," she said.

Jade reached out and touched Shane's hand. "Thank you though," Jade continued. "Thank you for thinking of me but I'll sort it out okay."

"Bullshit. How are you going to sort this out?" Shane piped up. "You've got no job and that bastard of an ex of yours left you in the shit and now Cody is paying for it. I'm not having Cody go without. We're going tomorrow, and that's the end of it."

Jade was speechless she knew Shane had a generous nature, he had shown that when they had first met, but after all that had happened between them, this was unexpected.

"I don't know what to say Shane, I really don't." Jade lifted her eyes to meet his. "Thank you, Shane," and wrapped her arms around him, the thoughts melting inside of her. "He really does care."

The next day Shane and Jade left for the city to buy a new car, they hunted and scoured all the car sales sites and finally, near the end of the day they found it: a shiny, well-maintained Mazda, within Shane's budget, that suited Jade's needs perfectly.

That night Jade agreed to the thrills of Shane's enticement and said a special thank you to Shane as she swallowed the ecstasy pills and slipped into their pleasures.

As Jade felt the effects of the little white pills expand and pulse through her mind she leant over to whisper in Shane's ear, "Stay here, I'll be back in a moment. I have a surprise for you."

Jade rose to her feet and walked from the loungeroom to her bedroom where she pulled out the sheer black, see through negligee she had been saving for a special occasion.

Jade smiled, a wicked glint shining in her eyes as she slipped out of her clothes and into the soft see through negligee, rolled the matching stockings up the length of her thighs and slipped into her high heels.

Jade walked back out to the loungeroom to Shane who was waiting eagerly for his surprise to which he was not disappointed.

Shane let out a loud wolf whistle as he sighted his woman, dressed up just for him.

Jade walked over to him slowly each sway of her hips, enticing him to reach out and touch the warm, curvaceous skin that lay underneath.

"I want you," Jade whispered in a soft, sexy voice as she pushed up against Shane and embraced him in a passionate kiss on his soft wanting lips.

She felt the heat serge through her veins, the lust cover her skin, as his hands trailed up the length of her stocking-covered thighs and over the curves of her womanly hips; his hands wrapped around her tiny waist as he lifted her from the ground, her long legs, wrapping around him still embraced in their fiery passionate kiss.

Shane placed her slowly down on the kitchen table, her warm skin connecting with the cold surface, making her arch her back and stiffen in response. "Mmm, oh, I want you there," Jade moaned as she slid her fingertips down along the length of her body to touch the now wet place between her legs.

Jade placed her feet on the table bending her knees and spread her legs as she ran her fingertips over the soft moist lips of her own pleasure before sliding her fingers inside of herself pleasuring herself while Shane watched in anticipation as he slid his jeans off his legs and allowed them to fall to the floor.

"Mmmm," Jade moaned as she slowly slid her fingers in and out of herself teasing and pleasuring the heat between her legs.

"Mmmm. Oh yes," she moaned. "I want you now," Jade purred as Shane lifted her by the waist and pushed his hardness all the way inside of her.

"Ohhh," Jade gasped as she felt the first entrance of his thrust, his length spreading her tight opening and entering her deeply.

Shane's fingers wrapped around her hips as he held her in place, thrusting faster and faster deeper and deeper, as her fingers curled around in a tight grip of the table's edge.

"Ohhh, yes, mm, yes. Harder, oh god yes," Jade moaned as she felt the clench of her hot pleasure tighten around him, pushing her closer and closer to her climax with each hard thrust.

"Ohhh that's it," she moaned as her hand reached down to tease her now-erect clit, begging to be rubbed, teased, pleasured. "Yes. Yes, ohhh god, yes," Jade moaned as the sensation drove her over the edge and into the wet pleasures of her orgasm. "Ohhh yes."

Shane stopped for a moment just long enough to feel the pulsating pleasures wrapped tightly around him before picking Jade up and carrying her to the loungeroom, placing her on her knees on the loungeroom chair. Jade gripped the back of the chair arched her back and turned her sultry eyes to look into his. "Take me," left her lips in a sexy enticement of erotic pleasure.

Shane grabbed her hips tightly as he viewed her long blonde hair that lay down the length of her back and pushed his hardness deep inside of her pressing his body hard against hers.

"Oh baby, you're going to make me cum," Shane moaned as Jade turned around to look at him, her eyes sultry, her lips parted, her breaths heavy.

"Cum baby. Mmm. I want to feel you…mmm…cum baby, cum," she moaned as Shane thrust deep inside of her harder and harder, faster and faster, then one last time before his orgasm exploded deep inside of her, mingling with hers.

"Oh baby, oh yes," Shane moaned, as he pulsed and throbbed inside of her as the succulent orgasm stopped him in one place breathlessly, one of many for that night.

. The previous month while Shane was absent and Jade was inconvenienced and struggling without the use of a car to drive the long distance into town to carry out her duties for the home and her family swayed her mind into making a decision, that she had thought would be beneficial to the whole family. That night Jade spoke to Shane about the idea and the reasons behind her decision.

"So what do you think?" Jade asked, pausing after the long discussion.

"It's up to you," Shane answered. "If that's what you want to do, then yeah, find a house. We'll shift when I get home next month."

Jade's week rushed by in a busy scourer of the rental markets day after day from the moment Shane had left once more for his four-week employment position.

Jade viewed many premises over that week in search of a suitable house within the town area but she could not find one that would accommodate all the factors she needed until finally on the Friday, a house was placed on the market that was suitable and in a good location within the township of Suisania Bay.

Jade rang the Real Estate agent and arranged a viewing of the property for the next morning.

"Yes, I'll take it," Jade said, smiling at the Real Estate agent. "When can we move in?"

The Real Estate agent smiled back at Jade. "Great, we are just finishing up with some renovations, but it will be ready in a couple of weeks," he explained.

"Perfect," Jade replied. "My boyfriend comes home from work in three weeks' time, so we'll move in then."

Jade followed the agent back to the Real Estate office and finalised all the details in preparation for the move. The contract was drawn up, it was official.

Over the next three weeks, Jade worked hard, determined to establish the business she had created, she was now in constant search of the specialists she required and spent her days, scouring the internet for reputable specialists, developing professional relationships with them and trying to convince them to join her business venture.

By night, Jade continued to work, packing the house and all their belongings in preparation for when Shane arrived back home, the move to the new house.

Finally, the day of moving house arrived and while Shane worked away on his shift, Jade had fully prepared the house to shift residence, the boxes of stored goods placed strategically around each room ready to be moved into the new house. With the help of James and Cody, the move went quickly and smoothly and soon they were settled into their new home.

As Jade busied herself unpacking the many boxes and setting up the rooms, Shane went to work, setting up his shed. The large steel shed was situated adjacent to the back patio area and facing out towards the road that ran along the side of the home.

As the day headed towards the evening, Jade had had enough of the unpacking of boxes and sorting out the house and decided it was time to stop for the day, and paused to look around at the house.

"Job well done," she said to herself.

She grabbed two cans of bourbon from out of the refrigerator and headed out the back door towards the shed door that opened under the patio area.

Shane had not heard Jade leave the house or approach the shed door.

As Jade approached the shed door, she came to a standstill as she overheard the conversation coming from Shane's phone, a voicemail, a smouldering, sexy female voice saying, "I had such a good time with you. I can't wait to see you again. Hurry back. I love you."

Jade stood to the side of the shed doorway, hidden from Shane's view as she listened to the unknown voice speaking seductively, saying those words to her man.

Jade's heart raced with anxiety as her fists clenched into tight balls and her stomach knotted.

Was Shane cheating on her again, this time while he was working away?

Jade hid secretly behind the shed's doorway as the words sunk beneath her skin and left a sour taste within her mouth.

Jade stood motionless, gripping tightly the two chilled cans of bourbon that froze her fingers, as her mind raced over the suspicious words she had just heard.

As she stood thinking of her next move, suddenly without warning a can of bourbon slipped from her grip and went crashing down on the concrete floor of the patio.

"Oh no," Jade called out. She quickly raced across the floor and retrieved the rolling cans, turning to flash a quick awkward smile in Shane's direction.

"How long have you been standing there Jade? I was just checking my phone. My stepsister left a message. She always sounds like when she's bloody drunk," Shane explained laughing nervously.

"Oh, Okay," Jade replied, smiling back at him. "I didn't hear, I only just came out."

A cunning lie spilt from her lips in her defence as her suspicious mind wandered back and forth over the details of the phone call and her eyes narrowed subtly.

"I'll just go get some more," Jade called out as she walked away, back into the house to return the shaken cans to the refrigerator and to retrieve two more.

Jade paused for a moment in the kitchen, as her mind ticked over the thousand thoughts that raced through her, she looked out of the large kitchen window facing the shed.

"You're a bloody liar," Jade said quietly to herself, swallowing hard at her emotions before returning to the shed.

Over the next couple of months, the distance between Shane and Jade had grown and the uncomfortable silence in their time together had turned to fidgeting and blank stares.

Shane's nightly phone calls from the mines had now turned to twice a week and Jade found herself rambling in pointless conversation, saying anything in order to remain the focus of Shane's attention.

Upon his return from his place of employment, Shane's endless blank stares, his lack of reaction and now his sexual disinterest in her, chipped away at Jade's confidence and pointed her mind in one direction.

"Was he having an affair?"

Jade's suspicions grew as one by one each member of the notorious motorcycle club had started to change towards her, a once welcoming friendly relationship that she had formed with them was slowly one by one, turning into quick chats, untrusting glares and their stand-offish behaviour.

Jade had not done anything to warrant such treatment she had formed her place amongst the club before she had met Shane but now things were different, something had changed, something was going on behind Jade's back, behind the scenes, even with Ryan.

Jade became increasingly jittery amongst the members of the clubhouse; her once haven of fun and friends now felt uncomfortable which sent inquisitive bewilderment through Jade's mind.

Was Shane doing this, what was he saying about her?

Shane had started to spend more and more time away from Jade, their relationship strained with constant battles and accusations choosing to retreat to the privacy of the shed.

Jade often found herself creeping outside to stand at the edge of the shed doorway, under the patio listening, watching for signs of Shane's deceit, thoughts of this other woman at the mines denting her, twisting her into a suspicious toil of paranoia and once again Jade's confidence began to unravel.

Jade listened silently while Shane was unaware of her being there, as Shane received phone call after phone call from the other woman. She listened as they chatted and laughed with each other as he had once done with her.

She watched as her stomach tightened into tight knots as Shane's chatter and laughter changed to a professional short conversation the moment she entered the room.

Upon returning from work one weekend, Shane sat Jade down to talk.

"Babe, I've been thinking, I might change my work hours, fly in and out on Tuesdays instead. The flights are less crowded and I can fly in and out earlier which means I won't have to drive on a Friday night anymore to come home. I can be here around lunchtime instead. What do you think?"

"Yeah, that's fine with me," Jade agreed. "It's up to you."

Jade had thought nothing of it at the time it made sense to her but her mind remained incessantly focused on Shane's behaviour and finding out if her instincts were correct. "Who was this other woman?"

Night after night, Jade tossed and turned in a sleepless summarise of each phone call, each conversation she had heard while standing behind the shed's doorway until the night she finally made a decision.

Jade had remembered the conversation she had shared with Shane and wondered whether she would qualify as a partner to the employees' protocol of the mines. While lying in bed one night, arm in arm, Shane had explained how his worksite allowed visitors of the employees' families and partners to stay on the site for a week at a time.

"That's what I'll do. I'll see for myself," Jade whispered to herself pulling at the quilt cover that lay strewn against the bedroom floor from over the edge of the bed.

Jade knew that Shane would never agree to such a plan and although she felt bad about going behind his back, her suspicious mind pushed her into a frenzy of a precise perfunctory of tactical moves.

That week Jade rang the mines and spoke to the manager to organise her visit to the mines, unbeknownst to Shane.

Jade waited for Shane's phone call the next day to give him the surprise news but Shane never rang. She waited for the next day but once again Shane did not ring.

Jade decided she would ring him instead.

Shane had given her the number and the extension that rang directly to a phone in his room, when he had first started his employment at the mines.

Jade had not called it before, as not wanting to interrupt his work pattern or routine but now curiosity had gotten the better of her; her mind would not rest on his deceits, his lies.

Jade called the number at the mines it rang and rang and rang but remained unanswered.

She stood still paused in her assumptions, holding the phone, staring at it, her mind rolling over every horrible scenario of what Shane could be doing.

The next night Shane finally rang. "Hey babe," Shane said down the phone.

"Hey Shane," Jade replied, her voice now tight with tension and suspicion. I have some news for you. I'm coming for a visit to the site. I rang your boss and we've arranged it, I'll be coming back with you next trip, staying for a week. Cool huh?"

Shane's voice went silent.

"Shane. Shane are you there?" Jade asked into the silence.

"Yeah. Yeah," his voice slightly shaky. "Ahh, okay cool. Next trip then huh?" Shane finally replied.

"Yes, with you next trip," Jade answered again.

"Ah, okay, cool," Shane replied once more.

Just then, Jade heard a noise, a voice coming from the back ground of the phone call at Shane's end.

"Who was that?" Jade asked.

"Umm. It's just one of the blokes, he was checking to see if the phones were working now. We've been having trouble with them, that's why I haven't rang," Shane explained.

"Oh, okay," Jade replied. Her mind, though, spitting the words "Bullshit."

"I have to go now okay, babe," Shane told her. "I'm really tired, I'm going to bed."

Jade said goodnight to Shane and hung up the phone but then waited for fifteen minutes before ringing back.

The phone rang and rang till it rang out. Shane did not answer.

Jade started to fume, the lies tangling her up in anger, she felt she was now being made a fool of.

"Does he think I'm fucken stupid," Jade said, her voice now stern and loud as she dialled the number once more.

It rang and rang and rang and just as she was about to hang up Shane answered his voice slightly out of breath and heavy.

"Hello," Shane answered as he picked up the phone.

"Where were you? I rang two times," Jade asked sternly down the phone.

"I was asleep babe. I only just heard the phone, you woke me up," Shane tried to explain.

"That's funny," Jade snapped down the phone. "It sounds to me like you're out of breath. Where were you? Hanging with your woman up there huh?"

Jade could not stop the accusation from leaping from her tongue as it seeped out from under her skin and spat in angry accusations. "I'm not a fool Shane."

"For fuck's sake Jade. I'm not doing this. I'm going back to fucken bed. Stop being such a fucken bitch. Talk to you next week, "Shane yelled at her down the phone before slamming it down in her ear.

"You fucken wanker," Jade yelled at the phone and slammed it down too, and rushed to the refrigerator to grab a can of bourbon before retiring to her bedroom, and inhaling the intoxication of the marijuana.

"Ahh that's better," Jade whispered to herself, her racing heart slowing to a single beat of relaxation, laying her head down upon the soft pillow upon her bed.

The following week, while Jade was busy preparing another batch of letters to be sent to the specialists that she had been seeking for her business, there was a knock on her front door. "Hmm. Who could that be?" Jade hummed to herself.

Jade walked to the door and opened it.

246

"Ohh hi Sonia," Jade said to the face grinning back at her.

Although Jade and Sonia had partied hard together in the previous years, Jade had not had a fondness for Sonia's ways as she offered numerous pills and lines of cocaine in their preparation for the dance clubs of Suisania Bay and had abstained from venturing down that path.

Jade did not trust Sonia as she had been known as being two faced with the woman whom frequented the club house and within her relationship with Ryan's son which left a cautionary measure to sit in the pit of Jade's stomach.

Jade had not seen Sonia for many months, her visit today at her door was a surprise and a question mark.

"Come in, how are you?" Jade asked, as she opened the door to let Sonia in.

"I'm doing really well," Sonia replied. "How have you been?"

Jade made a coffee for them both and they sat on the couch in the loungeroom, chatting and catching up on old times.

Sonia talked incessantly, as she always had but to Jade, a mindless dribble, that really held no interest to her. Something wasn't measuring up to Jade, why after so long, had Sonia come to see her, but still, Jade did not question her; she did not let on of her concerns, the questions that had seeped into her thoughts remained silent.

Jade sat and listened watching, taking in Sonia's endless babble of gossip and nervousness as she spoke. But Jade could not deny that feeling sitting within her. "What was Sonia up to? Why was she here?"

After two hours Sonia left leaving Jade standing and watching at the large lounge room window as Sonia's car drove away. "Hmmm," Jade hummed, her only words.

Three weeks later, Jade prepared for her trip with Shane to the mines. Although she held an air of nervousness within herself as this was her first time aboard an aeroplane, the suspicions that sat within the depths of her mind overwhelmed her senses; she had to know and abated her nervousness about flying.

Jade's nervousness held deep within her throat as she sat with Shane awaiting to board the plane rose and fell as the numerous other passengers rushed to and fro past them in a rush to their next destinations.

As Jade looked around at the vast amount of people also waiting, she noticed a woman staring straight over at her and Shane.

Jade turned to tell Shane of the woman's staring but noticed Shane was staring straight back at the same woman. Jade's eyes darted to and fro between the space that sat between the two, paused in her concern. Jade's face frowned with question. "Does he know her? How does he know her?" ran through her mind. Shane noticed Jade looking at him and quickly dropped his stare, his attention turning back around to Jade. Once more her facial expression asking the question before her lips even spoke. "That's the flight to the other mines," Shane explained.

But still Jade said nothing and had decided to wait and see just what she would find out at the other end.

Jade followed Shane down the long board walk to board the plane and sat in her seat next to Shane as her eyes darted over the many different functions upon the airplane's interior. Within moments of boarding the plane, the engines started as Jade's breath drew deep and the plane headed for the run way.

"Oh my, here we go," Jade said, looking over at Shane whose fascinated smile spoke in volumes.

Although nervous at first her nerves were soon soothed as Jade enjoyed the two hour flight, the views over the clouds, the land and sea so far below, now a beautiful site of shapes and colours, weaves and mazes of nature and manmade structures.

"The view is amazing," Jade said quietly, as the plane flew above the land below.

The plane arrived at the next airport and Shane and Jade departed the plane at this stop, a two-hour wait until their next departure.

The pair strolled together as Shane showed Jade through the many shops situated throughout the airport. Jade loved each moment of the new sites and the excitement of the adventure had soon washed away the very reason for her decision of visiting Shane's worksite.

After the sightseeing tour of the terminal and after having something to eat at one of the many cafes it was time to board the small plane that took them the rest of the way.

Jade enjoyed the two-hour flight on the small plane, taking in all the sites that flashed passed her, so many miles below until the end, the landing of the plane.

The small air strip at the mines site had been struck with a small amount of turbulence, that made the plane unable to land straight away. The small plane circled the air strip again, in a figure eight, a motion that did not sit well with Jade as the feelings of her motion sickness affected her adversely and her stomach started to turn.

"Oh god I need off this ride," she whispered her face turning pale as she turned around to look at Shane who looked at her with a laugh.

"You'll be right," he reassured her.

Within moments, the plane landed and the people exited the plane and walked through the gates near the baggage area. Jade looked around at the bustling people, walking this way and that way, leaving and arriving from the site, the first mine site of which Shane and Jade had arrived.

The whole experience, the adventure energised Jade's spirit, every new site, the bustle of the new people and sounds around her, turning her head from side to side in smiles until she saw an older woman walking straight towards them approaching from afar.

Jade felt her instincts send chills through the previous exuberance of her disposition as her smile fell into a frown of concern and her minds suspicion shot blazes of doubts through her confidence.

"Is this her?" Jade questioned quietly within her mind.

The older woman continued in her approach until she came to a standstill in front of Shane and her eyes darted up and down the contours of Jade's body and clothing.

"Hey Shane," the woman burst out, smiling from ear to ear.

"Hey Meg," Shane replied, returning the smile. Nervously, Shane introduced the woman. "Meg, this is Jade."

"Hello," Jade greeted the woman and smiled.

The two women smiled at each other but they did not have much to say as the air hung heavily between them.

"Are you ready to go Meg?" Shane asked quickly.

"I've just got to catch up with my husband first," Meg answered back.

Shane's face dropped slightly at the comment in an air of disappointment which Jade carefully watched with a suspicious mind, before ushering Jade off in the direction of the worksites onsite car that drove them to the site of the mines.

Shane and Jade walked over to the parked work car and climbed in the front seat, to wait for Meg.

Jade felt the coldness of her disposition creep within as the excitement and joy of the journey was replaced with a deep suspicion upon her meeting with Meg and witnessing her interaction with Shane.

As Shane and Jade sat in the car waiting, Shane sat quiet, patiently watching out for Meg's return. Shane sighted Meg as she was collecting her bags from the baggage department and rushed over to pick up her bags and place them into the back of the car. "You don't do that for me anymore," Jade mumbled under her breath, sitting in the front seat of the car.

Jade sat in the front seat of the work vehicle quiet, listening, as Shane, who was normally quiet with her, chatted and laughed endlessly with Meg.

Jade sat there silently unable to get a word in between Shane and Meg's constant chatter to each other making her feel like she was the third wheel within the realms of her own relationship; Now Jade was getting angry.

Her mind worked over time as she continued to analyse every conversation between Shane and Meg, every phone call and message he had received upon his returns back home.

Jade had listened intensely as Shane spoke endlessly about a co-worker at the mines a woman, he had said was just a friend until the day he called out to Jade in another name.

"What did you just call me? Whose Meg?"

"Ah. Uh. Um… Sorry babe, I'm just away at work so much it's just become habit. Really it's nothing, she's just someone I work with, it's nothing," Shane explained, stumbling over his words.

Jade's glance froze in instant disapproval of being called another woman's name, the co-worker he had continuously spoke of.

"Liar," Jade spat from her mouth. "Who's this other bloody woman you're hanging with?" Jade saw red, her mind already feeling the tension that had grown between them over the last couple of months, the distrust she had had of him since the voicemail.

Jade tried desperately to stay focused on her work, the establishment of the business she was creating, but often found herself drifting back in to her thoughts.

Shanes times of being home had increasingly become harder and harder, their time together, marred by constant spats of arguments and disagreements, their only good times being while in the company of their drug induced moments.

Their relationship was coming undone and now their prides were taking precedence. This was Meg.

Two hours later, they had reached the mines camp site.

Jade got out of the work car and looked around at the remote setting.

"Awesome," Jade whispered to herself. Free from the modern world, internet, phones, her everyday view of the familiar surroundings, Jade felt she had stepped into another world and she liked it.

Jade grabbed her bags from the back of the car and followed Shane to their sleeping quarters: a make shift, portable cabin one of many, scattered throughout the camp site.

"Are you going to show me around?" Jade asked, smiling at Shane.

"Yeah, sure," Shane replied.

She placed her bags on the floor next to the queen size bed and followed Shane out the door and along the dirt track that led to the camp site's meal quarters: a large room, filled with tables and a food display unit filled with a variety of choices of food, beverages and supplies for the mines employees.

Jade watched as many cooks busied themselves in the kitchen, preparing for that evening's meal. Jade introduced herself to the cooks, who were happy to meet the stranger who had entered their camp site and reassured her, "Anything you want just let us know we'll take care of you."

"Thank you," Jade said, smiling, as she followed Shane back outside and over to the bar facilities, a patio area filled with tall benches and stools, with a bar at one end: a place the miners enjoyed a get together at the end of their working day. Jade looked around at the mines facilities; she was impressed; the camp site had the feel of its own little community, catering for all the different activities that its employees enjoyed back home.

Next, Shane and Jade ventured down the long path that led to a gymnasium which had exercise machines strategically placed throughout the room, gym equipment, mats for stretching and a stereo, played in the corner of the room. Shane and Jade entered the room. Only one person occupied the room, working out in private before the next shift filled the small space. A blonde-haired younger woman who stopped, who's face froze as Shane and Jade entered the room.

"Hello," Jade greeted the girl, a smile on her face. "I'm Jade."

"Hello Jade. I'm Lucy," the woman greeted back.

Jade looked at Shane, who's face had frozen at the sight of the woman also.

Jade's mind started to tick; had Shane disappeared up here and started a life without her knowing?

Jade followed Shane back out the door as he led her down another dirt path and into another area situated in this area, a swimming pool and tennis court.

Jade couldn't believe it, the whole set up was like its own little town; once again Jade was impressed.

As the day rolled on, getting later and later, Shane and Jade sat outside their make shift cabin, chatting and relaxing from their long trip to the site, watching as the camp site filled, as the miners finished their shifts and returned to the site.

Jade had never experienced anything like it and although she had come under false pretence, her mind had subdued the suspicious notion of her initial presence on the site.

"Well, it's tucker time," Shane announced to Jade as the clock ticked over to 5.30 pm.

Jade followed Shane back over to the meal hall, the pair stood in line as the many cooks buzzed around, filling up the plates full of the menus of the day. Shane led Jade to a long table, that by now was quickly filling of employees, who all had their regular positions at the many tables scattered across the room.

Jade introduced herself to the men already sitting at the table as she joined them for the evening's meal.

She laughed at the talk and jokes being flung around the table, the buzz of all the different characters interacting in harmony with each other, an experience she was enjoying very much. Jade looked over at the door to the meal room as a familiar face caught her vision it was Meg who looked straight at Jade through sly, slit eyes something that made Jade giggle inside.

Meg walked over to the long caters bench and returned to the full table at which Shane and Jade were already seated.

"Full up tonight Meg," one of the men announced, whose face was not impressed and Shane, whose face had lowered.

Jade knew, she was sitting in Megs spot, as the only woman on the table of men straight across from Shane, and Jade soon realised Shane and Meg had been eating their meals together while Jade sat at home alone without him. "How could you," Jade muttered under her breath before lifting the fork full of food to her lips.

The next morning Shane's shift had commenced and Jade was left to her own devices to explore the camp site, something she was eager to do.

She got dressed into her exercise gear and quickly walked to the gymnasium to start the day.

"Oh, I have it all to myself," Jade cooed entering the gymnasium and turning on the stereo and proceeded to work out on the various exercise machines.

Jade had only been working out for a few minutes when the door opened and a woman entered the gym; it was Lucy.

"Oh hi," Jade greeted the woman, remembering her face from the previous day.

"Hi," Lucy greeted back, and before too long, the women were caught up in a conversation of getting to know one another and had related instantly.

Lucy informed Jade that she came from Darwin and had come on site as the cleaner of the camp site. She had told Jade all about her ordeal at landing the job, having failed the compulsory drug test screening the first time and was sent home but had been given another chance to which this time, she had passed.

"Oh, you naughty girl," Jade teased, as the two women giggled together and continued to chat and made plans to meet up the next day after Lucy had completed her cleaning duties.

That night, Shane and Jade joined the other miners at the bar. Jade sat with the many different characters that laughed and joked, teasing and stirring each other as if they were old friends and it wasn't long before her presence was known and accepted amongst the small mining community.

As they continued to talk and laugh Jade noticed Meg entering the bar area who quickly covered a scowl that had formed upon her face and spread across her lips in a tightened smile.

Meg's eyes darted across the scene before narrowing her focus in on Shane's direction before she started to approach. Shane's eyes followed her around the room in a silent reciprocation as his face dropped into a sheepish scowl and subtly shook his head no in Meg's direction.

Meg nodded in acknowledgement as she picked up her drink and excused herself from the bar and walked away.

"Now I see," ran through Jade's mind as her eyes followed the look that sat heavily across Shane and Meg's faces. Jade finally knew. Jade looked on smugly as their secret unravelled before her eyes and she sat astute in her accusations towards Shane's behaviour. Jade let out a giggle that had formed in her throat as she quickly covered the smugness that had formed across her face and gave her a sense of satisfaction.

The next morning Jade awoke early and walked to the gymnasium and done her exercises before quickly returning to her cabin and showered. Once dressed Jade walked over to Lucy's cabin as they had planned and knocked on the door.

"Coming," Lucy called out as Jade waited patiently. "Hello again," Lucy greeted her opening the door with a smile and grabbing her keys from the bench top next to the door.

Jade and Lucy traced around the long, winding dirt roads that wound around the campsite in a tessellation of walkways, roadways and mining sites.

As Jade and Lucy walked and talked, the trail loaders and dump trucks passed them by, rushing to and from their pick-up and drop-off stations as they collected the large piles of soil, dug out from the mine. Jade suddenly turned to Lucy as she watched the numerous trucks circle around them.

"Are we meant to be here?" she asked.

Lucy laughed. "I don't know," she replied as they both started laughing together.

Just then one of the busy dump trucks stopped right next to them and wound down the window. "Hey girls," the driver called out to them from his window. "You have to go back, this is a restricted area."

"Oh, okay, sorry, we didn't know," Jade called back to him as the driver drove off, leaving the girls giggling together like naughty school girls who had just broken the playground rules. As the two women walked back towards the campsite converged in their deep conversation Lucy suddenly stopped and looked at Jade strangely.

"You know it's very strange Jade but I have spoken to Shane numerous times at the bar and he has never mentioned that he had a girlfriend. He has never mentioned you at all, I actually thought that he was single. "Hmm" Jade hummed quietly and grinned but remained silent in her response as Lucy's admission swirled within her thoughts. "Shane had never mentioned me at all," Jade thought to herself. "I find that very peculiar, odd. Does anyone know about me, except for Meg?"

The next night, Shane and Jade ventured back to the mines bar facility and sat at the rounded wooden bar that wound itself around the patio area and began to socialise with the other miners within the bar area.

A group of emergency workers who had arrived at the mines site to conduct emergency scenario training exercises to improve their skills and to qualify for their emergency positions arrived at the bar, and sat along the long wooden tables and was quickly joined by their leader, who entered the room and remained standing at the front of the room. "Excuse me everyone," the man interrupted addressing the room. "I am looking for volunteers to participate in emergency scenarios as car crash victims for our training seminar. Would anyone be interested?" Jade jumped at the chance excitedly to show off her acting talents and to be part of the fun and raised her hand in the air quickly, followed by Shane and the other miners who sat around the bar.

The group of volunteers were led to the parked work vehicles, parked only metres away and were driven to the site that had been prepared for the scene of the emergency scenario.

As Jade stood in the darkened area of the prepared scene ready for the scenarios to take place, one of the emergency service men approached her and explained the role of which she had to fill.

Jade was informed that she would be playing the role of the kidnapped woman, a victim that was involved in a car roll over with two men, her captives. Jade agreed with excitement and enthusiasm and jumped in wholeheartedly. She climbed into the upside down car with two of the volunteers who were playing their role as captives, as the emergency crew got into position.

"Action," the team-leader yelled out and the volunteers quickly sprung into the simulated action of the emergency scenario. Jade crawled out of the upside down car, yelling and screaming as she escaped the clutches of her kidnappers and the emergency crew sprung into action and arrived, approaching the scene quickly.

Jade gave it all she had, acting the part perfectly as she ran down the darkened dirt track screaming and yelling, escaping as one of the emergency men chased her, catching her and led her to the planned safety zone within the emergency scene. The kidnappers were apprehended and taken to an area away from the vehicle while the emergency team went into action dispersing the fire that had set the vehicle ablaze, completing the training scenario perfectly.

Jade stood with the man from the emergency team that had pretended to save her, laughing and chatting while they awaited for the scene to be completed. She had enjoyed the exercise very much and felt the rush of the adrenalin still pulsing through her in excitement and enthusiasm.

"Oh my, he's nice," ran through Jade's mind and across her lips hidden within her smile. "Am I flirting with him?" The man stood locked in a smile as the small talk struck his interest and mesmerised his view in her direction. "Oh my, he's flirting with me too," Jade thought to herself as the smiles that had spread across their faces were suddenly interrupted by the group's leader shouting directions to the group.

Once the emergency exercise was completed the group returned to the bar facilities within the mines camp and placed themselves around the long wooden bar and sipped upon the bourbon which had been handed to them by the team's leader for the groups participation, before placing the recorded footage into the player.

As Jade sat next to Shane watching the footage Jade noticed out of the corner of her eye a glance of admiring attraction looking at her.

"Oh my," Jade thought. "That's the man that I was flirting with." Jade fluttered her eyes in the flattering attention before looking down coyly at the wooden bar in front of her. "I'm with Shane," she kept telling herself continuously but she could not hide the attraction that had dazzled within her eyes with each glance she made towards the handsome stranger that had caught her eye.

Jade pulled her eyes away as the footage came to an end before turning her attentions to Shane.

"I'm not in love with you, I can do better" ran through Jade's thoughts as she looked Shane in the eyes and flashed a fake smile of perfunctory in his direction.

Shane returned the smile with a tight lipped grin as his eyes darted back and forth between Jade and the emergency service member as he noticed the man's eyes captivated by Jade. Shane picked up the can of bourbon and gulped at the chilled alcohol quickly before leading Jade out of the bar facilities as they retired for the night.

Jade never saw the emergency services man again although he had remained in her thoughts.

The week spent at the mines site passed by quickly as Jade enjoyed her time away and frequenting the bar facilities to talk to all the different characters of the mines employees, and the time she had spent with Lucy. Jade awoke early on the Saturday morning in preparation for her departure from the mines site and travelled the two hour drive down the dusty dirt roads that led to the landing strip situated at the first mines site with the mines manager, Shane's boss, who she had made the visitation arrangements with.

Jade sat on the bar stool in her wait for the plane's arrival engaged in continual conversation with Frank. Frank had taken a fancy to Jade, an attraction that did not go unnoticed while Jade was on the mines site with Shane. Jade smiled at Frank as she tilted the conversation towards Shane's behaviour on the mines site in her absence. "We did not even known Shane had a girlfriend until now," Frank blurted out in his abreaction towards Shane.

Frank flowed into conversation as Jade led him into the lines of her questioning and continued to smile and flutter her eyes in his direction probing carefully and strategically for information. "We all thought that when the pair wanted to be placed on the new roster so they could fly out together that something shifty was happening," flowed out of his mouth as he gulped at another beer in their waiting.

"Who Meg and Shane?" Jade questioned. "Yes", Frank answered quickly. "Hmm, No he has a girlfriend alright Frank but I'm not sure for how much longer," Jade replied, her eyes narrowing slightly.

During the next three weeks in Shanes absence, Jade spent a lot of time in thought and focusing on the new direction of which she wished to seek. She had learned a lot about herself, her attraction to another man while at the mines site and also found what she was looking for, Meg. Jade knew she had to be strong this time and stand her ground at any cost and awaited for Shane to return.

That evening when the lights of Shane's car shone through the loungeroom window, Jade took a deep breath and remained seated in the loungeroom chair. Jade did not rush to the door as she always had and sat silent in her sternness, until Shane approached the front door.

Jade walked over to the door and opened it.

"Hey baby," Shane greeted her, a smile on his face.

"Hey Shane," Jade greeted back and turned her back as Shane followed her inside.

"I've got a few things to finish up, then we can sit down to have a drink together if you would like?" Jade coldly informed him, as Shane looked on, slightly bewildered by the stand-offish welcoming he had just received.

"Oh, yeah, okay, I'll just get my bags and things from the car then," Shane replied.

Jade walked back into the office and busied herself in a secrecy of avoidance until she had completed her work and felt ready to face Shane and be in his presence.

An hour later, Jade emerged from the office and joined Shane in the shed where he had been keeping himself busy while he waited. "I'm ready to have that drink now," Jade announced upon her arrival, handing a can of bourbon to Shane.

"So, how was your flight?" Jade finally asked, placing herself on one of the stools.

"Yeah, good baby," Shane replied. "I was glad to get home though. Work is starting to suck. It's getting boring up there."

"Hmm," Jade hummed through disinterested lips.

Jade sat swinging her legs as they dangled from the tall stool she had sat on, looking out of the large shed doors that over looked the street, the silence between them awkward, deafening; neither one thinking of anything to say.

Eventually, Shane broke the silence between them. "Baby. I'm leaving the club this weekend, I gave notice last month, this will be my last meeting. I'm a bit nervous though."

Jade's face suddenly showed interest. "Oh, okay. You told me you wanted to leave, time to do it hey," Jade replied.

"Yeah," Shane continued. "It's too hard with work and stuff, it's too much."

Jade paused for a moment, thinking about the last words Shane had just said, then slightly concerned, asked. "Why are you nervous?"

Shane's blank stare sat in Jade's eyes for a moment before he finally answered.

"Cause I don't know how it will go down; they're going to be pissed off with me. I might not be able to walk out of there by the time they've finished with me."

Jade's face filled with an instant concern for his safety.

She had no idea that that's how it was at the club house having watched many hangabouts and prospects come and go without consequence. Why was it different for Shane?

"Umm, what do you mean?" Jade asked nervously.

"Well, they might kick the shit out of me. I know too much, I'm in too deep, to make sure I keep my mouth shut. I might not leave there alive," Shane explained nervously.

Jade's face dropped, stunned by what she was hearing.

"What, what, really," she stuttered, her words now filled with anxiousness. Shane just nodded as they both fell back into silence staring at the concrete floor.

Jade chewed softly at her nails in a nervous pause as the unexpected news dawned upon her and sent her into a state of concern for Shanes decision and safety.

That night was spent in a state of restlessness as Shane and Jade spent the night laying restlessly next to one another in the bed locked in conversation over the coming weekend and Shane's decision to leave the notorious club house. Although Jade had felt the relationship was coming to an end, she could no longer hold on to the anger she felt in the wake of the current events, and the scowl of disinterest that had covered her face had disappeared to reveal a look of concern for Shane's safety.

The clock ticked slowly with a deafening silence as the hands reached for six thirty, as Shane and Jade sat together in the loungeroom in the deafening wait that Saturday night.

Jade wrapped her arms around Shane nervously, holding him tightly to her.

"Please, please let me know you're okay," she begged. "I have to know you're alright."

"Of course I will," Shane replied, holding her close to him before pulling away slowly to look her in the eyes. "We'll stick to our arrangement okay."

"Okay," Jade replied bravely, the concern hidden deep within her eyes.

Shane apprehensively and nervously walked to the front door as his hand reached for the doorknob.

"Shane," Jade called out, rushing to her feet and walking towards him. "I love you," wrapping her arms around him in a tight embrace before placing her lips upon his in a slow kiss. Shane smiled briefly before turning to walk out through the front door and climbed into his car parked in the front driveway and left, disappearing down the road.

Jade paced the width of her bedroom anxiously, tracing along the width of her bed continuously, clutching her mobile phone in the tight grip of her fingers as the minutes turned to hours in her wait for Shane's message.

Her mind darted over each horrible imagined scenario continuously, of Shane's graphic descriptions of how the nights ordeal could end. Would she ever hear from Shane again? Would he come back home safe?

"Oh god, please, Shane message me," Jade whispered, pacing the floor, once more unable to find any peace or stillness within herself. "Please god, let him be okay."

The hours passed silently and endlessly until finally at eleven thirty pm Jade heard the message notification of her mobile phone.

"Please let this be Shane," Jade whispered, as she rushed to open the message. Jade held a breath in her throat as she flipped open the message and began to read it.

"Hey babe,"

"I'm all good, a car will be around shortly to pick you up. Be ready okay." xx

Jade felt the anxiousness instantly leave her body and stream tears of unambiguous relief down her cheeks as she read the words over and over, and allowed her hand to relax down by her side.

"Ohh, thank god," she said out loud, as she began to breathe again and a smile spread across her face.

Within thirty minutes, Jade heard the beeping horn of a parked vehicle coming from the front of the house. Jade walked to the window in the loungeroom and pulled back the curtain. "Hmm, that looks like Trent," ran through Jade's mind as her hand left the curtain and it swung back into position.

Trent had always shown concern for Jade and had treated her with the up most respect at all times and Jade reciprocated the same in an offering of friendship and trust, as she dated his brother.

Jade locked up the house and walked out to the car, opening the door. "Is Shane okay? Is everything alright," a veil of concern still covering the corners of her lips.

"Yeah Jade. Shane's fine, everything's okay," Trent replied.

"Thank you, Trent, I needed to hear those words."

Trent flashed a smile in Jade's direction and giggled a little at her naivety as she climbed into the front seat of the car.

"Shane gave me this to give to you," Trent said, reaching his hand out sideways and placing two little white pills into Jade's open palm. "Oh thanks," Jade said reciprocating with a smile.

Jade paused apprehensively as she sat looking at the pills sitting in her open palm as she summarised her entry into the clubhouse. "I need to see for myself first. I think I'll wait," ran through Jade's mind, her hands reaching for her purse in her handbag placed at the side of her leg and dropping the ecstasy pills into the zipper compartment.

Within minutes, Trent and Jade arrived at the front gates of the motorcycle clubhouse.

Jade stood nervously at the gates choosing to stand behind Trent upon entry in her apprehension.

Upon entry into the clubhouse, Jade's eyes darted around the sectioned rooms of people standing along the walls, bar areas and tables, desperately searching for Shane's whereabouts.

She walked up to the long wooden bar where Damien stood in his tender of the bars facilities.

"Hi Damien. Do you know where Shane is?"

But Jade's words were met with silence as Damien remained tight-lipped in his approach and turned his back in an angry gesture of refute. Jade placed her hand against her mouth in bewilderment as her eyes directed onto the cold glares and stares she was receiving from her friends and associates who sat at the tables scattered around the rooms. "Something is wrong here," ran through her mind, as her body pressed harder into the bar's wooden frame.

A cautiousness crept through her, and sat in the pit of her stomach in a nervousness of fearfulness.

It was the first time Jade had not felt welcomed at the notorious clubhouse, it was the first time she had felt scared to be there.

Jade sat anxiously at the bar, slowly soothing the end of her fingers with the fingertips on her other hand in an attempt to ease the feeling of the thickened silence that sat within the glares of the other members and their wives, as she waited for Shane to appear.

Out of the corner of her eye Jade noticed Ryan, whose glare pierced straight through her, followed closely behind by Shane who appeared to be heavily intoxicated walking next to Rebecca who chatted incessantly to the men.

Jade noticed the coloured scribbles written all over Rebecca's exposed breasts and shoulders, her mind instantly sparked into an air of suspicion. "What had gone on here tonight in her absence?"

"Hey girl," Rebecca said to Jade laughing as she approached her, her stride remaining unbroken as she barely acknowledged Jade and headed towards the other women sitting around at the tables.

"Hey Rebecca," Jade replied, smiling, but bewildered at her avoidance.

Jade knew something was wrong, she could feel the tension all around her that cut through her in an air of apprehension and foreboding.

Shane sat down on the stool at the bar, wobbling as he came to a rest, his words barely recognisable, each word a slur as they left his mouth.

"I just wanted to see that you were okay," Jade said quietly in Shane's ear. "But I think I'll go home. I'm a bit tired tonight, is that okay?" Shane's blurry eyes followed her lips as he spoke the words.

"Yeah babe, I'll be home later. Trent, can you drop Jade home for me," Shane called out to his brother who sat quietly on the other side of the bar.

"Yeah mate," Trent replied as Jade gathered her handbag, threw it over her shoulder and walked out of the clubhouse without Shane.

That night Jade spent the night alone bewildered in the night's events as her mind constantly searched for the answers of the treatment she received at the clubhouse by the other members when she had arrived. Those answers never came and she remained dumbfounded as she tossed and turned in her bed that night all alone. Jades phone remained silent that evening and Shane did not return to the family home until the late hours of the following day. They never spoke of the events of that night and Jade remained unaware of what had really transpired in her absence.

The following week, Jade received an unexpected phone call from Monique. "Mum, I'm coming home for a visit." Jade could not believe her ears and was filled with an instant exuberance of excitement and anticipation. She leapt back into the bed where Shane lay peacefully dozing, jumping excitedly around him on the bed.

"Shane, Shane. Monique's coming home. Yes," Jade giggled as she leapt off the side of the bed and rushed to Cody's bedroom.

One week later, Jade walked into the Alterro airport and waited by the gates in eager anticipation. Her eyes darted throughout the numerous people boarding and arriving at each gate as she waited excitedly to see her daughter.

Jade's eyes came to a stop as a pretty teenage girl with shoulder-length brown hair caught her eye walking down the boarding ramps. "Oh my. It's my sweet girl," Jade whispered to herself, holding her hands over her mouth and wiping the trickle of a tear that had fallen from her eyes. Monique approached closer and closer as she walked along the boarding ramp towards the terminal.

"Mum. Mum," Monique suddenly called out as her steps quickened and hurried until finally she fell into the deep embrace of her mother's open arms. "Oh my sweet girl, you're home," Jade cried, holding her tightly within her arms, kissing her on the cheeks and looking at her daughters smile that covered her face from ear to ear.

"Let's go home," Jade said, taking her daughters hand into hers and leading her through the terminal as the happiness expressed in a broad smile covered their faces.

Monique had changed so much, now at thirteen, she was changing into a beautiful young lady. Jade could hardly recognise the young girl she once was and found herself in moments of just looking at her as she went about her way in the family home.

Over the course of the week Jade had lost all focus from the troubles of the household and her troubles with Shane and stayed focused on Monique, fussing over her daughter at every chance she got.

Each day Jade rose with a smile beaming across her face as the joy of having her daughter home filled her heart with extreme joviality and exuberance and lifted the dark clouds of the longing that had sat heavily within her heart in her absence until it was time for Monique to leave once more and return to Meltona.

Jade tentatively stood in the airport terminal watching her daughter walk the boarding lane to the plane that stretched further and further away from her until Monique disappeared and she could see her no more. Tears welled within Jades eyes and pain filled the cracks within her heart with every footstep that took her daughter away from her. Each goodbye harder than the next as her heart longed to never let her go.

No matter how well Jade became in Monique's absence, no matter how much she carried on with her life, each moment of watching her daughter leave again stirred and stabbed at her broken heart. Jade was suffering from separation anxiety from her daughter, which grew worse with each visit.

Two days later Shane left to head back to his employment position at the mines.

Shane and Jade stood on the small concrete front porch of the family home wrapped in each other's arms as they kissed each other goodbye, leaving Jade to her life at home without him once more.

That night after Shane had left, Jade's phone suddenly began to ring, flashing an unknown number. "Hello," Jade answered, frowning at the unknown caller.

"Is that Jade?" a woman's voice said before giggling and quickly hanging up the phone. A bewildered frown formed in Jade's brows as her mind momentarily paused before starting to focus on the pitch of the woman's voice.

"Who was that?" Jade asked, picking up her phone and looking at it as if the answers were written in black and white upon the screen.

That night Jade received three more suspicious phone calls from two different women asking the same question and giggling before hanging up which stretched out over the period of three hours.

Jade sat in her bedroom alone in a bewildered state as her mind searched for answers to the phone calls and who may have been behind them. "What's going on? Who are these women? How did they get my number?" Jade had not forgotten her unwelcoming at the clubhouse that evening when Shane had departed from his position and had not found the answers to her refutation and had felt the nervousness of the events which now ticked loudly within her thoughts.

Over the next month in Shane's absence, Jade received numerous phone calls late into the evening hours of the night in exact replica to when they had started, ending in the childish giggling before a silence sat between them and the phone went dead. Each night Jade tossed and turned in a sleepless tessellation of concern. Each night as Jade lay awake alone in her bed her mind focused endlessly on the conversations and events that she had encountered on a day to day basis with Shane and the clubhouse and compared the previous to the recent events. "Oh my god," Jade whispered to herself, coming to her own conclusion while lying under the soft warm protective covers of her bed.

"It's the women from the club." What had Shane done?

Jade felt threatened and uncertain of what to expect outside of the protective walls of her home and if she was being watched and started to become a recluse of the family home, leaving the house less and less.

On the Thursday evening while Shane was still away at the mines, unexpectedly Sonia came knocking at Jade's door. Jade had not seen Sonia since her last unexpected visit and had once again caught Jade off guard and unprepared.

"Hey Jade," Sonia greeted her, smiling.

"Oh, hi Sonia, come in," Jade answered back suspiciously.

Sonia sat down on the chair within the loungeroom, silently patient as Jade busied herself in the kitchen making them a coffee. Jade returned to the loungeroom with two cups of coffee and placed them on the coffee table in front of them and sat down on the end of the lounge.

"So, how's it all going?" Sonia asked.

"Yeah, good," Jade replied. "I'm still pushing on with the business plan, I'm close to getting it started now, but I'm still having trouble raising the funds but I'm getting there though."

"That's excellent," Sonia replied, smiling back at Jade. "Sounds like you've been busy, sounds like you need a break hey," smiling devilishly at Jade. Jade smiled warily back in her uneasiness and mistrust of Sonia's intentions of arriving on her doorstep.

"What are you doing this weekend?" Sonia asked.

"Staying home, I guess," Jade replied, shrugging her shoulders at the question. "I haven't really made any plans."

"Would you like to go out, come dancing with me?" Sonia asked.

Jade smiled at the idea, although she wasn't sure about Sonia's intentions, her mind focused on the fun of dancing which appealed to her senses and quickly overcome her hesitation. "Umm, Yes, I would love to," Jade finally replied. "Brilliant, I'll pick you up at around 9 pm then, would that suit you?" Sonia replied.

"Perfect," Jade answered smiling as they both rose to their feet and Jade walked Sonia to the front door. "I'll see you then," Sonia said stepping through the front door, waving as she climbed into her car and drove away.

Saturday night: "What am I going to wear?" Jade mumbled to herself, pulling out this outfit and that outfit from the bedroom cupboard as she watched the clock on the bedside cupboard. "Sonia will be here in a couple of hours." Jade had looked forward to her night out with Sonia all week but had not prepared for it at all until the last minute and rushed around her bedroom in a flurry of choices and indecisiveness.

Jade had decided not to allow the week's events of numerous phone calls weigh on her mind and her fears of the unknown that surrounded her and halted her life into a nonexistence of living outside of the family homes walls and although she felt a little nervous her excitement for the evening outweighed her fears and fuelled her enthusiasm.

Sonia arrived at Jade's house at 9 pm, full of smiles and warmth, which made Jade feel more comfortable in her presence. After consuming a couple of drinks and engaging in an ebullient conversation of laughter and playfulness the two women stepped out of the house and headed for the local nightclubs and hotels.

Jade and Sonia entered the first hotel, approaching the bar upon their entry and ordered their drinks before placing themselves at one of the outdoor table settings and looked around the room at the numerous patrons that frequented the venue, playing Eightball and enjoying one another's company.

"Do you want to go to the next venue?" Sonia suggested, pointing towards the end of the street.

"Yes," agreed Jade, gulping down the rest of her drink, gathering her handbag and weaving her way through the numerous people that surrounded her.

After arriving at the next location, Sonia grabbed Jade by the hand and led her into the confines and privacy of the facilities toilet block, leading her into one of the cubicles. "Here," Sonia said, handing Jade a mirror lined up with the temptations of cocaine. Jade held the cocaine out in front of her as her mind paused in her decision. "Well, might as well enjoy the evening," ran through Jade's mind, as she rolled up the fifty dollar note and proceeded to inhale the two lines of cocaine.

"Thank you," Jade replied, looking up at Sonia, handing the mirror back to her. Sonia giggled as she looked at Jade and took the fifty dollar note and placed it down onto the mirrors surface and inhaled two lines of the cocaine also before packing it back away in her purse. "Let's go dancing," Sonia said in exuberance grabbing Jade by the hand and leading her out of the toilet block and out onto the dance floor. Jade giggled freely as the events that had led up to the evening disappeared from her thoughts and she started to feel the comfortable familiarity of the night scene that surrounded her of which she had once enjoyed without hesitation.

Two hours passed by as Jade and Sonia danced joyfully and chatted to their friends as the cocaine rushed through their minds and sent them into a state of uninhibited intoxication. The lights flashed by quickly all around them in illuminated colours that danced within their eyes and swayed their hips in a methodical rhythm of rhapsody to the loud music that rushed through their ears in pure delight.

"I need a rest" Jade said, walking back over to their table and picking up her drink. "Oh c'mon, let's keep dancing," Sonia said, giggling, following Jade over to the table.

Jade giggled at Sonia's eagerness and quickly finished her drink. "Let's go outside a minute", Jade suggested, taking a step towards the front doors of the establishment, quickly followed by Sonia.

"I need a cigarette," she said, giggling, pulling one out of her handbag and lighting it up as Sonia stood next to her waiting for her on the footpath. Jade finished her cigarette and followed Sonia back into the venue which had become the most popular venue in the small local township of Suisania Bay in Jades absence of revelling in the night clubs since she had met Shane and was now full of people.

"C'mon, come shake it with me and make me look sexy," Sonia said, turning her smile towards Jade and grabbing her by the hand to pull her onto the dance floor. Jade followed and swayed to the music in a rhythmic seduction as the loud music reached through to her soul and swayed her to its seductive rhythms, as the intoxication of the cocaine lowered her defences and inhibitions and rendered her mind helpless to its effects.

Suddenly Jade noticed Sonia looking over at the corner of the bar, smiling audaciously.

"Who's that?" ran through Jade's mind as she twisted her head around to view the corner of the bar. Sonia reached her hands out quickly, grabbing at Jade's shoulders and turning her to face her once again.

Without warning suddenly a full can of alcohol came hurdling through the gap in the crowd heading straight for Jade's face. "Oh god," Jade said, ducking around the can of alcohol and stood motionless stunned as the can crashed to the floor just behind her before turning her head so that her eyes could narrow in on the direction of the throw. Within minutes of the can being thrown Rebecca, Tasha and Michelle stepped through the crowd and walked angrily in Jade's direction. Jade's eyes sharpened and focused on the three women that walked towards her and stood in a confrontational stance as she stood her ground angrily. Suddenly Tasha and Rebecca pulled out more cans that sat concealed behind their backs in their hands and threw them viciously at Jade, one after the other.

Jade dodged as the flying cans pelted past her head and fell heavily to the ground.

"Ohhh," Jade yelped, as one of the cans hit heavily against her cheek bone.

"Grrr," Jade growled under her breath. "You fucken bitches," flew out of Jade's mouth before she could contain herself and reached for one of the cans that had fallen to the ground and threw it back in Tasha's direction.

Michelle quickly stepped in front of the flung can and deflected it sideways away from Tasha and stood firmly between the feuding women.

"Go home Jade," Michelle pleaded quietly in Jade's ear. "Just go home okay? I'll take care of this," Michelle continued.

Jade rushed over to Sonia who stood to the side of the feuding women but within a comfortable distance from them.

"Are you coming Sonia?" Jade asked, angrily. Sonia's eyes darted towards Rebecca and Tasha quickly before returning her look back in Jade's direction.

"I'm going to stay okay," Sonia finally replied, dropping her eyes to the floor.

"No worries, see ya later," huffily leapt from Jade's mouth as she collected her handbag and quickly walked away down the long alleyway and out onto the footpath. Trent, who stood alone near the entrance of the gateway suddenly came unexpectedly into Jade's view.

"Hey Trent. Would you mind giving me a ride home?" Jade asked, her voice still trembling angrily from the incident that had just occurred inside.

"Yeah, sure," Trent replied. "Are you alright?" Trent asked as the pair climbed into the front seat of his parked car. "No. I'm really angry right now," Jade replied, turning the angry glare that blaze within her eyes in Trent's direction.

As Trent pulled the car to a stop at the front of Jade's house he paused momentarily as Jade proceeded to climb out of the vehicle.

"Hey Jade, watch out for those girls. They have got it in for you, watch yourself okay."

Jade paused, lifted her head slightly and breathed a deep sigh releasing the anger that had remained ablaze within her, before raising her eyes to look at Trent. "But what have I done Trent?" she asked. "What have I done to them?"

Trent's stare remained stubbornly stealth out of the front window of the car as his lips remained tightly shut. "I have to go Jade. I've got to get back okay. Take care."

A subtle silence fell between them as Jade stood there looking in through the crack in the half open front door.

"Thanks Trent for the ride home, I appreciate that," Jade finally said, breaking through the awkward silence that sat between them.

Jade slowly pushed the car door closed as she nervously bit on her bottom lip and watched as Trent drove down the road and disappeared around the corner.

On Tuesday Jade drove the highway to Alterro to pick Shane up from the airport as his vehicle had been booked in for repairs and he was unable to drive the three-hour trip back home to Suisania Bay.

Jade had not minded the drive, thinking it would be good for her to get out of town for the day as the tension of Saturday night's events still sat heavily within her thoughts.

Jade parked the car in the airport parking bay, arriving with just minutes to spare and rushed through the terminal and up the airport escalator, reaching the top just as Shane came into her view walking towards her.

A smile formed across Shane's face as he spotted Jade through the large crowd and walked enthusiastically towards her in his anticipation.

"Hey baby," Shane greeted her, throwing his arms around her in a tight embrace.

But Jade did not reciprocate the embrace and stood silently motionless and emotionless in her welcoming as her arms remained by her side and her kiss remained tight lipped.

Shane shrugged off the cold shoulder of her greeting as his eyes studied the tight lipped grip written upon Jade's face and continued to act the part of the oblivious, as he tried to engage in small talk through Jade's silence that continued while they walked through the terminal to the baggage area.

The three-hour drive back to the township of Suisania Bay was filled with silence except for the melodies that played upon the cars radio as the tension sat heavily between them in the front seat of the vehicle.

"So, what happened to your cheek?" Shane finally asked, breaking the silence between them. Jade raised her hand to touch the swollen grazed bruise that sat upon her cheekbone hidden under her makeup.

"Hmm," Jade hummed through tight lips. "I thought that would have been the first thing you asked me when you saw me if you bloody cared," the harsh words snapping from her mouth as her cold glare pointed its venom in Shane's direction.

"What the fuck's wrong with you?" Shane snapped back at her angrily.

"Oh, nothing. Why would there be anything wrong Shane," Jade replied, her voice condescending and irritated. "Have you any idea what's been going on while you're up there playing around on me," Jade snapped as each word spilt from the containment of her will and the anger boiled within her and lashed out in an attack of accusations.

"You set me up, you set me up, I went out and those bitches, our so-called friends, threw cans at me. I've been getting phone call after phone call asking if I'm Jade. Who the fuck is it huh? Who did you give my number to? One of your women you're doing up there or one of them here, huh? I hate you." Jade sat motionless and silenced in the front seat of the car, her eyes cold with anger, her skin flushed with her temper, her body stiff, her glare directed directly at Shane.

Shane slowed the car down and pulled over to the side of the road as the argument escalated between them into a war of words and accusations.

"Listen here, I don't know what the fuck's been going on here, I'm just up there doing my bloody work. I get home, and you're bloody accusing me of this that and the other. You're fucken crazy, you've got something wrong with you. You're paranoid woman. If you were a fucken man, I'd smack you to the ground right now," Shane growled and snarled, yelling at Jade in retaliation. "Shut your bloody mouth now girl or else."

Jade stared at Shane, her glare, a dagger of rage as she closed her mouth and bit down upon the venomous words that threatened to escape from her mouth. The car fell silent once more.

Three hours later, Shane and Jade arrived back at their home in Suisania bay.

Jade rushed out of the car, slamming the door behind her and stomped inside the house in a state of disarray and walked straight into her bedroom.

"You don't even care what has happened," Jade spluttered into the air, her face falling heavily into her hands as the tears began to flow heavily down her cheeks and over the swollen bruise that lay upon her cheekbone, as she sat upon the side of the bed.

Shane did not dare to enter the house and walked straight out to the shed in his avoidance of the confrontation of Jade's anger and emotional upset.

Over the following week Shane and Jade lived in stubborn silence as the tension between them escalated and they were unable to break through the issues that surrounded their now turbulent relationship.

That weekend in an emotional dishevelment Jade could not restrain from the temptation and reached out for the little white pill.

As the intoxicating effect of the ecstasy pill seeped through Jade's mind the heaviness of the oppugnancy that sat between the couple, fell to the floor in a beautiful, hazy illusion of peacefulness. Jade started to giggle and entice playfulness as she turned on the music and started to sway sexily to the melodies that lasted only moments.

All of a sudden Jade's eyes glazed over into a dark rage of animosity and the words that flew from her mouth snapped without a minute's notice.

"I know what you've been doing. You're a liar and a cheater. Up there screwing that woman. I saw it all, the way you both looked at each other. You disgust me; I'm home here faithful, staying home, doing right by you, while you're stabbing me in the back," Jade yelled, her temper out of her control.

Shane grabbed Jade by the shoulders and slammed her up against the wall pointing his finger straight into her chest. "You little bitch. You've bloody lost it. Shut your fucking mouth, or I'll shut it for you," Shane roared back at her, squeezing her skin in a tight angry grip.

Jade's eyes narrowed into a vindictive glare as her words left her mouth in a precise precision of oppugnant animosity.

"You think you're so clever, don't you," Jade growled as she pushed her body away from the wall, her moves slow and calculating.

Step by step, Jade moved calculatingly slowly towards Shane, as his face dropped into an astonished open mouth glare and turned a shade of pale as he loosened his grip and slowly moved away from Jade fearfully.

"How bloody clever do you think you're going to feel when Meg's husband kicks the shit out of you. Yeah, that's right, he knows. You see, I made a little visit to see him on my way back from the mines. I told him I was looking for a job and I got his phone number. We've been keeping in touch while you've been gone. My last words to him, before I left, were, You better keep a close eye on your wife, she likes to get extra friendly with her co-workers especially one called Shane," Jade continued coldly.

Jade smirked as the last words left her mouth a cold vindictive shadow cast itself all over her face as she rubbed the words deep into Shanes mind.

The realisation of Jade's betrayal froze Shane on the spot as the cruel words of animosity reached their depth in a twisted tale of his panic.

Jade stood there laughing a crazy, mean laugh that sent shivers up Shane's spine.

"You're crazy," Shane said, his eyes filled with a bewildering panic and quickly ran towards the front door and left. Jade had been pushed too far.

Three days later, Jade heard the familiar sound of the back gate latch lift up and click.

"Shane," Jade whispered to herself, standing at the kitchen sink, looking out of the large window that over looked the patio area.

"Jade," Shane said, standing in the open plan doorway of the kitchen. "I'm so sorry I ran out on you. I swear Jade, I swear to you that I have never cheated on you."

Shane stood in a profusely submitted state as he begged for Jade's forgiveness, profusely denying the accusations over and over, his eyes looking straight into hers.

Jade stood firm momentarily, her eyes locked on his stubbornly, until finally she relented and took Shane back in.

That month in Shane's absence, the phone calls started again.

Late one evening, Jade climbed into bed and turned off the bedside lamp when suddenly the phone began to ring.

"Hello," Jade said, sleepily picking up the phone and answering it. All of a sudden, the words trailed down the phone in a cold, shilling attack.

"You're fucken dead bitch, we know where you live. Watch your back bitch, we're watching you. We're coming."

"Oh shit," Jade whispered to herself, placing her fingers into the small of her mouth and nibbling nervously. "Who are you? "

Jade's mind raced fast as her heart beat quickened and her breath became shallow as she sat alone in her bed.

Although she feared for her own safety Jade could not focus on anything except her children who slept peacefully in their bedrooms, unaware of the turmoil of which their mother was enduring night after night, and the threats that had been placed upon her.

Each evening, Jade began to check the locks of each window and stood in the loungeroom windows searching for any shapes in the shadows watching her and her family as they slept.

Her weight began to plummet continuously, as she suffered from overwhelming anxiety attacks standing in the loungeroom windows alone every night, awaiting an attack from the unknown assailants.

Jade lay beneath the soft warm covers of her bed staring up at the ceiling locked in a sleepless restlessness as she tossed from side to side trying to go to sleep each night. One night in the late hours of the night as the phone lay silent on the bedside cupboard all of a sudden Jade heard the sound of the message alert tone. "Who's that?" Jade whispered to herself, a curious frown forming between her brows as she held the phone up to her face to read the screen.

Jade sat up in her bed and opened the message and began to read it out loud to herself.

"Mmm. I love it when your man goes down on me. We've been seeing each other for months. He's mine bitch."

"What," Jade said out loud, her mouth dropping in disgust. "You've got to be kidding me"

The cruel words struck there mark as Jade's temper flung her out of the bed and raised her to her feet walking back and forth along the end of the bed, growling to herself.

"How dare he," Jade growled. "Who does he think he is cheating on me," walking out to the back patio and lighting a cigarette.

Jade stomped back and forth along the patio cement floor as her mind filled with the tension of the words.

"So this is it Shane," Jade continued to growl. "Hang on."

Jade came to a sudden stop, as her eyes became focused before suddenly letting out a loud laugh.

"That's it," Jade said to herself, smiling. "You stupid bitch. You just messed up and gave me your phone number." All of a sudden Jade's message alert sounded again with a second message sent from a different number. Jade started to read the message.

"Don't fall asleep bitch. You're going up in flames and I'm taking your man." Jade's face tightened at the threat.

"Oh really bitch," Jade said smugly to herself. "Well, we'll see about that, won't we?"

The next morning after getting the children to school, Jade set out to unravel the mystery of the phone calls and messages. She wrote down the phone numbers of the messages and called the first number after blocking her own number so the recipient could not identify her.

"Hmm. That's strange. It went straight to voice mail," Jade said, holding the phone out in front of her face. Jade listened intensely for the recorded message but the phone had remained silent and a greeting on the voice mail box had not been recorded.

"Hmm," Jade hummed to herself. "Okay, I'll try the next one." Jade rang the second number, standing quiet and still, her ears focused and straining, ready to hear the name. The phone rang and rang until finally the phone was answered but once again, it went straight to voice mail without a greeting message. "Damn," Jade said out loud stomping her feet on the spot. "Okay, I'll call again later," looking at her phone and placing the piece of paper containing the phone numbers into her jacket pocket.

That evening Jade heard a knock at her front door. Jade walked nervously to the loungeroom window and pulled back the covers and looked through the crack of the curtain.

"Ohh, It's Lilly," Jade said to herself, a smile quickly forming across her lips.

Jade had known Lilly for two years now, having first met her at the local nightclub venue within Suisania Bay during her nights of dancing and revelling. Lilly had been a regular visitor of the notorious motorcycle clubhouse and had dated Bryan, who was one of the members of the clubhouse. Lilly was a friendly girl, who was much younger than Jade but it had not caused any concern within their friendship which had always remained honest, open and communicative.

Although Jade had disappeared while consumed within the deep depression that had gripped her and had been abandoned by her friends during that time, Lilly had remained a constant source of contact, sending messages and phone calls on a regular basis in her support. Jade trusted Lilly.

Jade walked swiftly around to the front door of the house and opened the door. "Lilly," Jade greeted as she opened her arms and welcomed her into a tight embrace. "I'm so happy to see you," Jade continued, kissing Lilly upon the cheek.

"So how have you been?" Lilly asked friendly and smiling, pleased to see her too.

Jade dropped her head and looked towards the floor. "Not good sweetie. Not good at all."

She quickly began to explain to Lilly of the confusing, fearful events that now surrounded her and of the infliction of her relationship to Shane, which had caused so much turmoil in her life and had now led to the terrible phone calls that she was now receiving each night, while Shane was absent from the family home and away at work. Lilly listened intently as Jade ran down the harrowing ordeals of the past and the present and the constant conflict of which she suffered with Shane.

Lilly's eyes drew into a stare of concern and astonishment which had rendered her speechless and lost for words.

Jade looked back at her with wide open eyes and just nodded. "Uh uh. Pretty bad hey."

Lilly spread her arms out open and wrapped her into a tight comforting embrace before finally speaking.

"Unbelievable chick, I had no idea. But you're a strong girl. You always pull yourself through. And the rest of us as well," Lilly giggled. "You know what you have to do, you always find the solution," giving Jade a reassuring smile. Jade's lips formed into a small comforted smile.

"Thank you Lilly. I love you. But I don't know what to do about the phone calls I have been receiving from these unknown women," Jade explained, pouring out her heart and concerns.

"They did send me messages though, which was their mistake and now I have their numbers," Jade continued, grinning cunningly.

"Would you like me to ring them?" Lilly asked, selflessly offering Jade her help.

"I. Ah. If you want to, but I don't really want to get anyone involved," Jade replied, indecisively.

"I don't mind chick, really, give me the numbers. We'll give it a go," Lilly replied, placing her hand reassuringly upon Jade's shoulder.

Jade reached for the piece of paper that sat within her jacket pocket and handed it to Lilly revealing the phone numbers of the unknown assailants and placed her phone into her hand. Jade sat quietly next to Lilly, anxious, nervous as Lilly proceeded to dial the first number. "It's ringing," Lilly said, looking into the anxiousness of Jade's eyes.

"Hello," a woman's voice answered.

"Oh hi, um, who is this?" asked Lilly cunningly.

"Who the fuck's this?" the voice quickly snapped back angrily.

"Oh, I'm sorry. I must have dialled the wrong number," Lilly nervously answered back, sitting straight up and startled in the angry response.

"Well get your bloody numbers right, you stupid fucken bitch," the voice growled at Lilly before hanging up in her ear.

"Oh God," Lilly muttered, her eyes wide with disbelief and concern, dropping the phone down from her ear and placing it down onto the kitchen counter. "She's one angry lady, I'd leave that one alone chick."

A worrying frown formed across Jade's face as Lilly reached out to touch her on the shoulder in a comforting concerned gesture. "Do you want me to try the second number?" Lilly asked, picking up the phone and looking down at the slip of paper.

"I need to know who they are," Jade replied. "This needs to stop, would you mind Lilly, please, I would understand if you don't want to get involved, especially after that last phone call." "Of course I don't mind Jade," Lilly replied, picking up the piece of paper and dialling the second number.

"Hello," the voice answered.

"Oh hi, who is this?" Lilly said, repeating the same words that she had cunningly used during the first phone call.

"It's Mary," answered the voice. "Who's this?"

"Oh, I'm really sorry Mary. I must have dialled the wrong number," Lilly replied and quickly hung up the phone, placing it into Jade's open palm.

Lilly looked at Jade, a worrying look spreading across her face and creeping into her eyes. "Chick, that was Mary, Tasha's friend."

"What," flew out of her mouth as she quickly leapt to her feet from of the kitchen chair, "Those two." Jade shook her head in disbelief. "You've got to be kidding me, how the hell did they get my number? How the hell."

Jade fell into a momentary pause as her mind searched for the answers. Suddenly her eyes quickly darted back in Lilly's direction as the words spilt from her lips. "Shane. That bastard," Jade yelled out as anger rose up her back and filled her senses. "That bloody little prick. Oh, you wait till I see him, it's gonna be on," Jade ranted, her feet now a quick pace back and forth along the loungeroom floor. "That's why I haven't been allowed to go over to the club until after a certain time anymore. They've been having an affair behind my back. It's Shane Lilly. It's Shane." "He gave them my number and set them upon me. That's what has been going on this whole fucken time."

Lilly looked at Jade formidably and speechless. "I can't believe he would do that to you. What are you going to do Jade?" Lilly finally asked, breaking Jade's angry focus on her thoughts as she continued to pace angrily upon the loungeroom floor.

Jade stopped and looked at Lilly, rage blazing within her eyes that quickly softened upon the view of the concern and compassion formed upon Lilly's face.

"Oh," Jade sighed. "I'm sorry Lilly. I haven't seen you for ages and you walk in on this. I'm so sorry."

"That's okay chick, I understand. I would feel the same way," Lilly calmly replied disconcertingly.

"But if Tasha is involved," Lilly continued. "I'd watch your back, she's crazy. You don't know what she'll do."

Jade looked at Lilly, staring, lost in her own thoughts before finally answering, "Yes, I know, but at least now I know who I'm dealing with and why."

That evening after putting the children to bed, Jade's feet paced back and forth across the bedroom floor as her thoughts tangled and tried to fathom the level of Shane's deceit and betrayal as many questions formed within her mind and ended in lashings of accusations towards him. Words of rage left Jade's mouth as quickly as they raced across her mind until she could stand it no more and lost her control.

"Fuck it," Jade growled to herself, quickly walking from the bedroom and into the kitchen. Jade reached her hand up to the kitchen cupboard and opened the door and stood staring at the half filled bottle of bourbon adorning the cupboard shelf. "Fuck it. Fuck it all," Jade raged, reaching her hand out to firmly grip the bottle of bourbon, placing it down onto the kitchen bench in front of her and filling up a glass.

"I'm going to ring the bastard," Jade spat as she stomped into the hallway and grabbed the phone from off the hallway stand and rang Shane's number.

"Hello," Shane answered wearily, his voice a tone of his disturbed sleepiness.

"You bastard," Jade growled. "You gave my phone number to Tasha. You set me up. How could you do that to me, I'm your girlfriend," Jade yelled, her rage spitting the words down the phone.

"Hang on. What the fuck are you talking about Jade? I didn't give your number to anyone," Shane yelled back, in his defence. "What's going on?"

But Jade could not contain her rage and continued to yell condemning accusations down the phone.

"So, your fucking her now too huh?" Jade yelled angrily.

"No," Shane yelled back. "I haven't done anything Jade. That depression has made you paranoid, you're losing it girl. Truly, your mind's playing tricks on you. I'm totally innocent of this. Give me the number, I'll ring it okay."

Jade went silent momentarily as Shane's words penetrated her thoughts and suddenly subdued her anger and forced questions of self-doubt and confusion to form within her mind. "Was Shane right? Am I disillusioned? Did he really have nothing to do with this?"

"Okay," Jade finally answered calmly, breaking the deafening silence that sat like a dark cloud between them, before reading out the phone numbers.

"I'll get back to you in a minute okay," Shane assured her and hung up the phone.

Jade sat back down on the side of her bed in her wait, nervously twiddling her phone between her rigid fingers as she gulped at the chilled bourbon held tightly within her other hand.

Thirty minutes later, the phone rang.

"Hello," Jade answered calmly, her voice now slightly slurred from the numerous glasses of alcohol that she had consumed while nervously waiting.

"It was bloody Tasha Jade. She's done this, not me. I had nothing to do with it. She's got your number from someone and thought it would be funny to stir you up. Don't worry, she copped a bloody mouthful from me, believe me, that will be the end of it," Shane continued, acting the hero of the situation.

Jade paused momentarily, her mind darting back and forth over the realisation, lost in the truth or lies of the moment. "I don't know what to believe," Jade whispered to herself, dropping her eyes to the floor in dismay and confusion as her eyes filled with tears.

"Alright, Alright," Jade finally answered. "I believe you. God Shane, that was nearly it for us. I was going to tell you to go to hell, don't bother coming home ever again. This nearly ended us, do you realise that," Jade sobbed down the phone, the tears that had welled in her eyes finally falling and rolling down her flushing cheeks.

"Baby, you need to calm down," Shane answered. "You haven't been yourself for a long time. That bastard of an ex of yours messed your mind up, you're paranoid and you're taking it all out on me. I love you, don't you know that. Just calm down girl."

Jade had not heard those words from Shane in such a long time, which flowed through her in a mellifluous state of comfort. "Oh Shane, I'm so sorry baby, I'm so sorry," the words falling from her mouth through the heavy flow of tears that rolled down her cheeks and fell heavily to the floor. "I love you too."

One month later, Shane quit his job at the mines and returned back home to be with Jade permanently telling her he needed to be there with her as he was worried about everything that had happened and her being left on her own. Jade's mind and emotional state had felt torn apart, embattled and now in a constant state of confusion, her trust shaken and destroyed, she no longer knew which way she could turn and felt in a continuous battle with herself, her mind, her feelings and thoughts now in question and doubt of her own reality as Shane wiggled back under her skin, taking advantage of Jade's current state of mind and blaming the depression for her irrational behaviour and accusations. Jade tried desperately to stay focused on what was important to her; her children; her business plan; her life, but the misplaced trust, the threats and Shane weighed heavily upon her shoulders, following her around like a constant bad dream, one from which she was unable to escape and shake herself awake.

Jade was lost, drowning in her emotional and mental confusion and self-doubt and constantly sought clarity and found herself pulled into the unfocused, scattered corners of her mind.

Shane, now home and not working, deemed a constant distraction for her, she had hoped his presence back in the home would start to rebuild their relationship, once more bringing closeness back to their lives and mend the shattered cracks that had formed in her heart, the shattered remains of his time spent at the mines and his indiscretion of his time spent with the other woman, Meg.

As Jade busied herself in the office still trying to build the business she was developing, pushing it closer and closer to the predicted start-up date of establishment, Shane potted around the house, taking back the roles that Jade had filled in his absence.

But Jade still felt the constant battle of the trust issues that Shane had cemented within her so deeply and her days in the office drew shorter and shorter as her mind was pulled out to the shed where Shane now spent most of his time.

Her mind, now on constant alert, her ears listening for any sign of Shane's womanising behaviour found herself standing secretly at the side of the shed door once again. Quietly sneaking to the entrance, standing for a moment each time, it had become an obsession as she held her breath and listened intently before she would enter. Jade hoped that time would heal the mistrust that had sat between them in a stalemate of animosity but continued in an endless battle of wills and pride.

One month after Shane's return to the family home, things had started to finally improve. Shane no longer left for days at a time and his attention was now focused on Jade and her young son, Cody. With his involvement with the notorious bikie club now dissolved, Shane had settled and seemed to be trying to rebuild the foundations of their relationship that had been broken and cracked and caused a distance to form between them over the course of their relationship and finally with time the trust that had been shattered was starting to heal and reform between them once more.

Jade smiled coyly as she stood at the shed entrance watching Shane as he potted around the shed, tinkering with his tools and motorbike.

"Hey baby. Would you like to have a drink with me?" Jade asked, announcing her presence.

Shane turned his head around to greet her with a smile as Jade stood holding two cans of bourbon out in front of her.

"Okay, thanks baby," Shane replied reaching for a can of the alcohol.

She sat down on the plastic stool, sipping at the cold can of liquor as the couple continued to chat as she watched Shane fixing the broken parts of his motorcycle.

"I'm thinking about selling this baby," Shane announced, raising his head and smiling at Jade.

Jade remained paused and silent as she reminisced in her mind over the many memorable moments on the motorcycle of which they had shared together, often taking off for long trips, riding through the beautiful scenery of the gorges and enjoying the freedom and views of the winding, hilly roads that surrounded the small town of Suisania Bay.

Jade remembered the two of them riding from town to town stopping at all the small quaint eateries that were scattered throughout the small townships located on the outskirts of Suisania Bay and stopping at a creek bed next to a large pine tree where Shane had declared his love for her by carving their initials, written in a love heart, into the bark that would grow with the tree as would their love.

Memories that were a part of them, their relationship and were sentimentality attached to the motorcycle Shane now wished to sell.

"Well, baby," Jade finally replied after her momentary pause. "It's up to you. You know that. But I will miss it though. We've had a lot of good times on that bike."

Jade smiled, her eyes a glow within the treasured memories.

"Yeah, I know baby but I'm not working now and I've quit the club. I have no reason to keep it anymore. It just seems impractical to keep it now," Shane explained.

Jade nodded, she could see the reasoning behind his decision but continued in her own sense of reasoning. "But just don't rush it okay. Give it a couple of months, see how you feel about it then."

Shane nodded in agreement. "Yeah, you're probably right. I do love my bike," he replied, smiling.

The following weekend Shane and Jade decided to go for a drive up into the hillsides that surrounded Suisania Bay to explore the many dirt trail tracks that wound through the bushlands and climbed up the hillsides to the top of the mountain peaks.

On the Saturday morning Jade filled fresh bread rolls with meat and salads in preparation for the outing and packed snacks to take with them in her anticipation and enthusiasm of spending the day together outside of the house and in the fresh air and beautiful surroundings.

Cody had decided that he would like to join them and opted to stay home that weekend instead of visiting his friends, which pleased Jade and filled her with happiness.

The thought of them finally having a family outing together seemed perfect; it had been a long time since they had all enjoyed each other's company without being engulfed by the difficulties of which they had faced throughout their relationship, which had also taken a toll on Cody.

They packed their things into the four-wheel-drive and all climbed into the car and drove out towards the highway and in the direction of the gorges and hillside.

They arrived at the bottom of the first steep track that wound its way up the bush-laden hillside and eagerly smiled at each other before proceeding up its narrow rocky path. Although this was Jade's first time at attempting four wheel driving she felt enthusiastic and excited as they slowly scaled the steep rocky terrain.

She looked out through the cars windows, viewing the tree laden valley below, the bright sun's rays that shone down illuminating the colours of the trees and flowers that grew on the valley floor, watching as the birds gathered upon the scrub of the bushland and scattered into the sky as they were disturbed by the roar of the car's engine as she listened to the sounds of nature that echoed from out of the scrub and dense trees.

"Okay, here we go," Shane said as they approached a part of the track that was more difficult to climb. "Hold on tight." Jade giggled in anticipation as she gripped the handle that was situated above her head on the car's interior as the car started its gradual climb up the steep, rocky dirt track. She laughed in her amusement and enjoyment as the car rocked and jerked her this way and that, bumping her in her seat as it scaled the rocky terrain, loving every moment of their adventure. Jade quickly leant forward and turned up the sound of the radio as she heard one of her favourite songs begin to bellow from the cars speakers and let go of the handle that was holding her steady in place, raising her arms into the air, singing and swaying to the rhythmic melodies of the loud music and the motion of the car as she looked around into the back seat at her son's broad grin that covered his face, smiling at his mother's antics and happiness. Cody quickly joined into the fun, singing and playing along to the music in joyous exuberance as they continued the steep climb up the hillside.

Shane laughed out loud as he watched Jade and Cody goofing around to the music and giggling at being rocked around as the car rolled side to side while making its way towards the top of the narrow rocky track.

"Look," Jade squealed in excitement and delight. "A wallaby. Stop the car, stop the car," she called out. "I need a photo." Shane pulled the car to a stop as Jade reached for her camera and aimed the lens at the wallaby capturing its natural beauty and the delightful memory in photographic colour. "Isn't it beautiful," Jade said smiling pointing at the wallaby as it sprung out of the bush and across in front of them, leaping its way through the dense trees on the other side of the dirt track before disappearing.

Finally, they reached the top of the hill where they all got out of the car to stand in the open, fresh air to view the valley below. Jade picked up a large stick from off the ground, stabbing it into the hard rocky ground and stood holding onto it. "I declare me queen of this hill," she giggled, standing playfully smiling at Shane and Cody, who laughed in their entertainment shaking their heads. They unpacked their lunch and the snacks they had brought with them from the back of the car and sat down on a grassy patch and began to enjoy their packed lunches on the open hillside, as the sun shone down upon them and the slight warm breeze wisped softly through their hair. Cody quickly devoured his lunch within minutes, passing Jade the wrappers of the freshly made rolls and raised to his feet. "I'm going exploring," he announced, rushing towards the dense bushes and trees within the natural terrain that surrounded them. Suddenly Cody came marching from out of the bushland, displaying two sticks in his hands and draped in a large bushy vine that wrapped around his waist, laughing.

"This is my village and you are my prisoners," Cody teased pointing at Shane and Jade who flung their heads backwards laughing at his crazy outfit and antics. Shane jumped to his feet and grabbed one of the sticks from Cody's grip, who laughed with playful excitement. "On guard prisoner," Cody yelled playfully charging towards Shane who stood on guard with the other stick ready to battle him laughing. As the two played joyfully under the bright sunny skies that illuminated the ground of the valley and surrounded them with the warmth of the beautiful day Jade watched on giggling in the delight of Shane and Cody's playful antics.

After a day of exploring and trekking up and down the numerous rocky dirt tracks that wound around the hillsides of the valley embraced in the exuberance of the natural sites and the fresh air that surrounded them, they parked the car on the top of the hillside and watched as the sun began to fade behind the horizon, spreading it's beautiful colours across the sky for all to see, before the night sky began to rise and fill the land with darkness.

Jade leant across the console in the front seat of the car and placed a kiss upon Shane's cheek.

"Thank you for a perfect day," her eyes sparkling as a glorious smile spread across her face.

Shane smiled back. "You're welcome baby. I'm glad you enjoyed it." Jade tilted her head slightly towards her lap, a girlish smile covering her face as Shane started the car's engine and drove down the rocky tracks towards the bottom the hillside and out of the valley towards the highway, heading for home.

Over the next couple of months, Shane and Jade's relationship flourished as they dined at restaurants, attended the various theatre productions that were held in the local theatre of Suisania bay and Shane took her to all her favourite places, absorbed in each other's company and placing their once formidable past behind them. As the business plan drew close to completion, Jade secured the premise to establish the business and secured the specialist to commence on the predicted start-up date of the business.

Jade worked endlessly and tenaciously as she designed the advertisement necessary to market the business and attract the clients she sought in anticipation of the commencement of the business in the small township of Suisania Bay. One by one Jade

270

began to receive contact from people within the township and surrounding districts upon the release of the advertisements and she watched excitedly as her clientele base accelerated and grew beyond her expectations.

Although at times, memories, ghosts of the past of the troubles that they had encountered within their relationship would come back to haunt her, niggling at her senses, threatening to unfocus her mind and pull her sideways, she stayed strong, sweeping them away as each memory poked themselves into the corners of her mind and tried hard to forget and lock the memories away forever. Shane had not returned to the workforce, choosing to instead to take the time to concentrate on their relationship and re-build the shattered remains of their love. A move that served well at the time, over the course of a few months.

But all of a sudden, without warning Shane's behaviour started to change towards Jade as she noticed subtle indifferences forming between them once more and the ambience of the home started to change once again.

One afternoon Jade returned to the family home after her appointment with the Real Estate agent ecstatic at securing the premise for the commencement of her business. Jade bounced out the back door to tell Shane the fantastic news.

"Shane," Jade called out, walking towards the shed door. "Shane? Where are you?" as her eyes glanced around the empty shed. "Hmm," Jade hummed to herself, turning from the shed doorway and glancing around the small backyard. "Hmm," Jade hummed again, scratching her head, wondering where Shane may be.

Jade walked around the corner of the garden and looked down the side of the house towards the corner of the bedroom but she could not see anyone. All of a sudden Jade heard voices nearby which sounded like Shane talking to somebody.

Jade walked towards the voices, following the sound's direction and rounded the large tank that stood next to the fence, blocking the view of the small patio area that was located outside of their bedroom. As Jade walked around the corner of the tank next to the fence, concealed by the obstructed view of the tank stood Shane, chatting and laughing with the young, married woman that lived next door to them, who was standing on the other side of the fence.

Jade had tried numerous times to be friendly to the young woman, saying hello as she walked past the house or they sighted each other over the fence line of the back yard but had been met with a snobbish glare on each occasion, to which Jade had found to be unusual but shrugged it off.

"Shane," Jade called out as she spotted the two engaged in joyful chatter oblivious to her arrival.

Instantly, without haste Shane and the young woman dropped their heads and the woman quickly walked away into her home as Shane re-directed his attention towards Jade. "Hey baby," he greeted, smiling as he kept on walking, placing his hand around her waist as he led her around to the back of the house. "Oh Shane, not again," rushed through Jade's mind conversancy. "Please not again."

Over the next couple of weeks, Jade noticed an impertinence in Shane's behaviour as he favoured spending more and more time within the dwellings of the back yard, shed and the garden, which was well maintained and did not require any maintenance to be done. Jade lay restless in her suspicion and apprehension as she woke numerous times in the middle of the night to find the bed beside her empty and cold and Shane's whereabouts unknown, and the plants that lay trampled next to the next door neighbour's fence-line after the lock of the bedroom door that led to the outside of the house, remained opened on numerous occasions unexplained.

As Jade's suspicions grew so did Shane's distance from her as his attentions towards her faded into a disposition of infatuation with the outside world of the family home.

The silence and distance between them grew in momentum as Shane no longer asserted his interest in taking her places or complimenting her and their sex life had ceased to exist as Shane's sexual performance emasculated to impotency. Jade knew deep within the pit of her stomach that something was wrong.

Day by day Jade snuck to the outside corner of the shed to stand by the door in her attempt to hear the reason for his impertinence and lack of interest in her, as she had once done before.

She watched tentatively and secretly hiding behind the covers of the loungeroom window and peeking through a crack as the younger woman who lived next door, continuously walked the perimeter of their home and past the open double doors of the shed that faced the narrow side road leading inconspicuously down the side of their home.

Jade stood at the loungeroom window everyday looking out into the world, her mind entrenched in the suspicious behaviour of Shane and the girl next door. "Where have I gone wrong?" she questioned herself, her mind searching for the answers to the self-doubt that grew inside of her.

One morning as Jade stood surreptitiously at the loungeroom window she saw the young woman from next door walk along the footpath in front of their home and come into her view. Jade's eyes widened as they followed the younger woman down the footpath that led around to the narrow side road that led towards the back of the shed. "I have to know," Jade whispered to herself, rushing to the back door, sneaking towards the entrance of the shed, where she stood quiet, out of Shane's view watching, waiting for the woman to walk past.

As the next door neighbour rounded the corner and walked the length of the footpath past the open shed doors, Jade watched then gasped, her jaw dropping open as the sound coming from out of the shed constricted her into a knot of anguish.

"Weit wil," Shane whistled, letting out a wolf whistle as the younger woman walked past the shed doors.

The woman smiled a devilish grin and waved in Shane's direction. A devilish smile formed across Shane's face as Jade looked on in horror.

Jade's face fell into a bitter entrapment of disappointment and anguish. "How could you Shane, after all that we have been through, all the effort and time that we have spent mending the broken bridges within our relationship, your doing this again." Jade turned her head away, leaning her back against the shed wall and closed her eyes as bitter tears of disappointment began to fall and flow down her cheeks and her hopes for their relationship dashed and sat in ruins upon the floor in front of her.

"How could you Shane, how could you?" she whispered to herself, placing her forehead into her palms. "No more, please, no more," her stomach knotted and painful within the ruins of that moment.

Over the next few weeks, Jade's confidence in herself diminished, her mind tormented and twisting under the weight of Shanes infidelities and emotional desecration until, she began to unravel into a downward spiral of confusion and betrayal. Shane's presence in the home dwindled as he regularly found excuses to leave the house to places unknown to Jade, which often led to heated arguments between them which remained unsettled.

No longer content with the exuberant sexual effects of the little white ecstasy pills, Shane introduced Jade to the world of LSD, the little square tab that he held out to her in the palm of his hand each weekend in his attempt of quelling the situation of their continual perturbation towards each other while sober. Jade spiralled helplessly into emotional declension as her life turned into a torrent of endless weekends of exuberant hallucinations of surrealism, only to be returned to the reality of the week days that were filled with tiresome, volatile arguments between herself and Shane and then also of her son, James, whose life began to unravel uncontrollably back into the unlawful realm of crime and drugs.

Jade was overwhelmed and consumed in a tessellation of continuous bitter battles with Shane and now also her son, James, and little by little, piece by piece, Jade's morale and emotional state wore down as each stone thrown chipped away at her, as each cruel word bore its hole and mark within her heart and soul, leaving tear after tear, jagger after jagger until Jade's soft nature finally fell to the floor. Torn to strips, embattled beyond repair Jade's disposition turned into an uncontrollable fiery rage that lay deep within her soul, fused by the bitterness and emotional cruelty of her world.

Simmering and boiling Jade turned silent, cold and sat quiet and still, the only emotion visible sat trembling in her tight, motionless lips until she could take no more. As the days turned to weeks and the fun of the intoxication of the drugs and alcohol turned sour and bitter, every smirk, every comment, every put-down, every shove that Jade had endured at the hands of Shane, came roaring out of her in a torrent of unstoppable venom and rage.

Jade placed the little square tab of LSD into her mouth and slipped under its hallucinogenic spell as it slowly dissolved against her tongue. This time, it did not take her to the technicoloured, imaginable, beautiful place she had come to know; this time it took her to hell unleashing the bitter demon that ate away at her soul, unleashing the rage of all the betrayals, the lies she had swallowed over and over again and all of a sudden Jade's blue eyes turned to black.

"Get the fuck out," Jade growled deeply, turning her head slowly and meticulously, her eyes a narrow slit that looked directly into Shane, her face covered with the anger that raged inside of her, her eyes blackened with the bitterness and coldness of her damnation.

"What," Shane said, leaping quickly to his feet.

Jade rose to her feet in a picture of slow motion, her steps, steady and precise as she slowly walked towards him as if stalking her prey, fire raging within her eyes, piercing and narrow as she coldly spat the words at him.

"I don't love you anymore. I know everything that you have done. You think you can break me. I hate you. You're nothing. Get away from me now. Get the fuck out."

Shane stepped backwards, step by step by step as each word, every cold precise glare of Jade's cold eyes burned through him, terrorising his every sense, his every thought he had of Jade, her weakness, her venerability now stood before him in a calculated strength of stone cold rage.

"Calm down girl. Jade, calm down," Shane stuttered, his voice shaking with panic, stuttering as he tried to calm the situation that had erupted in front of him. "Please Jade," Shane begged as he reached his hand out to touch hers. Jade threw his hand away from her as quickly as he had reached out to touch it, still walking, step by step, backing him up until he was hard up against the wall, her breath close enough to taste the bitterness of her words as her words drove daggers straight into Shanes eyes.

"Don't you ever touch me again. You worthless man. Get the fuck out NOW"

Jade stood motionless, calculated and stern, her face tight, her eyes glaring into his with all the rage of his betrayals and the pain of which he had inflicted upon her. Shane's face turned a shade of white, his eyes widened as he trembled, pressed and cornered hard up against the wall before he suddenly and quickly stepped sideways and ran towards the front door, fleeing from the house in over whelming panic fearing the woman he had pushed and pushed and pushed, this time, way too far.

Jade slowly walked to the kitchen and grabbed a can of bourbon from the refrigerator, returned to the loungeroom and sat down on the couch sipping at the cold liquor, staring blankly at the wall in a trance-like state. She had no emotion, no movement, except for the slow motion of the can of bourbon being lifted to her lips.

Jade had not known where Shane had gone that night; she did not care. She had not known where he had been since or if he would dare come back; she did not care, she just wanted him gone. She needed him gone, to leave her life and to leave her alone this time for good.

Jade spent the next week packing up Shane's belongings into the large plastic crates that he had arrived with when they had first met, collecting piece after piece of all the memories she had shared with Shane from the house, removing it from her sight, as her face displayed the bitter contempt of his behaviour cold and still, her voice silent, frozen in the bitter depths of her soul as the hot blood of her rage and Shane's betrayals ran through her like an unstoppable storm.

Five days later, Shane returned to the house. Jade watched as his car pulled into the driveway and he slowly climbed out of the car door and hesitated before approaching the front door of the house. Jade stood motionless and waiting, watching until finally Shane knocked on the door. She walked to the front door of the house and slowly opened it, her cold glare directed straight at Shane as he stood there in his apprehension and nervousness.

"Give me the house keys," Jade demanded, her first and only words spoken in that moment. Shane removed the house keys off his key ring and placed them in Jade's outreached hand. Jade slipped the keys into her pocket and stepped sideways allowing Shane to enter through the doorway her eyes piercing his every movement.

Shane entered the house nervously to find all of his belongings stacked in a pile in the corner of the loungeroom. He turned his face around to look at Jade his eyes suddenly softened and filled with sorrow and sadness.

"Jade," Shane pleaded. "Don't do this." Jade stood impregnable and stern, her eyes glaring at him, full of hatred, anger, bitterness and just shook her head no, but remained silent and cold. She walked towards the kitchen and sat at the kitchen table, her back facing Shane as she listened to him remove the crates one by one until he had fully packed his car of his belongings.

"Jade," Shane said softly, his voice filled with remorse. "I'm sorry baby, I'm so sorry," he cried as tears of sorrow rolled down his cheeks. Jade stood from the table in a stiff-like motion, her back still turned on the sound of Shane's tears and apology and walked silently to the front door and opened it, without saying a word.

"Okay," Shane sobbed. "I'll be back in a couple of days to clear the shed." Jade just nodded again but spoke not one word. Shane walked out of the front door and left.

Jade waited each day, sitting in the lounge room all alone after her children had left for school, just waiting, day after day after day, watching for Shane's car to pull up in the driveway, waiting for it all to be finished. Finally on the fifth day, Shane arrived. This time he did not walk slowly, this time he did not hesitate, this time he marched straight to the front door and knocked on it hard. Jade stood up and walked to the front door, opening it. Shane stood firm in his stance, angry and fiery within his own disappointment and disapproval of the dissolution of the relationship.

"I've come to get my fucken stuff," Shane snapped before turning away and marching to the backyard to stand at the shed entrance. Jade grabbed the keys that hung on the hook on the kitchen wall and quickly walked to the shed entrance to open it and walked back into the house.

Thirty minutes later, Shane knocked on the back door. Jade rose from off the kitchen chair and walked towards the back door and opened it. "I've emptied the shed except for my motorbike. "I can't get that today," he said angrily. "I'll pick it up tomorrow."

"Yeah, okay," Jade replied, nodding her head.

Shane looked at Jade, his face cased in a frown. "I didn't fucken do anything Jade. You're fucken wrong. You're throwing us away for some fucked-up reason, you're fucken wrong," Shane snapped at her coldly.

Jade stood up stiff. "I've got this fucken wrong huh. You think you can fuck around on me over and over and then point this back on me. You're the one who's fucked up, you're the one who's fucked all this up," Jade spat back viciously, entering into another ferocious, vicious attack of words that escalated into a tackle of a physical scramble for the shed keys.

"You stand there accusing me of fucking around on you, you fucken bitch. You're nothing but a dirty little slut that's fucked around on me. You let Michelle kiss you that night and what else huh. Why are you on your computer so much, you fucking someone on there too you fucken little bitch," Shane yelled loudly at her in a torrent of vicious words, grabbing the keys from the shed door and running into the house, snatching Jade's computer off the office desk. Jade ran in after him, pushing him as she tried desperately to get her computer back from Shane's grip.

"Fuck off," Shane yelled viciously at her, pushing her back, knocking her backwards to the floor and ran out of the house with the computer before jumping into his car and speeding down the road.

Jade quickly picked herself up from off the floor, running after Shane, yelling, "Bring my computer back, it's got all my work on it. Bring my bloody computer back. Shane." But Shane did not come back and continued speeding down the road until he disappeared.

Jade frantically paced the house, looking for her phone, worried that she had lost all of her hard work. With her computer gone so was her business plan, all her information, her contacts, the data, all sat within the files of her computer. Now she was frantic. Jade had no way of knowing where Shane was staying nor where he had taken her computer she could not chase him she could not find him, her only option was to ring him and hope that he would bring it back. Jade grabbed her phone from the kitchen table and rang Shane's number.

"Answer you fucken prick," she yelled frantically at the phone. "Bloody answer." Jade rang Shane's phone three more times before finally Shane picked up the phone, answering in only two words, "Get fucked," and then hung the phone up in Jade's ear. Jade growled loudly then yelled in frustration. "Ahhh, you prick, you fucken little prick."

She paced the house back and forth, her mind hell-bent in fury, hell-bent on getting her computer back. Then suddenly, Jade stopped, stood still within her frustrations as her eyes widened and her mind snapped into gear. Jade's eyes quickly darted towards the shed and raced outside.

"Take my computer, will you. Won't give it bloody back huh," she growled angrily. "Yes, you bloody will," growled out of her mouth as she marched around to the side of the shed to stop at the louver window. Jade stood looking at the window, accessing the area before stomping back around to the patio area and grabbing one of the outdoor setting benches and placed it under the window. She stepped up onto the bench and pulled at the metal frame of the glass louvers, prying the window open and carefully removing the glass panels, one by one by one, muttering under her breath, "You fucken bastard, now you'll bring it back."

Jade climbed through the open window and onto the large bench that sat beneath it and climbed down into the shed. She stopped and looked at Shanes motorbike still locked in her shed as she let out a vindictive, clever little laugh. She walked over to the draw that she knew concealed the key of the motorbike. She grabbed the key and shoved it into her pocket and climbed back out the window and rushed back inside, picking up her phone. Jade rang and rang until finally Shane answered, "I told you to."

"Ut ut ut, shut your fucking mouth," Jade said coldly, smugly, interrupting his words of compunction. "You listen to me now Shane. You'll bring my fucken computer back, and you'll bring it back right now. I have the key to your precious motorbike. I broke into the shed," slamming the phone down, silenced.

Ten minutes later, Shane pulled up in her driveway with Jade's computer in his hands, his head down as he walked it over to Jade and handed it to her. Jade snatched the computer out of Shane's hands and handed him the motorbike key.

"I'll be back in a minute to get the bike," Shane said, his voice now submissive and beaten.

Jade just nodded her head replying, "Leave the shed keys out on the back table when you leave," and she turned away and walked back inside the house grinning smugly as she walked.

Twenty minutes later, Shane returned, removing his motorcycle from the shed and left the keys on the back table, and rode away.

Over the next two months Jade suffered from the terrible relentless cravings of her drug addiction withdrawal, her body ached as her mind craved the intoxicating toxins of each drug she had induced with Shane and their wild nights together but still, she struggled on. By day, Jade threw herself into her business venture which had now attracted a clientele base strong enough for her to conduct an information day of the specialists to meet with the clients in order to discuss the procedures, products and pricing of their desired specialists treatments. But by night, Jade suffered long and hard, unable to sleep, the threatening phone calls returning late at night that had now escalated into violent death threats against her and her children. Jade had started to find screens off the house windows, groups of women standing on the footpath at the front of her home yelling profanity at her, threatening to slit her throat and that of her children while she slept, glass bottles being thrown at her house by cars driving past in the middle of the night and knifes found on the front and back porches. Jade watched out of her windows hiding in her house, checking the locks and windows nightly, her eyes searching for shadows in the dark for movement and sounds. Her terror grew day by day, night by night as the threats and violence continued and escalated around her. Jade was terrified for her children's safety but she feared to involve the police as the threats had come from the club house and she was still friends with Ryan.

James continued in his destructive behaviour, often not returning to the family home at night, night after night. Police knocked at the door at all hours of the day or night, dragging James to the police station for questioning as Jade stood by helplessly unable to help her son, tangled in her own hell.

As each day came, it grew worse and worse as Jade struggled with the mess of her home life, her drug addiction, her son, the constant threats of the club house and her lustful addiction to Shane.

Jade had not seen Shane at all since that last day, her activities now restricted, hiding in fear at home, avoiding the ugly violent scene that surrounded her in bloodshed threats against her and her children. Until the day Shane rode past the house, two months later.

Jade heard the rumble of the motorbike engine as it rumbled down the road and approached her house each day. She pulled back the curtains looking out of the large loungeroom window as Shane rode back and forth, passing her house, day after day, after day.

Over whelmed, unravelled by all the stress and pressure and with her mind in an emotional daze, Jade's guard gave way and she stepped outside, back into Shane's view and back into the arms of drugs, his betrayal and lies.

Shane had told Jade that he had now moved in with his brother, Trent, who also lived in the same town and that he had never left, hoping that one day Jade would realise that he had done nothing wrong and that he truly loved her. Jade didn't know what to think anymore, twisted upside down she no longer trusted anyone, not even her own judgement and found herself in a constant daze, desperately seeking and searching for the truth, the end, her soul. She felt lost, trapped and felt there was no one she could turn to help pull her from the vicious cycle she had so helplessly fallen into as she fell deeper and deeper into Shane's manipulation of sex and drugs, a puppet for which he pulled the strings. But Jade did not allow Shane to move back into the house. She had agreed to continue with the relationship without the pressure of living together. They decided to slow it down, give each other space and see if they could rebuild their relationship from scratch.

For the next three months Shane and Jade continued seeing each other, going on dates and catching up throughout the day as often as they could. No longer living with the pressure of continuously being in each other's company, the casualness of the relationship seemed to work well but still Jade suffered at home and had not told Shane anything of her troubles.

James had been in trouble with the police numerous times, assault charges, stealing and destruction of property and Jade seemed to be in constant battles with him as she tried desperately to pull him from the bad crowd he had gotten tangled up with. Jade paced the house nightly, waiting and watching for James to return with James often not returning home for days on end. On returning to the house, James was often intoxicated or suffering the effects of the drugs he had been taking while absent from the home. Jade had often retuned to the house after running errands for her business venture or for the family, finding James and his friends sprawled all over the loungeroom floor, drinking alcohol and passing packed bongs of pot from person to person with Jade having to chase them off out of her home. James had lost all respect of the family home, himself and for Jade as he followed his bad crowd's behaviour. Their quarrels worsened each time, ending with profanity, thrown viciously from her son's mouth at her. Jade was beside herself, finding all the pressure unbearable, weighing her down in a heavy weight of helplessness.

Her only control left, Jade's only option left to try was to ban her son's friends from the family home and regain control. One by one as James' friends arrived at the house, Jade hunted them off, telling them they were not welcome there anymore and to never return. Jade did not care how James's friends had felt about not letting them in the house and would tell them in front of James, her only concern was saving her son and pulling him from the bad lifestyle he had fallen into, the bad crowd.

Jade tried everything to regain control of her home, to keep Cody safe and return James back to the young man he once was. Over the course of a few weeks, Jade had started to win the battle. James had stopped bringing his friends to the house. They no longer knocked on the front door and James was coming home almost every night until the terrifying night it all went horribly wrong.

Jade was sitting in her bedroom after she had just finished with her work for the day. A long day of writing the invitations for the information day she was conducting with

277

the specialists, the first introduction of her new business venture she was establishing within the local area.

As Jade applied the finishing touches to the invitations, she sat back to admire her hard work. "Yes," Jade whispered excitedly, seeing now that finally her dream was forming. Jade closed the computer and walked to the bathroom to take a shower. After her shower, she made herself a cup of tea and wandered off to bed, tired from her long day in the office. She had not been in bed very long when she heard a noise at the back of the house, the back door. "Oh no," she whispered into the dark, sitting up, startled by the noise.

Jade reached for her dressing gown, wrapping it around herself and softly crept down the dark hallway to the back door. She reached out to pull back the curtain that hung covering the large sliding glass windows of the back door to see who was there.

"James, what are you doing?" she questioned, watching her son and his friend trying to sneak through the back door. "James," Jade piped up. "You scared me. Come on, but no, you know the rules. Your friend has to leave."

"Mum, come on. We just walked all the way here," James replied in dispute.

"No James. Jay has to go home. No one is to come here, you have to go Jay," Jade said, standing firm on her refusal to allow Jay into the house. James entered the door fuming at his mother.

"This is ridiculous Mum. I should be able to have my friends over. Don't go Jay," James yelled as he tried to push past Jade to open the door to let his friend in.

"No," Jade said, standing her ground. "Go home now Jay, I mean it," and Jade locked the door and walked back up the hallway with James following behind her, yelling at her.

"It's not fair Mum. You can't tell me what to do," James screamed through the house, his anger escalating into a bitter tangle of words as they stood within the narrow confines of the hallway.

"No one is to come here James," Jade said loudly and sternly. "And that's the end of it," walking off into the bathroom to wash her face from the upset of the argument.

Suddenly Jade heard a loud smashing sound come from the loungeroom. James came running into the bathroom. "Mum," he whimpered, his face pale and covered with fright and fear.

Jade froze, looked at James then looked down at his arm. "Ahhh, oh god, no," Jade screamed, as she saw her son's arm covered and gushing blood all over the bathroom walls and vanity, his wrist gashed and ripped wide open, his veins and tendons exposed through the ripped jaggered gashes of his skin.

"Oh my god James," Jade cried out as she quickly grabbed the towel that was hanging on the towel rail and wrapped it as tight as she could around the gushing wound. "Get in the car, hurry," Jade shouted. "Cody get in the car," she yelled out through the house to her young son as she ran from the bathroom.

Jade ran to the kitchen grabbing the car keys and her handbag that sat on the kitchen bench and ran out of the front door with her two boys and quickly got into the car. "Lock the house up Jay," Jade yelled in a frantic panic, who was still standing in the backyard, startled by the sound of the breaking glass inside the house. Jade started the car and slammed it into reverse, rushing backwards out of the driveway and onto the road before slamming it into gear and drove as fast as she could down the streets, round the roundabouts, pushing the car as fast as it could handle the roads, rushing straight to the hospital emergency.

"Hold on James, squeeze it tight, oh god, we're nearly there," Jade cried out, panicked but still in control as they rounded the corner and into the hospital emergency parking bay.

Jade rushed James inside, running to the emergency room window. "Help, Help," she cried out and the nurses immediately let them through the doors as the now-blood-soaked towel wrapped around James' wrist filled with his blood left trails behind them, dripping all over the hospital floor.

"Oh god, we need a doctor," Jade cried out to the nurse in a panic. "Hurry, we need a doctor, he's done an artery, he's done an artery, hurry."

The nurses rushed around, placing James on the emergency bed as another nurse wrapped a large padding around the wound, holding James arm in the air as he applied pressure to the wound to try and slow the bleeding as they waited for the doctor to arrive. Jade stood by James rubbing his head. "It's going to be okay, it's going to be okay, the doctor's coming," Jade said, trying to keep him calm, to help slow down the tremendous flow of blood that was still gushing from the wounds in his wrist.

Jade stayed by his side holding onto James' other hand as she watched her son slowly getting whiter and whiter and then start to go into shock. "Sweetie, oh god James, hold on, the doctor's nearly here, you're okay," Jade cried out, trying to give James a little reassuring smile through her trembling lips and trying to stay calm herself for her son as they endlessly waited, while Jade watched her son bleeding to death in front of her eyes. Thirty minutes later the doctor finally walked through the door, rushing to take over from the nurse that was applying the pressure to the wound. Jade stepped away and stood to the side of them as the team of doctors and nurses rushed to bring the wound under control and stop the bleeding.

"Blood transfusion. Surgery now," the doctor ordered the nurses. "Hang in there buddy, okay," the doctor said to James as he inserted the first lot of needles into James' wrist and quickly applied the make shift stitches to slow down the bleeding in order to get him to surgery. Jade looked on in horror as she watched all of the colour drain from her son's face and his eyes roll back in his head. "Oh god. Oh god no," Jade gasped, placing her blood-soaked hands over her mouth. "God, James no," Jade gasped again as she watched James slip into shock and pass out.

"Surgery now," the doctor yelled as the nurses rushed the surgery trolley into the emergency room and placed James onto it, rushing him straight up to the surgery theatre. Jade just stood there watching, her whole body feeling every terrifying emotion of her son's tragedy, tears rolling down her face as the horrible thoughts slammed down on her. "Oh god, he's dying, I could lose my son, I could lose my James."

Jade rushed over to Cody who sat worried and scared on the chair outside the emergency room and wrapped him up in her arms, holding onto each other tightly. "It's going to be okay," Jade sobbed, trembling as she held Cody in her arms, her dressing gown soaked with James' blood. Jade and Cody waited silently in the hospital waiting area, waiting endlessly as Jade held her breath, her body wracked with knots and fear as they waited for news of James, news that he was okay. An hour and a half later, the doctor entered the waiting room and walked over to Jade, who stood, her hands covering her mouth, holding her breath as her eyes filled with fear, waiting for the doctor to tell her the news of the surgery.

"He's going to be fine," the doctor started to explain. Jade let out a heavy sigh of relief then took a breath. "He did a lot of damage Jade," the doctor continued. "He punctured an artery and lost a lot of blood. We nearly lost him on the surgery table."

Jade froze, her face staring at the doctor in horror. "He's okay though," the doctor kept explaining, reaching his hand out to touch Jade's shoulder. "We've given him a blood transfusion and we managed to close the artery and the large gash across his wrist. I have to tell you though Jade, if we were ten minutes later, we would have lost him, but he's okay, he's resting now, if you'd like to see him." Jade nodded her head, the shock of the situation hitting her like a ton of bricks as she and Cody followed the doctor to the room to which James had been placed for the night.

On the walk to the room, the doctor explained to Jade that James had also cut and damaged tendons and nerves in his wrist and that he would have to be transferred to the hospital in the city in the morning for more surgery but tonight they were stabilizing him.

Jade walked into James' room and looked at her sleeping, pale son laying on the hospital bed now peaceful, now okay after his life saving surgery. "I'll see you tomorrow Jade," the doctor said as he left the room, leaving Jade and Cody alone with James. Cody stood back a little, still dazed and scared by what he had just witnessed with his brother, oblivious that they had nearly just lost him.

Jade stood by James' bed stroking James' arm, his head. "I love you," she whispered to James as she leant over him to kiss his cheek and forehead. Jade and Cody left the hospital an hour later, staying while James slept, placed under sedation for the night to help his recovery for the second round of surgery the next day.

It was three thirty am when Jade and Cody got home from the hospital and stepped in the front door. Jade covered Cody's eyes as she led him through the blood covered walls and floor of the hallway and up to his bedroom and placed him in bed.

"Good night sweetheart," Jade said as she closed his bedroom door and walked back into the hallway to face the picture of the near fatal injury of her son, the blood covering the hallway walls and floor. "Ohh James," Jade cried out as tears rushed to her eyes and fell down her cheeks, as she viewed the horrifying sight of the jaggered smashed glass door panel that James had put his fist through and her son's blood pooled and covering the length of the hallway walls, floor and sprayed all over the bathroom vanity. Jade stood motionless in shock, crying as she looked at the splattered walls and floor, the horrifying picture of what her son had just endured. She walked back to the laundry to fill a bucket of soapy water, picked up a sponge and walked back into the hallway and dropped to her knees, sobbing as she wiped away her son's blood from the walls and floor, washing away the terrifying picture of her son's almost fatal tragic night.

Two hours later, Jade finally crawled into her bed, closed her eyes and fell asleep emotionally exhausted.

The next morning, Jade awoke early still exhausted from the night before but still she rushed around getting herself and Cody ready to get back to the local hospital before James was transferred to Alterro Hospital. Jade and Cody rushed out the front door, driving straight to the hospital and walked straight up to James' room hoping he was now awake.

"Hey Mum," James said in a quiet voice as she walked through the door.

"Oh, hey sweetheart," she replied, smiling bravely at her son, holding back the tears. Jade walked over to James wrapping her arms around him holding him tight. "I love you," she said softly.

"I love you too mum," James whispered back. Minutes later the nurses came to the room. Jade stood back looking at James, the tubes poking from his body, his heavily bandaged wrist, his pale, hallowed face, just thinking, did that really happen. It seemed all too surreal as she watched the nurses unhooking all the tubes before placing James on the trolley bed and pushing him down the long corridor to the exit of the hospital and loaded him into the back of the ambulance that had been waiting to transfer him to the city hospital. "I'll see you soon sweetheart okay," Jade called out to James as the nurses closed the ambulance doors and it drove away. Jade and Cody quickly jumped in the car and drove back home. Jade packed two bags and placed them in the boot of the car, ready to leave for the city to meet James at the hospital.

"I'm just going to ring Shane okay," Jade called out to Cody. "Then we're leaving, so be ready matey."

"Okay, Mum," Cody replied and continued with the game he was playing on his handheld game set.

Jade picked up her phone and rang Shane. Shane answered straight away.

"Hello Shane," Jade started. "Something terrible happened last night with James."

Jade continued to tell Shane about the horrifying events that had happened as Shane listened speechless and shocked by what he was hearing.

"I have to go to the city for a couple of days though. I'm leaving now," Jade continued.

"Well, I'm already here. I've been visiting Mum for a couple of days. You can stay here with us if you like?" Shane told Jade, inviting her to stay at his mother's house.

"Yes, thank you Shane," Jade replied, relieved she had somewhere to stay and for the support. "I'll be there in a few hours. Then I'm going straight to the hospital okay."

"Okay, I'll see you when you get here. Drive safe," Shane replied and hung up the phone.

Three hours later, Jade and Cody arrived in Alterro and drove straight to Shane's mother's house where Shane was waiting for her in the front garden. Jade got out of the car and walked straight over to Shane, falling into his open arms, seeking the comfort she so desperately needed after such a horrific ordeal.

"I'll come with you to the hospital if you would like?" Shane said, looking at Jade with concern.

"I'd like that," Jade replied, a small smile turning the corners of her mouth. Shane, Jade and Cody got back into Jade's car and drove to the hospital and went straight to the reception desk to find out where James had been placed. The receptionist told them which room and pointed them in the direction towards the ward where James had been taken.

"Hey Mum," James said as he saw his mother enter the room.

"Hey sweetie. I told you I was on my way, I wouldn't be long," Jade replied, smiling back at James. Jade sat chatting with James as they waited for the doctor to arrive. Two hours later, after James had been examined, James was back in the surgery theatre, his second operation to repair the tendons and nerve damage he had suffered from the puncture wounds of the glass-panel window. The operation went well, a success. The doctors had managed to fix all of the damage to James' tendons and nerves and he was now doing well and suffered no permanent damage, but because James had had two operations in two days and the blood transfusion, the doctors required him to stay in hospital for an extra two days, to keep him monitored and help with his recovery.

On the third day, Shane, Jade and Cody arrived at the hospital ready to take James home. They sat and waited as they watched the nurse buzz around James, removing all the needles and plasters and finally the heavy bandage that still lay wrapped around his wrist. Jade's eyes stopped and stared as the last layer of bandage was unravelled and she sighted the many heavy black stitches that trailed over the three large wounds on the inside of her son's wrist. "Ohhh," Jade sighed quietly at the sight dropping her head, remembering, just how close James had come to losing his young life that night at only sixteen years of age.

Jade looked at Shane, looking for support but Shane wasn't looking at James or Jade. His eyes were not on her son's stitches, they were fixated straight on the nurse, following her as she walked back and forth around the room until he had noticed Jade watching him. Shane quickly broke his stare at the nurse, dropping his head to the floor; his face covered with the guilt of having been caught. Jade couldn't believe it and just shook her head in dismay, stood up and walked out. "I'm going to get a drink of water," she announced as she left the room. Upon returning to the room, where James was now ready and waiting to leave, what Jade had encountered left her speechless. In Jade's absence, Shane had got up and started talking to the nurse, they were both chatting and giggling with each other and the nurse sneakily slipped a slip of paper into Shane's hand which he concealed very quickly into his jeans' pocket. Jade's eyes glared straight at Shane as anger rose throughout all her senses. "How could you, how dare you, in front of my sons and James, who had just nearly died, who they were there for," flashed through her mind. The sight disgusted her as she lost all respect for Shane, right there, right then.

But Jade said nothing, she swallowed every word, pushed down all her anger and walked over to comfort James, ignoring Shane completely. Minutes later, the doctor entered the room, giving James the all-clear and he was discharged from the hospital and they were on their way back to Suisania Bay. Shane had asked Jade if he was able to come back with her and stay with her for the night, telling her that he was worried about her and that she shouldn't be alone. Jade had agreed to Shane staying with her for the night but the truth was, she didn't really care anymore. Shane's intentions, she did not believe; her only concern was for her son, James.

That night while back at the house, as Shane lay sleeping next to her, Jade quietly slipped out of bed and crept over to Shane's jeans that hung on the chair in her bedroom. Jade slipped her hand in the pocket and felt around for the slip of paper that she had seen the nurse hand to Shane at the hospital, she felt it sitting in the pocket and pulled it out and crept quietly into the next room. She unfolded the piece of paper as her eyes widened into a stare of disbelief. Shane had gotten the nurse's phone number that day, while her son lay in the hospital bed and with Jade having suffered the thought of losing James only three days earlier. Jade saw red, her emotions reeling in anger, disgusted. Jade raised her dismayed eyes to the ceiling as the words left her lips. "I have to clear my heart, I have to break free of this, free of Shane."

Over the next month, James slowly recovered, regaining all his strength. His wrist healed and grew stronger with each passing day and he was now back to the young man she had tried so desperately to bring back from the badness, the crowd he had fallen into. Jade had stayed home constantly, only leaving to get supplies or attend appointments. She stuck by her son's side, shielding her children from the threats that had continued from the women at the clubhouse who still rang late at night and now followed her wherever she went, when she left the house. Sonia had become a regular visitor to the home, turning up out of the blue, at all different times of the day or night. Jade kept Sonia close as a precautionary measure but remained cautious in her approach. Unbeknown to Jade, it was Sonia who had been informing the women from the clubhouse of Jade's coming and goings from her home, until the night Jade followed Sonia to a party.

Suspicious of how the women from the clubhouse always knew of her whereabouts and when she had left her house, Jade had to know, she had to find out, which prompted Jade to make a decision.

This night was the night. Jade snuck out of her house late that Saturday night, and out to her car, climbing in, and closing the door quietly behind her, as not to make a sound and drove to the night club venue where she knew Sonia would be. She sat in her car, outside the local night club venue, patiently waiting, hiding, watching as one by one the people started to leave the venue at the end of the night. Jade sat watching, waiting to see the women from the club house. She quickly ducked her head as low as she could go, her eyes staring on the door's entrance as she saw them, the ones she had been waiting for, walk from the entrance: Tasha then Rebecca followed by Mary and then finally Sonia.

"I knew it," Jade whispered bitterly to herself. "I knew she was in on it."

Jade sat quiet and still, watching as the women piled into Tasha's car and reversed out of the car park on the other side of the road.

She waited a little while longer, quietly watching before she started her car and pulled out to the road steering her car in behind another car and followed the group of women to see where they were going. Jade followed them down the back streets, along the dark stretch that led to the outskirts of town and watched as they pulled up in the driveway of a house, a house Jade had not been to before. She parked her car behind a parked car on the other side of the road and watched as the women got out of the car and walked to the front door of the house. Jade tried desperately to see the person that stood on the other side of the now opened door, but it was too dark and she was unable to see the figure that stood behind the screened door. "Damn," Jade whispered, waiting and watching as the women entered the house.

Within minutes of arriving at the house, another car pulled up, coming from the opposite direction from which Jade was parked across the road from the house, and pulled into the same driveway as Tasha and the other women. As the men started getting out of the car Jade noticed a very familiar face.

"You're kidding," Jade whispered quietly. So this is where you have been going all this time. All the pieces suddenly fell into place instantly. "Shane, it was you."

Parked in her secret position Jade watched as Shane and the group of men from the notorious motorcycle clubhouse walked to the front of the house and knocked hard on the front door. "Okay, okay," Jade whispered to herself before starting the engine of the car and drove off.

Within minutes, Jade parked the car in the driveway of her home and sat silently, eminently as the rage ran up her spine and twisted within her mind. "How dare you Shane," Jade whispered, exiting from the car and walking inside the house.

Pacing back and forth along the perimeter of her bedroom floor, the images flashed through Jade's mind over and over in a lashing of anger, confusion and then rage. "How could you do this to us Shane, how could you," repeated over and over in her mind as the thoughts settled deep within her disposition. Jade did not know who she could trust anymore.

Rage roared through her, burning and scolding like hot fire running up her spine, pulsating through her every sense until it turned into a coldness within her heart. "I hate you Shane Devio," Jade said to herself. "How could you betray me and lie to me. This is it. I've had enough."

Two days later, Jade drove over to Trent's house looking for Shane. She marched up to the door and knocked loudly. Shane opened the wooden door, carefully sheltered standing behind the screen door. "Oh hey babe," Shane said with a smile, looking through the screen door.

"Don't hey babe me you prick," Jade shouted, her hands on her hips.

"What the fuck is wrong with you?" Shane answered, raising his voice slightly.

"Come out here you gutless wanker," Jade yelled, shaking the door, kicking out at the bottom steel railing of the screen door with her foot. "Come out here and face me."

"You're fucking crazy," Shane yelled. "Go home. Get the fuck out of here Jade," he yelled again as he opened the door and stepped out under the small patio area of the front door entrance.

Jade's eyes opened wide in astonishment from the narrow slits of which her anger had held them before returning to their narrow position as she spotted the marks at the bottom of Shane's neck, just above the collar of his T-shirt.

"You bastard," Jade yelled. "You bastard. So who was it huh? Who are you fucking? Mary or Sonia, or both of them," Jade continued to yell at Shane, taking in the views of the love bites strategically placed on the bottom half of Shane's neck slightly concealed by the curve of his shirt collar.

"What," Shane yelled back. "I've done nothing. The blokes held me down, they're twist marks from their fingers, not fucken hickys you stupid bitch. Get the fuck out of here."

Jade's feet dug into the ground in a stance of subornation as her words stung the air in a rage of abusive language, hatred and accusations which escalated in a retaliation of vicious assaults of words.

"You bitch come over here and accuse me of fucking around on you and setting you up. You're the fucking lying bitch," Shane yelled. "I know what you've been doing, you filthy little bitch. I read everything. Who's fucken Max hey?"

Jade froze on the spot, her mouth dropped open in a gasp of shock as her hand raised to cradle her forehead.

"Yeah. I read all your fucken emails the day I stole your computer. I fucken saw it all, you disgust me. I've got it all. I downloaded the lot onto my hard drive. I've had nothing to do with anything that's happened to you, nothing. But you," Shane continued yelling viciously.

Jade's blood boiled as each word that spilt from Shane's mouth settled under her skin in a fit of rage.

"How fucken dare you go through my computer. Max is just a friend. I've known him longer than you. You and I are done. It's over. Go fuck one your secrets, you fucken bastard. I hate you. Don't ever come near me again," Jade roared, viciously picking up a pile of dirt and throwing it in his face, before jumping in her car and speeding down the road and coming to a stop in her driveway. Jade stomped into the house cursing as she walked into the kitchen and reached for the bottle of bourbon that had sat idle in the kitchen cupboard and quickly poured herself two shots of the liquor.

That night Jade did not leave her room, she did not speak and sat on the side of her bed until the bourbon finally hit its mark and slumped her in an inert mess across the bridge of her bed.

Over the next two months, Shane stayed away. Jade had not seen him at all around town when she had snuck out to carry out the household duties. She did not see him near her home but still Jade's mind spiralled out of control, fuelled by betrayal, hatred and aggression.

As she sat in her bedroom, sipping from the bottle of straight bourbon and racking up the lines of cocaine that sat in front of her, the addiction that had clung to her mind and her body in an unstoppable, relentless craving, Jade planned and plotted her revenge.

That night Jade lost all control as her heart filled with the viciousness of her vengeance as she reflected upon each harsh word spoken, each cruel act of betrayal and the lies of which she was sold.

Jade paced the bedroom floor back and forth as her mind weighed heavily under the strain and twisted under the intoxication of the cocaine and alcohol that drew her away from all logical reasoning. She walked to the shed door, placed the key into the lock and opened it.

Jade entered the shed, looking around on top of the benches and under the tables that sat on the cement floor of the shed, knowing what she was searching for.

"Hmmm," Jade hummed through her tight angry lips. "There you are," she said as she picked up the empty fuel container and walked to her car to place it into the boot before walking back into the house.

Jade picked up her mobile phone, a cunning grin forming across the bridge of her tightly held lips before her fingers started to punch at the letters forming a tightly woven conspiracy of a planned attack of revenge.

"Hey girl. What are you up to tomorrow? I thought I'd come for a visit?"

Within minutes Jade heard the familiar ring of her mobiles message bank. A devilish smile formed across her lips as she reached for her phone and read the reply.

"Hey," Natasha wrote, "I'm not busy tomorrow, love to see you."

Jade answered with calculated strategical precision as she organised her visit to the city with Natasha, as she hatched her planned revenge. "Okay, tomorrow it is," Jade said, laughing out loud, her eyes narrowing in a vindictive slant.

The next day Jade drove to the city to see Natasha, staying until the darkened hours of the evening. While in the presence of her friend, Jade sent a calculated message to Ryan on her mobile phone.

"Hey Ryan. I'm not going to be home tonight, I'm staying at my friend's house in Alterro. Would you mind swinging by my place, just to have a check on things for me please." A reply returned to her phone within minutes.

"Yeah sure, have fun. See you soon."

Jade smiled at the message as her twisted, tormented mind formed into a planned strategic extract of her revenge.

That night, Jade said goodbye to Natasha and left, heading back out on the highway, as the night sky fell into a darkened cloak of disguise.

Five miles from the township of Port Winifield Jade stopped at the service station situated out of site on the highway and filled the fuel can with the potentially fatal fuel and continued on her way along the highway towards the small township of Suisania Bay.

Three hours later, Jade arrived back in the small township of Suisania Bay but she did not drive home, she did not enter the inner streets of the small local township. Jade veered off the highway, drove down the long narrow back roads that led to the outskirts of the township and parked a block away from a house, the house that she had followed the women to on the Saturday night.

Jade waited and waited, sitting quietly in the dark hovering low in the front seat of her car until she sighted a car travelling down the narrow long stretch of the darkened road. Her eyes narrowed in hatred as the cars lights lit up the view to the house and a woman parked the car in the driveway and walked to the front door. "Tasha," Jade whispered through gritted teeth, lowering herself into the car's seat.

Jade's heart thumped nervously and heavily within her chest as her mind embarked upon the contemplation of her planned attack.

Her eyes darted back and forth as her mind raced through the thoughts of her planned attack, as her hands started to tremble and her heart beat faster and faster, before her hands started to reach out for the filled fuel can that sat on the floor in the back seat, before suddenly hesitating.

"Oh my god," she whispered, placing her hand to her open mouth. "What am I doing? This is not me. What am I doing?"

Jade placed her head in her hands in disbelief as all her logic returned in a flying rush, pushing out the illogical rage that had driven her to the point of the calculated revenge.

"Oh god," Jade cried out, realising what she was about to do. Jade turned the rear view mirror sideways, facing it towards herself and looked at the reflection of the face staring back at her worn down, beaten down, the twisted and tormented woman that had been driven to the edge. "This is not you," she whispered at the reflection. "This is not you."

Jade placed her hand upon the key in the ignition and started the car and slowly drove back down the narrow darkened road and pulled the car to a stop in her driveway as the tears started to roll down her hallowed, pale cheeks. Jade searched for her mobile phone inside the depths of her handbag and typed a message.

"Ryan, I need to speak to you. Now," Jade pleaded. "Can you please come over. Urgent."

"Give me a minute," Ryan answered quickly and was on her doorstep within moments.

"Hey," Jade said calmly, opening the front door. "Come in."

"I thought you were staying at your friend's house tonight," Ryan asked as he entered the house.

Jade shook her head in her own disbelief. "I lied," she confessed before dropping her eyes to the floor as the guilt overwhelmed her and held her in a state of regret.

"I really need to talk to you. Come sit down," Jade continued, pointing Ryan towards the kitchen table. Ryan sat down at the table, a worried look forming on his face.

"What's going on Jade?" Ryan asked concerned, knowing something was terribly wrong.

Jade sat down at the table placing herself across from Ryan and broke down into inconsolable tears as she started to tell Ryan the whole story of what had been happening.

Ryan sat silenced as he listened in disbelief as Jade poured out every detail of what had been going on with Shane, the threatening phone calls that had escalated into attacks on her home and the horrible extreme events of what she was about to do that night and why she had sent him that message.

"I just snapped," Jade sobbed, tears flowing down her pale thin face. "I could see nothing but revenge, hatred, for all they had done. I went there. I sat there. But all of a sudden, I couldn't do it. Logic kicked back in and I couldn't believe what I had thought about doing. I would have lost everything, my children, my business, everything. And for what. Shane. Oh Ryan, How did it get this far," Jade cried out, her tears flowing in an endless stream of uncontrollable weeping. Ryan was speechless as he sat there staring at Jade walking back and forth crying and pouring out the terrible tale of the ordeal she had been suffering at the hands of his friends, the clubhouse members and their girlfriends. Finally Ryan spoke.

"Come here," Ryan said as he pulled Jade to him and hugged her firmly. "You poor little bugger. I had no idea Jade that this was going on. That this was done without my knowledge."

Ryan stood back and looked into Jade's tear-soaked eyes. "I'll get to the bottom of this okay. And believe me, it will be stopped," Ryan reassured her, his voice filled with anger and concern as he held Jade tight.

Over the next two weeks Jade plunged into despair. She hid in her house, fearing the world, unable to break free of the shame, the fear, the drug addiction and once again, was trapped in her prison of depression on the side of the bed. She no longer smiled, she no longer slept, she no longer ate and stood by helplessly as her weight once again plummeted her to skin and bones and her mind shattered under the weight of all that had happened. The life that had once shone so bright inside of her now tarnished and blackened and tilted her in a day to day struggle of an emotional rollercoaster of guilt, shame, betrayal and anger. Her faith and hope lost all place within her soul as her life brought her to her knees with nowhere to turn.

After three weeks, Ryan returned and sat Jade down to talk. He had done what he said he would do and found out everything that had been going on at the clubhouse. As Ryan and Jade compared notes on all they knew, they both realised Shane was the catalyst behind it all. It had been Shane who had set her up at the club that night, he had told them that he had left because Jade had asked him to and that he had pinned the whole decision of his leaving on her shoulders causing the club to turn on her and blame her for his leaving. It was Shane who had given Jade's number to Tasha and Mary and that he had been having an affair with Mary the whole time and that's how the women had known when Shane was with her and when he had left for the mines. Everything that had happened was Shane's doing. Jade just sat there stunned, shocked, her mind unable to fathom the depth of Shane's deceit, cruelty, and callous nature until she questioned. Why? Why had Shane done this to her when he had told her that he loved her? Jade just couldn't believe it.

Ryan reassured Jade that he had taken care of it all though and told her that Shane had now moved back to the city to live with his mother again but he couldn't assure her that the women would stop altogether.

"That girl's fucken crazy Jade. They were planning on coming over here in a group and knocking you off. I don't trust Tasha hey, she could do anything behind my back. I think you should move, stay low until this all blows over," Ryan suggested. Jade just nodded her head in agreement.

"Yes, I think I should," Jade finally replied quietly, trying to fathom it all.

One month later, Jade found a house on the other side of town, hidden away within the boundaries of a quiet neighbourhood. She had not told a soul of her moving and stipulated to her children the importance of keeping quiet about the move. Jade had never told her children about the violence she had endured and the threats that had been placed on their lives but instead had explained to them that the move was a fresh start away from Shane and it was him who she didn't want to know of their new location. James and Cody had promised their mother to keep it a secret but Jade knew that Cody was very upset by the breakdown of the relationship. That he had formed a strong bond with Shane and the pair had become very good friends, enjoying activities and outings together and spending time together. Shane had become like a father to him and now Cody was placed in the position of letting go of him as well and he was hurting. Jade had felt guilt over her son's anguish, she felt that she had failed him for not being able to save the relationship and had allowed her son to get hurt by getting close to Shane and now carried that weight as well and was trying to console and heal Cody's loss as best as she could while dealing with her own.

Over the next month, Jade's health did not improve, she felt constantly on guard and unable to relax within her new environment. She watched and listened all the time for any little sound, every car that came towards the house and had become paranoid of everything. She trusted no one and kept to herself more and more, isolating herself from the outside world, only leaving the house to shop and pay bills on the days she knew the crowds would be few and quiet. Her work on the business venture suffered, unable to concentrate and focus, her mind wandering continuously, stuck in the torment of all that had happened and now Jade leant heavily on her drug intake. She had given up all hope on life and even her once long letters to her best friend, Max, now withered into short notes of hopelessness and mistrust even of him. Jade was slowly shutting out the world piece by piece and everyone she had once known had disappeared; she was all alone. Although the violence had stopped and no one knew of her whereabouts, the scars had remained, haunting Jade day and night and often waking her in the middle of the night, startled, terrified and shaken in nightmares and eventually, Jade broke for the second time, depression her only friend.

James' behaviour since that night at the hospital, his near fatal injury, had improved and he had not gotten into any more trouble with the police, choosing to stay away from the local bad crowd that he had previously fallen in with and he seemed to have turned his life around until the day his girlfriend broke off their relationship after three years of being together.

James returned that night red faced and tear stained, refusing to allow Jade into his room.

As the weeks rolled on, his grief over the relationship became anger as he had found out that the relationship had ended because his girlfriend had met someone else at a party that she had gone to. That night James had gone to the same party and watched as his girlfriend flirted with the other young lad, who in return, taunted and flaunted his conquest in front of James. James had lost his temper at the other young lad who had stolen his girlfriend and a fight broke out between the two which resulted in an assault charge being laid on James. Jade watched as her son's happy disposition slowly faded day by day and once again turned to anger towards her. Day after day their arguments grew worse and worse, louder and louder until James lost control. He yelled and roared at Jade, blaming her for everything that had gone wrong and started throwing things at her from his bedroom. Jade tried desperately to defuse the argument, to calm her son down but it had gone too far. James was boiling with anger and started kicking and punching through his bedroom door, destroying it beyond repair. Jade ran to her room, escaping the violence that was targeted in her direction. Unable to cope and already under emotional distress from all she had suffered, she was beside herself, frantic and didn't know what to do or how to stop James as she helplessly listened to him smashing his room into pieces.

"I've got to get help," Jade cried to herself, her head in her hands. "Oh god, what do I do, what do I do?" Jade paced her bedroom floor back and forth, thinking and thinking, helplessly not knowing just what to do to stop her son from all this violence he had brought into the family home and towards her. Jade grabbed her handbag from off her dressing room table, grabbed her car keys off the hook in the kitchen , yelled out to Cody to get in the car and jumped into her car and drove to the hospital begging to see the social worker.

"Please, I need help," Jade begged. "My son has lost control and is smashing up the house. I need help."

"I'm sorry," the social worker replied. "We can't help you." Jade stood there stunned.

"I thought that's what you did," she cried out to the social worker.

"I can't. There's nothing I can do. I'm sorry."

But Jade didn't wait for her to finish and let out a heavy sigh before running back out the door and back into her car. Jade drove to the children's support shelter and ran into the reception office.

"Please, I need help, my boy's smashing up the house. I need help, please help me," Jade begged to the lady standing at the desk.

"I'm sorry," the lady replied. "We can't help you. You'll have to go to the police."

Jade just stood there, her face filled with exasperated worry and bewilderment. "What do I do?" she asked herself over and over frantically. Jade did not want to involve the police, this was her son but she had no one to help her, nowhere to turn. As the tears flowed down her face, overwhelmed with the emotional turmoil, frustration, the battle within herself, the battles she faced around her, Jade was left with no choice and drove to the police station for help. Jade rushed through the large sliding doors of the police station and up to the counter. "Please, I need help with my son," she cried out to the officer standing behind the counter. "I need help. No one will help me," Jade cried, her face falling into her hands.

"What's wrong. What's going on with your son?" the officer asked quickly, trying to console Jade at the same time. Jade sat down on the chair in the waiting area with the officer and explained the argument she had had with James and the violence she had suffered at the hands of his father and what had happened with her children, with the continuous violence that they had continued in the family home.

"I just need him scared, shocked into stopping this," Jade explained, the tears falling from her eyes. "I need to break this cycle. They watched their father do this over and over. I need it to stop," she sobbed. The officer looked at Jade with concern.

"What would you like us to do Jade?" he asked.

Jade looked back at the officer pausing for a moment before speaking the words she had dreaded to speak. "Remove him from the home. I have a person, his friend, he can go stay with tonight, then the children's services can help me." The officer looked at Jade, noted her emotional state and then nodded, agreeing, telling Jade that they would follow her back to the house. Once arriving at the house, Jade walked inside as the officers followed her in and saw the damage James had caused to the home.

James came rushing from his bedroom and saw the officers standing there. "You dog Mum. You called the cops on your own son. I'll never forgive you for this," James yelled as Jade stood there, crying uncontrollably, shaking from all the stress of the situation of what she had to do.

"I asked you to stop James. I asked you to leave. You won't stop, you won't stop," Jade cried out back, distraught, beaten by all the turmoil of her troubled life and the guilt she felt by having to remove her son from the family home.

Jade stood in the face of her failing, crying helplessly. She stepped into the loungeroom as the officers marched her son out of the house and placed him in the back of the police car while the other officer stood with Jade, crying helplessly into her hands. "Oh god James. How did it get this bad," she wept as she dropped into the chair beside her and hung her head towards the floor.

The officer accessed the damage to the house and the door that James had destroyed before walking back over to where Jade sat in the chair.

"Do you want to press charges?" the officer asked her.

"No," Jade sobbed. "No, I don't. He's my son, I just needed help."

The officer looked down at Jade. "We have to charge him tonight Jade. In order for us to remove James from the premises, we have to press charges for the damage. But if you come to the station tomorrow and drop the charges we can withdraw it and nothing will come of it okay," the officer explained. Jade paused momentarily before finally nodding her head and agreeing. The officers left the house, taking James with them to the police station.

Two hours later they rang her, explaining that they had taken James to the address that she had specified.

The next day Jade drove around to her son's friend's house and knocked on the front door.

James stood tight-lipped, glaring at his mother. "How could you do that to me Mum. I'm your son," he said loudly. Jade dropped her head, she had already felt the shame of what she had to do the night before, the depth of the failure, she felt it sink deep into her heart.

"I'm sorry James," Jade cried, breaking down into tears. "But I told you last time when this happened. Anymore, and you'll have to go live with your father. You won't go there. You left me no choice. I'm not going to have this around me or your little brother anymore."

"Whatever Mum," James said back angrily and slammed the door in his mother's face. Jade left, upset and crying at the whole situation. Jade returned one week later.

This time James had calmed down and was ready to talk. "Can I come home Mum?" James asked, looking at Jade as he waited for her answer. Jade dropped her head, she wanted to wrap him in her arms and just take him home, but what if it happen again like so many other times she had given in to him. Jade took a deep breath and stood firm in her stance.

"No, no, I'm sorry James. You have to go live with your father or at the children's support shelter. The choice is yours." James looked at Jade, the glare returning to his eyes.

"True. You're kicking me out Mum. That's fucked," James ranted, pacing the front pavement of the house. "I'm not going to Dad's," James continued. "I'm not."

"Then I'll take you to the support shelter today," Jade replied, watching as James temper started to flair again. James paused, stopped, and stared at his mother before finally replying. "Fine," and walked back into the house to collect his things.

That day Jade helped her son pack up his room and moved him to the children's support shelter; he was only seventeen years of age.

That week Jade went to the police station and asked for the charges to be dropped, twice, without success.

One month later, Jade and James entered the courthouse once more. James had been charged over the assault he had committed when he attacked his ex-girlfriend's new boyfriend who had flaunted their relationship right in front of James which had caused the fight to break out. This time because of all the previous trouble that James had been in when hanging with the local bad crowd he did not receive community service or a way out he only had one choice left. Leave town and live with his father or they would lock him up for twelve months in the juvenile detention facility. Jade had no choice but agree to send her son across state to live with his father. The judge gave the order and gave Jade one week to shift James to his father's or he would be locked up. That week Jade drove her son to the airport. She stood in the airport terminal holding James in her arms tightly not wanting to let him go and said goodbye. As she watched him board the plane, her heart sank as her eyes filled with tears, not knowing when or if she would ever see James again.

Two weeks later, unable to free herself of the blackened cloud of depression that had plagued her and gripped her so tight, feeling the failure of what had happened with James, distraught and scared by all that had happened with Shane and the clubhouse, Jade planned her own death desperate to be free of the hell that had now become her life. Day by day, Jade slowly disappeared, she no longer saw the world in all its beautiful colours, now replaced by a black, hazy, dark fog; her smile disappeared, now a thin line of disappointment and failure; her blue eyes, now a window of grey sadness and her once body of curvaceous glowing skin, a thin, drawn out shell of grief, drug addiction and hopelessness. Each day grew harder and harder to face as each moment of her eyes open started in tears that rained until closed again. Jade no longer felt love in her heart, she no longer felt anger pulse through her veins, she no longer felt the glowing spark of life within her. Jade no longer felt anything, nothing mattered to her anymore as her own self destruction took hold and beckoned her to end it all and be the nothing she felt she had become.

As Jade sat on the rocks at the edge of the bay she stared into her own emptiness, day after day, her mind blank of thought, she saw nothing no one only the call of how she would take her own life. Jade walked the winding dirt trail that weaved its way around the dense marshes of the bay each day, planning her escape and her final resting position until the day came.

Jade sat in the spot on the edge of the dense marshes that over looked the bay as she stared at her grey, dark world that surrounded her, her mind empty, her spirit broken and lost. She reached into her pocket, and pulled out the bottle filled with the little white pills and emptied them into her hand.

"I love you kids. I'm sorry," Jade whispered as her eyes dropped to stare at her death sitting in the palm of her hand.

"Ooui," a voice called from the distance. "Jade, what are you doing?" Jade raised her head slowly and turned towards the sound of the voice as her hand slid the pills back into her pocket and she broke down into tears; tears that came and came, falling down over her cheeks and down to the ground below.

Ryan walked quickly over to Jade and sat beside her, his face filled with worry and concern. "I've been watching you for days girl," Ryan said, in a quiet comforting voice as he wrapped his arm around her sobbing shoulders.

"Oh Ryan. I can't do this anymore," Jade cried, her words muffled and broken through her tear stained breath. "I just can't do this anymore," she continued to weep, placing her face into her hands.

"Yes, you can Jade. You'll be okay," Ryan comforted her. "Look at me."

Jade lifted her red eyes slowly to look at Ryan. "Your son needs you," he said, his eyes soft but worried. "Cody needs you, don't you give up on him. Don't you give up. Do you hear me?" Jade nodded her head slowly as Ryan's words began to sink in bringing her back from the brink of her demise and despair as she lay her head upon his strong shoulder.

Jade and Ryan sat in the spot at the edge of the marshes overlooking the bay, just sitting together, quiet and still, as Jade rested against her friend's arm wrapped around her shoulders until the tears stopped.

"Come on. Come with me, back to the club," Ryan said as he helped Jade to her feet and back to her car where she followed him back to the club and spent the day until Cody finished school.

Ryan never knew about the little white pills in Jade's pocket, she never told anyone about that faithless day but Ryan knew and he had followed her that day and saved her life.

That night when Cody arrived home from school, Jade rushed to the door and stood still, staring at her young son, realising the depths to which she had fallen, taking in his smile, his loving eyes, of the one thing she knew she had to live for: Cody, her children. Jade wrapped Cody up tight in her arms, and whispered, "I love you."

Over the next two months, Jade's tears dried. She continued to battle everyday with her depression and the relentless cravings of her drug addiction as she forced herself to her feet and back into her work and her daily routines until she was once again standing and started to rebuild her life once more.

Jade had still not found her smile, she did not feel the same anymore, the warmth from her heart had turned hard, building barriers between her and the outside world. Her senses, her emotions had thickened, shielding her, guarding her from any form of deepness and connection with the people she came into contact with except for Ryan, Max and her children. Although Ryan had started to fix the damage Shane had caused between Jade and the other members of the clubhouse, Jade had not relaxed, her guard stood firm and strong, frowning protectively as she stood away from the people she had once trusted and knew, and Jade was no longer the sweet, caring, talkative woman she once was.

As the weeks passed, Jade changed, day by day. She no longer dressed in her usual fashion of flair, her dresses and high heels now locked in her cupboard, replaced by denim and sandshoes, T-shirts and jackets; her eloquent speech, now slurred with profanity and crass as she spent most of her time mending the broken bridges with the members back at the club house.

Piece by piece, person by person, Jade's relationships with the clubhouse members mended but Jade was now a different person, the once kind, sweet woman, replaced by a broken disguise of a sharp-tongued rebel of hardened feelings, wayward actions, drinking and drugs, which continued for six months.

Six months later: Jade had not sighted Shane or heard from him at all as her phone lay silent, void of his number and messages until unexpectedly one day a message flashed upon her phone. Jade picked up her phone, a small smile forming on her face as she opened the message expecting it to be from Ryan.

"Hey Jade, I'm sorry for everything that happened between us. I'm so sad without you. I think about you every day. I miss you and Cody so much… Please, can we talk? I still love you. Shane."

Jade's face froze as she stared at the unexpected message, reading the words again and again as her heart beat faster in a sly anticipation. "Hmmm," Jade hummed as the soft words left no sweetness to her senses or temptation of love to penetrate the hard shell that she had built around her heart. Jade's mind jumped from thought to thought as she hesitated and contemplated her answer.

"Hehe," Jade giggled a devious giggle as she placed the phone back down on the kitchen counter. "I might answer you. I may not," she giggled to herself, now caught up in her own taunting of the message from Shane.

Jade went about her day; that day unaffected or fazed by the message she had received from Shane, placing the thought from any meaning or moment and did not answer, content with making him wait and wonder.

The next day Jade received another message.

"Hey Jade. I understand if you don't want to talk to me, I don't blame you. It was all my fault. But I miss you so much. Please baby. Give me another chance. I love you. Shane."

Jade felt nothing as she stood back holding the phone message in front of her eyes laughing out loud in a devious, devilish manner. "Do you now," she said laughing to herself. But still Jade did not answer and remained silent as her mind forged a precise strategical plan of her next move.

That night Jade carefully hatched a plan of her own revenge before she devilishly carved the words into the message.

"Hey, how are you?" Jade started to type. "I got your message. I've just been very busy," and sent the message to Shane.

Over the next two weeks, Shane wrote to Jade every day, declaring his feelings for her, apologizing profusely and trying to win back her affections but Jade did not sway from her hardened heart, she did not return his affections her messages had remained short but sweet, precise and leading.

Then Shane sent another message, this time inviting Jade to see him.

"Hey Jade," the message read. "Would you like a weekend in a hotel, just you and me. I need to see you, I'll pay for your petrol and everything. You just need to bring yourself. Love Shane."

Jade sat for a moment smiling at the message, a hardened, devious smile forming upon her mouth as she sat thinking about the offer. "Hmm," Jade thought. "A weekend out in a hotel and a spa, nice food. Hmmm," Jade continued in her thoughts. "That would be nice." Jade picked up her phone and sent a message back in her reply.

"Yeah okay. That would be nice. See you this weekend. But I'm only coming as a friend with benefits lol."

Jade sat back against the wall covering herself deep with the pillows that sat on her bed and giggled.

"You're a bad girl Jade but fuck him. Take what you can get girl," she said laughing quietly under her breath.

That weekend Jade met her son's friend's mother, Susan at their usual meeting spot out on the highway, leaving her son with his friend for the weekend, and drove to the city for her planned rendezvous with Shane. On arriving in the city, Jade drove straight to the hotel, Shane had told her, he had booked for them and walked up the stairs to the room and knocked on the door.

"Hey," Jade said, greeting Shane as he opened the hotel door.

"Hey Jade," Shane said back smiling a happy smile, pleased that she had come. She walked into the room smugly and confidentially and placed her overnight bag on the floor next to the hotel couch.

"Nice room," Jade said as she looked around at the settings of the hotel room. "So, how have you been?" she asked smiling.

"Yeah good. But missing you like crazy baby," Shane replied. Jade just smiled, an uninterested smile as she walked to the bathroom to view the spa that sat in the corner.

"Mmm," she hummed, a sexy glint entertaining her eyes. "It's been a while huh," she said, pointing to the spa.

"Too long," Shane replied.

They stood together in the bathroom as Shane poured Jade a drink and offered her all off their creature comforts first, displaying his best behaviour, before re-entering the bedroom of the hotel. Jade stood within the bedroom smiling, looking smugly down her nose at Shane, feeling her own power in his presence, her absence from Shane rendering him soft and unable to resist her charms as he sat helplessly in her hands like putty and stood strong within her liberation of power refusing to budge and let her heart soften to his charms. As they smoked the pot that Shane had supplied and drank the bourbon that Shane had supplied, they chatted and laughed together, staying clear of any subject to do with their previous relationship. Shane reached his hand out to Jade, touching the warmth of her hand.

"Would you like one of these?" he asked, placing the little white pill into Jade's hand. Jade smiled as she took the pill from Shane's hand, placed it on her tongue and swallowed it without hesitation. Twenty minutes later Jade felt the intoxication of the ecstasy seep through her system and uninhibit her mind and step her towards Shane and into the seductive lustful embrace of their lips. This time Jade did not feel the tingle of Shanes lips as they pressed against hers or the emotional pull of her heart to the man that she had once loved and remained heartless in her seduction and felt nothing but the sexual lust that rose between her legs induced by the little white pill. Jade pulled at Shanes T-shirt ripping it from his body and pulled up her skirt, removing her panties and throwing them to the floor. Shane took a step back at the dominating woman that now stood before him, looking at Jade through startled eyes. A giggle slipped from Jades mouth a sexy devilish giggle as she stepped forward and undid Shane's jeans, pushing them to the floor before dropping to her knees and opened her mouth seductively tasting and teasing his hard length that she held against her warm tongue. Her eyes lifted up the length of his body to meet his as he looked down towards her and watched his enjoyment as she knelt on the hard floor, his hardness filling her warm wet mouth as she pleasured him, her fingers playing with the warm wet pleasure that sat between her own legs. Jade suddenly rose to her feet, softly pushing Shane on the shoulder in a stance of seductive power and turned around giggling as she bent over the bathroom vanity placing one knee on top of the vanity bench. "Mmm," she moaned as she stared into the mirror at their reflection and mouthed the words. "Take me." Shane's face filled with excitement and the sexual lust of the moment that flashed through his eyes as he gripped the skirt, hitched up around Jade's hips and thrust his hardened length deep inside of her. Jade gasped loudly as he took her and she continued to watch their reflection in the mirror. "Ohh, yes," she moaned. "Ohh god yes, oh harder, harder, that's it," Jade moaned louder and louder, taking what she had come for. As the sexual excitement grew through every hard thrust, she felt Shane start to swell inside of her, pushing him closer towards his own climax. Jade reached out her hand behind her and pushed Shane away, sliding his length out of the wet warmth between her legs. "Mmm," Jade moaned. "Not yet, you don't," she whispered in a sexy dominating voice as she lowered her leg from off the bathroom vanity and slid her skirt back down to her knees and walked out of the bathroom door, turning her head to smile at Shane, a sexy glint beaming within the smouldering look of her eyes.

Jade walked slowly seductively from the bathroom and sat down on the couch in the adjacent room, her eyes focused on the movement behind her as Shane followed in her footsteps shaking his head in disbelief.

"You wicked woman," Shane said, laughing, as he entered the room. Jade's eyes flashed a wicked glint as she lifted the glass of bourbon to her lips and sipped at the cold liquor.

"Mmm," she giggled, devilishness gleaming in her eyes. "I'm getting hungry. How about you?"

"Yeah, I am a bit too," Shane replied still smiling. "How about we get some room service hey?"

"Yes, that sounds good," Jade replied picking up the menu that sat on the table next to the couch. "So, what can I order?" she asked, smiling once again, raising her eyes to meet his.

"Anything you want naughty girl," Shane teased returning the smile and placing himself down on the couch next to her.

"Hmm," Jade hummed smugly, her eyes staying directed at the menu in front of her ignoring Shane's presence and startled expression as she looked over the different options. "Hmm. I think I'll have that, that and that," Jade said pointing to the different dishes that she had chosen upon the menu.

"Okay sexy," Shane replied, picking his own choices from the menu before ringing through to the hotels reception and placing the order.

Twenty minutes later, they heard a knock on the hotel room door as their room service announced its arrival and their meals were placed upon the dining table. "Mmm. Oh, this is delicious," Jade cooed throughout the three course meal until finally she came to the dessert. "Oh god this is good," she continued as she placed a spoonful of the fresh strawberry and cream cheesecake she had ordered into her mouth. Full and satisfied they both sat down upon the couch to allow their meals to settle as they continued to engage in small talk that held no interest to Jade and acted nonchalant as her eyes secretly rolled in her mind at the endless dribble that permeated her ears.

Jade rose to her feet and walked confidently back towards the bathroom seductively wrapping her leg around the frame of the door. "Mmm. I think it's time for a spa, don't you," she said giggling as she suggestively stroked her finger up and down the painted door frame, her eyes smouldering and seducing, tempting Shane to rise from the couch and join her. A seducible smile spread across Shane's face as he shook his head slightly and raised from the couch and stepped towards her. "I don't know about you girl," he said his mind bewildered by the seductive power of Jade's sexuality of which he had not seen before.

Jade laughed, a sexy little laugh, knowing exactly what she was doing, what she wanted and what she had come to get. As Shane entered the bathroom Jade stepped in front of him her fingers trailing up the length of her shirt until they reached the top button. One by one she slowly undid her shirt buttons and slipped the sheer fabric from off her shoulders dropping it to the floor as she continuously seduced him with her eyes.

Jade slowly turned around placing her back towards him and slowly slid her hands around the curves of her waist, following the contours of her body until her fingertips found the top of her skirt zipper. She giggled seductively as she turned her head around to look at Shane, a little sexy smile forming on her pouty lips as she slowly, inch by inch, lowered the zipper of her skirt, revealing the tiny lace G-string that lay underneath and slowly started to slide the skirt down over the curves of her hips then came to an unexpected stop just before her skirt lowered past her thighs.

"Ohh," Jade said with a sexy smile. "Before we forget. Petrol money please," tilting her head slightly sideways, smiling sweetly at Shane. Without haste Shane pulled his wallet out from his jeans pocket and placed the petrol money into Jade's outstretched hand emancipated in the excitement and anticipation of the sexual seduction and lust that flashed through his eyes in eagerness. "Thank you," Jade said smiling a devilish little smile before walking over to the bathroom vanity, placing the money into her purse. "Mmm," Jade hummed through her moist soft lips as she walked seductively back towards Shane, swaying her hips with each step that she took. "Time to get these off," she whispered, pulling at Shanes clothing. As Shane started to quickly remove his clothing his eyes stayed focused on Jade, watching her intensely as she continued to slowly remove her skirt, her bra and G-string, dropping them to the floor and stepping into the spa sinking beneath the warm, bubbling water, waiting for Shane to join her. Jade sighed as the warm water soothed her and the bubbles tantalised her skin, her body her senses. She looked over at Shane, naughtiness flowing through her inhibited mind and flashing in her smouldering eyes as she slowly crept over to Shane's side of the spa and slid into his lap. "Mmmm. Now where were we," she softly whispered in Shane's ear reaching her hand down between her legs to stroke Shane's arousal. "Mmm," she moaned placing his hardened length up against the moist pleasures between her legs and finished what they had started on the bathroom vanity.

Over the next four hours, Shane and Jade embraced in an erotic sexual frenzy of pure sexual pleasure, teasing and playing, touching and tasting, thrusting and grinding until their bodies were totally spent and they could give no more to each other and finally, they lay down together in the hotel bed and fell asleep exhausted but satisfied.

Early the next morning Jade awoke and crept out of the bed quietly as Shane lay peaceful and sound asleep within the bed. She gathered her strewn clothes from around the hotel room placing them into her overnight bag, picked up her handbag from off the dining chair, gently kissed Shane on the cheek and left a note on the side table beside the couch. "Thank you for a brilliant night. Bye for now, Jade," and snuck out the door and left, heading back to her home town of Suisania Bay.

Two weeks later, Shane invited Jade to join him again in the hotel room for another adventurous sexual weekend; his treat, offering to pay for Jade's petrol and all of their commodities over the course of the weekend. Once again, Jade accepted the offer and made the arrangements for Cody to stay at his friend's house for the weekend and Jade left for the city, joining Shane in the hotel room once more. Jade entered the hotel room smiling devilishly at Shane, who stood near the doorway entrance after closing the door smiling back at her, holding a package in his hands.

"I got you a present," Shane said stepping towards her and placing the package into her hands.

"Ohh what is it?" Jade said, looking at the package smiling before sitting on the couch to undo the wrapping.

"Ohhh," she cooed as she pulled the sexy black negligee and toys from the box, smiling devilishly up at Shane. "We are going to have a good weekend aren't we. I'll go put it on," she said seductively, smiling as she rose to her feet and walked into the bathroom, slipping out of her clothes and into the little, black, lacy negligee. Jade slipped on her high heels and slowly, seductively walked out of the bathroom to join Shane in the adjacent room, who was eagerly waiting for her on the bed. She slowly walked towards the bed as the little lace negligee hung delicately over the curves of her hips, swaying with each sway of her steps as she approached closer and closer, looking into Shane's eyes as they lit up with excitement and anticipation. Tantalising him with smouldering sexy eyes and painted parted lips she slowly crawled onto the foot of the bed.

"Ohhh baby. You are one sexy woman," Shane said through an excited gasp, eyeing Jade as she crawled closer and closer towards him. Jade smiled seductively as she knelt on her knees and picked up one of the vibrators and trailed it down the length of her body.

"Mmmm," she moaned as she switched on the vibrator and felt its tantalising vibrations against her soft warm skin. "Mmm. This one first," she whispered as Shane rose to his knees and excitedly dragged her down upon the bed and into a night of wild adventurous, lustful passion of erotic, tantalising sex that continued into the early morning hours.

The next morning, Jade gathered up her presents, her overnight bag, her petrol money and the bag of pot she had asked Shane to buy for her and walked out of the hotel room, leaving a note on the side table next to the couch and drove back home to Suisania Bay, while Shane still slept in the hotel bed.

The following week while running numerous errands for the family home and attending the numerous appointments she had made with the various businesses within the township for her business plan, upon leaving from the Real Estate agents, her last appointment to which Jade had just completed negotiating a contract on the premise she had chosen for the initial start-up of her business, she walked out of the office and was suddenly startled by an unexpected familiar face standing before her.

"Hey Jade. I haven't seen you for ages. How are you?" Sonia greeted her, her voice tinged with an intention.

Caught off guard and startled Jade took a slight step back but quickly regained her composure and stood firm holding her new found confidence in the air.

"Oh. Hey Sonia. I'm really well. Yes it has been a long time. How are you?" Jade replied politely.

As Jade and Sonia stood on the footpath engaging in idle chit chat, Jade's mind darted in many different directions. Her thoughts engulfed her as the memories came flooding back and filled her once again of the guilt she had felt of the night she had almost twisted and snapped, stalked the house on the outskirts of town and nearly threw away everything for revenge. Jade stared at Sonia, her surreptitious thoughts hidden behind a veil within her eyes, as she watched the words flow from Sonia's mouth, her endless gossip just an uninteresting blur to Jade's ears as her mind drifted in its own direction.

"Um, I'm sorry Sonia," Jade eventually said interrupting her mid-sentence. "I'm in a hurry, you've caught me on the hop. I've got to go. Nice to see you though. Take care," taking a step backwards and stepping into a stride to leave.

"Oh, okay," Sonia replied a blank look forming across her face. "We'll have to catch up soon hey," she continued, waving to Jade as she walked away.

"Oh yeah. For sure. As soon as I get some free time," Jade replied in her stride turning her head around to look at her giggling, portraying a fake polite laugh followed by a roll of her eyes as she turned her head back around out of her view.

Although Jade had remained friendly and polite within Sonia's unexpected presence she had not forgotten the part that Sonia had played in Shane's deceit and attack upon her family home which had nearly driven Jade to her final demise on that nearly fateful day on the edge of the marshes and held onto a side of caution and suspicion.

That night Jade sat in her bedroom comfortable and relaxed smoking the pot that Shane had bought for her as she wrote a letter to Max. Jade sat patiently on the edge of her bed as she waited for Max to reply, desperately needing to hear his words of reasoning and wisdom, his guidance to the unanswered questions that continuously swirled within the depths of her mind.

An hour later, Jade heard the familiar tone of her computer's email alert and eagerly rushed to read the reply.

"Oh Max," she whispered to herself as she turned to face the computer screen and started to read his written words

"Hey Jade,

Firstly, I just want to say, 'Are you crazy!', I thought you were done with this joker. What are you doing?"

As Jade continued to read Max's letter, every sentence, every word, reached into the logical recesses of her mind and tugged at the woman that was trapped inside locked behind all the anger, bitterness and betrayal.

Jade could see the wrong path she had in her hardened, twisted soul, so foolishly stepped down again in her need to empower herself against the cruel deceitful reality of Shane's behaviour. Jade sat back against the pillows that lay on her bed, staring into the computer screen, staring at Max's words her mind absorbed in thought as her eyes read the last sentence of Max's letter.

"Jade you deserve better. Don't do this to yourself again. He'll never change."

"Hmmm," Jade hummed as the words sank deep into her mind, her psyche and touched at the very roots of her soul, words she needed to hear, words she needed to be told.

"You're right Max," she whispered laying down upon her bed her eyes lifting towards the ceiling in an omniscient stare. "Yes Max, your right," she whispered once more closing her eyes to sooth the restlessness of her mind.

That weekend Jade received another message from Shane.

"Hey Jade. I've booked the hotel room. You up for it again? I'd love to see you. Shane."

Jade opened the message, reading the words continuously as if the words could define an answer before her mind re-focused and drifted to the words of the letter that she had received from Max. Her fingers hesitated over the key pad of her phone as she contemplated her answer and the consequences of her actions. This time Jade was not so sure.

"What should I do?" Jade whispered to herself, her mind darting between the sexual pleasures and the aberration of her behaviour that had her so hopelessly hooked and the logic of her own self-worth that Max had reminded her of, that still lay deep within her hidden. Jade rose to her feet and walked from her bedroom and out the back door to sit on the chair under her back veranda, sitting still, motionless and silent looking at the trees, the soft blow of the breeze gently swaying the leaves in rhythm with the swirling currents, watching as the world around her cast shadows under the twinkle of the stars, the beam of the moon and the silence that surrounded her that slipped her into deep thought.

"Max is right," Jade whispered to herself shaking her head slightly in the realisation. "Why am I doing this to myself? I'm worth more. A lot more. But. But." Jade placed her fingertips to her mouth pensively her words stuck for a moment within her throat the devilishness within her sounding it's voice and pulling at her again. "Maybe just one last time and then I'll end it, I'll walk away," she told herself giggling nervously but seductively the glint flashing into her eyes. Jade rose up off the chair and walked back inside to her bedroom and picked up her phone, stopping to study the message that Shane had sent one more time, as her mind once again split between wrong and right in the face of the message.

"Ohh," Jade sighed. "I hope you know what you are doing girl," she said softly to herself as her fingers started to glide over the keypad.

This time as Jade replied, she did not giggle with a confident air, this time she was not so sure, but still she said yes to Shane and sent the message, accepting his invitation.

That weekend Jade dropped Cody off to spend the weekend with his friend and headed to the city, this time, meeting Shane at his mother's house instead of the hotel room. Shane smiled as he greeted Jade in the front garden of his mother's house before following him down the driveway towards the shed at the back of the house that had now been converted into Shane's bedroom. As Jade followed Shane down the long cement driveway, approaching the shed's entrance, she could hear two voices coming from inside the shed walls that had intrigued Jades mind as to who they were. Upon entering the sheds doorway the mystery of the voices came into Jades view as she was unexpectedly greeted by Simon and Kay who had jumped to their feet from off the chairs placed within the room in front of the television set. Jade's eyes opened wide startled by the view of the couple of who greeted her and of who she had not seen since the day of her daughter Monique moving to Meltona to live with her father.

"Hey Jade," Kay greeted her, a polite smile forming on her face. "How have you been?"

Jade felt instantly awkward in their presence, having had no contact with them for over a year, and was uncertain and hesitant to be more than just polite as she didn't know where she stood with them in the aftermath of her dissolved relationship with Shane.

"Oh, hi," Jade replied politely, fiddling with her own fingers that sat together hidden behind her back. "I've been doing really well," she continued. "And how have you been?"

"Yeah, good," Kay replied, a reply that led into a continuum of awkward moments and long pauses within their pointless conversation.

As the conversation with Kay drifted back into the awkward silence once more, Jade quickly took advantage of the moment to slip out of the awkward situation and excuse herself from the room. "I'm just going to go say hello to your mum okay," she said looking in Shane's direction.

"Okay," Shane replied quickly interrupting his conversation with Simon.

"Oh, I'll come with you," Kay said smiling. Jade smiled back politely and nodded her head while the discomfort of Kay's following stayed hidden within the depths of her mind in a gestural rolling of her eyes that was not displayed upon her face as they headed for the back door of the home.

"Hello," Jade called out announcing her arrival as she opened the door and took a step inside.

"We're in the kitchen," came a reply from inside the house. Jade walked through the small foyer of the house entrance that led straight into the kitchen as Kay followed closely behind her.

"Hello stranger," Bev said welcomely as Jade walked through the kitchen door.

Jade's face lit up instantly with a broad smile, her happiness at seeing Shane's mother recognisable and written all over her face.

"Hi, how are you?" Jade replied, giving Bev a big hug.

"I'm doing well," Bev replied smiling and wrapping her arms around Jade in a reciprocating hug. The interaction between them quickly flowed into a mellifluous banter of jokes and giggles of which they had always shared while she was dating Shane and had come to visit on regular occasions.

Within minutes, Kay, who was standing at the other side of the kitchen, pushed her way in on the conversation, joining in the joking and giggles, taking over and unabashedly throwing herself into the spotlight of the attention.

"Hi, ma and pa," Kay said loudly, throwing her arms around them pushing Jade to the side. "Hmmm," Jade thought to herself, her mind bewildered by Bev's reaction to Kay, surprised by the reciprocated sudden closeness of their relationship that had previously been so distant in the past in the abstinence of Kay's presence within the family home, of which she did not frequent or venture. A bewildered frown formed within Jade's brow as her fingers raised to her bottom lip in thought as she stood back watching the strange behaviour taking place. Feeling uncomfortable within the inconsequent moment Jade quickly interrupted walking towards Bev who had stayed seated at the kitchen table.

"Ok, we better get back out there. The men will be waiting and wondering," Jade said with a giggle. "It was so good to see you," she continued, placing her arms around Bev's shoulders hugging her goodbye.

Jade and Kay walked from the house and back into the shed where Shane and Simon were still engaged in conversation while appreciating Shane's collections of memorabilia that hung on the shed walls.

"You're back," Shane said as the two women entered the shed. "We were going to send out a search party," Shane teased. Jade faked a smile and stood politely near the shed's entrance, eager to leave for the hotel room and away from the presence of Kay and Simon.

Although Jade had portrayed herself in a polite manner within the moment and their presence deep inside of herself she had not forgiven Kay for the vicious onslaught of abusive text messages which she received upon the break-up of her relationship with Shane, of which Jade felt was not her place to interfere and now wished that she had answered with a no instead to Shane's invitation, as she stood uncomfortably in their presence. Jade felt the foreboding warning run up her spine and tangle in the depths of her mind as she stood silenced and trapped in the situation and fought the urge to just walk out and not face the truth that swirled within her, that this was a mistake.

"Come sit down girls," Shane said as he sat in one of the four chairs that where situated in the front of the room and patted at the seat next to him.

As Jade took a step forward to sit in the chair next to Shane, Kay impertinently rushed ahead of her and quickly sat in the chair next to him. Jade's eyes glared at Kay dubiously as her initial thoughts flashed in quick succession. Shane had always been indifferent to Kay and Kay to Shane, their interaction with each other in the past being one of few words. During their relationship Shane had confessed his true feelings to Jade about Kay and had said that he thought Kay was an 'airhead' and only put up with her because she was in a relationship with his mate, Simon, and the two had never really seen eye to eye or talked that much because of it. Jade believed what Shane had told her as she had seen their lack of interaction or liking for one another firsthand on the occasions that they had visited the couple, whilst they were still in a relationship.

As Simon had taken the next chair next to Kay, Jade walked to the last chair, sat down and placed her hands in her lap, feeling bewildered and curious as to the exact interaction that had been taking place while Shane had been vacant from her life and living in the city close to Simon and Kay.

As they all began to talk engaging in light, polite conversation that really held no quality or definition of anything intellectual or intriguing, Jade watched and listened as Shane and Kay leant into an individual conversation privately held between themselves. As the conversation continued Shane and Kay got louder and more playful with each other leaning against each other as they viewed and joked about the different pictures and messages they had on each other's phones, laughing, offering each other cigarettes, locked in their own little private affair of conversation and laughs and acted as if totally oblivious to Jade and Simon sitting in the same room.

Simon continued talking to Jade as if all was normal, as if this is how it was and always had been. Although Jade remained polite, beneath the surface she was furious as she watched on as Shane continued with his womanising ways with the woman of whom he had once stated that he didn't even like.

Jade's eyes formed into a cold glare of disapproval and anger as she sat disgusted and disrespected at the outwardly display of affection and attention Shane lavished towards Kay while in her presence.

Ignored and feeling separated from the loop as if her presence in the room had meant nothing to Shane, Jade's mind started to recant over the lengthy conversations of which she had shared with Shane during the last encounter over the previous weekend within the privacy of the hotel room.

Shane had proclaimed his undying love for Jade, that he had understood how he had made her feel while they were together and that he had now changed his ways, confessing of his need to stay in the city to be close to where she was, waiting for her to come back to him and that there had never been another woman in his arms or charms, that his heart belonged to her.

But Jade had not believed him, having witnessed firsthand while they were in a relationship Shane's deceitful ways as she felt emotionally exasperated, suffering and struggling as she was engulfed by the overwhelming suspicious paranoia that grew within her as she watched in silence at Shane's philandering ways, and she had hoped that he was now suffering, hurting without her, something she had felt during their torrid relationship in the small town of Suisania Bay.

But now Jade did not feel so clever or empowered in her own deceitful rebellious act of her vengeance for all of the pain she had suffered during the course of their relationship. As she continued to sit there silenced in the flirtatious repugnance of their behaviour, Jade felt foolish and wished that she had never come or agreed to see Shane ever again.

"I should have said no," the alarming whisper sounded within her mind but did not reach her lips as her eyes dropped to the floor before raising up again into Shanes direction.

"Well, time's a wasting," Jade announced her giggle stained with the annoyance that swirled within her and raised her to her feet, her unimpressed glare remaining within the depths of her eyes as she glanced at Shane and Kay. "I'm on limited time. We better get to the hotel hey Shane," Jade continued as she walked closer to the shed door.

"Oh, yep, okay. We better go hey," Shane replied, breaking his attention from Kay and rising to his feet also. Kay glanced over at Jade, who looked back at her, the unimpressed glare now written all over her face as Jade shrugged her shoulders in a gesture of annoyance and impatience.

"Oh, okay," Kay and Simon replied in unison, looking at each other, as they gathered their things quickly and rose to their feet. "Okay, have fun," Simon continued as he stepped towards the doorway of the shed with Kay following directly behind him. "We'll see you soon then," Simon said as they walked along the footpath towards their parked vehicle at the front of the house, got in and drove away.

Jade's eyes looked over at Shane as a small smile formed across her lips in a disguise of the anger that lay hidden beneath her skin.

Jade followed Shane out of the shed, down the cement driveway and got into his car, leaving for the hotel.

Silence sat between them within the confinement of the vehicle, until they arrived at the hotel moments later.

That night after Shane and Jade had enjoyed their room service meals, Shane offered Jade the little white pill that had become a regular part of their rebelliousness together. "Would you like one of these? Time to party yeah," Shane giggled, holding the pill out to Jade in his open palm oblivious to her anger.

Jade paused momentarily looking at the pill sitting in Shane's hand in front of her. Jade's mind busied itself in deep thought as she hesitated.

"No. I think I'll pass tonight." And for the first time Jade had refused the intoxicating effects of the little, white pill that fuelled her into the fantasy of their sexual world that had held her so tightly in Shane's grip. This time she was determined and whispered within the depths of her mind, "No more, Max was right." Jade watched as Shane slipped into the intoxicating effects of the little white pill and was alarmed as his actions changed his speech into a slur and the stark realisation sank beneath her skin.

"Enough," Jade said within her mind. "I don't even like the man that stands before me anymore."

As the evening grew later, Jade's awareness grew as she watched in her coherent state as Shane received many phone messages on his mobile phone that lay unanswered and face down on the bathroom vanity unit within the hotel room. Jade knew something was odd as her mind flooded back to Shane's behaviour while working at the mines and the other woman, of whom she discovered, Meg.

This time she did not doubt herself or the actions which she witnessed.

Jade heard the alarm bells within herself, the rising of the red flags, her senses felt the tremulous trouble bubbling once again. Within that moment she knew Shane was never going to change and this was the last time she would ever come to see him, he just wasn't worth it.

That night Jade did not fall into the intoxicating pleasures of the erotic fantasy, the sexual adventures she had once shared so lustfully with Shane, that night she was not turned on by him; every kiss, a sour reminder, every touch, a burn of his betrayal, every thrust, a bitter taste of deceit as she faked every moment, every sound, every movement until the end, her last one with Shane.

While Shane slept heavily beside her in the hotel bed Jade crept silently into the bathroom where Shane's phone lay on the vanity bench upside down. She secretly picked up the phone nervously, quietly and quickly searched through the messages that Shane had received, ignored and hidden throughout the night while they had been together. One by one Jade searched for the names of his hidden secrets until the truth stared back at her right in the face.

"What. You never use to talk to her, or her, or her, and who's this woman," Jade whispered to herself as each new name flashed across the screen of the phone.

Within moments, flashings of the past began to swirl within Jade's mind as she sighted each new message from the other women until finally reality slammed her feet back onto solid ground. This was never going to stop. "I hate you Shane," whispered from the scalding corners of her mouth. "I really hate you."

Jade stood silently, staring at Shane's phone, nodding her head knowingly before placing it back upside down on the vanity bench where she had found it. She walked back into the other room where Shane still lay sleeping oblivious to her actions and sat down in the chair at the table, motionless, silent, smoking a cigarette as she stared at Shane, the man she had once loved and had once believed had loved her back.

Within that pause of the silent moment, each memory of their togetherness, each moment that they had shared, dissolved and turned to dust as Jade turned her back on it all and whispered. "Goodbye Shane."

She packed her overnight bag, picked up the petrol money off the dining table and quietly walked out the door of the hotel room. Feeling foolish and demoralised of her own self-worth, Jade returned to her life in the small town of Suisania Bay, determined this time would be the last time that she would see Shane and that she deserved better.

Jade had not left a note that night on the hotel table. She had not contacted Shane at all nor answered any of the numerous messages he had sent to her phone of his proclaimed love and invitations to see him again in the hotel room.

Jade stood firm to her decision and was trying to drift away, hoping Shane would just disappear and was out of her life forever. This time Jade knew she could say no.

Each night Jade wrote her letters to Max, the one person she knew would hold her head above water and steer her from the mess, sadness and confusion and away from her lustful addiction of Shane.

Everyday Jade fought the lust within her mind as her body ached, craving the drugs she had helplessly allowed Shane to drive to addiction within her.

With each passing night, she drifted further and further from Shane's grip as the animosity began to fade with each sweet mellifluence of Max's words that beat louder and louder within her heart, pulling her back into a world of sweet admiration, peacefulness and love.

Each day Jade stayed focused, concentrated and ignored the constant pull of Shane's temptation, the pull of the rage and vengeance that once roared through her like an angry fire, wanting to strike out and hurt the way she had been hurt. Each day, Jade rose closer and closer to the woman she knew she once was; strong but soft, sweet but sassy and finally Jade found herself and smiled again.

Three weeks after Jade had left Shane in the hotel room that morning and after receiving relentless messages on a daily basis, Jade finally answered.

Jade picked up her mobile phone as she softly bit her bottom lip nervously, hesitated, then began to write.

302

"Shane, I'm sorry I haven't answered you, but I have something to tell you. I've met someone. I can't see you anymore. I wish you luck in your life, but this is goodbye. Take care. Jade."

Jade placed her phone down on the bedside table and breathed a sense of relief.

Within that moment Jade felt a resonating peacefulness sweep over her as she took a deep breath and relaxed, and sat back against the pillows that lay at the top of her bed.

She walked out to the kitchen and made herself a cup of tea determined this time she would be free; free of Shane's lies, free of the betrayal and free of the lifestyle that had surrendered her to weakness, free of Shane.

Although Jade had lied to Shane, her message a fabrication, a reason to let go and be rid of him she had felt no guilt she felt no shame. Jade felt the finality of the situation and knew that she had done the right thing within her deceitfulness and walked away from the path of her own destruction that she had succumbed to for so long. This time she was free.

Shane did not answer her message, he did not call her phone and once again Jade's phone sat silent, void of Shane's number, void of his endless messages and finally, void of Shane. He had let her go. One week later; Cody had decided to go to his friend's house for the weekend and after going to the designated meeting spot to meet his friend's parents and drop Cody off, Jade returned back home for a quiet peaceful night of relaxation.

That evening while sitting alone in her bedroom writing a letter to Max, she suddenly heard a knock on the front door. Jade stood up quickly, startled by the knock.

No one had known of her new location, she had snuck away that day from the other house that she had shared with Shane, hidden herself away and the only person that knew of her whereabouts, was Ryan.

But as it was a Saturday night, a gathering for the members at the clubhouse, Jade knew it couldn't be him. She walked to the front door, a nervousness filling the pit of her stomach as her heart beat faster and faster and she reached out her hand to turn the door handle and open the door.

"Hi there," a voice came from the other side of the locked screen door. Jade's body stiffened as her tongue tied and her words stuck in her throat at the sight of the unexpected visitor.

"Uh-uh, oh hi Sonia," the words finally stumbling from Jade's mouth. "What are you doing here?"

"I was wondering how you were. I haven't seen you since that day we ran into each other. I thought I'd come for a visit, are you busy?" Sonia replied in a chirpy tone, smiling at Jade.

"I, ah. No, I'm not busy," Jade replied nervously, her mind racing as the questions beat through her head as fast as her pounding heart.

Jade did not know how Sonia had found her nor did want to let her in but politely, reluctantly opened the door and let her into the house.

As Sonia walked through the door Jade looked around behind her, her eyes scoping the street, her driveway, fearful that Sonia had not come alone.

The streets remained empty, silent and the only shadows that lay in the dark remained innocent of any wrong doing. Jade took a deep breath before closing the door and joining Sonia inside.

"So how long have you been here?" Sonia asked, looking around at the interior of Jade's new home.

"Not long," Jade answered, her words short, defensive, careful not to divulge any information.

"How did you find me?" the curious words flying out of Jade's mouth before she could stop them.

"Oh, I have a friend that lives just up the road," Sonia replied with a smile. "I saw you out the front of this house the other day when I was visiting her and drove past."

"Ohh," Jade replied, a worrisome smile forming across her lips. "Would you like a coffee?" she continued as Sonia sat down on the couch in the loungeroom.

"Um. Well, I thought you might like to have a bit of fun with me," Sonia replied, reaching into her handbag and pulling a bottle of wine from its contents. "And maybe some of this," Sonia smiled, also pulling a small bag out of her handbag filled with cocaine and shook the bag in temptation.

Jade stopped and stared at the wine and the cocaine filled bag Sonia was holding in the air, the temptation surging through her in an unrelenting sting.

"I, um. No. No thanks," Jade finally replied, biting down nervously upon her bottom lip. "I'm not doing that anymore. I've quit," she continued smiling proudly. "But feel free if you want to. I don't mind. Really."

Sonia's jaw dropped as her face flew into a look of astonishment. "You've quit?"

"Yeah," Jade nodded, as she walked into the kitchen and made herself a cup of tea before returning to join Sonia on the couch, handing her a glass for her wine.

Jade sat down on the couch next to Sonia, sipping at the cup of tea within the tight, nervous grip of her hand as she listened to the endless stories of her conquests, while Sonia continued to indulge in the cocaine and wine in front of her. She watched as she noticed the drugs and alcohol start to take effect as Sonia's demeanour started to change, her actions, her words, her personality and for the first time, Jade was faced with the stark realisation of her own behaviour.

"Was that really me? Is that how I want to spend my life?" the thoughts rolling around Jade's mind as she dropped her head, breaking her glance from Sonia and the sight that sat before her.

"No, that's not what I want to be. That's not the life I want for me. I'm better than that." Jade raised the hot cup of tea to her lips and began to sip, feeling proud of herself. Jade lifted her head and began to flash a proud smile in Sonia's direction as the addictive temptation that had clung to her heavily fell from her shoulders like clothing to the floor.

"Oh, that's my phone," Sonia said suddenly, her smile beaming as she placed her hand into her handbag and searched for the beeping phone. Sonia flipped open the mobile phone and began to read the unknown message out loud as Jade sat and listened. "She's acting strange," Jade thought as she watched on, listening to Sonia's every word. "What's going on here?" Jade's mind boggled.

Although Sonia had portrayed the visit as one of innocence Jade had become suspicious and in light of the previous events had not believed her intentions were that of an innocent formulism.

"Oh," Sonia cooed. "Hi sexy," she giggled reading the message out loud as a devious glint entered her eyes and glanced her eyes sideways in Jade's direction.

Jade's ears pricked up instantly, the words rang a familiar theme of deception within her. "Shane," ran through her mind but withheld within her throat. Jade smiled nervously at Sonia but not a word leaving her lips as she hid the thoughts in the depths of her suspicious, ticking mind.

"So, that's your new guy huh?" Jade asked politely, suspicious curiosity sitting firmly and secretively within her thoughts.

"Yeah," Sonia replied. "We met a couple of months ago in Alterro. He's really hot, strong and mmm, muscles all over," she continued unconsciously bragging, giggling childishly and smiling at Jade. Jade's senses were sent into a tremulous state as alarm bells rang through her like flashing red lights and she fell into a deafening silence.

"This was no accident," ran through her mind in a formulated evaluation of the moment, as her eyes once again suspiciously glanced over at Sonia.

"Ohh, watch out," Jade yelled suddenly, taking a swipe into the air between them, knocking the mobile phone out of Sonia's hand. "Spider!" Jade yelled again, as Sonia leapt off the couch with a squeal.

"Oh god. I hate spiders," Sonia cried out, jumping from side to side upon her feet looking for it.

"Oh, I'm sorry," Jade said as she leant forward to pick the phone up off the floor, her eyes intensely focusing on the screen.

"Oh I hope it didn't crack," Jade said, her eyes focusing on the name within the message before handing the phone back to her. A formidable smile spread across Jade's lips as she placed the mobile phone into Sonia's open hand and reached for her empty cup that sat on the small coffee table in front of them.

"Well," Jade said standing up, her stance strong, her eyes precise, staring straight into Sonia's eyes. "I hate to cut this short, but I'm really tired tonight. I've had a big week and was going to have an early night. I'm sorry Sonia," Jade smiled again as she stepped in the direction of the front door.

"Ohh, okay, I thought you might want to go out with me tonight, have some fun and go dancing," Sonia replied as she picked up her handbag off the floor.

"No, not tonight," Jade replied back strongly but smiling politely again.

"Um, well. I've sort of had too much to drink and." Sonia stopped and subtly pointed towards the remnants of the cocaine that still sat on the glass mirror on the floor next to the wine bottle.

"Would you mind if I left my car here for the night? I'll be back first thing in the morning and," Sonia asked awkwardly.

"How are you going to go out, get up to the night club without your car?" Jade interrupted, her head tilting in a questionable manner.

"Well, um, would you mind driving me please?" Sonia asked, a smile of question forming on her face.

Jade had not wanted to help Sonia at all, she had wanted her to just leave. Against her best judgement, Jade agreed to help her and was handed the car keys and they left.

Within minutes, the two women arrived at the local night-time venue where she dropped off Sonia and returned home seething from the surprise visit and the name that had appeared on Sonia's phone.

"What a bitch," Jade said to herself stumbling as she lifted her feet up to the small steps that led into her back door. As the evening drifted into the early hours of the morning, Jade could not relax. The unexpected visit from Sonia at her new location had left her nervously on edge, her mind could not rest as it continuously raised question after question analysing every word of Sonia's conversation, her excuse of how she had found her and the message on Sonia's phone, the message from Shane.

"I knew it," Jade said loudly as she paced the house from end to end, her mind a formidable saturation of questioning and suspicion. "This is not over. What are they up to now?" Jade said to herself, her fingers nervously reaching for her bottom lip.

Jade looked over at the clock hanging on the kitchen wall and breathed out a heavy sigh. "It's 4 am."

"I've got to stop this," she said to herself, trying to unwind the mess that was forming in her mind.

"I won't let them get to me, I won't let them destroy me again. I know what their trying to do, it's not going to work you bitches. You come near me, I'll call the police," she continued to rant, turning on the kettle and making herself a hot chocolate.

Jade walked to her bedroom, climbed into her bed and rested her head on the big, soft pillows that had now become her sanctuary away from the rest of the world. She closed her eyes and started to drift off to sleep, peaceful, calm as the night slipped away into the darkness of slumber as she lay curled in the warmth of her bed, alone.

Startled by a loud noise coming from the front of her house, Jade's short slumber disturbed, she sat up right in her bed, her heart pounding hard in her chest as if awoken from a nightmare.

"What was that?" Jade whispered, her eyes darting around the room looking for the source of the sound that had awoken her suddenly. Bang, bang, bang the noise thumped through the house once more.

"Oh god," Jade whispered again, her breathing racing as she quickly scrambled in the dark to find the bat that sat in the corner next to her bed. Jade picked up the bat and quietly, softly tiptoed over the wooden floor boards of her bedroom and headed towards the front door of the house.

As she neared the door, bang, went the sound again this time, followed by a voice.

Jade jumped at the sound startled as she placed her hand to her mouth, her breathing erratic, her heart pounding as her senses went into full alert.

"Who is it?" Jade called out, her voice trembling with anxiousness.

"Jade. Jade, let me in, let me in. It's Shane. I need to talk to you," came the voice from behind the door. Jade froze, standing still as the bat dropped from her hands to the floor by her side.

"What are you doing here?" she called out nervously.

"We need to talk. Please baby. Let me in. I need to see you, please," Shane called back as he stood on the other side of the closed door, his voice gentle, pleading with Jade to let him in.

Jade stood dumbfounded and hesitant in her silence before her eyes came to a focus on the front door, and her feet took the first step before stopping once more, her eyes filled with anxiety and hesitation.

"You can do this Jade. Just tell him to leave," she whispered to herself, her back falling against the wall next to the front door.

"Please Jade," Shane begged once more. "Please baby. I just want to talk. Let me in, please."

Jade rubbed her head with her hand, as she picked up the bat and placed it against the wall, uncertainty swirling through all of her senses as she tentatively reached for the door handle and slowly opened the door.

"Hey," Jade said softly, looking at Shane standing there. "Come in."

Shane quickly entered through the door and wrapped his arms around her in a warm embrace.

"Hi baby," Shane whispered in her ear, holding on to her tightly. Jade stood still, her arms staying by her sides in an unwelcome gesture of animosity.

Shane looked at Jade with bloodshot eyes as his words began to fall from his mouth in a familiar slur.

"Have you been drinking?" Jade asked. Shane reached out his hand and pulled Jade's into his as his eyes softened to a loving hue.

"I needed to see you baby. Please baby. Take me back. I love you girl." Jade stared back at Shane, he had caught her off guard, not yet expecting to face the man she had once loved but walked away from. Jade's heart beat faster and faster in her chest as her mind recanted over the bad memories, her eyes staring into his. Suddenly feelings of disgust, anguish and hurt came flooding back in a revelation of empowerment. Jade's stance lifted as her back bone straightened, her hand left Shanes touch and her feet took a step backwards.

"No," Jade said firmly. "No Shane. This time we're over. I told you I've met someone. I'm with him now. You have to leave. You have to go."

Shanes eyes quickly changed into a dark shade of black within the bloodshot view as his mouth dropped into a vicious scowl.

"So that's it. You're fucking someone else you fucken bitch. The bed's not even cold and you've put some other fuckhead in it. Where is the fuckhead hey? I'll fucken kill him. Is he in there?" Shane yelled abusively, marching straight into her bedroom.

Jade rushed to stop Shane as he pushed past her, yelling abusively. "No, he's not here Shane," Jade yelled. "Get out. Get out of my house."

But Shane just ignored her, stomping through her bedroom as he pulled the blankets from her bed throwing them to the floor.

"Stop it," Jade yelled, picking up the blankets and throwing them back onto her bed. "Get out Shane, I mean it; It's over. You have no right to be here. You have to go. Get out."

"Or what, you fucken little slut. Or fucken what? What the fuck are you going to do hey," Shane roared back at her, walking towards her, anger burning in his eyes. "You really think that's it huh. You think you can just get rid of me and go fuck someone else. I'll fucken kill him. You are nothing but a stupid fucken bitch. You belong to me bitch. You're mine," Shane roared and roared, sweeping his hand viciously across the dressing table crashing her belongings to the floor smashing them, before picking up the coffee cup and smashing it against the wall.

"Grrr," roared from Jade's mouth as each action and word burnt deeply into the scars of the memories of their tremulous relationship as her belongings went crashing to the floor.

Jade stood up stiff, her face tightened as her glare bore daggers into Shanes eyes.

"Get the fuck out now Shane," Jade roared, her voice boiling with rage. Shane rushed towards her, pushing her against the wall hard.

"Or fucken what bitch," he yelled in her face, his finger pointed straight at her. Jade glared back at him, her breathing heavy with rage as she placed her foot against the wall and pushed her self forward straight towards Shane, her hands falling on his shoulders, knocking him backwards away from her.

"Or I'll call the fucken cops," Jade said sternly, her voice now calm and precise. "Get out," Jade growled again loudly, pointing towards the door. Shane took a step backwards, distancing himself from the angry woman in front of him, the woman whose rage had once made him flee.

Shane stomped from the bedroom his abusive rant spilling from the scowl that covered his mouth.

"You fucken bitch. Call the fucken cops on me will you? You fucken little bitch," Shane roared again as he stomped into the loungeroom, pushing over the furniture and knocking the pictures off the walls and throwing her belongings to the ground, smashing everything in his path.

Jade looked on with disgust as the rage started to boil through her veins. "You bastard, you fucken bastard. Get out now," she roared behind him, rushing towards him.

But Shane did not leave. This time, he did not run, he turned, facing Jade, his face contort with anger, red, his eyes full of flames, burning into her, full of rage as he grabbed

Jade by the throat and rammed her up against the wall, holding his fist over his shoulder, aiming it at Jade's face.

Jade glared back staring directly into Shane's eyes, her own rage now stone cold angry and bitter.

Jade's eyes narrowed as her body tensed and her arm raised her hand, pushing Shane's arm away from off her throat and she took a step forward towards him. "You gutless bastard," she growled, her words cold as ice, as she quickly raised her open left hand and slammed it down hard against Shane's cheek twice in quick succession, swift, fast and furious in her attack, knocking him off balance and tumbling him backwards. Shane stopped and paused momentarily looking at Jade before taking another step backwards, stunned and shocked by Jade's strikes to his face. "Now get out," Jade growled through gritted teeth, staring straight into Shane's eyes. Shane took another step backwards then stomped out through the side door of the house. Jade rushed to the door, slamming it shut and locked it behind him.

She stood at the big glass windows of the sliding door watching as Shane continued his abuse of vicious words in the driveway of her home, continuing his rampage of destruction as he kicked in the panels of Sonia's car and slammed the large pot plants on top of the bonnets of both their cars.

Jade shook her head in disbelief, disgust, outraged at his acts of childish destruction. Shane climbed into his car and sat in her driveway, roaring out of his car window. "I'm still here you fucken little slut. I'm still here. You're fucked now girl. You fucken bitch. You're fucked."

"No, you are," Jade said to herself before turning from the window and walking to her bedroom, picking up her mobile phone and dialling.

"Hey," Ryan answered. "What's up?"

"Ryan," Jade replied. "Your boy is over here wrecking my place and threatening me. Come and get him now or I'll call the cops. He's left me no choice, I have kids. Stop this Ryan, tonight," Jade's voice ran down the phone, calm, stern and serious.

"Okay. Calm down. You don't need to involve them. I'll take care of it okay. Just stay inside," Ryan replied and hung up the phone. Jade walked back to the large window of the sliding door to watch as Shane remained sitting in his car, still yelling out the abuse and threats. Suddenly all went quiet, Shane stopped yelling and placed his phone to his ear. Jade watched intensely as Shane's face dropped, changed, calmed, before he reached down started his car and backed out of Jade's driveway and disappeared down the narrow streets of Suisania Bay.

The next morning when Jade awoke, she looked around at the damaged furniture, her belongings that had been smashed and scattered all over the floors, the picture frames pulled, hanging in shreds upon the walls, the coffee stains up the walls and the remnants of the smashed cup spread upon the floor.

"Unbelievable," Jade said. "Unbelievable. What a bloody jerk. But I'm free, I'm finally free," Jade cried out, spinning on her heels, a proud relieved smile filling and lighting her face as she felt her future come rushing into her thoughts, one without Shane.

Over the next year, Jade focused herself back into her work, trying to rebuild her confidence, her shattered soul, her life. Each day she struggled and ached as she pulled herself from the grips of the relentless drug addiction and the dark depression that had plagued her and had almost cost her life.

Day by day, Jade forced herself to leave the safe barriers of her home and wander back into the world. Although the sense of being watched, being followed, never left her and sat in her mind in a defensive front of continuously watching over her shoulder, she kept on trying, she would not give up.

Jade changed her phone number and kept it hidden, keeping it private and only allowing the closest people to her to have access to the fiercely guarded and protected number.

Day by day, Jade returned to her normal routine of healthy eating, exercise and daily walks around the small town of which she lived and slowly piece by piece, Jade's soul started to heal and shake the terror and damage of the emotional scars of what she had suffered within her life, her relationship with Shane.

As she stood in the mirror every day, staring back at herself, the woman that now reflected in her stare, the stranger staring back into her eyes, each day, bit by bit, Jade slowly started to shed what she had become.

The sandshoes, the T-shirts, the denim, all got locked away and were now replaced by her colourful tops, her pretty flowing dresses and skirts and finally her high heels. Jade had returned to her former beauty.

By the end of the first year, Jade had shaken herself free of the drugs that had held her so tightly in their tragic grip, she had stopped drinking alcohol and no longer felt the need to escape through the means of the intoxication of alcohol and the little white pills.

Jade sought the help of her physician to rid herself of the debilitating, dark depression that spiralled her up and down endlessly, like a never-ending nightmare of sadness, paranoia and isolation and slowly, Jade's health started to improve. Her thin, hallowed body began to fill and once again glow in her curvaceous style, her bleak, grey eyes disappeared and returned to the shining blue they once were, full of spark and flashing life, able to once again see the beautiful colours of the world around her.

Although Jade was healing and the memories were fading, the wall, the guard around her heart had remained her defences had remained and she now found it hard to connect with people, staying distant and in reserve, not allowing any form of closeness and trust to enter her world and spent the next two years alone, single, devoid of love separated from friendship and distant from anyone who tried to enter her life. Jade and Max had remained friends. Their once secret, adventurous affair had ceased and now cemented and remained in a bond of true friendship, admiration and respect for one another.

Although at times they still teased one another with sexy little taunts, it had remained to them just that, a tease of what they had once shared, of what they once had and it never went any further. They had become just friends, best friends.

Ryan had mended the mess that had occurred amongst the members at the clubhouse and Jade never saw Shane, Sonia, Tasha or Rebecca again. No one ever knocked on Jade's door or stalked her house and all of the threats, stares and glares ceased, replaced by friendly smiles and welcomes from the members at the clubhouse.

Jade had tried many times to finally start her dream, the business venture she had developed and pushed on with, her tremendous ambition. She sought help from numerous development boards, councils, members of parliament but all to no avail. Unable to rouse the support or gain the financial funding she needed in order to establish and start the business, Jade placed it all on hold, hoping one day she would eventually find the right channel, the support she needed and her dream would come true, become a reality.

With her business now placed on hold, Jade turned her hand to drawing, sketching and spent her days in her office in long hours of design, until the day she had sketched her vision; the new business venture she would now embark upon.

Day by day, Jade drew and fine-tuned the drawings until finally it was complete and she started developing her new venture of clothes designing.

As the months passed, Jade had designed her own brand of clothing and had developed business contacts and contracts in order to launch her new idea. Jade transformed her office into a homebased business of designing and retail for the markets, catalogue and internet sale outlets and had found her new direction and interest, a new passion, to fill her life of the empty space that had been formed in the closure of the direction she had once dedicated herself to previously.

After two years, Jade's confidence within herself had finally returned, the dark depression that had plagued her had lifted as her mind once again balanced and her happy demeanour returned, glowing once again with life. Now focused, absorbed in her new business idea and the raising of her son Cody, Jade felt she was now ready to finally step back into the world and meet someone special.

At night Jade started to surf the internet, researching the possibilities, the open fields of internet dating, the chance of finding the one thing she craved the most: true love. Jade joined four dating sites, placing her profile on each one and soon the messages of interest started to roll in. One by one Jade chatted nightly with the men that had sent her letters, compliments and interest from all over the world. Jade loved hearing their stories, their day to day lives and had soon formed many friendships but still no one had captured her interest, close to where she lived, close enough to meet, until the night she met Daniel.